I Couldn't
Love
You More

I Couldn't Love You More

Esther Freud

BLOOMSBURY PUBLISHING
LONDON · OXFORD · NEW YORK · NEW DELHI · SYDNEY

BLOOMSBURY PUBLISHING
Bloomsbury Publishing Plc
50 Bedford Square, London, WC1B 3DP, UK
29 Earlsfort Terrace, Dublin 2, Ireland

BLOOMSBURY, BLOOMSBURY PUBLISHING and the Diana logo
are trademarks of Bloomsbury Publishing Plc

First published in Great Britain 2021

ISBN: HB: 978-1-5266-2990-6; TPB: 978-1-5266-2991-3; EBOOK: 978-1-5266-2993-7

2 4 6 8 10 9 7 5 3 1

Typeset by Integra Software Services Pvt. Ltd.
Printed and bound in Great Britain by CPI Group (UK) Ltd, Croydon CR0 4YY

To find out more about our authors and books visit www.bloomsbury.com
and sign up for our newsletters

For GS

Being with you and not being with you is the only way I have to measure time.

Jorge Luis Borges

The past is but the beginning of a beginning.

H. G. Wells

Prologue

Summer 1991

My daughter is suspicious. She sits beside me in the taxi, squinting at the mist of rain as we wind our way through the straggled outskirts of Cork City. 'Who are we visiting?' she asks again, but my heart is beating, leaping – I'm surprised not to see it bucking through my shirt – and my voice is caught up in my throat. The driver answers for me by turning in beside a sign: CONVENT OF THE SACRED HEART.

'Not far now.' He starts along the humped slope of the drive and I stare out through the window at hedgerows, saplings overshot, cows, legs folded, fields green with wet. Fence posts flash past white; there's a curve, a mesh of wire, and there it is: the home. 'Here we are, right enough.' The man gets out, and he lifts our bag from the boot.

I wait until the car has turned before ringing the bell. It shrills, and we can hear it, startling on the other side. When no one comes I ring again, longer, louder, and even before the drill of it has died I seize the handle, and I twist. 'Hello?' There is no hint of give, and so I bang a fist against the wood. 'Hello!' I shout, and would have gone on shouting if Freya hadn't tugged at my coat.

I spin round for the car. It's gone: there's nothing but the plume of its exhaust, and desperate for what else there is to do, I see a gate in the fence and rush us both towards it.

'Was no one there?' Freya has to run.

I look back and on the second floor, I catch the dim glow of a lamp.

The latched gate opens easily, and we find ourselves in a shaded glade of trees, a mulched path leading between pine and rhododendron, and in the distance, the low hum of the road. At the far end is a rectangle of lawn; beyond it, the ruins of a tower.

'A castle!'

'Wait!' Around the edges of the lawn are black encircled crosses. I bend to one, my breath caught high, but the graves are inscribed with the names of nuns. Sister Augustine. Mother Euphrasia. The most recent, Sister Gerarda, buried two years before. I speak the names, and wonder what it was that brought them to their vows. Poverty, chastity, obedience.

I saw a face, I'm sure of it, peering out beside the lamp.

On the castle wall there is a plaque:

IN REMEMBRANCE OF ALL BABIES WHO DIED HERE BEFORE OR SHORTLY AFTER BIRTH. I GATHER YOU IN YOUR FRESHNESS BEFORE A SINGLE BREEZE HAS DAMAGED YOUR PURITY.

'Freya!' But Freya has stepped inside and is standing with her hood up in a leak of rain.

We wait until the sky has cleared and walk back the way we came. A pale sun has broken through the cloud and the house sits huge and solid in the light.

'Excuse me!' There is someone striding out. 'Can I help?' The nun is tall, white hair wisping on her upper lip. 'It's private property you're on.'

I swallow and my heart skips, painful. 'I was hoping for some information. I'd like to speak to someone who might know … my mother, she was here …'

Her eyes widen, and I see her flash a look across the knuckles of my hand. 'Shame on you, dragging the child along.'

'I've come from England to talk to—'

'This is no talk for innocent ears. Now off with you.' She ushers us, with unholy strength, past the front of the house, round to the side, and points us down the drive to the main road.

'She was here.'

The nun stands squarely. 'You'll find you have it all mixed up.'

My blood rises and I'm swirled round in a sea of red. 'And so was I.' I'm flailing, falling, holding out my arms, and when I'm steady, and my vision's cleared, the nun has turned her back, and we are left alone.

Aoife

1939

I met you at a dance in Ilford. I saw you as soon as you walked in. Black hair, the curls oiled down, the flash of your green eyes. I was there with Clifford Bray, but as soon as he released me to step outside and smoke, there you were at my side. 'Cashel Kelly.' You put out your hand, and I took it as the music started. '"Begin the Beguine",' the bandmaster announced. Our own version of Cole Porter. And so we began.

You weren't tall, I could look you in the eye in my new heels, but you were strong, and you could dance. We swooped away to the lilt of the trombone, the clarinet smooth, talking, pleading, as we floated around the room. I'll never end, it told us, peeping high and low, two voices, mine and yours, and then the trumpets blasted and the notes slid into a swing and we were roaring, laughing, our fingertips on fire. Next was that dreadful song by Eddy Duchin about not waiting till Christmas to be good, and we were arranging ourselves, ready to start again, when I felt a hand on my arm. My eyes must have closed because I remember the surprise as they snapped open and there was Clifford.

I'll take over now, thank you. Cliff was always the gentleman, always polite, I think I only agreed to marry him because he asked so nicely, but politeness, that was never your style. Your face darkened and your grip tightened, but I looked at you, and I gave you a sign. What was it? I'm not sure I know, but you understood, and you released your hold.

Who's your new friend? Clifford held me, stiff and disapproving, as we clinked round the room.

Just someone … How could I explain? Someone I know. We left early. Cliff was working the next morning and he wanted to drop me home. I had a room with Mrs O'Shea on the Broadway, and he had to get to Epping where he lived with his mother.

I didn't see you again till the New Year. I'd been home. Spent a week on the farm at Kilcrea, and when I got back – I'd warned Clifford I'd be tired from the ferry, sitting up all night on a wooden seat – and I *was* tired, but then when Eileen asked, did I want to come to the dance, I'd be lying if I didn't wonder … maybe … what if you were there? I hardly dared look up as I stepped in. I was wearing a red dress. If you've two eyes in your head you'll see me, that's for sure, but you didn't come over, not at first. We waited out the first dance. Eileen was hoping to set up with a fella she'd met, a lad from Dun Laoghaire, not that that ever worked out. They were playing 'At Long Last Love', and we were mouthing the words, *Is it an earthquake, or simply a shock? Is it the good turtle soup or merely the mock?*

And there you were, your eyes bright. I don't think I waited for Eileen to find her man, I was away with you, sweeping round the room, and no one this time to tell us to break it up. Eva, you murmured into my ear, and I didn't have the heart to set you straight: Aoife – the name is pronounced Eefa. Hadn't

I said it a hundred times since arriving in England? But I didn't want my voice to come out sharp.

I wrote a note to Clifford the next day to say the crossing was desperate rough, I was the colour of the sea still, but needed nothing – I didn't want him knocking with powders – only a rest and some weak tea which Mrs O'Shea was kind enough to supply. I'll be well enough, god willing, I told him, to start back at work Monday. Do you remember I used to dress the window at that department store in Kensington? Pontings. Closed down now. Then I took myself to Confession and was given three Hail Marys for my lies.

You wanted to be married that first summer, in June. It was the talk of war that was hurrying people up, but Mavis announced that she'd be marrying in June, although she and Bob had been courting five years and could have tied the knot at any time. But Mavis was the boss. We set a new date, 9 September, and didn't Chamberlain announce that very week we were now at war with Germany? This time you wouldn't cancel. Your sister could interrupt your plans, you said, but not Hitler. So the service went ahead, and lovely it was too, with Joan and Doris in palest pink. They wanted to wear those awful buttercup affairs they'd worn for Mavis, with the sash bows at the back, but I wasn't having that. I bought a roll of crêpe de Chine and we started again. Hundreds of tiny buttons. Spain was out. Too dangerous to travel, so instead we treated ourselves to two nights at the Strand Hotel. Squeeze my hand if you remember. What a two nights they were. The first morning you wouldn't let me out of your arms. What about breakfast, isn't it included? I thought someone might come and thump on our door, and you laughed and said that if I cared so much what people thought, we'd go and have our tea and toast and then get back into bed. There was raspberry jam, and strawberry jam, and the butter was moulded into shells, and in the years that followed, when there was hardly a raisin to sweeten a scone, I'd think of that breakfast and wish I'd eaten more.

I'd been engaged before, twice as it happens, and you weren't going to let me forget it. What stopped you marrying that Dennis fellow, then, or Clifford Bray? You didn't miss a chance to remind me. But the truth was that I'd never really known them. Maybe that would have come later. Or maybe not. But either way the Good Lord had other plans.

That first month after the wedding we lived with your family. We were glad then to have had those two nights at the Strand because I was put in to sleep with Isabelle – your mother – while you were in the box room. I would have crept in beside you if I'd not been so afraid of Mavis, all settled in with her new husband, in the big room at the front. I was still working for Pontings, that was a lovely job, and you had work as an engineer. Trained for it, to step into your father's shoes. Cashel Kelly. You were named for him. Dead before you were born. But it wasn't until we had Rosaleen that I thought of Isabelle, a stranger in this country, four little ones, and not a bit of help.

We'd have stopped in Ilford for the duration of the war if there'd been a bedroom for us, and then didn't my brother Joe write to say he'd taken on the lease of the Bull and Gate in Islington, and there he was when we dropped round, Elsie all togged up and leaning on the bar. You saw a future for us then. How hard could it be to run a pub? The beauty of it – we'd never have to be apart. Men were being called up – boys, at least – and within a week you'd volunteered for the fire service, and that was it. You'd stay at home.

It didn't take long to find our pub. The couple who ran it were keen to get away. Off to Devon, they were. Her nerves were shot from the first war, and she wasn't going through it again. We signed the papers then and there, and afterwards we stayed and had a drink. Met the locals. Brixton. The shopping capital of the south. Lovely big houses out along the main road, and down by the station the first street in London to be lit by electric light. We stayed till after closing and even then we were too excited to go home, couldn't sit still long enough to board a bus, and so we walked, our arms linked, listening, waiting for what was to come.

If I close my eyes even now, Cash, I can feel it, your first kiss. We were outside the dance hall and you had hold of my hand, and as we said our goodbyes you pressed your lips against my hair. A heat went through me, over in a flicker, but the imprint of it stayed. Bye then, I said all breezy, and as I walked away I put a hand up to my temple and felt the burn of it right there. It woke me, I didn't know I'd been asleep, travelled through my skin and down into the pit of me. I could blush to say it, a fire raged so fierce I was hardly able to keep still. What's with you, you dope? That's what they said to me at Pontings, because I was away with you, wondering how it might feel, whatever came next. Give me a sign, Cash, if you remember our night in the Strand Hotel. There was me, sitting up in bed. No wonder God declared this to be a sin before marriage, or we'd all be at it, day and night.

It's not always like this, that's what you said, it can be a sordid business, if it's not right. I thought of Clifford Bray, and his politeness, and I wriggled down and lay against your chest. It was only later did I think: how do you know? But it wasn't expected that the men resist, it was only the girls that had to wait. Cash? I'll whisper it to you – that night in the cellar with the sirens wailing, the place to ourselves for once with Margaret away visiting her sister, that's when I gave up being careful. What was the use when none of us might get through to the morning? One in the eye for Hitler. I didn't buy into that. But I knew straight away, when silence fell, and we wandered out into the sulphur and the smoke and there was one star glinting high above us in the dark. We clung together and gave our thanks and for all that I'd determined I'd not bring a child into this world, not till the war was over, I knew we'd made a start.

* * *

Rosaleen was quiet as they boarded the train. She sat by the window and looked out. No, she shook her head at the offer of a sandwich, again no to a drink. It was a long slow journey from Harrogate to London. By Leeds the girl had still not said a word. 'I spy with my little eye,' Cashel leant forward in his seat, 'something beginning with ...'

'She's too small,' Aoife whispered, although of course Rosaleen could hear. 'She won't know her letters, she's only just turned four.' She moved closer to the girl. 'Something the *colour* of ...' She glanced around and her eyes lit on the leather bag Elspeth Stead had packed for her. It was the same bag Aoife had handed over when Rosaleen was three months old, and inside were the clothes she'd sent up to her over the years. There was the winceyette nightdress with the pink sprigged flowers and the ribbon bows, and a cardigan she'd paid Mrs Winstanley next door to run up in double-knit wool to keep her warm through that last freezing winter. She'd knitted a doll too, for today, with embroidered eyes and mouth which she'd handed her when she arrived. 'Will you keep it with you for the journey home?' Aoife had asked, but that too was met with a shake of the head. No.

'I'll give you a clue,' Aoife tried. 'It's inside the carriage.'

Rosaleen kept her eyes on the passing fields.

When they reached Leicester Aoife and Cashel ate the sandwiches they'd brought with them, although they kept one back, with a glug of tea, in case the child woke. Aoife's fingers itched to draw her down across her lap, lay a palm on her forehead, admire the shell of her ear. Instead she unwound the scarf she had around her neck, and folding it into a square she slid it between the window and her daughter's cheek. A wave of satisfaction threatened to engulf her, and when she met Cash's eye and he nodded his approval she had to stop herself from turning to her neighbour, to everyone in the carriage, and telling them: I'm her mother, do you know? This is my girl, Rosaleen Mary. But the man beside her had only one leg, his crutch sticking out into the aisle, and two young women, thin and pale, shared the seat opposite. They looked over at her, sour, and Aoife glanced away. Of course they must be thinking why didn't she lift the girl on to her lap, make room for someone deserving, but the child had a fierceness about her, and she couldn't risk it.

It wasn't until they pulled into King's Cross that Rosaleen's eyes flew open. She looked round, wild, as if she might run, but it was dark outside, shadows reflected in the windows, porters with cases, soldiers in uniform, groups of children herded along.

'Almost home now.' Aoife put a hand on her arm.

There was talk of a taxi, but the crowds in the station, the queue out by the rank, lost them their courage. We'll get the bus, they decided, and without warning Cash took hold of the girl, hoisted her up into his arms and ran with her across the street.

'Wait for me, you two!' Aoife was exultant.

'Would you like to sit upstairs?' Cash asked as they clambered aboard and, gentle as anything, he set her down.

'I would not.' Rosaleen stuck her chin out. It was the first time they'd heard her speak since she left Yorkshire, since she'd said goodbye to Elspeth Stead.

'So we'll sit downstairs.' Aoife could see two seats near the back and, taking courage from Cashel's example, she lifted the girl on to her knee.

'I'll sit over there.' Rosaleen wriggled down. There was an empty seat over the way beside a foreign man, a hat like Cash's tipped back on his head.

Cash grabbed her wrist. 'No, young lady,' he said. 'You'll sit where you're told.'

'This is your daddy,' Aoife tried. Maybe the girl was muddled.

'He's not my daddy.' For a four-year-old she was full of scorn, and she pulled away. 'He's my daddy.' She pointed, and before they could stop her she was away over the floor of the moving bus and had climbed up on to the seat beside the stranger.

Cash's fury threatened to derail him. 'Leave her,' Aoife held his arm, 'she doesn't know what she's saying.'

There were twenty-seven stops before they reached Brixton. Aoife had counted them that morning, in the long-ago time when it was her and Cash. A swirl of nausea caught hold of her, and she closed her eyes, and to distract herself from the creep of sickness, she pictured the delight in Rosaleen's face when they told her that before too long she'd have a brother or a sister. There was a new bed too, in a room all of her own, and Mrs Winstanley had made curtains. In Harrogate she'd not had her own room. She'd slept in with Mrs Stead, not that Aoife went upstairs, just once when the girl had mumps, and there she was, swollen and lost among the pillows, with Mrs Stead's stockings – had she forgotten she was coming? – hanging over the side of the chair. Mostly they sat in the parlour that didn't look as if it was used from one year's visit to the next, and she spent the hours attempting to coax her daughter on to her knee. She'd taken ribbons for her hair, long and thickly waving even by the age of three, yellow ribbons to plait into the ends, but the girl would not stay still. She wanted to be out, racing away across the country with the cowman's son, his neck and ears grubby as the earth. Aoife took a breath and remembered herself, sweeping the yard, washing down the doorstep, forking straw from the chicken coop, all so she'd be free to tear across the fields with her brothers where they'd make their own fun over at the creek, or climb into the hay barn and lie in hollows of warm hay, shrieking as they pushed each other off a precipice of bales. She could smell the hot, dry smell of the twine, feel the itch of it in her nose, but hadn't she got away from all of that? Put herself into college. Walking across those same fields to catch the train from Killumney into Cork, studying, taking jobs, anything that would fit around her classes, saving up her fare to London, avoiding marrying the first one who asked, waiting, waiting, for a man who might rise up in the world with her, make a better future, work hard for their children – not a filthy horde running wild, like this one – but who would get everything that was for the best, good food, smart clothes, an education, a job that meant she'd not be stuck at home, cutting peat from the bog, swabbing floors, old at thirty-five – her mother – with nine children, and those the ones that had survived.

The bus rattled to a stop and, shaken, Aoife twisted around expecting to find Rosaleen vanished, but there she was, although the man — where had he even come from? — was gone. She eased her hand from her husband's. 'Is there room on that seat for your mummy?' she asked, and the girl looked up, her eyes flecked with fear, and, with the smallest quiver of her lip, she nodded.

They sat side by side, not speaking. Four years was too long. Aoife cursed the war, the greed of it, crossing herself as she did so, and thanking God in his wisdom to see fit that they'd survived.

'Are you getting off, then?' It was Cashel. 'Or will you wait and travel back to King's Cross?' Aoife looked into his face and smiled, and before the child had time to protest they had hold of a hand each and they were swooping her down the step and out on to the street.

Rosaleen

Summer 1959

Rosaleen knew Felix Lichtman was dangerous. That was what she liked about him. 'Will you have a drink?' he asked and before she could answer he'd ordered her a Kir Royale. They'd talked, pressed against the bar of the French pub, and whatever she told him, he wanted more: her family, the move to Ireland, the girl who helped her mother with the paying guests – Frances – one of seventeen surviving who lived in a two-room cottage on the border of their land. She told him the farm had been her parents' dream; they'd saved the whole of her lifetime, running the Black Horse in Brixton, her father spending every hour between shifts studying *Farmers Weekly*.

'And now they've gone and left you here ...' Felix Lichtman creased his eyes.

'My father, he's still ...' he mustn't think she'd been abandoned, 'I told them I had to finish ...' She couldn't say *school*, not here, in Soho. 'We still have the pub, till Daddy sells the lease ...' her body felt heavy with the dread of that, 'and then I'll be going to join them, I suppose, unless ...'

'Unless?' She could feel the heat of him through the fine cloth of his clothes.

A tall man pushed in beside them. Felix turned to him and spoke, and as he did he reached across and laid his hand on her. The other man leant forward, intent on telling him some news. Felix's grip tightened, his thumb pressing warm against her wrist. Rosaleen sipped her drink and did her best to appear calm, breathing in the babble of the room, the doors swinging open on to the street, stray drinkers gathered on the pavement. Her father would be home by now, bleary from the boat train. She'd better not stay out too late, although Margaret would be there to cover for her, telling him what a grand girl she'd been, studying all the hours, going out only once with her friend Michele.

'We could go somewhere for a bite?' Felix had turned to her. 'If you're hungry?'

Rosaleen nodded, not because she was hungry, but because she felt herself hypnotised, her pulse quivering, sparks like darts storming up inside her, and as they snaked their way through the crush of people, his hand on her, she dreaded the moment when he would, by necessity, let go. But he didn't let go. He held on to her along the street, through the bright glass-patterned door of a restaurant, steering, as if her life depended on it, which quite possibly it did, towards a table where she gratefully sank down.

'Are the oysters fresh in today, Henry?' Felix smiled up at the waiter.

'They are, Mr Lichtman, come in this afternoon.' Felix raised his eyes to Rosaleen and, when she nodded, he said they'd have two dozen, and a bottle of champagne.

All food should be like this, she thought, as sunshine and sea brine slipped down inside her, and she reached for another oyster and tipped it up.

'So,' Felix was smiling, 'what will you do, when you find a way to stay?'

'In London?' She took a sip of champagne. 'I'd like to be a journalist,' although really, and she told him this, she'd wanted to be a dancer. Her parents would never … they were thinking she might work in a bank! She had to stop herself jumping up from the table and doing a cha-cha-cha right there in the room. A one, and a two, and a … His eyes encouraged, and as she looked into the amused blue of his irises, she gulped another oyster, the rawness of it filling her with courage, and confided how she'd been taking classes on a Saturday, paying with money saved from shifts behind the bar. As she talked she felt him with her, travelling towards Covent Garden, tugging on her silver leotard, lacing her shoes. There was nothing like that at the convent, she told him, and she nearly choked on the flute of the champagne as it struck her there were girls at St Joseph's now, rows of them, tucked into their metal beds, some of them as young as four, crying for their mothers who couldn't know, surely, what a desperate place it was.

'Hey.' Felix's hand was stretched across the table, his fingers moments from her own. 'Where were you?'

'Nowhere.' She felt herself chilled, and she looked at him and took a quick sip to bring herself into the glittery now.

Felix had two rooms at the top of a building opposite the British Museum. You pushed through a heavy door and climbed, and climbed, until your legs were screaming. 'What will you do when you're old?' Rosaleen laughed as she followed him up, the scuffed soles of his shoes slipping away above her, and she bit her lip because, of course, he was already old.

'What will I do?' He seized her round the waist, and he said there'd be so little time, he'd run up faster.

There were no curtains in the flat, and the rooms were full of sky. There was almost no furniture – a narrow bed, a chair, one leg of which was loose — but it was crowded none the less with Felix's work. You could smell it as you neared the landing, the reek of stone and scorching, and as soon as the door opened it enveloped you. In the first room was a stone figure of a man, one knee bent to form a hollow, his mouth open in a roar. The other room was full of animals — frogs, owls, foxes — their bodies mottled, their eyes unnaturally large. Rosaleen turned to survey Felix — what could he possibly expect her to say? — but he was filling a kettle, spooning tea leaves into an old pot, and when the tea had brewed he eased up the sash window and lifted in a pint of milk. 'May I offer you a drop?' he asked in his elegant old-world accent, and she thanked him, although really she knew that she should leave. The cup he handed her was white and fluted, there was no sign of its saucer, and she sipped from it, spitting small swelling leaves into her hand.

'That's it,' he nodded slowly, his eyes on the work, and when the tea was drunk he escorted her down the stairs, flinging up his arm at an approaching taxi, instructing the driver to take her home to Brixton, pressing the fare into her palm.

★ ★ ★

That summer the sandstone pillars of the museum, illuminated, acted as a lamp, filling the rooms of Felix's flat with stripes and pools of light. 'Will you go to hell?' Felix lay propped on an elbow the first night she stayed, and she watched the smooth planes of his face and said she supposed she might, if she didn't get to confession first. 'Well then,' his mouth was warm against her ear, 'it had better be worth it,' and he kissed her, travelling the length of her body, setting off small sparks and shudders of desire.

The next morning Rosaleen was woken early. She lay still, unsure why she was lying alone in this bright room, with no one for company but the back of a stone man, and then, with a sharp pang of remembering, she looked up at the ceiling. There was Reverend Mother, her eyes brimming with disgust. *Will you look at yourself? You always were a rotten one*, and she assured her there'd be punishment to come. 'Felix?' Rosaleen wrapped a shirt around her and, walking through to the next room, she found him chiselling a block of granite. Who carried that up here? she wanted to ask, but his back was rigid with intent and she didn't like to disturb him. Instead she washed herself at the sink, slapping cold water under her arms, between her legs, using the shirt to dry herself.

She made tea as he did, heating water on the gas, lifting in the milk, considering what she would do if she were to live here with him. A small table by the window, another chair. She imagined the two of them sitting on either side, a candle lit, a dish of cauliflower cheese – it was the one thing she felt confident about cooking. I'd buy new cups, she inspected the stained brown chips of these, but then she thought of her parents, the silver service saved for best, smothered in its velvet box, and she decided she'd buy nothing at all.

'Here,' she offered him a cup, and he looked at her and his face cleared.

'Rosaleen!' Had he forgotten she was there? His smile had mischief in it, his eyes were full of unspoken words and he leant in towards her, and setting the tea aside, he led her back to bed.

For weeks, and then a month, she spent her every spare minute with Felix. When she wasn't standing beside him in the French pub, or eating oysters in his favourite restaurant, she roamed with him through London, examining carvings and statues, seeing the monuments of the city with new eyes. She learnt how Eros had spent the war in Egham, had only been restored to his Piccadilly plinth in 1947, and how when this small winged god had been erected he'd not been Eros at all, but his twin brother Anteros, a symbol of selfless love. But whatever his name, and no one could take the trouble to remember Anteros, the statue had been so ridiculed its creator was driven to financial ruin and had emigrated to Bruges. In Trafalgar Square they'd examined the four lions that surrounded Nelson's column, cast from bronze by Landseer, an artist renowned for horses and dogs, and had made an expedition to the City to inspect two golden unicorns guarding an apothecaries hall. He'd taken her to look at an Edwardian pub sign, swinging from its bracket, the sinister face of a fiddle-playing cat crossing its eyes at them, and in turn she'd risked a visit to her own pub, its name carved in the stone parapet above her bedroom window. They'd stood on the far side of the street, in the shade of an awning, and much as he'd threatened to cross and examine the gold letters: Henekey and Co's Port Wines and Madeiras, and to explore the side alley with its amusing name of Beehive Lane, she'd begged him to stay hidden.

Summer was tailing to an end when Rosaleen hurried along the High Street, the heels of her new boots clipping as she skirted the crowds at the entrance to the market. She glanced back at three West Indians, smoking as they leant against a wall, so handsome, so sharp, she caught her breath. 'Excuse me, sorry.' She pushed her way through a knot of women huffing up the hill, and fearful that anyone might know her as the daughter of the man who'd placed the sign NO BLACKS, NO DOGS in the window of his pub – would have scrawled no Irish if his wife hadn't been Irish herself – she kept her head down and ran.

It wasn't easy running in high heels. She should have kept her old shoes on, tatty amongst the rustle of the boots' white paper, but once she'd seen herself, tall and straight in the shop mirror, she didn't want to take them off. 'You like them?' Felix had asked. He was standing behind her, and she'd met his eye and seen that, more importantly, *he* liked them. He liked her. 'I do.' She was still standing, admiring the brown suede, the zip so neat against her calf, when he went to the till and paid.

'And what time do you call this?' Daddy glanced up at the clock, set fast to wish away the drunks, and she saw to her relief there were still ten minutes till opening.

'I'll change.' She moved towards the stairs.

'A word with you, young lady.' He stepped out from behind the bar.

'Yes?' She held her head up and found she could look him in the eye.

His face turned red, his hand sprang up, and before she could back away he'd slapped her, hard, across the ear. She staggered, one ankle buckled, but she stood her ground. 'Is that all you have to say?' She held his stare, and it wasn't until she was in her room that she allowed herself to cry.

All evening Rosaleen worked, clearing glasses, replacing spirits as the bottles emptied. She poured a pint of Guinness for Mr Moynihan who sat on his same stool, and served a pickled egg to Tim O'Doyle who had no one to feed him now his wife had run off home.

'So what'll happen to Frank here,' Moynihan wiped the froth of Guinness from his lip, 'once the establishment is sold and himself away to Ireland?' Frank was her mother's youngest brother. Twelve months in, and he still had the same surprised look as when he'd first arrived.

Frank shrugged, although he must have thought about it, and continued counting out the change. 'He should marry Margaret,' O'Doyle nodded, 'then they could keep the old place going.'

Frank's face blazed.

'So how's yourself this evening?' O'Doyle turned his attention to Rosaleen. She had her admirers among the regulars, although there were some, more than others, that she dreaded.

'Be civil,' her father hissed as he passed her with a pair of dripping pints.

'I'm grand, thank you.' She smiled swift in his direction and moved through to the saloon bar where there was a party of four, dressed in their finery, the women with matching shoes and bags, ready for a refill.

As Rosaleen sliced lemon and scooped ice into glasses, she considered how Felix might fit in. Would he choose the saloon bar, or sit with the working men next door? Neither, she smiled. Or both. It was what was most remarkable about him. He didn't fit, and yet he was comfortable anywhere at all.

'And something for yourself,' O'Doyle called after her as she took the money for another pint, and she added a tomato juice and put the price for it on a shelf. Always choose something inexpensive, Margaret had told her, but not the very cheapest; that would offend. She'd smiled at her then: we don't want that. Margaret was small and freckled. Her hair, which she wore parted to one side, was dark and light as straw. She had a strong flat body, with bowed legs under her flowered dress, and never once had Rosaleen thought of her even needing to be married. She looked differently at her Uncle Frank as she passed him in the galley between bars, and catching her staring, he blushed and his ears, two jug handles on either side of his head, tinted red.

When every last customer had gone, her father sat himself at the table by the fire and took out his glasses. 'Young lady.' He sounded cheerful enough.

Rosaleen draped a towel over the pump and slid her tips into the pocket of her skirt. 'Daddy?'

He had a whisky in a cut-glass tumbler and the smell of it was high as peat. 'Young lady,' he said again, and she saw his good humour was a trap. She dropped her eyes, and there it was, a pale blue sheet of paper printed with squat words.

'*Dear Mr Kelly,*' he began to read. '*I thought it would be of interest to know your little girl is thought to be carrying on with an unsuitable person. A foreigner, twice her age – dirty fellow, taking advantage I should say – and if it was my daughter, I'd want to know.*' He looked at her over the top of his glasses. '*Ask her if she was up West, at dinner last Thursday evening with a Mr Felix Lichtman, a Jew of no known occupation, and see if she denies it.*'

Rosaleen held his hard green stare. 'It isn't even signed.'

'Right from the start, disobedient, rude, and now … What will I tell your mother?' He raised himself up on his stool, and if it wasn't for Margaret sallying in with her broom, she was sure he would have knocked her to the floor.

'It's not your business.'

'It's my business, all right. You'll see.'

Rosaleen took off her apron and hung it on a peg, and as slowly as she could she walked out through the double doors.

★ ★ ★

The Loreto convent was opposite the sea on the road leading out of Youghal. It was tucked into the hillside, a long low building, the nuns' accommodation at one end, the girls' at the other. 'It's not so bad,' Angela told her, 'now that we don't have to board, and anyway, it'll only be a year, and you'll be done.'

It was raining, a fine, light September rain, and Angela and Rosaleen had walked on to the beach. The tide was out and there was a stretch of treacly sand. They reached the edge of it and looked back across the road and up at the school.

'Sure.' Rosaleen felt a stab of irritation. Nothing was ever too bad for her sister, not even St Joseph's, about which she'd set off such a storm, begging her parents to take her away, refusing to return when they let her home for Christmas. 'I won't go back,' she'd tried, 'unless you make Angela go too.' She'd known they never would. Wasn't it Angela that they'd kept close, no scratchy knitted pullovers sent up to Yorkshire to remind her who they were, but when January came, and the date of the new term, there was her sister, four years old, her stub nose and halo of dark curls, ready with her case.

'Better now?' Her mother's voice was ice, and Rosaleen had hung her head because she'd always known that having Angela with her wouldn't help. She'd be put in with The Babies, at least until she was five, and the babies lived in their own separate house with their own babies' nuns.

'The food is nice,' Angela said now, 'and Sister Antony, you'll see, she's about a hundred, but she's—'

Rosaleen walked away, the footprints of her treasured boots evaporating in the sand. 'They're all bitches,' she threw over her shoulder and, flushing, Angela crossed herself before hurrying to catch her up.

Their parents were waiting in the back bar of the Moby Dick. 'So, you've found someone to take over that pub of yours then, Mr Kelly?' The landlord nodded to Daddy as he drained his glass.

'Aye, that I have.' He rested his eyes on Rosaleen as if it was her and her alone that had forced him to take the lower offer.

'Mrs Kelly here's been doing a fine job with the farm, or so I hear,' the barman winked. Was this somehow improper? Rosaleen looked at her mother, her hair newly set, a tiny fleck of lipstick smudged against a tooth. 'A capable one you've got there.'

'Well, stands to reason – the woman was raised on a farm. Up at Kilcrea.'

'The Herlihy place?'

'The same.'

The barman leant across and called to her that only last week he was out at Kilcrea, collecting a kitten for his youngest girl.

Aoife smiled coolly. 'That'll be my brother Jim's place so.' She tilted her chin and gave her new smart hair a little shake, as if to say, I've had a life over in England and I might be back, but I'm not the local girl I was.

'Aoife Herlihy!' An older man glanced up from his Guinness. He peered at her, and his worn face brightened. 'I remember you, walking into that shebeen down by the docks. No women allowed, but Aoife Herlihy, back from London, the clothes on her, there wasn't a man, let me tell you …'

A rage of love and fury swelled Rosaleen's throat. Why couldn't she see that woman: *back from London!* But before another word was spoken Daddy placed himself between her and the bar. 'Have you met my wife Eva Kelly? I'm not sure that you have?'

'Is that right?' The man folded himself back over his pint, and the talk turned to farming, the weather and the mart.

'What shebeen was that then?' Rosaleen asked as they drove home.

'Don't be getting any ideas, young lady.' Daddy scraped the gears.

'It was my brother's bar, in Cork, that's all it was.' Her mother gave her that, but as she had so many brothers it was of little help.

'I'm feeling sick.' It was Kitty, who'd been in the car all this while, gobbling down lemonade.

'We'll not be long.' Their mother stretched a hand to her youngest girl, and Angela, who hated anyone to vomit, wound down her window and stuck her own head out.

Daddy made a piffling sound as if they were all too much of an irritation, and they stayed like that, in silence, till they drove in through the gates of Barraghmore and parked in front of their new home.

Lord save me! Rosaleen said it to herself as she stamped up to her bedroom, and she counted the months from September round to June when she'd be finished with school forever, when her parents would have no hold on her, and she'd be free.

★ ★ ★

Rosaleen had the room above the kitchen, in the old part of the house. It was low-ceilinged and looked out over the farmyard, with its own crooked staircase that led up from the back hall. Her sisters had the smart rooms at the front, on either side of the landing, but what did Rosaleen expect when she'd stayed behind in London?

'Come on down.' Kitty was banging on the door. 'Mummy says to come now, the dinner's on the table.' Rosaleen didn't answer. She was reading her letter and she was not to be disturbed. She'd read it before, that morning when she'd snatched it from the mat, and then again as soon as she'd come in, but now she wanted the words – the jumping, wildly pleasing shapes of them – needed to breathe them in like air. 'Are you even in there?' Her sister's voice had trickled to a whine and, defeated, she slipped the letter into its envelope, taking a quick moment to admire it – Rosaleen Kelly, Barraghmore – and sighed her way downstairs.

Everyone was seated when she came in. 'And what time do you call this, young lady?' Daddy, as so often, was spoiling for a fight. Rosaleen ignored him. She pulled out a chair on the far side of the table, and bent over her soup. It was oxtail and the nubby knots of ... was it really tail? caught unpleasantly in the broth, but she knew better than to leave it. If there was one thing, and there were many that her father could not abide, it was his daughters toying with their food. Spoon after spoon was swallowed as she thought of her small, determined self – *I only like white meals* – not knowing it was a sin, and from nowhere her elbow – also a sin – was smacked away from under her. *You'll eat what's in front of you.* But she couldn't eat it, and so she'd sat all afternoon at the table until Margaret had tiptoed in and secreted the greying meat and the green mound of cabbage into the pocket of her skirt.

'How was your mathematics test?' It was her mother, her arched eyebrows hopeful.

'Fine.' Rosaleen was nearly through the soup, could see the glassy bottom of the bowl.

'Is that it?' Her father was leaning in towards her. 'Is that all we're going to get?'

'What do you want?' She couldn't help herself, she was a mirror of his snarl. 'Take the square root of eighty-one, divide it by seventeen … It was boring. It's done.'

Kitty, her littlest sister, giggled, but Angela, who loved Rosaleen with a fear, choked on her spoon. Daddy leant across and thumped her on the back, so hard the piece of oxtail that had been troubling her flew out across the table. 'Praise the Lord.' Mummy dropped her napkin over it, and Rosaleen, seeing her chance to avoid the last greasy mouthful, cleared the bowls. The next course was already served: one chop, a mound of mashed potato, a spoonful of carrots, arranged in the warming oven of the Aga. Mummy, with her heatproof hands, lifted out each plate, and Rosaleen set them down.

Through the rest of the meal her father talked about the farm. One of the men might have to be let go. He, himself, never would have hired him, could spot a slacker at a glance, but he'd come with the land so what was to be done? He'd need another hand with milking. The Charolais were giving a good yield. Cream two inches thick. 'Eva, for God's sake, woman, are you listening?'

Mummy jumped. 'Of course I'm listening, what else would I be doing?' She nodded after that with every word and made encouraging clucks, while the three girls sawed at their meat and stabbed at the soft flesh of their carrots.

'Kitty?' Her mother deemed it safe to rise. 'There's a pet, help me with the sweet.' And because it was Friday, with the worst of the week over, she brought out a jelly from the pantry: lime, with a tin of nectarines set into it. Kitty, who, to be fair, was only nine, made a great show of bringing the dessert bowls to the table, and her mother served, and Angela handed them round.

Rosaleen could hardly face another thing but she knew better than to say so. Slowly she sucked at the cool, fluorescent jelly, thinking of when she might be dismissed, when the washing-up was done, the table wiped, the floor swept, the mush of the dogs' dinner – Humphrey the house dog, the others must live in the yard – put on the slow plate to cook. Only then could she retreat to her room and, with the door safely locked, draw out her letter, sniff it, smooth it, maybe even lick it, so that Felix's words – *What news of the great escape?* – could thrill her back to life.

Kate

Spring 1991

I'm on the bus when it happens, the knot, bound tight, unravelling. I catch at my breath, surprised to find I'm standing. How does anybody stand? My skull is open, the air gone from my lungs. I clutch at a pole. Would it help if I lay down? I get off, step out into the traffic and, finding no relief, I climb back on. The bus jolts forward. We're crawling along Gower Street, past the Slade where in another life I was moulding figures from the debris of my clothes. My stomach hollows. I need to cross the road, find my way home, but Matt will be waiting outside the cinema and I can't leave him there, wondering, worrying I've died.

A woman glances at me, sideways, and I do my best to smile. We cross the lights and pick up speed. *I can do this*, I tell myself.

'Hey!' Matt is cheerful. He kisses me, and flicks the tickets in my face.

I swallow. 'I'm feeling a bit …'

'What?'

I look round for an escape. 'I won't be long.'

Oh God, I'm on the toilet, my head dropped between my legs. There's a queue outside. I can hear shuffling and then a child asks, can they get popcorn to eat on the way home? 'Salt,' her mother tells her and I hear the grumble through the door.

The water runs cold as I splash my face. The child waits beside the basins. She wears a hairband with mouse ears, the insides of which are pink.

'I like your ears,' I say.

She rewards me with a gappy smile. 'It's my birthday,' and I tell her it's my birthday too, and for a moment I'm inside myself again. Hope flares.

'What did *you* get?' She fingers the pink felt.

'A knife,' and before I can explain that it's a special kind of knife, for stencilling, her mother has sailed from her cubicle and is bundling her away.

I stare into the mirror. Pale skin, dark hair still curling – outwardly I haven't changed – although my pupils are so huge the black has almost blotted out the blue.

I feel my way along the carpeted corridor, back into the lit-up foyer. 'Bloody hell.' Matt ushers me towards Screen 2. 'What kept you?'

People stand as we squeeze through to our seats. I've wanted to see this film. It was my idea, but even as the titles roll I'm afraid I'll have to leave. The music helps. It's melancholy and hopeful, but the dark-haired woman has a look about her of my mother, my real mother, the one that gave me up. I scrabble for my coat.

Matt takes my arm and holds me down. 'For God's sake, wait …'

I can't wait. If I wait I'll scream. I push along the row. Matt follows, I can feel him at my back.

Grim, unspeaking, we stand out on the street, and when a cab steams by I flag it down.

'I was on the bus ...' I start, but I daren't name it, the terror of dissolving. I lean forward and stare out at the night.

'Kate,' Matt tries. 'Let's stop somewhere. Have a drink. It's your birthday, for Christ's sake.'

If I could cry it might convince him, but I'm holding on so tight there's nothing left for tears.

Celine is at the kitchen table. I can see her through the glass of the front door. 'Sorry.' My voice comes as if from a great distance, and with no further explanation I pay her for three hours.

The bath is as hot as I can bear it. From downstairs there is the drift of the TV. Gunshots. Shouting. I close my eyes and lie still as it cools. I have three books borrowed from the library. No, I had to explain, for me, not for the child, and I've been keeping myself up late, extracting tips on how to sleep. A river. That is what I need to summon, but it seems I'm choosy about rivers. Mine must be turquoise, slicked with silver, its current flowing not towards me, but away. I'm still searching when Matt creaks open the door. I swallow as he climbs into bed, the mint cutting through the waft of beer, and I think how I could reach out, stretch an arm across his chest, feel the warm cotton of his T-shirt, have him clasp my hand with his own. Instead I press hard into the pillow. Stay calm: I force my mind through fields, ploughed furrows, marshes, scree. I'm searching, swooping, low-flying as a plane, and then with a shiver of relief I find one – a translucent streak of water, two swans, their curved necks reflected in its depth. The swans drift, and I drift with them, through bulrushes and sedge. I'd continue drifting if the next instruction didn't require me to find a tree. Flowering, leafless, spindly, giant – I accept whatever tree arrives. Tonight it is a yew. An ancient, dark-green yew of mythical proportions, its branches hanging down to create a cave. I creep inside and press my face against the trunk, spread my arms, my fingers, breathe in the lichen and the peeling bark – *Kate was here*, scratched with a penknife that might have been my own. I'm safe. And I lie myself down in the cradle of the roots and let them wrap themselves around me.

Aoife

Summer 1960

Aoife prided herself on the quality of her breakfasts. The glass orange plates, brought over from London, the crisp rashers of bacon, the frill of the eggs. There were mushrooms softened with salt butter, and toast in a rack, with marmalade and jam. 'You spoil us.' Eamon slapped his big washed hands together and Patsy, who'd taken a shine to her, blushed.

Cashel was glum. The rain was fierce that summer and the stream on the border of their land had burst its banks. Aoife stood by the range and thought how it might have been her father talking. Foot rot, silage, milk yields, clay, and she was seventeen again, packing the few things she had into a case. She was leaning against the rails of the ferry, the belt of her coat tightened, her bag stowed in the cabin, and below her on the quay, her three closest brothers, waving to her, shouting they'd be following her to London soon.

'Will you not check the toast, woman?' Cashel's voice knocked the daydream out of her. She lifted the round dome of the Aga to release the blackened bread and, mortified, tossed the useless things into the slop.

Once the men were gone, the washing-up done, every last dish put away, she sat down on the low chair and went through the post. Her heart jolted to find a letter from Rosaleen, and then, in amongst a fold of bills and pamphlets, another letter, also from Rosaleen, this one addressed to Angela. The waste! Why couldn't she have slipped the page in with her own, and she tutted to herself as she eased open the thick cream paper of the envelope. *Dear Mummy and Daddy.* How smart that looked. She thought of her own mam, never the leisure to answer the letters she herself had written home. *Dear Mam and Da*, she'd told them about her life in London, the Christmas window display at Pontings, the fine dress she'd slipped over the body of a mannequin, the same dress, in red, she was saving up to buy herself. It was the winter she'd become engaged to Clifford Bray. She'd not mentioned that when she wrote home, and she imagined the two of them, married, still living with Cliff's mother, their children, boys for sure, engaged as clerks in a law firm in the City.

Dear Mummy and Daddy
Work at the Express *is going well. It's exciting to be at the centre of everything, knowing the news as soon as it comes in. There are a lot of interesting people here, and I'm making important contacts which will no doubt come in useful in my future career. I hope you're both well. I'll write again soon.*
Love from Rosaleen

Angela's letter felt thicker. She could hardly have said less. Aoife pressed it between her fingers, examined the seam of glue, and sighing in loud exasperation — what could be so private? — she propped it on the dresser where Angela would see it as soon as she came in.

It rained all morning and into the afternoon, but all the same Aoife pulled on her mac, covered her hair with a scarf, and with a hood of plastic purchased the week before in Youghal, she walked Humphrey up the lane. The whole world was a haze of grey and green. Fat drops sloshed down from branches, and the sky was close. Humphrey plodded beside her, head down, tail down, nose occasionally twitching. She'd got him as a pup and brought him across when they moved, his lion head resting in her lap, his great fur body pale if such a thing could be. Where are you taking me? his soft eyes seemed to ask as the boat lurched, and she'd stroked his ears and whispered that never again would he stay locked in a back room, allowed out only after closing where he'd sniff the scratchings and loll up the spills of beer. Cashel would have nothing to do with him. What's the point of it, great useless thing? Now there were two trained collies, living in an outhouse, Moss and Mo, quick and slippery as ferrets, expecting nothing, needing nothing but to be told what to do.

Aoife passed the Kerry place. A white, wrought-iron gate. A Protestant couple living in that big house. No children. Or maybe they were gone. In the cottage further on were the O'Malleys, a nice woman, the son was a good boy, and the husband, Patrick it was, a foreman over at the cotton factory in Youghal. He had a twinkle in his eye; Aoife smiled and shook her head at the memory of their first Christmas back, how they'd been standing chatting after Mass, when he'd looked at the two of them, she and Rosaleen. 'So I see your sister's come to stay?'

There was a gust of wind and the leaves above her rustled. Aoife tilted her face into the rain, catching a warm drop on her tongue. Humphrey looked up at her. No, she told him, we'll go on until the turn, and she fixed her eyes on the fields beyond and kept up her pace.

★ ★ ★

Do you remember the day she turned up out of nowhere? I was wiping down the bar – dead on my feet, I was, with Kitty not more than a few months old – when there was a tapping on the glass. I might not have noticed but, whoever it was, they kept on until I slid the bolt. Who is it? I know you never liked me to open during closing, and there she was, in her school uniform, bedraggled from the rain.

What in God's name are you doing here?

The child was smiling as if she'd been clever, and if I'd had my coat on and my purse, I'd have taken her by the arm there and then, and marched her back to St Joseph's.

I caught the train, she said, smart as anything. And a bus from Victoria.

I called to you then, do you remember, and the first thing you wanted to know was where she got the money. You better not have stolen it, you said, but she looked scornful, and she told us that the uncles had given it to her, every time we saw them for a visit they'd pressed a coin into her hand. She'd been saving for an emergency.

What kind of emergency is this? you asked. It was a Tuesday. A perfectly ordinary Tuesday. A little rainy, that was all.

She didn't say anything. Not at first. Just looked at us with those round eyes. Her hair was in plaits. They did a lovely job with the girls' hair, you couldn't fault the nuns for that. Did you not get my letters?

We got your letters; I wanted to kneel down to her then, her lip was quivering, but you kept your hand on my shoulder. So I told her what smart handwriting she had. I told her I was proud.

I said to come and bring me away!

Now, young lady. You wouldn't stand for that, not after the sacrifices we'd made, and before her temper flared, or yours, I shouted to Margaret to get the child cleaned up.

I called the nuns then, they were frantic, and I told them not to fret, I'd be bringing her right back.

She didn't say a word all the way to Dorking, not on the bus or the train, and I explained to her, although I'm sure I'd said it before, that she was lucky. There was fresh air in Dorking, not like at home where the place was broken up with craters from the bombs, where rats ran riot through the weeds, and the dust from the wrecking balls, flattening what was left, was enough to make you choke. They had vegetables and eggs in Dorking, and above all else she'd get an education. An education, we believed that, an education would see them straight.

When we arrived at St Joseph's she marched straight past that lovely Sister Benedict, do you remember her, she hardly came up to my shoulder so tiny she was, and up to her dorm. It was evening prayers. I could hear the voices floating out of the chapel. So pure. But no one shouted at her, although maybe they should have; they just smiled and said the child was most likely tired. It was best she got herself to bed.

It was only a month or so and she was back. Tapping on the glass. This time I knew who it was. Mummy, she wailed when I looked out. Why don't you come for me? I was too fearful to let her inside, I'd never prise her out again, so I shut the door, ran back for my coat and shouted to Margaret to mind the others while I was gone. Right, I caught her by the hand

and we were away, running down the street to the bus stop. Which train did you get anyway? Who sold you a ticket? We'd taken her money off her the last time, told the uncles not to give a penny more, but she said she'd stood on the road and put out her thumb, and a nice man had driven her all the way to London, dropped her by a place called Ealing, and she'd taken a bus, and when the inspector got on she said she'd lost the penny for her ticket.

I was glad you weren't there to hear that. Your own child lying, plain as day. I was too taken aback to speak, and this time it was me sitting on the train in silence.

Wait for me in the vestry, Sister Benedict told her when we arrived. She gave me a look as if to say, Leave it to me, I'll be dealing with her. You'll not be worried again.

How quiet she was when she came home for the summer. She stayed in her room, reading mostly. Tales of ballet dancers, and princesses. Although she talked to Angela. She always talked to Angela. I used to stop outside their door at night and listen to them, whispering. Angela told me later, much later, when we'd lost her, that it was scary stories her sister was telling, hauntings and murder, and then, in the middle of the night, having frightened her own self witless, she would climb into the big bed where the other two were sleeping and lie there, shivering between them.

★ ★ ★

There were paying guests arriving. The wife of a man who read the news, and their awkward teenage son. Aoife would give them the smart room at the front, the same as last year, move the girls into the attic, while she and Cash could sleep in Rosaleen's old room.

Rosaleen's room was much as she had left it. Her school uniform hanging in the cupboard, a heap of books on the table by the bed. The bed Aoife had stripped the day she'd left, and now she made it up, easing on a fitted sheet, pulling it tight at its corners. She floated down the top sheet as her own mother, God bless her soul, had taught her, and used the flat of her palms to mould it in under the pillows. When they'd first moved to Barraghmore she'd gone to Youghal and chosen bedspreads for each room. Peach, Lavender, Barley and Harvest, and now she eased the Lavender into the dent below the pillows, cutting a sharp line, then allowing it to swell so welcomingly she felt inclined to let her own tired body fall into the embrace. Instead she sat on the very edge and shuffled Rosaleen's books, wiping away their outline, looking around for where they could be stored. *Gorky*. Whoever was that? *My Childhood*. Aoife flicked through the pages. *She was a clean, smooth, large person like a horse*. The cheek of it. That was his mother he was describing, but as she read on she saw the poor woman was pregnant. *It's not cholera, she's in labour*. Then the same person, the grandmother. *In the name of the son and Holy Ghost. Try and bear the pain, Varyusha. Holy Mother of God who prays for us …* At least the family were Catholic, however poor and wretched. Aoife bit down a stab of irritation. If Rosaleen wanted stories she could have come to her, and she thought of her mother the year after she lost Maeve, her hair so thin, the teeth loose in her mouth, and Aoife herself getting the little ones up, giving them an apple and a square of cheese and nothing more till tea. The next book was French, Madames this and Mademoiselles that, and Aoife wondered when she'd last had time to read. One Christmas in London, that was it, she'd sat with the younger girls and read Patricia Lynch – *Brogeen and the Green Shoes* – a chapter a day, between the lunchtime and the evening shifts. She'd been homesick and it soothed her.

Aoife got up to place the books on the window ledge and that's when she saw it – a small, plain volume, but dangerous as sin. *The Country Girls.* Surely it was banned? *The book is filth and shouldn't be allowed in any decent home.* Who was it that had said that? The Minister for Justice, that's who it was, and the author an O'Brien, only a girl herself, and she from County Clare. Aoife opened it and saw the scrawl of an inscription.

MY ROSE, I THOUGHT I'D BETTER SEND YOU THIS AS I HEAR
THEY'RE BURNING COPIES IN THE STREET. HARD TO IMAGINE
THAT WOULD HAPPEN AGAIN, SO SOON. BUT AS YOU'RE
OVER THERE GETTING AN EDUCATION, THEN YOU MIGHT AS
WELL MAKE SURE ALL ASPECTS ARE COVERED. LOVE TO THE
NUNS. LOVE, AND SO MUCH MORE TO YOU, FELIX X

Aoife slapped shut the book. Hadn't they put a stop to that? Bringing her away as soon as they were warned, but then Felix Lichtman was a foreigner, and what did he care for their ways? She slid the book into the top of the cupboard, slamming a pillow in after it, and then a heavy folded blanket. 'There!' She swung the wardrobe closed, and as she turned the key she did her best to push the whole nasty business from her mind.

Wearily Aoife made up the other rooms. Peach she chose for her guests, the girls could have Barley, but as she lifted their linen into the warm space of the attic, she felt overcome with such an ache she left the sheets in piles – let them make up the beds themselves. 'Angela,' she shouted as she came downstairs. She'd tell her no, she'd not be stopping with Rosaleen that summer, but Angela was not in the house. She must have gone on up the road to have a cup of tea with Mrs O'Malley. She was popular, that one, and welcome wherever she went.

There was a walled garden to the side of the house and Aoife took a trowel to the weeds, thrashing and digging and tugging them out by the roots so that by the time the guests drove through the gate and pulled up she had a nice clean border, but the dinner still not on, so that she must run round into the back yard, in through the kitchen to scrub her hands and tidy her hair and race through into the hall to pull open the door just as the boy, whose name escaped her, heaved their one heavy bag on to the step.

'Grand to see you again,' she greeted them. 'I've given you the front room to the right. The same as last year. Dinner will be a little later tonight. Seven o'clock. I hope that's all right. I thought you might want a rest after your journey.'

The woman still hadn't said a word, was only nodding, and Aoife blushed as she led them up the stairs, sure they could smell it on her, the fume of that filthy book, the only copy, as far as she knew, in all of Ireland not to have been tossed into the trash. 'Will you be wanting a cup of tea?' she asked, although that wasn't a service she provided, not at ten past five when she had food to prepare, and the woman smiled greedy and said she could kill for a cup of tea. Would they come down?

'Come down to the lounge, that's it.' What did they think, she'd be bringing up a tray? She swung into the kitchen and thumped the kettle on to the hot plate of the range.

★ ★ ★

Aoife didn't see the car until it was almost upon her. A white saloon, and wasn't that Mr O'Malley winding down his window? 'Fine weather for ducks,' he smiled. 'Can I give you a lift?' He was heading back the way she'd come.

'I have the dog.' She hesitated, and Humphrey looked up at her, his brown eyes willing.

Patrick O'Malley got out of the car. He creaked open the boot and stood there under the shelter of its hood. 'Come, boy.' He made a sort of cluck with the corner of his mouth, and Aoife joined him. 'Come now.' She put an arm round the dog's wide girth, 'good boy,' and she encouraged him in.

'That's very kind,' Aoife told him once she was in the front seat, the plastic headscarf she'd tied over a silk one dripping in her lap. 'I didn't know I'd come so far.'

'Got carried away, did you?' He smiled at her, as if he too lost himself in thought. 'So, I'll drop you home, is that it? Or were you wanting to come into Youghal?'

'Oh no!' The idea.

Mr O'Malley drove on as if he hadn't heard. 'I have to pick up some baking soda for the wife, I'll only be ten minutes, and I'll be turning round again.'

'Thank you,' Aoife said more quietly. 'I'd better get home.' She looked out of the window at the drowned fields and the shivering trees and thought how as soon as she got in she must check the stew slow-cooking in the Aga. They'd need it, come dinner time, her paying guests, and she wondered how they were getting through the day. Sitting in their car, most likely, looking at the strand. They were a couple from Armagh, the man jolly, full of news, his wife silent, nodding and agreeing with everything he said. Did it always have to be that way, one half of a couple doing all the talking, the other one shut up?

'You like your walking.' Mr O'Malley was looking at her. 'I've seen you out and about before.'

'I didn't know how much I'd missed it, not till I was back.' They glanced out through the swish of the wipers.

'Sweet Youghal Bay, sweet Youghal Bay,' he had a low slow
   voice.
'Beside your Blackwater, I'm longing to stray
Soon I'll return, until that happy day
My heart's in your keeping, oh sweet Youghal Bay.'

They laughed, and floundered for the rest of the words.

'Sweet Youghal Bay,' Aoife started in again on the chorus.
'Sweet Youghal Bay …' They were still singing when they
swooped past the gates to Barraghmore. 'You know what?'
She glanced over her shoulder. 'Maybe I will come into town
with you. I could pick up something from the chemist if you
don't mind dropping me.' They turned on to the main road,
the dog suspicious, his ears down, his nose pointed back the
way they'd come.

Rosaleen

Summer 1960

Rosaleen hadn't been entirely truthful about her job. She *was* working at the *Daily Express*, but not, as she'd told her parents, putting together stories for the news desk. She'd been there six weeks and she'd not seen a typewriter, busy as she was from morning to night, sorting mail in the post room. Each day before eight she entered the building on Fleet Street, passed the uniformed doorman and hurried through the marble foyer to the lifts. However early she arrived, Betty the postmistress was already there, her peroxide hair piled high, a cigarette hanging from the corner of her mouth. 'Good morning,' she'd glance at the clock, and Rosaleen, fearful of disapproval, looked too. The post room was hot and airless, its one window facing on to a central shaft, and there were two other girls, Sally and Meg, whose job, like hers, was to sort the mail: letters to columnists, packets from photographers, information from overseas which all needed to be placed in the wooden pigeonholes along the walls. Often the letters were addressed to the newspaper itself, without any hint at a department, and it was Rosaleen's job to open and distribute them. Occasionally it was clear from the first line – a sorrowful letter for the Agony Aunt, grainy images of a faraway conflict for News – but sometimes the contents were mysterious. Stones, out-of-date coins, visionary messages of calamity. Once there was nothing but a length of string. The most prized letters were for the proprietor himself, Lord Beaverbrook, unseen in an office far above them. These Rosaleen would place prayerfully in his pigeonhole, sending with them the hope that one day he would flick through his own paper and see her byline – Rosaleen Kelly – below a front-page report.

By ten o'clock the worst of the mail had been sorted, and there was a minute to sit down. Betty put on the kettle and, as soon as it had boiled, the printworkers –who surely couldn't hear the whistle above the rolling of the presses – would sidle in. It was Betty they came to see, to hear her teasing and her raspy laugh, although she liked to pretend it was the young ones they were courting, to make Meg blush and Sally stutter. Rosaleen, they all knew, had a boyfriend. Felix Lichtman had rung on her first day; he'd placed a call to the paper from the South of France where he was on some kind of business and, rare as it was for anyone to telephone from abroad, he'd been put through to Lord Beaverbrook. *Hello?* Rosaleen imagined the old man picking up the phone, and she smiled at the thought of his surprise when Felix, in his lightly foreign tones, had asked to speak to the girl in the post room.

'It's for you,' Betty mouthed to her when the call was redirected. 'Hope it's nothing serious.' Rosaleen had swallowed, involuntarily smoothing down her hair.

'Made the news yet?' Felix was laughing, and she'd had to turn away from the curious faces of the others. 'Felix,' she whispered, as sternly as she dared, 'you're not allowed to call me here. It's emergencies only.'

'This is an emergency,' his voice was low. 'I'm travelling back today and I need to be sure that you are free for supper.'

'I may be,' Rosaleen said with due solemnity, and before she replaced the receiver she amended her reply. 'I am.'

It had been Felix who had found her the job. She'd written to him as soon as she'd finished at Loreto. *I'm ready for my escape, although I'll need something to come back for.* And he'd replied by return to ask if it wasn't enough that she was coming back for him? She'd sat in her bedroom and held the letter to her heart, and this time when Kitty banged on the door she'd ignored it. She didn't want another discussion about her future, about what college she might apply to now she had such astonishingly good grades in her matric. 'There's no better place than Cork.' Her mother was determined and Rosaleen had been unable to resist derailing her by suggesting she might try for Trinity.

'Trinity? They've a ban on Catholics attending, you know that.'

'Church restrictions,' Rosaleen came back. 'It doesn't say a ban. There was a girl from the convent whose brother got a special dispensation.' She could see she'd sown a seed of hope. Aoife Kelly's daughter, Aoife Herlihy that was – graduating from Trinity!

'I could talk to the priest.' She was all a-scatter, and when Daddy came in she passed on the news.

'You always were trouble.' He looked at her, impressed. 'You'll have us writing to the Pope for you, is that it?'

'Or maybe I could try ...' she couldn't help herself '... for the Sorbonne in Paris?'

'Paris?' he spluttered, and he saw then, a moment too late, that what she wanted was to get away.

'At least go and look at Cork?' her mother tried again, but her father slammed his fist against the table. 'That's enough!'

Within a week Felix found a man who knew a man who said she could come and work at the *Express*. A job.

A professional position. Her parents hadn't a word to say against that, although they might have if they'd known who had arranged it. Her father bought her a ticket for the ferry while Mummy wrote to the aunties to ask if they could put her up, until she found herself a room closer to her work. Her work on the news desk. Her work as a journalist for a national newspaper. Auntie Mavis wrote back to say, of course, Rosaleen was always welcome. She could sleep in with her Nana Isabelle. There would always be room.

On her last day Rosaleen drove with her mother to Kilcrea. They sat side by side, wordless in the car, watching the fields and the narrow roads. They parked on the lane outside the priory and, passing through the wishing gate, walked along the soft avenue of grass. She knew Mummy liked to say her prayers alone – her parents were buried here – Joseph and Cathleen – and beside them, a sister, Maeve, lost before she was grown. On the other side were a multitude of Horgans. There'd been a Horgan at Loreto, and here, surely, were the girl's relatives stretching back through time. As her mother knelt beside the Herlihy grave, mumbling her messages, Rosaleen wandered through the ruins, stepping in and out of the ancient rooms, reading the writing on the tombs. She sat with her back against a flinty wall and closed her eyes. *Not long now*, she told Felix, *and I'll be on the ferry.* She thought of the letters she'd composed this way, and she blushed to remember how she'd described to him the progress of the crops, the hogs, the ewes and lambs, and the settling in of the new pale cattle – Charolais, they were – which produced such creamy milk that her father kept it separate from the rest, driving the churns to Castlemartyr first thing in the morning. *Sorry*, she told him now, *there's not a lot of news in these parts*, although of course she could have mentioned Declan Shaughnessy who drove over last Saturday and whisked her away in a sports car to a club in Cork where they'd danced so long and late even her father had given up waiting and taken himself to bed. *Will we take a trip to France ourselves?* He'd promised her they would, but here, in the damp green silence of Kilcrea, it seemed too much to ask.

'Well look at you!' her Auntie Mavis greeted her. 'A job as a real-life journalist. We'll have to watch what we say around you.' She'd shown her to her nana's room, where there was the one lumpy bed, and the old lady herself, her silver hair held in a bun, sitting by the window. Rosaleen kissed her worn cheek, and felt the squeeze of her hand. 'You always were the clever one,' there was her soft breath in her ear. 'I'm glad I lived to see the day.' By the time Rosaleen arrived on her first morning at the doors of the *Daily Express* she had to remind herself it was in fact the post room she was working in, and not on a story for the front page.

★ ★ ★

Felix was preparing for an exhibition. That first weekend Rosaleen waited all morning for him to stop work, and when he showed no sign of it, she slipped on her shoes and opened the door on to the stairs. The creak of it caught his attention. 'You should see the look on Auntie Mavis's face,' she told him as he set aside his chisel. 'She leaves the hall light on for me, although I ask her not to, and when I do come in she tells me off for wasting the electric. I'll not hear the end of it, staying out all night.'

'I do see that could be maddening.'

'For her?'

'For you.' He pushed the hair back from her face and kissed her with such tenderness, pressing the sudden hardness of himself against her so that she thought how marvellous it was – why did no one ever say? – to be alive.

Within a week Felix had found her a flat in Maida Vale, furnished, the walls, the furniture, the carpet, in softest grey. 'Who lives here?' she asked, walking from one room to the next and out on to the narrow wrought-iron balcony that overlooked the street.

'You do,' Felix smiled, and when she persisted, 'they're abroad.'

'They are? Who are?'

Felix would not be drawn.

From then on mostly they met in Maida Vale, or returned there after dinners out, and when she did visit his flat, to collect him, or something he'd forgotten, racing him up the stairs, trying her hardest to overtake, arriving gasping and laughing, always second to the top, he never liked them to stay long. 'I won't be a minute,' he warned, but even with only a minute she was able to check on the progress of his work, wander among the fearful flock of creatures, chart the expression of the stone man.

As the summer wore on there were days, and then more days, when he rang through to the post room to say he was working and had no plans to stop. Rosaleen made herself toast and got into bed early, taking a pen and a notebook and that day's copy of the newspaper which she trawled through for ideas. *Betting shops legalised. Is Alan Bates the future for our leading men?* She hoped to present a sample article to the *Express*, send it via pigeonhole to the appropriate department, and she pictured her name in small serious type. Rosaleen Kelly, she wrote, and then, blushing, Rose Lichtman. She was back at school picking petals off a daisy. 'Loves me,' Teresa Donnelly was saying. 'Loves me not,' she chorused back, until they were delirious with laughter, and the face of their beloved, the son of a dinner lady who had once been drafted in to mow the lawn, was obscured by their tears.

Rosaleen folded the paper and allowed herself a dream of Felix. She had to ration herself or she could lose whole days. The cool blue of his eyes, his eagle nose, his shoulders shaking with some silent joke. Enough. She turned back to her notebook. *Barclays: the first bank to adopt an in-house computer system.* She imagined the bank manager in a space suit, giving orders in a jerky automated voice. She mapped out an article about the planned redevelopment of London. A motorway flowing through the centre. Old buildings cleared. When this was done she rewarded herself with a letter. It had only been two days but she gave Felix all her news: the gossip from the post room, what new and mysterious item had arrived in the mail. She described her lunch with the aunties, her cousins' blushes when she wore her new short skirt, her nana who stared out of the window and didn't say a word. When there was nothing else she told him that she missed him, and as she signed her name she stopped and listened for it – Rosa – the way it sounded on his lips. Rosa-leen, she tried to catch his accent, or was it just his voice, for hadn't he arrived here as a boy? She sealed the envelope, wrote his address and, unable to wait till morning, ran down to the postbox, her coat over her nightdress, her feet in pumps.

The night was warm, the street lights hazy. She turned to hare back to her front door, and there he was, leaping from a taxi. 'Felix!' He looked dusty and dishevelled, and as he rounded on her his eyes were cold. 'Where have you been?' His fingers

51

pressed into her shoulder, and she wished she had the letter so that she could tear it open and read him the last lines.

'I missed you.' She looked back at the postbox, red and solid. 'I sent you a letter.'

'Is that right?' There was a sharp edge of disbelief, and it was only her panic and the trim of her white nightdress that eased his mood. 'I missed you too.' He took her hand and, using his own key, let them both in.

That night he made love to her in fierce and mournful style, his body burning, his eyes grown black. 'Be careful,' she gathered courage to say as she felt him still and gather, and then, 'Thank you,' as at the last moment he withdrew. She smeared the pleasing stickiness across the white skin of her stomach, and thought of Teresa's sister who'd been with a man who'd not cared it was the wrong time of the month, and when she'd gone to him in trouble, fearful of losing her job, he'd given her the number of a woman who'd told her to shoot soap water up inside with a syringe. She'd been so bad the girl she lived with called a doctor, and the doctor had ordered her to hospital where she'd stayed so long her job had gone.

Teresa Donnelly had started at St Joseph's the year after Rosaleen.

'God help us,' Bridie had hissed from her bed that first night when the girl would not stop crying. 'Sister Benedict will be in here in a flash.'

There was a hush as the eight girls in the dormitory considered the vengeful figure of the nun, but Teresa had no idea what awaited her, was not to know that the punishment for crying was to be pulled up by the ear and slapped. Within minutes she was at it again, sobbing loud enough to wake the dead.

'Shhh.' Rosaleen slithered to the floor, and crawling – who knew who might be listening for footsteps? – she knelt beside Teresa's bed. 'It's not so bad,' her stomach hollowed at the lie, 'once you get used to it.'

Teresa looked at her with a tear-stained face. 'I wrote,' she said, 'and told them to come and get me.'

'Write again,' Rosaleen nodded, 'but this time,' and she spoke quiet into her ear, 'don't give it to the nuns. They don't send those letters, not if they're sad. Write, and put it in the post yourself.'

'But I've no stamp.'

There was a rustle in the corridor and they both froze.

'Sometimes the postman takes them anyway.'

'Is that right?' The girl looked at her, hopeful, and as Rosaleen crawled back to bed she wondered if it was wrong to give encouragement when not a single one of her own letters had got through.

The cold had crept in between her sheets and her teeth chattered as she hunched into a ball, composing one last letter. Maybe this time … She imagined her mother hurrying up the steps. 'Be quick and pack,' she'd call to her. 'You'll not spend another minute in this place.' There would be Daddy testing out the slipper on his arm. 'Why did you say nothing?' they'd ask as they walked out through the gates, Angela rescued from the Babies, her socks unravelled, her face surprised. 'Why did you not let us know before?'

The next day Teresa found her, the letter in her hand. She'd drawn a stamp on the envelope, the kind face of the Queen, and on the back she'd written the address of the convent.

'What if it's sent back?' Rosaleen worried. 'What if the nuns read it?'

Teresa began to giggle. She was a plump girl with a freck-led face and the smallest, brightest eyes. 'I told them Sister Benedict was a lizard dressed as a bat.'

Rosaleen put a hand over her mouth.

'That the Mother Superior freezes soup with a single look.'

'I'll post it for you.' Rosaleen took a pen and scribbled out the return address. 'There's a gate at the back of the garden on to the main road.' She stowed the letter under the bib of her pinafore beside one of her own.

The following Sunday Teresa slipped her a sweet at Mass. It was a strawberry sherbet, a little fluffed on one side. 'I saved it for you,' and Rosaleen pushed it fast into her mouth. 'Thank you,' she smiled around its edges, and she sucked slowly, in the hope that she could make it last through the morning hour of prayers.

That term every girl aged eight and over was to partake in three days of prayerful silence. Three days of consider-ing your sins. Rosaleen tore two sheets of paper from her workbook and secreted them under her vest so that in the afternoon, when they were out in the gardens with their rosary beads, she might find a spot behind the rhododen-drons to distract her from the day. Now, with no one in sight, she slid a pen out of her sock. *Benedict the Batwoman*, she wrote, and every chance she got, she spun a tale of daring and adventure, herself and Teresa the fearless heroines, embroiled in an elaborate revenge. Rosaleen whispered the story to her new friend in instalments. 'I could do drawings.' Teresa's voice, like hers, was scratchy from the days of quiet. 'What do they look like … under their habits? Do they have hair? Or is it shaved?'

Rosaleen wasn't sure it mattered. She could see the Batwoman flying through the sky, her face with narrow lizard eyes, dragged back by her cape.

'Do you think,' Teresa whispered, 'they keep their veils on at night, being God's brides and that?'

Rosaleen put her hands over her ears but the image wouldn't leave her.

That night she was almost asleep when she felt a pinch on her arm. 'Pssst. Come on then, if you're coming.' Teresa led her from the dormitory.

'Where are we going?' She caught hold of her friend's hand, and Teresa ran, over the shiny floors, through the swish of swing doors, past the office and the slipper room and into the nun's corridor. Rosaleen's heart was beating so hard she thought for sure somebody would hear it.

'Nothing.' Teresa was bending to a door, her eye to the keyhole. She straightened up, and moved on to another. Almost at once she looked over at Rosaleen, her mouth a small round O.

'What?' Rosaleen whispered, but Teresa gestured for her to look. At first she could see nothing. A streak of light, a square of wall, the corner of a bed, and then she shifted her eyes sideways and there was Sister Angelica in a white nightdress, her hair loose about her shoulders. She was brushing it, slowly, thoroughly, her body swaying with the effort. 'She's getting ready for Himself,' and the two girls, shocked, ran, skimming over the corridors, back to their beds.

The next week at Confession Rosaleen's cheeks blazed. *I took a piece of bread from the refectory. I told a lie to Dolly Burke.* She ran through the usual sins and was given three Hail Marys, but it was possible that Teresa had been less able to dissemble because the next week when they snuck out of their beds, tiptoeing from door to door, pressing their eyes to keyholes, a hand came down and grasped each girl by the shoulder.

The slipper room was where the nuns did the girls' hair. They plaited it and tied it up with ribbons, pulling it so tight across their scalp it was impossible to sleep, but that was nothing to the slap of leather against skin, nothing beside the sickening humiliation of lying across Sister Annunciata's lap. 'So you're not sorry, is that it?' She gave Rosaleen an extra wallop. 'You're not sorry to be peaking and sneaking.' Rosaleen would not cry, not since the time she'd jolted her bowl and soup had slopped out over the table. Not since she'd stood on shaking legs after the shock of that first thrashing and seen the smirk on the nun's face as she'd wailed. Never again would she give them that pleasure, and as she lay in her bed, the welts on her skin rising, she pinched her arm and bunched her mouth into a knot.

★ ★ ★

Rosaleen had to ring three times before Felix answered. 'Yes?' His voice travelled flatly, uninviting through the grille, and she swallowed hard before she spoke. 'I thought you might be hungry …' She stepped into the road and looked up at his window for the keys to come hurtling down. 'Careful!' A bicycle swerved, and a car on the other side hooted as she leapt to catch them.

It had been a week since she'd seen Felix. *Working, not long now.* There'd been notes in pencil with kisses roughly drawn, and on the back of one a sketch of his rumpled bed, and on another an empty plate. Rosaleen had taken this as an invitation to visit the delicatessen on Brewer Street, and with the help of the man who ran it bought some of his favourite things. Liver pâté, pickled cucumbers and a dark, seeded loaf of bread. She had a bottle of wine, and glasses wrapped in a scarf, and as she stopped on the last landing to recover her breath, she did her best to still the flutter of apprehension as to how she might be greeted when she reached the top. 'I thought you might need—' she started, but Felix was waiting for her, his face pale, and he shook his head and, slipping an arm around her waist, moved her bodily inside. 'They're coming to take them tomorrow.' His foot was tapping, and with one distracted kiss, he took up his tools and before she could say more he'd turned to the smallest of his creatures and was chiselling the corner of its mouth.

Rosaleen found a tin plate on which to put the bread, and using her scarf as a tablecloth she spread out the picnic. As quietly as she could she searched for a bottle opener. She found three spoons, a rusted knife, a hammer and a ball of string. Surely if she attached the string … but then she saw the spiralled end of it lying on the floor. Rosaleen thought the plunk of the cork escaping might alert him but Felix was lost to her, muttering, clearing his throat, swatting away imaginary flies. 'No, no,' he bent to his work. 'That's not it.'

She poured herself a glass of wine and walked through to the next room. The stone man was unchanged. Knee bent, mouth open, his head so fierce and tender she stroked it as she passed. The bed was filthy, seamed with grit, as if Felix had lain between the sheets wearing his boots. She stripped them off and shook them, and as she tucked the cover over she heard the scolding voice of Sister Benedict. *Hospital corners. What have I told you?* The nun's eyes swam bald behind her glasses and Rosaleen felt the stubborn jut of her lip, and the word sorry, bitten to the quick. There. She laid a hand on Felix's quilt.

Felix was crouched down, knocking at the chisel with a hammer. With each strike a flicker passed across his eye. Rosaleen watched, wincing with him as he blinked, and then an arrow seemed to strike him. 'Aghh, damn that.' He put a hand to his head.

'Felix?' but he warded her off and, with a grimace, bent to his work.

It was dark when Rosaleen let herself out. 'Will I see you, then, before the opening?' She was on the landing, looking back.

'What's that?'

She took another step away. 'It's all right.' She touched her finger to her lip, the top one where he'd first kissed her, and as she ran down the stairs she wondered if tomorrow, when the figures were removed, he'd remember she was there.

Kate

I wake early and tiptoe down the stairs. My workroom door is closed, the handle smeared with paint, and even as I wrap my hand around it I am soothed. Inside, the trunks of trees stretch tall on their boards. I roll up the blind and let in the first light, and loosening a hardened nub of brown I mash my brush against the palette. I'm working on a severed branch and, with an old shirt buttoned over my nightie, I bend to the grooves of bark. This branch was once attached to the Big Oak, lost – or not entirely – but with this limb, for which it was renowned, wrenched off and slammed into the ground. It happened in the storm of '87, three days after Freya's birth, and once the roads were clear I'd made Matt drive me back to the village where I'd grown up.

'Will we visit your parents?' Matt had eased Freya from my arms.

'No.' My breasts were leaking, my body pulped, and even when we were diverted – a horse chestnut had fallen by the church – and forced to drive right past their house, I wouldn't change my mind. Now I attempt to recreate the knots of the oak, the polished bark where I'd come to test my courage, and as I do I can feel it, the snag and bobble as the wood caught on my tights, the terror as I lay flat, my arms outstretched, the close of my eyes as I swung under and dropped.

The last time we'd visited I'd been pregnant. Triumphant, nauseous, unprepared for the blanched look on my mother's face when we told her our news. 'What are you planning to do?' She'd drawn me into the garden, and I'd rounded on her. 'What's your question? Will I keep it?'

'I didn't mean … Congratulations, darling.' But when my father followed he was grinning as if he'd won some wager, as if he'd always known how I'd turn out. 'So?' He'd stood before Matthew. 'Are you two planning to get married?' And Matt had turned and put an arm around my shoulder and I'd loved him for it. 'That's between me and Kate.'

'Muuum.' Freya is awake.

'Muuuuuum.' She has her own special drawn-out name for me, and with each repetition it gets longer.

'Coming!' Three more strokes and I force myself to stop.

Freya is sitting in her bed, a fearful bird in the nest of her quilt. She has her back pressed against the wall, as far as she can get from the terror of the carpet. 'Come on, you.' I give my voice a cheerful lilt and she wraps her arms around my neck and hangs there as we make our way downstairs. I boil her an egg, butter toast, and we sit at the table with the radio murmuring while I calculate how soon I can get back to work. Neil Kinnock has condemned John Major for allowing small business interest rates to rise as high as 17 per cent. Three IRA gunmen have been shot dead. Soldiers opened fire on their car as it …

'When *you* die …' I turn the radio off, too late. 'Will you wait for me, when you get to heaven?'

'Of course!' I wonder if it's right to indulge the idea of heaven when I'm not sure what I believe, and to distract her, and myself, I shuffle and deal a pack of cards and we play Snap as loudly as we dare.

It's lunchtime before Matt appears. 'Feeling better?'

I nod. I am. A bit.

Freya is colouring. 'Smello.' It's true, he smells powerfully of beer, and she sticks out her tongue.

'Don't be like that.' He doesn't pretend to be amused, and when he leans across to see her page, she covers her picture with her hands.

Matt sits at the table and takes out his tobacco. He eases a pinch into the crease of the paper.

'Anything you'd like to do today?'

'I'm meeting the boys,' he tilts his chair, 'rehearsing.'

'And tomorrow?'

The legs snap back against the floor. 'What are you trying to do, ruin my weekend?' In the silence that follows we listen to the furious colouring of our child.

'Sorry,' he says later. 'Bit of a bad head.' He goes to the sink and, pressing two aspirin from their pack, he gulps them down.

That afternoon, once Matt has set off to corral the members of his band, I curl up with Freya on the sofa, and when, half-way through *Pinocchio* she falls asleep, I extricate myself and slip into my workroom. Ten minutes, I promise, and I bend to my branch, to the curve above the dip where, much as a chicken keeps on strutting after its head has been lopped off, the leaves still cling.

It's late when I hear Matt fumbling with his key. He hates it when I double-lock the door, thinks it's him I'm shutting out, but tonight the lock felt flimsy with its one loose catch, and Freya had alarmed me with her fears. There was a monster waiting underneath the bed, and she couldn't hear her story until I'd made myself safe.

'Matt,' I hiss from the top of the stairs as he swings his jacket and a plant pot shatters to the floor.

'Shhhory.' All around is earth and the jagged shards of clay. 'Katie, damn, I didn't mean … listen, Kate, I love you.' He sounds like everyone who was ever drunk but tonight he's my drunk, home, and I believe him. Three-legged we shuffle to the sofa where he does his best to pull me down. 'Let me get a quilt at least.' I'm laughing, but by the time I'm back he's asleep.

'Do you know,' Freya starts the next morning as soon as she's awake, 'it's easier to die standing up?' She crawls to the top of the stairs, and I have no choice but to follow as she bumps down on her bottom, pads along the hall, only stopping when stray beads of earth catch on her palms. She looks at me accusingly as if to say, be it on your head, and she stands up.

It's cold today, the pale sky striped with cloud, but with Matt still on the sofa, the safest thing to do is leave the house. We walk through the morning-after streets, grey paving strewn with stains and litter, but once we're through the railings, trailing up beside the first expanse of the heath, the sun breaks through. There are joggers, cyclists, two small football-kitted boys using their father as a goal. We wind along the path beside the ponds, stop to watch a Labrador plunge in after a stick, heaving in his big brown body, his mouth a smile, his tail wagging even as he shakes himself dry. There are men swimming in the next pond. We wait for one, in minuscule red trunks, to stop strutting and dive, and when he does, and the blue pond closes after him, we shiver as we watch to see where he'll come up. Three, four, five. He reappears in an arc of spray and, with only a second's pause, strikes out.

We walk uphill, curving away from the terraced pools of water towards a circle of trees. Last year's pine cones are scattered on the ground and I crouch down with my back against a trunk.

'I've been thinking … ' Freya's face is hopeful. 'I think you'll die when I'm eleven.'

'Let's have a race.' I'm determined to distract her. 'First one to the bottom of the hill is a—' She is off, and I am after her, knees jolting, hair flying, London stretched before us, a frieze of stark black towers, the mess of houses on the far side of the railway, our own tucked in between two blocks of flats. I let Freya hurtle ahead of me, bouncing and lunging over the uneven ground so that I have to stop myself calling out *Careful* as my mother would have done. *Careful*, until I wanted to harm myself to show her I'd survive.

As if I've conjured her, that afternoon my mother calls. She wants to know if it's safe to park outside the house; she doesn't want to be towed away, or broken into. 'Don't worry.' I'd forgotten she was coming, and I look around the kitchen with her scrutinising eyes.

Usually my mother stays with Alice when she visits London, but Alice is abroad with work. Her firm has sent her on a six-month placement to Atlanta, a promotion which has made our parents inordinately proud. I open the fridge and stare in at its contents.

'Morning, my lovelies.' Matt has staggered up from the sofa and Freya, who is icing digestives, puts a whole biscuit into her mouth and bares her teeth around it.

I'll make soup, I decide, and I go upstairs. I strip Freya's bed. Tonight she'll have to sleep in with us, and I'm grateful that last night took place *last night* because it means tonight will be better. 'If you want to be helpful,' I shout down to Matt when I've calculated the mix of food, coffee and aspirin will have set him straight, 'you could take Freya out for half an hour.'

I turn on the Hoover so that I'm spared any response and I follow it over Freya's carpet, into the corners, grimacing as it sucks up the lid of a miniature china teapot which I must retrieve. The inside of the Hoover is a world unto itself. I sit and stare into the bag. The fluff of the carpet, dark strands of hair, a penny gleaming in the dust, and I imagine myself at art school attempting to find a way to frame it in a Perspex box. Now I pluck out the lid, replace it on the china pot, and close the Hoover up.

'NO,' I hear Freya scream. 'I don't want my coat. Mummy never—' I drag the Hoover across the landing and into our room and wander it round the base of the chest of drawers, nose it under the bed. There is a shrilling as the nozzle blocks. I tug on its slinky neck and peel away a square of paper that will not be swallowed. *Call me.* The words are written in blue biro. *Bastard.* There are three kisses and the letter S.

Downstairs the door slams. I switch off the Hoover and listen. 'The fart went rolling down the street, parlez vous. The fart went rolling down the street …' Matt's voice sails up to me and I hear Freya giggle. I twist the note and throw it in the bin.

The morning after the first night I spent with Matt I woke to find a page of kisses on my pillow. I held the pencil crosses to my mouth, and later, as I dressed, my body liquid, my thoughts unspooled, I folded the sheet of paper into the pocket of my jeans. Do I still have it? I wonder now, and I lift down the box into which from the age of ten I've placed my most treasured possessions. As a child I'd kept it locked with its own key. And No One – I was fierce with my instructions

– was allowed to look inside. Now the key lies carelessly on top. Without Alice, without my mother, there is no one to keep out. I creak open the lid. On the top is a note from Freya, *I luv yuo Mumy*. And below this, as if there has been nothing in between, the plastic anklet she was labelled with when she was born. I sniff it, hoping to find a trace of her, the blood and milk, her embryonic nails, or failing that, the scent of hospital, of disinfectant, tears. There is no smell, only the silk slip of the plastic, the nub of the button. Below this is an assortment of necklaces, earrings, a choker I'd made myself from beads, and there, at the bottom, weighed down with foreign coins, is a picture of my mother. It is small and square, a photo-booth image, hand-drawn. Dark hair. A smile unnaturally wide. I uncurl its corners. It was the first thing I placed here and I am seized again with the same violent desire no one should know. *Mother*, I'd written on the back, and I look at it now. Who are you anyway? I take her to the mirror where my eyes surprise me with their wildness. I attempt to smile. Wider. But it's as false as the woman I have drawn, and although I'd like to scrunch it into nothing, I replace it care-fully, covering it feature by feature with my ornaments until it disappears from view. It is only then that I remember the kisses. Where did they go? I slam the lid, and seizing hold of the Hoover I pull it to the top of the stairs, scratching and rattling as I bump it down.

The sitting room smells like a bar. I draw the curtains, plump up the cushions, and vacuum it so thoroughly the reek of beer is replaced by hot, scorched dust. In the kitchen I fill the sink. Bacon fat, the clog of beans. In need of help, I slam Patsy Cline into the CD player and as I scour the grill pan I roar out the words of 'Crazy' and, cheered, sweep everything off the table and put each item in the place that it belongs. By the third verse I'm positively happy. I wipe the cooker, polish the knobs, and I have to stop myself from squeaking clean the glass in the back door.

I turn the music loud and run upstairs to clean the bathroom. *Are you all right?* Mum's concern fills the room. I scrub the basin. Scrub the bath. Wipe down the shelf and rearrange the bottles of shampoo. *I'm fine!* I pack the towels into the laundry basket and hang fresh ones on the peg, but I'll not be able to fool her, however brightly I smile.

Aoife

We were glad they were away in the clean air of the country. Do you remember how bad it was that winter when the smog came down? Not bad for business, we thought they'd never leave, and who can blame them, stumbling out into the street, feeling their way with fingertips and toes, and that poor fellow, the Murphy lad, God rest his soul, who never did reach home. That's when we started saving, every penny we could spare. The farm was your idea. Hadn't I spent my life trying to get away from the peat bog and the harvest, and then what do I do, go and marry a man with Ireland in his blood? It was Mam's funeral the first time we made the visit – too dangerous with the war to get back for my da – and there we were on the train to Killumney, the same journey I'd made all those years before but in reverse, walking over the fields to Kilcrea. My brother Jim had the farm by then, he'd worked it half his life, and he was welcome. A low place, with chickens messing as they pecked into the kitchen. I was ashamed for you to see where I'd been raised, but you showed it to me fresh. Through your green eyes I saw how bright was every blade of grass, how rich the soil, how ancient were the hills.

The next summer we sent the girls over as soon as they were done with school. Rosaleen and Angela, Kitty was too small, and the report came back that they were grand workers, our eldest if you can believe it, out in the fields the whole long day, pulling wild oats from barley. We'll put you on the pay roll, you told Rosaleen, when we have our farm. She was eleven, thin as a reed but strong, and she said she'd do it, if she could have a donkey. You riled at that. There was always something, but there'd been a donkey at Kilcrea and she'd fed it an apple on the flat of her palm. She'd call it Teddy, she said, and ride it through the lanes, and once she was back at St Joseph's she wrote to us about him, page after page, as if he was already hers.

It took too long, that was the truth of it. Sixteen by the time we'd saved enough, seventeen when we moved, and at seventeen there isn't a girl alive wants to go from London to Youghal, but that's what she had to do. By then she cared nothing for donkeys, although I found one for her anyway. Meet Teddy. He was a dusty old mule, stubborn as the day, and she only glanced at him, made a sad face at the droop of his head and left him for the rest of us to tend. Teddy, I'd coax, as if I didn't have better things to do, walking backwards with a carrot, Kitty sitting straight as a sergeant, kicking with her heels. Even Angela did her best, heaving her whole weight against his flank. It was only at night he'd waltz away to stand under the oak for which the house was named, and we'd wake in the morning to see him nosing out to reach a clump of thistle.

We'll send him to the knackers, you'd say to rouse her, but Rosaleen would only shrug. She had other things on her mind by then, if you remember. Dear God.

Rosaleen

Rosaleen ate her lunchtime sandwich at a pub in Fleet Street. She'd brought along the paper, the front page of which covered the trial of the American pilot Gary Powers, accused of espionage by a Russian court. 'If Eisenhower had just apologised.' Three newspapermen had joined her table.

'If Khrushchev hadn't made him look a fool …' A heavy, bald-headed man was squeezing in beside her.

'But you've got to admit it was funny … Weather research!' His friend was smirking.

'Not funny,' the man to Rosaleen's left cut in. He wore a shimmery blue suit. 'They were going to be discussing nuclear arms reduction, for Christ's sake.'

The first man was watching her. 'Will you have a drink?' He picked up his empty glass and turned to the others. 'Same again?'

'Thank you.' Rosaleen shook her head.

'Go on.' He looked disapproving at her lemonade. 'Something stronger? What will it be? A gin and tonic?'

Flustered, she conceded. Maybe this is it, my chance to talk to an actual journalist, and as she waited for her liquid courage she compiled a list of questions. Isn't Gary Powers a scapegoat? Is nuclear war a real threat? Who should I approach if I was to publish an article myself? But the men, once they were on their second pints, talked harder, faster, lighting cigarettes, one from the last, the only attention she had from them, the hand of the man in the blue suit creeping lazily across her lap.

The next day Rosaleen ate her sandwich by the river. She sat on a bench overlooking the Thames and unfolded that morning's paper. She flicked through the pages, studying the photographs beside each byline. She found two of the men from the pub – one was Sport, the other Money – but it was the women she examined more particularly. Their hair, their clothes, their confident smiles. Surely not one of them was so cowardly as to leave her drink half finished, slipping away with a small murmur of thanks as the blue-cuffed hand disappeared under her skirt.

'Nice lunch?' Betty had greeted her when she'd returned to work, and she'd nodded and continued sorting through the post.

That evening on her way home she stopped outside a hair salon. In the window was a picture of Jacqueline Kennedy, her black bob swept up off her forehead, flicking in under her ears. Rosaleen looked at her own reflection in the glass. A curtain falling to her shoulders, a fringe that dropped into her eyes.

'I'd like it short,' she said once she'd been ushered to a chair, and the neat man, his mouth pursed, lifted the dense mass of her curls. 'Yes,' he agreed and he reached for his scissors.

Felix was appalled. 'Where's my Rosa gone?' He'd been waiting for her in the street, smart in a dark suit, freshly shaved.

'It's the latest style. It's how Jackie—'

'You're the latest style.' He held her head in his hands. 'At least you were.'

Her cheeks flamed. 'It'll grow. I just wanted to see who I—'

Felix was surveying her, a long serious look. 'Promise me you won't cut it again?'

Never? Hope hurled her into the future and she pressed her face against the smoothness of his cheek. 'Is it true, you've finished?'

'For tonight, certainly.'

'I promise.' She grinned, and he kissed her, hungrily and for so long she was forced to wriggle away.

Angela, when she arrived, was equally shocked. 'Oh Rosaleen.' Her hands flew to her mouth. 'I'd hardly know you!' She slipped out of her shoes so as not to mark the pearl-grey carpet. 'You look ever so smart.'

It was the nicest thing, to have Angela with her. They made food from home, mashed potatoes and a chop, and they ate it on the sofa, laughing to think of Mummy's face as they propped the plates on their knees.

'The private view isn't till next week,' Rosaleen told her, 'that's when the exhibition opens, but Felix says we can sneak in and see it while you're here. He'll show us round on Sunday.'

'But I promised.' Angela's face clouded. 'The aunties, they're expecting us for our dinner.'

Rosaleen's anger flared. 'And why would you agree to that? You're here with me now and it's none of anyone's business what we do.'

'I suppose we could send a note and say we're sick?' Angela was pale.

'Then they can pray for us. They'll like that.'

'For all they know we *are* ill.'

Rosaleen leant over and squeezed her sister's hand. 'The gallery's in Mayfair, and if Felix can get away he says he'll take us out for lunch.'

'He'll take us both? You sure of that?'

71

'I'm not sure of anything, but it'll be more fun than the aunties.'

They smiled at each other and, leaving their dishes on the floor, lay on the sofa, one at each end, and talked about the farm, about school and Cork and Declan Shaughnessy who still called by to ask when Rosaleen was coming home. They talked about the nuns, and the newspaper, and Mr O'Malley up over the way, who'd pinned Angela to the wall while she was kicking off her gumboots, and when she pushed him off, he'd looked at her, aggrieved. 'It was only a kiss I was after!' They laughed, the greasy fellow, and to think she might have been hoping for more.

'I feel bad for his poor wife. She won't know why I've stopped going on over for a cup of tea.'

'She married him.' Rosaleen stretched. 'She'll know what he's like. Although look at our mother: she'd have us believe the sun shines out of Daddy's arse.'

'Rosaleen!'

She pressed her toes into her sister's side and tickled, and hard as she tried Angela couldn't stop herself from laughing.

Sunday came round in a flash. 'What should I wear?' Angela wanted to know. 'I've never been to an art gallery.'

'Your blue skirt, you'll be fine.' Rosaleen glanced at her own reflection, at her hair which was already flipping up below her ears. She had a cotton dress in black and white with short capped sleeves and a tight band around the bodice. There were ballet pumps that matched, and for once she felt just right. Angela stood beside her at the mirror. 'You look swell.' The sisters smiled into the glass.

FELIX LICHTMAN. His name was in large letters on the gallery wall, and beside the door, restless, shuffling from one foot to the other, was Felix himself. 'Are we late?' Rosaleen ran towards him, and he caught her round the waist and kissed her. 'This is Angela.' Her sister came panting behind, and fearful she may have pulled her backwards into childhood, Rosaleen blushed. But Felix looked at Angela with a clear, appraising eye. 'It's very nice to meet you.'

There was no one else at the gallery. They stood in silence, the work arranged in the old familiar order, the stone man filling the whole of the first room. Rosaleen put her hand out and drew it back. 'It's all right,' Felix said and she rested her palm lightly on its head. It was cold, and quickly warming, every chiselled pang rising through her arm, and turning to Felix she saw in his face the days and nights, the weeks, the years of work.

Angela walked through to the next room and when they followed they found her backed away from the creatures. 'Could you tell me what they are, Mr Lichtman?'

'I couldn't,' Felix didn't smile.

They all three circled, examining their movement and their horror, inspecting them as if they might have found a way in on their own.

'Lunch?' Felix suggested. They filed out into the heavy summer day and, leaving his name emblazoned, climbed into a taxi and sped through the Sunday streets. Rosaleen didn't ask where they would go. She sat with Angela beside her and let the rush of air from the open window mess her hair. Felix leant forward on the tip-up seat and talked to the driver: London talk, sporting talk, talk of the world. She reached across and squeezed her sister's hand.

The café had red Formica tables and a counter behind which large snowy cakes were arranged. They found a table at the back and sat in silence as they examined the menus. Omelette, soup of the day, croque-monsieur — whatever that was – and a list of gateaux. 'I think I'll have cake,' Felix decided, and he looked round for a waitress. Rosaleen saw Angela's eyes widen. Is that allowed? In answer she pushed away her own menu. 'Let's see what they have.' The two girls slithered from their seats and stood at the counter staring at the frosted flowers, the stripes of sponge seamed with jam and cream.

In the end all three of them had cake. One slice, and then another. 'Anyone for pudding?' Felix asked when they had scraped their plates, and Angela, giddy with freedom, jumped up to have a look.

'So?' Rosaleen leant across. 'Are we alike?'

Felix turned and glanced thoughtfully at Angela. 'The gentle sister.'

It had always been the case. 'The favourite.' The old despondency descended.

'Not with me.' He nudged her foot.

Angela was back with a tall almond pastry, and Felix waved over for the bill.

It had started to rain, light and warm. 'A day for the park, I think?' Felix tilted his face to the sky, and they walked through Marylebone and, dodging traffic, ran across the Euston Road. Once or twice when they were children they'd been to Regent's Park, dressed in their best, on a day out with their parents to meet Uncle Joe and Auntie Elsie, and their cousin, Patricia. Rosaleen remembered the rat-tat of Daddy shouting to them: not to walk on the grass, disturb the flowers, drip ice cream on their clothes. Patricia was a boarder at St Joseph's too, a shy girl cowed with misery, and they'd trudged dutifully ahead, the adults behind, the two couples, arm in arm, laughing and talking about what she'd never know.

They were halfway across the grass when the rain gathered strength and they raced for cover, huddling in under a tree. Rosaleen closed her eyes and let the thud of the down-pour surround her. It filled her ears and tingled her scalp and she longed to stand close in to Felix, feel the heat of him, steal some for herself. She pushed against the trunk and let the damp raise her curls to a frizz. 'Rosaleen?' Angela's voice drifted as if from far away and she found the rain had quieted and Felix was stepping out from the shelter of the tree.

'Wait for me.' She shook herself and, slipping off her shoes, took her sister's hand and raced with her across the grass, and along the road to the inner circle of the park where the roses were winking and heavy with wet. Felix had kept pace with them, running as if in some crazy kind of dance, twirling and swooping and tapping both heels in the air, and now he leant down and snapped off a dark red stem and, his fingers bloody with stray thorns, slid it between the buttons of Rosaleen's dress. 'A white flower for you,' he turned to Angela.

Angela was shivering. 'What if someone sees?'

There was no one on the path, and no one on the lawn, and so he found a smooth white rose and tucked it behind her ear.

They walked on until they reached the lake. Boats bumped against the shore, their plank seats oiled with water. The boatman sat smoking in his hut. 'Good afternoon.' Felix raised his hand, and the man nodded, flicked his cigarette. They kept on walking as the park came back to life, dogs, bicycles, children free of macs, and on the lake, boats launching off, couples, families, a man and his daughter, rowing round and round.

★ ★ ★

The private view was less glamorous than Rosaleen expected. She'd imagined women in cocktail dresses, men in pinstripes, but for the most part there was the same dishevelled crowd that packed into the French pub. 'Has anyone seen the artist?' a woman, loud and drunken, called across their heads.

'He stepped inside, saw that lot,' the man beside her pointed to a trio of old ladies, 'and vanished.'

'Get me another glass of this disgusting plonk.' She held out her empty glass, and he hurried obediently towards the makeshift bar.

Rosaleen circled the three women. They were dressed in black, their silver hair elegantly arranged. They talked in an urgent, guttural tongue and as she hovered Rosaleen slid her eyes sideways and found herself caught by a pale blue stare. She swallowed and put out a hand to touch the stone head, and then, remembering, balled her fingers into a fist. She wanted to look again, see the proud way the woman held herself, the familiar mouth, the curve of her chin. Instead she sipped her wine and moved away.

A new troupe of people had arrived. The door was left open on to the street as others crowded the pavement, smoking, laughing, hushing a little as they stepped inside. Here they waved to each other and swiped fresh drinks from the tray.

In the second room it was harder to ignore the art. A small group stood quiet before the creatures. The flock looked different when in company, more terrifying, more afraid. Rosaleen collected words, compiling a list for Felix. *Fury. Persecution.* The three old women came through and stopped abruptly at the door. One swayed and raised a hand to her head, and the others held tight to her and glared. There was another one. *Revenge.*

They came no nearer but stood blocking the door, and for the longest time it seemed no one could move, but then a woman with a stick, a regular at the French pub, burst past and swore. 'Bugger it. No wine in here either!' The spell broken, the woman with Felix's sharp eyes turned and, with the others following, moved through the crowd.

Rosaleen waited on the street. Surely he would come back now? She stood on the corner as the last guests straggled by, some in couples, others sauntering off alone, a large group arguing over where they might go on to. She caught sight of a few she knew, but they didn't look her way.

When everyone had gone she walked through the quiet streets of Mayfair. Her arms were chilled and her ankles slipped against the straps of her sandals. She'd dressed for a taxi. She glanced into gentlemen's outfitters, wood-panelled barbers', the glossy window of a department store as she wound her way towards the British Museum. It was dark by the time she arrived, the sandstone pillars lit like torches, the sentry boxes empty. Felix's building was dark too, only one flicker of a light three storeys up. Rosaleen waited, unable to decide whether or not to ring the bell. What if he was sleeping, or he'd started some new work? Or maybe, her stomach hollowed, he was entertaining a guest? The pavement slipped beneath her feet, and she clung to the handle of the door.

'Hello.' Felix's flat voice came through the grille. Did he think by deadening the vowels he could make himself unknown?

'It's me,' and before she could explain he told her he'd be down.

He must have run because she'd hardly had time to smooth her hair before he was with her on the step.

'What took you so long?' With a hand on the small of her back, he steered her ahead of him up the stairs.

The flat was empty, she'd forgotten to expect that, but on the one small table there was a bottle of champagne. 'There really was no one else I wanted to see.' He looked at her so intently she felt her limbs dissolve.

'I wanted to see you too.' She berated herself for doubting. 'I needed to see you.' For a long time they stood wrapped together and then, calmed, they hobbled through to the next room and fell down on to the bed.

'It was good …' Rosaleen told him.

'What was good?' He held a button in his mouth.

'Your exhibition.'

His fingers were undressing her.

'Your mother …'

He stopped.

'Was it your mother?'

He drew away from her although he hadn't moved. 'I told them not to come.'

'But why?'

A needle struck him in the eye. 'Aghh.' He reared his head as if to shake it out.

'What is it?'

'Nothing,' he said, severe, but his strength had drained away.

'I'm sorry.' Rosaleen lay with her head on his shoulder. She glanced at him. His eyes stayed fixed on the ceiling.

'Everyone loved it,' she tried, and when he didn't answer she turned and curled into his side.

'We'll go away.' He folded himself around her. 'The two of us.'

She wasn't sure that she believed him. 'What am I to tell them at work?'

'Compassionate leave,' he whispered. 'Your Auntie Mavis. The funeral is in the South of France.' And although she protested, she was still smiling as she fell asleep.

They went by train to the coast, and took a ferry from Dover. The sky was clear, the crossing smooth. They ate lunch in the ship's restaurant, grilled sole with peas, potatoes scalloped into shells, and after coffee they stood on deck and watched the waves, deep green and breaking, rolling from the prow. Gulls flew out to meet them as they neared Calais, sleek and fat, circling for scraps. From Calais they took another train, first class, the curtains drawn against the sun. Felix read the papers in English and French and Rosaleen took out her notebook. *Hovercraft travel. Will it catch on?* She looked out of the window as they trundled south and did her best to see into the future.

★ ★ ★

Rosaleen had bought the bikini with her first month's wages, and if she didn't wear it now she may never have the courage. While Felix shaved she lifted it from its tissue wrapping, her fingers trembling with the need for speed as she slipped the ruched bra over her arms and fastened the catch against her back. Felix was singing in the bathroom, one side of his face gleaming, the bright lather deepening his tan. Her own skin was pale, flecked with freckles, and before he could finish and catch sight of her surprise, she'd slipped on her dress and buttoned it up.

Later, when there was a chance for a swim, and Felix had settled himself on a restaurant's terrace, she raced across the coast road, her towel in a string bag. The beach was narrow and deserted, and self-conscious she flung off her dress, not looking round as she waded out in her flimsy covering of cotton. It was as good as swimming naked – and she thought of Angela and how at the end of the school year they'd swum out from the beach below Loreto, pulling off their rubbery black costumes under cover of the water, laughing as the sea's silk fingers slunk around their waists. 'I dare you to get out like this,' she'd shouted to her sister, the thought of the nuns watching from the hill above making her laugh more, and Angela had splashed, horrified, and refrained from returning the dare.

Rosaleen floated on her back and looked up at the sky. Light skipped across the water as she stretched. If she was truly one of God's creatures then how many sins had she accrued in the last two blissful weeks and, she wondered idly, would her life be long enough for penance? She flipped over and swam down under the water, following shoals of tiny glinting fish, tracing the dappled light across the seabed. It was then she remembered she had intended keeping her head dry. Surely Felix didn't want to dine with a girl dripping water into her plate? She burst up and glanced towards the terrace but the sun was in her eyes and there was nothing to be seen. Back on the beach she dried herself and, flushing to find she'd forgotten any underwear, pulled on her dress. *Our Father, who art in heaven …* The prayer unspooled as her nipples hardened and cool air swished between her legs.

Felix greeted her, amused. 'It was an itsy bitsy teenie weenie yellow polka-dot bikini,' he crooned in his pleasing, oddly tuneless voice, 'that she wore for the first time today,' and she laughed as she remembered that despite his many years – in the New Year he'd be turning forty! – he was the most ageless person she knew.

'Eat.' He pointed to the lobster they had chosen, bound and menacing in its tank, now bright and broken open. Her stomach growled, obedient, and she pulled out a chair.

'Marvellous.' He looked at her, his eyes glittery with sun, and she lifted his fingers and kissed them one by one.

All afternoon they wandered through Marseilles, down to the port where fishermen were finishing their day, while in the cafés opposite sailors were beginning theirs. They walked through narrow streets and peered into shops, and every time they crossed a road, Felix took her arm and, holding it tight, whisked her wildly over. 'Is there anything you long for?' he asked, as they stared at a collection of glass figurines, but apart from underwear, which she had at the hotel, there was nothing in the world she needed.

They stopped at a patisserie and bought a bag of vanilla-scented cakes, eating them straight from the paper, savouring the fluted yellow sponge. Felix told her they made him think of the *Sandkuchen* he'd eaten in Berlin before the war. 'My *Oma* would make it in a loaf tin and bring it to the house still warm.' Rosaleen slipped a last cake into her mouth and knew that if she were ever to eat one again she'd be reminded of today.

The need for tea drove them back to their hotel, but the hotel didn't understand about tea, and so Felix ordered champagne. It arrived as Rosaleen was pulling off her dress, and naked she leapt into bed and lay still under the covers while Felix ushered the boy in. '*Oui, c'est tout.*' She heard the rattle of coins, and with a '*merci beaucoup, Monsieur*', and some happy steps, the door was closed behind him. 'It is imperative this champagne be drunk immediately.' He poured two glasses and, kicking off his shoes, slid in beside her and, as the bubbles rose, he enfolded her salt body in his arms.

Kate

Where is that fucking river? Tomorrow I have work and I press a hand between my legs, comforting, hard, but I know I'll sleep more deeply if I can quieten my thoughts some other way. *Don't wake me.* I've left a note on the stairs, and I think how, when my mother was here, Matt was his true charming self. 'Just a quick rehearsal,' he'd said, not long after she had gone.

I glance at the clock. It's almost one.

My river, when I find it, is flowing over boulders. I cling fast, but they are slippery and green, and I'm rushed through reeds and minnows, catching at an overhanging branch, watching as it curves around a headland and is gone. Shipwrecked, I turn to my tree and start to climb, and soon I'm on a ladder, balancing against the dirty whitewashed wall of the yard where my people go to smoke. *We'd plant a real tree*, I tell them, *if the yard hadn't been paved over*, and Beck, who runs the centre's café, providing soup and flapjacks, has abandoned his kitchen to hold the ladder steady. 'You OK there?' he calls, and I look into his upturned face, and I see his eyes are beech-nut brown.

'I am.' I'm blushing, even in my sleep. 'I'm fine.'

'Muuum.' Like a miracle it's morning. I flick off the optimistic alarm and stretch out a foot to Matt. There's nothing but the smooth cool width of sheet.

'Muuuuum!' Freya is as pleased to see me as if we've been apart for years. She winds her arms around my neck and presses her mouth against my cheek as we stagger downstairs. 'Shhh,' I whisper as I duck into the sitting room, but Matt isn't there either.

Iced with worry, I leaf through my address book. Might he have stayed at Andy's? I listen to the ringing of the phone, and when there is no answer I try Ian. 'No,' comes the gravelly reply and I apologise. It's six a.m.

Unsure what else to do, I run a bath.

'Mum.' Freya has a bubble beard. 'I'll love you even when you're dead.'

My heart is heavy but I smile. 'I'll love you when I'm dead too.' I give myself bubble eyebrows and a bubble moustache. 'And even after that.'

'Forever and a million years.'

'A million and one.'

We stay in the bath until it's time for school, trickling in hot water when the temperature cools, making lists of fives – five favourite sweets, five favourite suppers, five favourite children in her class. 'Five favourite names,' Freya demands and I close my eyes, using the time to tip my head into the water. 'Freya: number one. Kate.' I read her lips, and I smile so that water seeps into my mouth.

'Catherine?'

I test it out, but I'm trying to retrieve that other name, the one I was given first.

'Grace.' Freya adds her own middle name.

Maybe Kate is all there is.

It's only later when I've dropped Freya at school, reminded her it will be Celine who will be collecting her today, that

I'm overrun by fear. I stare through the window of the bus, imagine I might see Matt in a side street, beaten, lost, in need of help. My stomach quakes, and then I pinch myself. I've been through this before, not often, but I have, and there has always been an explanation. Too tired to get the night bus. Didn't want to call and wake me up. And that's when I see her. My mother. She's an old woman, hunched over, her hair grown sparse. 'I'll not accept it,' she mutters to herself, 'they can't make me do it,' and she balls one hand into a fist. I look away but she is there, reflected in the glass.

A girl gets on. She glances at the empty seat and skips upstairs. Her hair is dark and straightened to a sheen, her arched eyebrow familiar as my own. I rise to follow, then catch myself, and sit back down.

When I next look the woman has gone. There's a stain where she's been sitting and no one has taken her place. I huff my breath against the window. Of course she's not my mother, and I summon up the managing director of a company, dogstooth jacket, belted skirt, standing at the head of a boardroom table while her employees sit with their pens poised to hear what she will say. I draw a face in the steam. Wide mouth, fierce eyes, and when I reach my stop I wipe it out.

'Are you all right?' Beck looks up as I come in. He's wearing a green shirt, the same shirt he was wearing in my dream.

'Early start, that's all.'

He makes me coffee. Black. One sugar. 'Thank you.' I could cry, and I take a sip too soon and scorch my lip.

I've brought along a stack of books and I set them on the table of my designated room. I unroll a poster that I found folded into the glossy segment of the paper. On it are sixteen varieties of tree. Birch, larch, hornbeam, cherry. There's a Scots pine, a crack willow, a bright red-berried holly. *Holly plants are either male or female, explaining why some never bear the familiar scarlet berries.* I stand before it as my group files in, but before I can suggest what they might do, Jen has her hand up. She's not feeling well. Jen is never feeling well. I sit beside her and ask that before she goes back to the hostel she could copy a leaf. Mute, she points to a maple. I sit with her while she leans over it, breathing heavily as she presses her pencil down, the cuff of one sleeve riding up to reveal a fine white mesh of scars.

Sam is standing by the poster, reading the words out loud. *Silver birch. The twigs are hairless but warted and the leaves are double-toothed.* He laughs, and I laugh. I have hopes for Sam.

It helps if I draw too. I take out my sketchbook and open it. I've been painting animals for Freya. A hippopotamus, a leopard. Naina wheels herself closer. She says she'd like to paint a leopard but she knows hers will be shit. She demands I do the outline. 'Why not trace it?' I pull a sheet of paper from my book. Tracing is the perfect combination of difficult and easy, and as I watch, I see her troubled self pulled into the sharp end of the lead.

Alec and Marjorie are both sketching the Scots pine.

'I'm Scottish,' Alec says.

'I'm pining,' Marjorie explains.

Neil arrives late. He smells hotly of spirits. He pinches out his roll-up and puts it in his pocket. 'Right.' He rubs his hands together and, ignoring my suggestions, takes a pen and sketches the naked outline of a woman.

It is only when we stop for coffee that I remember Matt. The shock of my forgetting propels me into the office where I must log the number and the time into a ledger so that the cost of any call can be deducted from my wages. I needn't have bothered. The answerphone clicks on. 'Matt, it's me. Pick up.' I wait, and say it again, louder, and then a third time, my voice rising to such a pitch the very inside of me is rattled: 'Matt!!' But he's not there, or if he is, he's upstairs, sleeping, deaf, or dead.

'Fuck you,' I say, because I know he's not dead, and I write *10 seconds!* and I dial the number for his work. 'Sorry,' the receptionist tells me in her singsong voice, 'he's on lunch. Can I suggest that you call back?'

I press my head against the cooling wall.

Donica is in the foyer when I emerge. It's been three months since she was enrolled into the class, but as yet she hasn't ventured through the door. A large, hunched woman, she rustles through the flock of plastic bags she carries with her at all times. 'Will you be joining us today?' I ask as casually as I can manage, but Donica continues sorting, and when I try again she kisses her teeth and looks away.

I release the CD player from a locked cupboard and plug it in so that the first strains of the music swell as my people trail in from the yard. All through that afternoon we listen, Bob Marley, Eurythmics, David Bowie, Wham, spiralling up on a rush of Dolly Parton, proclaiming she will always love us, always, so that soon we're warbling and screeching as we sketch and smudge and colour.

Rosaleen

When Rosaleen arrived at the French pub with her news, Felix was surrounded by people. There was the tall man, who she now knew to be a film-maker, and his wife, Anastasia, a loud, chaotic woman whose name her husband had suggested she change to that of his first wife. There was a photographer, mostly silent, who, if everyone was drunk enough, raised his camera to capture them with a click.

'Another glass,' Felix called to the proprietor, and as Rosaleen waited for her drink Anastasia put an arm around her and kissed her smokily on the cheek. 'Doesn't she look darling,' she proclaimed, and she began to whisper about a really rather horrible man she'd had sex with in the toilets of the Gargoyle Club. 'He smelt dirty as a bike chain. I can't get him out of my mind.'

Felix held a glass of champagne out to Rosaleen and they pressed into a circle. 'Cheers!' they clinked and Felix lowered his voice and told them his stone man had sold. Rosaleen reached up to him, thrilling with this unexpected luck, but rather than bend to her she found that he was tensed. The sinews of his arms were taut, heat scorched through his shirt. 'Felix?' she tried, but he had turned away.

Others crowded in. An artist with a fading bruise, his boyfriend – *Love* and *Hate* tattooed on his knuckles. 'Congratulations,' the word was passed around. *Stone Man.* Sold.

Later they flocked from the pub, and waltzed along the street to the restaurant. 'Mr Lichtman.' Henry the barman came out to greet them, and he suggested the oysters, fresh in from Wexford, and what would they start with, three bottles of champagne? They'd hardly sat down when others joined them, a girlfriend of Anastasia's, and a man with a lopsided smile. An adjoining table was pushed against theirs, more oysters ordered, more champagne. There was bread in baskets, butter in pale furls. Anastasia wanted steak, and so did her husband. An actor asked for lobster, the photographer soup, and Rosaleen watched as Felix's fee was almost certainly devoured. What would it cost, she wondered, to have a baby? An article she'd read, an interview with an Unmarried Mother, swam into her mind. The girl, nineteen, pictured with her smiling naked toddler, reported her life to be 'super'. What does anyone need anyway, she'd said, apart from love?

'What are you smiling about?' It was the artist, whose bruised face did nothing to disguise his sharpness.

Rosaleen flushed. 'I was thinking,' she had no idea what she was going to say, 'how glad I am to be here in London. Now. In this new decade.'

There was a silence, and everyone held up their drinks. 'The sixties,' the artist said, and when he'd drained his glass he threw it at the wall.

Henry rushed out, his face turned red. 'I'll cover it,' Felix nodded, and Henry crept away, returning with a dustpan and brush, with which he carefully, tenderly swept up the shards.

Soon the cloth was dense with glasses, trails of spinach, spills of wine. Anastasia was whispering into the tattooed boy's ear, while the tall man leant across the table and talked intently about film to the man with the lopsided smile. Felix and the artist were discussing a fight. The elegance with which the men danced around each other, the pulpy swelling of their blackened eyes. A realm of tiredness descended on Rosaleen. She slipped away and found the ladies and sat there on the toilet seat. She knew the others would soon move on to a club, the Gargoyle or the Colony, and although she longed for nothing more than to go home, it wasn't safe tonight, of all nights, to let Felix go alone.

'You all right in there?' It was Anastasia, twisting the handle. 'I'm bursting.' She pulled open the door which Rosaleen had failed to lock. 'Hey,' her face softened when she saw her, 'what's up with you then, duck?'

'Nothing. I'm just … I'm …' There were tears on her face.

'You're just what?' A knowing look sobered her. 'Happens to the best of us. Come round to me, and I'll give you a number. I've got a woman, she'll sort you out.'

'No, it's not …' Rosaleen flushed.

'It's all right. She's good. And not as dear as some. Don't wait too long or she'll charge extra. Happened to me last time. Bloody cleaned me out.' She winced then, and a shadow darkened her. 'Now get a move on or you'll have to fetch a mop.'

Rosaleen dabbed at her eyes with water and patted them dry while Anastasia, whose real name, it came to her, was Phyllis, sang to drown out the sound of her pissing. 'Oh dear, what can the matter be, three old ladies locked in the lavatory …'

'They were there from Monday to Saturday …' Daddy used to sing it when he was in a good mood, and Rosaleen remembered something the unmarried girl had said. *My father has been very supportive. I don't know what I'd have done without his help.* 'Nobody knew they were there.'

Anastasia bustled out of the cubicle. 'Oh dear, what can the matter be.' They smiled at each other in the mirror. 'Don't bother with all the gin and cod liver oil business, even falling down the stairs. I've tried that, it doesn't work.' Without washing her hands, she held open the door.

The sale of *Stone Man* catapulted Felix to a new level of success. A private collector made a bid for several of the creatures, but Felix was determined they remain together, and after some negotiation they were bought by an American museum as a flock. Felix responded by going to ground. He ordered a block of marble and spent all day and half the night winching it up on its cradle of ropes and staring at it. He turned it, lowered it, ran his hands over the rough surface. Sometimes he took a point chisel to it and burst away a corner, and then he faltered. 'What's in there, I don't see,' he muttered as if the image was already lurking, and Rosaleen swallowed in case it was her he was addressing. 'Come on, that's it.' His forehead was creased, his eyes two boreholes, and Rosaleen, who'd hoped they might go out for supper, turned away, nibbling on the dry black bread she'd taken to eating to settle her stomach.

'Did they pay you huge amounts of money?' she tried later, hoping to cheer him with the facts, but he continued feeling for the seams of stone and told her the money was of no interest — it was the gallery who'd taken the gamble, it was only right they had the bulk of the reward.

Rosaleen walked through to the next room and lay down on the bed. Her breasts pricked and itched against her bra.

The single mother, she remembered, had tucked her baby to sleep in a drawer, had lived on meat pies from a vending machine, had used Milton to soak the nappies, and when they became too grey had dyed them pink. She'd fed the child on National Dried Milk. *Super*, she'd declared the whole experience to be.

When she woke Felix had curled himself around her. 'My love,' she murmured, but his limbs were restless, and before she could turn to him and whisper that she had some news, he was up and through to the next room, pacing round his block of marble, staring, unblinking, to see what it contained.

For a whole week Rosaleen left him alone. She met her friend Michele who mentioned she looked pale, and when she went to Auntie Mavis for her lunch she pinched her cheeks and smiled between each mouthful.

'I have something to tell … to say …' Rosaleen practised as she walked towards the British Museum. 'I've been wanting… I need …' She rang the bell, hopeful, but as soon as she heard the cool flat tones, 'Hello' – more of a warning than a welcome – her heart sank.

Tonight she didn't try and catch the keys, but let them smash into the gutter. Slowly, heavily, she walked up the five flights of stairs.

'What is it?' Felix stood, bemused, in the doorway, a rasp in one hand, a hammer in the other.

Her mouth was dry, fear fizzed along her arms, but she had no words left other than to tell him. 'I'm going to have a baby.'

Felix dropped his tools.

'What?' She was laughing as he fell to his knees.

'You are?' He pressed his ear against her coat and she listened with him to the galloping of her blood. When he looked up his eyes were wet. 'It's mine?'

Rosaleen cuffed the dark crop of his head. 'What did you—'

Grinning, he swooped her off the ground. 'Why didn't you say?'

'I'm saying now.'

He walked them through to the empty room and fell with her on to the bed. 'Christ,' he said, 'it's cold. I'd light a fire, if there was any fuel ...' He peeled off her dress, her slip, her stockings, trailed a finger over the small rise of her belly. 'I thought it was the oysters that were fattening you up.'

'It wasn't the oysters, as it happened.' His touch was so light it sent shivers through her. 'Whatever the nuns would have us believe.'

'So it would seem,' and he kissed the bone of her shoulder, butterflies fluttering, warming her with the sharp scratch of his chin.

Afterwards she pulled the quilt around them, the spines of feathers catching at their skin, and Felix slept, his head thrown back, his limbs abandoned. Did he know, as she did, the moment it had happened? She wondered if they might give their child a French name. Celeste, she'd always liked that. Emile. She lay against his shoulder and allowed herself to dream.

'Damn.' Felix woke with a start, squinting through the window at the fading light. 'I need to get on.' He pulled on a sock, but as he reached for his shirt, a flash cracked against his eye.

'What is it?'

He stayed still, one arm warding her off, the other pressed to his forehead. 'Nothing.' He forced a smile. 'It's gone.'

'Felix.' She followed him, naked. 'Can you stop a moment ...'

He turned to her, a beat of anger, and then he froze. 'That's it.'

She was shivering.

'Of course. Stay there.' He dashed back into the bedroom and returned dragging the quilt cover and an old stained pillow out of its case. 'Sit here. Can you do that? Sideways.' He tugged at the rope pulley and lifted the block of marble so enthusiastically it swung.

Rosaleen didn't dare speak, only watched him as he took the only chair and, flinging it on to its side, stamped it into splinters with his boot. He flung the shards into the fireplace, adding the scrunched pages of a newspaper.

'Better?' he asked as it flamed, and then he started, taking up his point chisel, swimming through the stone.

Rosaleen sat still. Even her breathing she kept shallow.

'Yes,' Felix muttered. He was rasping, smoothing a corner to a curve, and she stared out of the window at the blackening night, wondering when they'd stop for supper. The fire had smouldered into embers. He threw in a bevelled leg and watched it spit.

'Felix?' She caught him. 'Do you have anything at all that I could eat?'

He shook himself and looked around. 'Of course.' To her surprise he opened the door to the oven and, reaching in, brought out a loaf of bread, a block of cheese, a small bowl of tomatoes. They sat together before the fire and ate.

'Ready?' He leapt up as she licked the crumbs from her fingers, and she resumed her position, sitting back on her heels, her stomach rounded, her nipples hardening with cold.

Now Felix wanted to see her every night. He caught the coalman on his rounds and filled the scuttle, and each time he passed through Covent Garden market he lifted a crate which he cracked apart for kindling. There was always bread in the oven cupboard, tins of anchovies, jars of olives, capers. That first Saturday Rosaleen made cauliflower cheese and brought it to heat through, but when she'd removed the items she found the oven didn't work. They ate it cold. It had never tasted more delicious, or was it that she was always hungry? One night she arrived from work to find that he'd bought oysters, and was prising them open with his chisel.

Time raced and slowed as he worked his way into the stone, rasping and tapping, smoothing away edges, revealing a knee, an elbow. Rosaleen watched as he turned the marble on its harness, setting it down, releasing hands, wrists, the drop of her chin. She didn't speak – it was as much as she could do to hold the pose – but slowly, as her body showed itself, the tilt of her hips, her belly swelling, he began to talk. He told her about the school he'd attended in Berlin, the seriousness with which he took his studies, his family's determination he choose medicine. He described how he'd seen Hitler in the street, a small man surrounded by his guard, and when he'd returned home and told his mother she'd put a hand before his eyes as if to wipe away the sight. Once in London, his father, a biologist, had found it impossible to get work, although his mother, who played the violin professionally, took a job in a canteen. He was seventeen when they arrived, eighteen when the war began, and he and his father had been interned, first on the Isle of Man, and then sent by ship to Australia, where the conditions were so harsh – Felix faltered and for once his hands were still – his father could not survive the voyage. It was in a camp there that he began to carve. He'd found wood from an abandoned piano and had used it to make a series of reliefs. It eased his mind, stopped him from worrying about his mother, although, on his return, when he told her that he would no longer be pursuing medicine, she took to her bed and mourned.

'Will I meet her? Rosaleen asked.

Felix didn't answer. He'd caught the wave of her hair, curling on her neck, and he was teasing it out with the small teeth of a rasp.

We should have made this sculpture in the summer, Rosaleen thought, as the days shortened, and the nights chilled, and high as they stoked the fire it only served to scald one side while the rest of her body shivered, but then by next summer there would be no bump to carve, only a baby, and the baby, after that first night, was never mentioned. *What am I to do?* The question assailed her at odd moments of the day or night – at work when the stuffiness of the post room caused her to feel faint; in the mornings when she wound a scarf around her breasts and tugged on her tightest vest. She'd stitched a length of webbing to the waistband of a skirt, moving the hook and eye to keep it up, and then today she'd received a letter from her mother, asking what date they might expect her home.

Felix was working on her feet, turning each toe, smoothing the one visible nail.

'Will they notice, do you think?'

Felix paused.

'When I go home at Christmas.'

He turned to her, frowning. 'That seems to me an exceedingly bad idea.'

They looked at each other.

'If *you* didn't notice …'

'It's not so much that I didn't notice, but with a woman …
It's best not to presume.'

Rosaleen winced at the thought he'd known another
woman. Any other women. 'You'd hardly believe it,' she said
to distract herself, 'but my parents, really, they never notice
anything about me.'

'Let's hope that is the case.'

'If I don't go, they'll be suspicious.'

'As long as you come back.'

'So you can finish your sculpture?' she flared.

'Not at all. I'll finish it before. Sit up. That's it. Exactly right.'

Later, when he'd taken her by taxi to Maida Vale to
warm herself and lay new clothes out for the morning, he
came and stood beside her as she ran hot water into the bath.
'Rosa-leen,' he held her face between his hands, 'I want you
to know …'

She swallowed. There was a look in his eyes that made her
reel. 'Know what?'

'I couldn't love you more.'

It was lucky he had hold of her or she'd have fallen, and it
was only when he'd careered away down the stairs, the heavy
oak door slamming behind him, that she realised she'd still not
asked her question: *What am I to do?*

Aoife

There was a man selling Christmas trees behind the Moby Dick. They took the farm truck with its open back, Cashel driving, the two girls squeezed in beside Aoife in the front.

'Will your big girl be coming home for Christmas?' It was Mr O'Malley, swaying out of the pub, and Aoife looked right at him as if he hadn't taken her hand, only the week before, and pressed it to his lips. 'Please God,' she told him, 'she'll be over next week.'

'Be sure and come up to us for a drink. We haven't seen so much of you this last little while.' He smiled round at Cashel, at her daughters, who, she was ashamed to say, looked down at their shoes. 'I have a nice bottle of …' he lowered his voice so that the word *poteen* was swallowed, 'finest in the country.'

'We'll be sure to,' Cash told him. He liked a drop. 'Say hello to Mrs O'Malley.' They all watched as he ambled towards his car, and stalling once, the gears screeching, he manoeuvred out on to the road.

'She'll be over when?' Cash was frowning.

'I've written to her. I told you. '

'I know you've written to her, woman.'

Aoife felt her daughters shrink, and she stood tall to show them how a husband could be managed. 'I've told her it gets busy this time of year, that if she lets us know, we'll be there at the boat to get her.'

'Will we now?' He turned his attention to the choosing of a tree.

'A big one,' Kitty dared, and they watched him as he ran his eyes over the green firs.

'Do *you* know when Rosaleen's coming home?' Aoife turned to Angela who had pulled up her hood and pushed her hands into the ends of her sleeves.

'She hasn't said.'

'Is that right?' Aoife wondered what else Rosaleen hadn't said.

'Nothing but trouble. Right from the start.' Cashel never tired of saying it, and as a great bristling fir was loaded into the open back Aoife thought of those desperate first weeks of her mothering, with Cash out in the blackening smoke, and she alone, feeding and shushing and walking up and down while Margaret ran the bar, and some oaf they'd brought in to help her pocketing the change. Aoife gave her usual sniff of disapproval, but there it was between them, the terrible peace of it, when the child went north to Elspeth Stead.

She could hear it, even now, the silence of that first morning. She'd lain there, Cashel's arms around her, one second, two, before the jolt of what they'd done had forced her up. She'd write. Tell them there had been an error, and seeing the delay in this she determined she'd go to Harrogate herself and bring the child back. She'd slipped on last night's dress. She could smell it, the scent of old tobacco, feel the run of her stockings as she tugged them on. The bar was dark, the till empty. Cashel locked the money in a metal box. Kept the key ... where did he keep the key? She'd stood looking at the compartments, wondering that she'd never thought to ask if it was her he didn't trust, or Margaret, over from Cork, just as she'd come herself at seventeen, to see the world.

'Eva?' His voice had made her jump and he'd come towards her, his face shaggy with sleep, and held her by the shoulders. 'I miss her too.' She'd felt the quake in his chest.

'I can't ...' But her voice was swallowed by a siren, and there was the wrench of Margaret's door and her petrified feet as she came running. They'd snaked into the cellar and sat there with the kegs of beer.

'In a neat little town they called Belfast, apprentice to trade I was bound ...' If Margaret could get through two verses before another siren started they were free to climb back up to the bar, but up it rose, a hum of panic, worse for the waiting, like a second scream. Aoife pressed herself against Cashel's side, and imagined the terror travelling through into her baby. No. She'd sat up straight. She's better where she is, and she smiled encouragingly at Margaret who'd come down without her slippers, and whose bare feet peeked out below the fringes of the rug.

The next morning at Mass, Aoife heard her husband telling the Fitzgeralds, 'News doesn't stop for Christmas now, does it? They might not be able to spare her at the *Express*, that's the thing.' The little group around him nodded. How could they not be impressed? And the priest, when he came out, shook both their hands, and lingered. 'A lovely service, thank you, Father.' Aoife felt grateful, as if it was him and not the Lord who had intervened in lightening Cashel's mood, and they went off to the pub where she bought crisps and lemonade and took them out to her daughters waiting in the car.

★ ★ ★

That was a happy time, out on the farm, just as we'd dreamed it all those years. The two girls at Loreto, and Rosaleen over in London all set up in her job. The news desk! Weren't you after telling everyone who'd listen what a grand girl she was – the brains of the family – you'd mention it each Sunday after Mass, and if anyone was making the journey from England they'd know to bring you a copy of the *Express*. It wasn't long before I wished they wouldn't. Red in the face – I thought you'd have an attack – demanding to know who they'd be letting in next. Four hundred and ninety-two West Indians was how it started, you never tired of telling me, as if I'd not been there myself in Brixton, in 1948. They took over the houses on the High Street, whole families to a room, more in the rooms next door. Brixton was never the same after that, you'd say, lucky we got out, although those buildings were pitted and unsteady from the doodlebugs, and I didn't dare mention how your own mother came over from South Africa the year you were born. She'd thrown herself on her dead husband's family, even though they'd not approved the match, and there she was, four little ones and nothing but the coldness of their shoulder. She whispered it to me in those first weeks of the war, the blinds fastened, our gas masks near, and maybe it was fear that loosened her because she didn't speak of it again. Not even when they bombed us, fifty-six days out of fifty-seven. I say days but it was nights. I hardly need remind you. The days were for raking through the wreckage, clearing away bodies, lying down to sleep. There was a woman, buried to the neck, who'd not leave your dreams. She had a hat on, a turban it was, grimed with dust and you found her fingers below the surface of the rubble and you held them in your own. A photograph was taken, but they didn't put it in the paper. Only happy pictures. Lads sticking together, and if there was a fireman, he was a hero.

Thank you, that was the last thing she said, and she closed her eyes, and she was gone. All around there were men digging. The ground was sharp as needles, turned to splinters, beams and brick. Half a street demolished. No wonder you couldn't sleep.

Women joined the fire service. Fire watchers. Van drivers. That would have done for me, but someone had to run the pub and who was going to clean you up when you came in? There was no one who knew how bad you really were. Not your mother, or Mavis, not even Margaret, the way you teased her with your singing. I'd sit beside you in the cellar, and I'd lean against your arm, and we'd guess how low the Thames was by the bombers flying over. Double the amount when the water was at its lowest, and it sickened me to think there was a man, over there, noting down the tides, and I'd think of my own diary, kept in with my stockings, the danger days circled round with red, so God forgive me, for who would want a child born into such a world?

Kate

I bend to my work, sketching in the veins and blades of leaves, and as I do I feel the heat of Matt's repentant kisses, the scorch as he impressed on me the true depths of his regret. He'd fallen asleep at Andy's, woken early and gone straight to the office. 'I'm so so sorry.' Tonight he's promised the rehearsal will be short. There's one song that needs attention, and he'll be back.

It had been an unusually mild autumn, the year Freya was born, trees in mid-October still in leaf. The gale caught them like a sail, lifting their branches, ripping up their roots. Fifteen million. I stop my work and listen. Was that a taxi screeching on the road? I stand on a chair and attend to a high branch, and as I work I find that I am weaving back through every man I ever loved, in an attempt to find out how I ended here. I dismiss myself, aged seven, passing a gift to a boy who seemed to have no friends, flinching, even now, at the horror on his face when I slid the unwieldy homemade farm into his arms. I skip forward over the years, past a heart-shaped biscuit left, misguidedly, in Peter Dunphy's desk, and not long after, a night spent in a sleeping bag beside sleek, popular Max Ravell, for which I was teased so mercilessly when I mentioned it at school that I never spoke to him again. I flashforward until I reach thirteen and set eyes on Freddie Agar at a half-term holiday camp on the Downs. It was his friend that the girls fancied – Paul, tall, in bright blue denim, flushed with their attention – while behind him, frowning at something no one else could see, stood Freddie. We spoke, a few hesitant words about the too-long, too-boring hike along a cliff path that secretly I had enjoyed, and then, at the beginning of the following year, there he was, at my school. My heart leapt as he filed into assembly, his blazer hanging from one shoulder, his shirt half tucked, and when he smiled a flash of recognition, I decided in that moment he was mine. I track over the months that followed. The weeks when only Thursdays mattered: Thursday at two forty-five, when his class streamed out from biology and mine waited to go in. I smile myself now to remember how I teamed up with Melinda Matthews, and we planned a Valentine's party, cleared out her father's workshop, hung batik bedspreads at the windows, lumped in her box record player, made a dip with sour cream. Did we dance? We must have, before the lights went out, and then, as if it was an order, everyone began kissing. Freddie and I looked at each other. There was nothing else to do, nothing to say, that was certain, and I close my eyes as I remember the clang of our teeth hitting, our noses bumping, and the warm sweet engine-oil smell of him as our mouths met. That was the end, and the beginning, of the party, lost as I was in a new language, following seams of pleasure as fine and white as that cliff path about which we'd moaned.

I sketch the buds and scars of twigs even as I luxuriate in the three spring months of Freddie Agar, the kissing as we walked back and forth from bus stops, the hours lying on his bed while he read motorcycle magazines, the weekend of my fourteenth birthday when I watched him assemble a moped from two others that he'd taken apart. How I wished I could have been satisfied with that, but I wanted more, or I wanted him to want more, and rather than ask, I tried another tack: 'Maybe we should break up?' I was calling from a phone box, away from Alice's inquisitive ears, away from my mother. There was a long pause. 'All right.' His voice was hollow, and although I had a tower of coins, it seemed there was nothing to add. 'Bye then,' I said and, stricken, I walked away along the empty road, watching my feet slapping against tarmac, my knees bending, my hands as they swung useless at my sides. I almost fell as I struggled up the hill, and when I balled my fists into my stomach the unused coins clinked in my pocket.

I stood in the kitchen and waited for my mother to look round. What happened? she would surely ask, but she was busy snipping the stringy ends from beans, and my father was rearranging the contents of his shed, rakes and trowels, paint pots in order of their size. I walked through to my room and lay down on the floor, and I felt the knife that lay, cold steel, inside me, twisting as it turned.

The door slams and Matt is home. 'There's a very small chance,' he bursts in, 'that it's going to be good.'

'What's going to be good?'

'The gig!' He dances me along the hall to the kitchen where he opens the fridge and stares thirstily in. 'I hope you'll be there.'

'Of course.'

'You're in my head,' he croons, 'you're in my heart …' It was a song he wrote when we first met – and he squints past the lettuce wilting in its plastic sheath, and finding no beer he shuts the door so fiercely it flies open and hangs there on its hinge.

Matt's band is playing in the basement of a pub. Andy is on stage, tuning and retuning his guitar; Ian too, shivering a brush across the drums. I stare down at the floor. We've been warmed by a support band, one girl with a soaring, raspy voice. What if we're left to cool? There's the squeal of static but Matt doesn't appear. I close my eyes. It's more than two years since they last played. Not since Ian started ward rounds at the hospital, not since Matt joined his brother's firm. All around is a restless shuffling and I dig my nails into my palms. When we first met there'd been gigs several times a month, tours around the country, festivals, supporting other bands. In the slow times Matt worked on a building site and he'd come home, caked in paint and plaster dust, and we'd embrace, pressing our gritty selves against each other, squeeze into the same shower. There's a whoop and a cheer and I open my eyes. Matt has bounded on to the stage. He takes the microphone and draws it to his mouth and he is singing, straight in without a pause. Keep going. I form the lyrics as if he is my child, but he doesn't need me, he has stepped into himself. I see his smile, shy – I used to think it was for me, but I see now it is for anyone who wants it. His voice reaches out over the crowd. He's good. He's gorgeous – I'd forgotten – even with his leather jacket drenching him in sweat. Beside him Andy leaps and spins, a boy lost in his bedroom, while Ian, a small man, prematurely bald, thrashes at the drums.

'"Whatever the Distance",' I shout my request. He played it one morning a month after we met. *You're in my head, you're in my heart … Whatever the distance, we'll never be apart* … and I imagined him driving past cactus-strewn motels, not knowing there were other kinds of distance, lands so cold and barren they could not be traversed. Matt plays his new songs, restless, jangled, and I dance, I have to, there's no space to stand still, and then there is a song I haven't heard before. 'I'm Missing You'. I wait for him to catch my eye. 'I've been missing you.' He stares into the lights, and I think how I've been missing him.

Afterwards I have to fight to get backstage. 'Matt …' I hold up my hand as if my ring is proof. 'The lead singer, Matt Jensen … he's my—' The bouncer waves me through. Matt has his shirt off and he's rubbing his hair with a towel. Annie, Andy's girlfriend, is cracking open beers.

'Babe!' Matt pulls me to him. 'I didn't think you were here!'

'I was here.' My face is against his shoulder. 'I am.' We exchange a friendly, beery kiss.

Everyone is going back to Ian's. He doesn't live too far away and we walk through the dark streets, the band of us, revelling in success. 'You were fantastic,' I tell Matt in the quiet moment when Ian searches for his keys and I put my arms round his neck and check to see if he believes me.

There is beer at Ian's, spirits and wine. I pour myself a splash of vodka and I gulp it down. 'I haven't seen you for bloody ages.' It's Annie, husky, effortless in faded jeans. It sounds like an accusation although she's smiling.

'I've been busy. Freya, you know, and work, I'm—' Annie is pulling the cork from a bottle. The doorbell rings and more people force in. 'How about you, what have you been up to?' Annie has turned away to wave to someone else.

I take my vodka and find Matt. He's in a thick circle of people, none of whom I know. They are talking about music. The bastards from their label. The shitty contracts they were stupid enough to sign. Matt nods and sucks at his beer.

However ugly their stories, it's what he wants, and I want it for him too. A red-haired woman joins the group. She stayed behind to watch the last band. 'I shouldn't have bothered,' she says, and she smiles dreamily at Matt. 'Should have left on a high.'

The music is turned loud and people start to dance. I wander into the kitchen for another drink but instead of getting drunker I seem already to be sobering up. I gulp down a glass of water and there is Andy behind me, leaning in with his mouth open, steadying himself against me as he drinks from the running tap. 'Hello, sexy. Where've you been?'

I pull away. 'You know …' I shrug, and drift through the rooms. I dance, I shout over the music to Ian who is already so wasted he won't remember that I'm here. Annie passes me a joint. 'How's your little girl?' Before I can answer I have a vision of her, sitting up in bed, calling to me. I'm certain I can hear her now.

I find Matt leant back into a sofa, the red-haired woman sitting on the arm, a squash of people craning round to talk to him. He still has his jacket on, and his smile is bleary. I kneel down before him. 'I've got to get back.' For one sweet second I think he may be about to stagger up.

'All right, darl.' He stays where he is.

I feel the others' eyes on me. 'See you later then,' I tell him, and I smile so convincingly I'm still smiling when I step into the night.

I see my mother outside the locked and gated Tube. She's a small woman, hair scrunched into a knot, and beside her on a cardboard pallet there's a white and tan dog, its head in her lap.

I dig into my pocket and gather all the change I have. 'Do you have somewhere to go?'

My mother's eyes are rheumy. She looks at me as if she hasn't heard. 'Fuck off,' she hisses when I suggest I could come back, with a sandwich, and when I still don't move, the dog lifts its head and growls.

The next morning we arrive at the playground so early it's still closed. Freya hangs over the railings and we stare in at the obsolete equipment: a see-saw wrapped in hazard tape, a merry-go-round with warning signs for people to Keep Off. There is a red-brick hut stocked with plasters and disinfectant and an attendant who flies out the moment anybody falls. She appears now, keys clanging, to open up, and I follow Freya from one activity to the next, stand by as she rocks on a virtu-ally immobile horse, dash after her when she runs towards the sandpit where she seizes an abandoned spade and proceeds to dig with it, fast, and rightly so, as within minutes a small boy, solid as his father who hovers on the sidelines, appears and snatches it back.

Saturday, I've noticed, is a morning for men. I push Freya on the swing and picture the wives luxuriating in bed, stretch-ing out for magazines and tea. 'Higher!' Freya demands, her sandalled feet pedalling, and I use all my strength to fling her into the blue sky. Matt arrived home as it was getting light. I'd heard the car, and lain there, listening to it idling, a murmur of music drifting up, until I'd kicked out of bed and, inching back the curtain, peered out. The car was red, two tyres on the kerb, and as I watched, Matt uncurled himself from its interior and, stooping down for a last word, loped towards the house.

It's midday and we stop to buy lunch from the deli on the corner. Bread, cheese, salami, olives. 'How are you, darling?' the owner asks so tenderly I feel myself buckle, and looking down at Freya he tips a bowl of miniature chocolate bars towards her. She turns to me, pleading, and unable to resist her pearly smile I tell her she can choose one if she saves it for pudding.

I make a salad. Pick mint to float with ice and lemon in a jug, and lay the food out in the garden. 'Go and wake Daddy,' I tell Freya — if I thought he'd wake I'd go myself — and as I wait I listen to the messages on the machine. Mum has rung to remind me about dinner. Alice arrives on Friday for a week-long visit and she's bringing someone with her. Who could it possibly be? There's a message from Annie, her voice huskier than ever. Matt left his wallet. She's not sure how he got home.

Freya is looking up at me. 'Daddy says he's coming.'

We wait another fifteen minutes. Relax, I tell myself. What does it matter? The salami is sweating and the cheese has turned waxy in the sun. I cut a slice and lay it on bread, I halve olives and form them into a face. 'Where's her hair?' Freya wants to know. I peel a carrot and arrange the orange curls and she shakes her own curls and eats an eye.

We are on the sofa by the time Matt comes down, the curtains drawn, Freya watching *The Little Mermaid* while I slip in and out of sleep. 'Mum.' She pokes me and my eyes spring open and I watch the film intently as if to make up for the bits I've missed.

'So this is what you're up to on a sunny afternoon?' Matt has on a crisp white shirt and jeans.

'We were out, first thing, we went to—'

'Shhh!' Freya scowls.

'Coffee?' Matt mock-whispers and I uncoil myself and follow him into the kitchen.

I watch him fill the kettle, arrange the cups. He looks happy. Lighter. 'Well done last night,' I tell him. At dawn I'd pretended to be asleep.

'It was a good night.'

But I can't help myself. 'So, what happened, the party lasted … till …?'

Matt shrugs as if surprised by time, that it can slip away so easily, that here he is on the other side of a new day. He brings the coffees to the table. 'I'm glad you were there.' He takes my hand.

'I'm glad I was there too.'

He leans forward and kisses me and I can taste the heat of spirits burning through mint. Are you still drunk? I hate myself, and I bat away my question and I kiss him back. His skin is smooth, his hair dense with damp, and when he draws me up and holds me hard against him I close my eyes and, with one ear out for the familiar finale of the Mermaid's song, I move my body against his. 'So good,' he murmurs as he manoeuvres us against the wall, between the fridge and the dresser. 'That's it.' My skirt is hoisted up, his belt unbuckled. 'Yes.' He lifts me, my arms are round his neck, bare skin cool against the wall, and then we are sliding, lowering, laughing as we stumble to the floor where soon everything is speed and need and if I had a worry it is rattled from my head. In the cool slippery aftermath he wedges his hand between my legs, circles his fingers, stroking, gentle, fast, so that I am drawn up out of myself, overflowing, exquisite.

'Ow.' I smile up at him. The sharp edge of the cooker is cutting into my thigh, and there is the plaintive sound of Freya calling.

We look at each other and laugh.

'Your turn,' I tell him, and light as spring I skip away upstairs.

Aoife

The day after Christmas, Aoife herded her family up the puddled lane for a drink with the O'Malleys.

'Hello there!' Patrick O'Malley stood at the door, alerted by two spaniels barking fit to burst. 'See the wanderers approach.'

'We're not putting you out?' Aoife called to him, although wasn't it he himself that had insisted on the visit?

'Not a bit of it.' He threw an order to the dogs who skittered away, ashamed. 'Come on now and get yourselves inside.' He flattened his large body against the frame and ushered them into the porch. The girls went first – sullen was how Aoife would describe them, could they not raise a smile as they squeezed past?

'Sweet Youghal Bay,' he crooned into her ear as his fingers caught her wrist.

'That'll be enough of that,' she shushed him, but she was smiling as she tugged off her galoshes, and still smiling as the two men slapped each other on the back.

Mrs O'Malley was pleased enough to see them. She must be lonely, home with her one son, and himself away over at the Moby Dick most every evening of the week, but this afternoon she had the lot of them at home, and a cake too, on the sideboard, dark and dry, there was no disguising that, even in its shell of icing. Mrs O'Malley cut two slices which she quartered and presented on a plate. 'No thank you.' Rosaleen shook her head, but Angela took a square, the crumbs cascading down on to her saucer, and Kitty helped herself to a corner and, before anyone could stop her, peeled away the icing and gobbled it up. Aoife winced in expectation of a reprimand, but Cashel was leaning against the range, deep into his favourite conversation – what it might mean for the farm if the rain went on bucketing down all year.

'Mrs O'Malley,' Kitty was made bold with sugar, 'is it right one of your dogs is sick?'

'That's the truth.' The woman's face softened. 'We've done everything we can for her.' She lifted the lid off a blackened pot. 'Why don't you take her out a scrap of food?' and she scooped out a spoon of slop and dropped it into a bowl.

Kitty looked doubtful.

'That's it.' Mrs O'Malley pushed the bowl across the table. 'Kevin will show you. You'll take the child into the outhouse, won't you now?'

The O'Malley boy slouched over his teacup. He was a tall young man with a cowed face.

A fleck of marzipan clung to Kitty's lip. 'Go on then, pet,' Aoife encouraged, although there was nothing she liked the idea of less than her child going off into the wet with this great gangling fellow. There was silence as Kevin unfolded his long legs, and with a terse nod he led Kitty out along the hall.

'So …' Patrick O'Malley stretched, expansive, as the front door slammed. 'How've you been keeping?' and right there in plain sight, he turned to Aoife and winked.

'We're grand, aren't we?' Aoife flashed a smile at her husband. 'And why wouldn't we be, with the girls all home.'

Cashel took his pipe from his pocket and began packing in tobacco. 'A house full of women!' He made a strangled noise and clutched at his throat as if he might expire if he wasn't soon given a drink.

Patrick O'Malley opened a cupboard and leant in. 'I got this off a man from Kerry, who got it from a man …' He pulled out a bottle and tapped his nose, and Aoife thought what a fool he was, playing the bog Irishman – half an hour and he might break into a jig. He moved behind her then and lifted the good glasses from the dresser and as he turned he brushed his hand across the silk of her blouse, and there it was, the shock of him, electric.

The clear liquid was poured with practised ease, and glasses set down before the three of them. Cash lifted his to his lips.

'Forgive me,' O'Malley stopped, his hand in mid-air, 'there's a young lady here that we're forgetting.' He turned his gaze on Rosaleen. 'Will you join us in a drop of poteen now that you're grown?'

'No thank you,' Rosaleen answered in the same imperious voice she'd used to turn down cake, and Aoife shot a quick look at Mrs O'Malley who'd also been forgotten, and found her sipping tea as if the idea of spirits on this afternoon, or any other, was so far out of the question as to be absurd.

'Cheers!' O'Malley drew them in. 'To peace, prosperity …'

'And a clear sky,' Cash intervened, and they all tipped up their glasses.

Aoife's throat burned, her eyes stung. 'Well,' was all she allowed herself when she could speak, and a rush of fire roared up inside her and forced out a laugh. 'Well, indeed,' Cash was laughing too, and she had a pang for those nights when they'd lock the doors and sit in the bar, the two of them, and no one else.

Rosaleen got to her feet. 'I'll go and check on my sister.'

Kitty! Aoife's face was flushed. Had she been gone long?

Angela stood too. 'We'll see how the dog is doing,' she said, placating, and they could hear them, out in the yard, slushing through puddles in their boots.

★ ★ ★

I said nothing when I saw her walking down the gangplank, pale, with her coat buttoned to the neck. Let her be rid of it, I sent up a prayer, although with my next breath I asked forgiveness for the wickedness of my thoughts. Maybe I hoped I'd got it wrong, but all week she wore that orange jersey with the roll-neck, and a pair of slacks – would have worn them to Mass on Christmas morning if I'd not insisted that she change. Rosaleen! who loved her clothes. She borrowed a skirt of Angela's then, the green kilt with the giant pin, and a black cardigan that struggled to do up. All her life till then, scrawny as a stick. You'd sit with her – do you remember? – from lunch to dinner if that's what it took. But would she eat? Not a bit of it. I blame Elspeth Stead. Spoilt the girl, spoon-fed her mashed potato, warm milk from the cow. She'd make a special custard, sent me the recipe, a vanilla pod, as if they grew on trees. Did they not have rationing in Yorkshire? She'll eat what she's given, we decided, but we didn't know then, how could we have guessed, the trouble we were in for.

Your Rosaleen's blooming! O'Malley's eyes, they were on stalks, and that's what everyone was saying. It suits her, you agreed, the *Daily Express*. I didn't want to be the one to contradict you.

I was glad when she went off again. My own daughter, glad to see her board the ferry. We all went, waved to her, waited until the boat began to move, and she stayed out on deck, friendly now that she was leaving.

Kitty cried on the way home. Why'd Rosie have to go? and I couldn't find the words to comfort her because I knew, if she'd stayed another week, there'd have been no hiding it.

I shouldn't be saying this. Not now. But I've fretted over it, all these years. The thing itself. And the not telling. Cash? Was that …? Nurse! Nurse, I think it was a squeeze. Cash, blink then, if it's easier, blink if you can hear me. Is it an earthquake or simply a shock? Do you hear me, Cashel?

No?

I'll leave you be. Maybe it's God's will that you don't know.

Rosaleen

Rosaleen went straight to Felix from the boat train. *Not a single person noticed!* She could see his face when she gave him the news, but Felix wasn't there. She rang the bell, and called up to his window. She leant against the door, and then, undaunted, sat down on her case to wait. It was cold, and getting colder. *Where are you?* They'd made a plan to meet. Here, on New Year's Eve, and certain he'd appear at any moment she slipped a hand between the buttons of her coat and held it over the warm bump of her belly. Her stomach had swollen in the hours since leaving Ireland, relief releasing her, all subterfuge gone, and she caught her breath as the scudding quiver of a kick rippled up under her skin.

A couple swung by, arm in arm. 'Happy New Year!' The man touched his hat, and the woman, leaning into him, smiled covetous.

'And to you,' she returned, and she blew on her fingers for warmth.

After half an hour Rosaleen rang the bell again. 'Felix!' She threw her voice up towards his window, and then not caring what anyone might think, she yelled louder. 'Felix!' She was sitting back down when it occurred to her. Of course. He was at Maida Vale. He'd be there with a bottle of champagne, cheese wrapped in white paper, crackers with poppy seed, the ones she liked best. There'd be a fire, and he'd be lying on the sofa, waiting for her to slide her body alongside his. A wave of longing propelled her up. Her feet had lost all feeling, and her hands, even inside her gloves, were ice, but even so, she ran, heaving her suitcase towards the bus stop. There was one old man, lost inside an overcoat, and two couples, dressed for a night out. They nodded to each other, shivering, but when the bus did come its windows glowed warm as a lantern, and the passengers on board were festive. 'Happy New Year,' they greeted one another. Even the conductor was jolly.

Rosaleen sat behind the driver and tapped her feet. 'Come on,' she murmured, sighing each time they rattled to a halt. She stared at the curtained houses, flickers of light seeping at the seams, the occasional bright tree. When they reached her stop she ran, the case banging against her leg, her fingers so eager to unlock the door the keys flew from her hand. The stairs she took more slowly, winding up their carpeted width, the image of Felix flying up before her, his rackety Charlie Chaplin gait.

The flat, when she entered it, was cold as hell. 'Hello?' She flicked on the light in the tiny kitchen, turned on the gas and rubbed her hands. She switched on the oven, although there was nothing to put in it, but she knew if she waited long enough her legs would warm. The door to the bedroom was closed. Was that how she'd left it? She pushed it, hopeful, but the room was empty. She sat down on the bed and with a hollow lurch she remembered she'd not eaten, not since that morning at the terminal when she'd bought herself a bacon roll. There was one potato in the larder, sprouting, but she peeled and chopped it and put it on to boil. There was a pat of butter, half frozen in a saucer, which she mashed in when it was soft, and spooning the food into a bowl she sat on the grey sofa and ate. *Where are you?* She had enough fuel now for outrage and, still in her coat, she picked up her keys and walked out into the night.

The warmth and chatter of the French pub hit her with force. Rosaleen reached out a hand to steady herself. 'Hello, love.' She was clutching at the shoulder of a man, big and leery, a feather in his hat. 'Sorry.' She made her way towards the bar, easing along the length of it, craning for anyone she knew. She came out in a little hollow beside a wooden table. They'd sat at this table, she and Felix, one night after hours, and the proprietor had come over with a tray of teacups and a bottle of gin. Cheers, they'd laughed as they clinked china, and the quiet photographer had snapped his shutter, and there they were, their faces blazing, their eyes lit by each other.

'Hello!' It was the tattooed friend of the painter. He laid a knuckled hand on her arm. 'What are you doing here?'

'It's New Year.' Didn't she have the right to be anywhere she chose?

'So it is,' but even as he smiled, his eyes were wary. 'You've not got a drink?'

Rosaleen wasn't sure she could manage a drink. 'I'll have a gin and tonic.' She'd do her best, and she put her hands in her pockets and stretched the sides of her coat so the material didn't fall too close.

He took his time at the bar. She could see him talking, teasing, at one point he got caught up in a scuffle, but it was warm in the pub, and she leant against the wood wall of the staircase and waited.

'Rosie!' It was Anastasia, her neck wound round with a fur stole. She cast her eyes down the length of her body. 'Oh darling,' she kissed her savagely on the cheek, 'now what the fuck are you going to do?'

Rosaleen was saved from answering by the arrival of her drink.

'Nothing for me?' Anastasia kissed him in turn, and he held out his pint of Guinness and watched her while she gulped the white froth.

The door swung open and Rosaleen looked up.

'Over here!' Anastasia waved to her husband who pushed his way towards them.

'I've come from the hospital,' he was breathless. 'They let me see him. I said I was his brother. His bruzzer,' and despite themselves they all smiled.

Whose brother? Rosaleen wanted to ask but her voice lay swallowed.

'They wouldn't let *me* in.' Anastasia took another slurp of Guinness. 'I said I was his wife but his wife was already in there. God! "I mean his wife's sister," I tried, but they weren't having it – one more minute and they would have stretchered me out.'

Rosaleen pressed the cold glass against her face.

'What is it, do they think?' Another man had joined them.

'Some kind of stroke.'

'Or quite possibly exhaustion. There was a commission he was determined to finish.'

'But he can speak?' Anastasia raised a hand to her mouth.

Slowly the tall man shook his head.

There was a silence, and they all turned to look at Rosaleen.

'What hospital is he in?' Her voice was small.

'Barts. You know it?'

She nodded, and they watched as she pushed her way through the crowd and out into the street.

The wind had risen, carrying with it the hints and drifts of celebration. Music through an open window, a car crammed with people cruising slow. Rosaleen reached a bus stop, and studied the routes. There was one bus that would take her to St Paul's, from where she could walk through side streets to the hospital. She waited, restless, quickly freezing, and after ten minutes she began to run. She kept in close against the buildings, cutting across the edge of Covent Garden, rising up at the broad cross of High Holborn, her eyes scanning the road ahead. A printworker from the *Express* had once been taken to Barts. He'd been sitting in the post room chatting to the girls when a wasp landed on his sandwich and, without noticing, he had taken a bite. He was halfway through a sentence when his mouth fell open, and a cascade of buzzing spluttered out. Sorry, he'd tried to say, but before the word was finished his throat was swelling closed. 'Get an ambulance!' Betty had shouted, and she'd manoeuvred him towards the lift.

Rosaleen thought about this now as she rushed on towards Chancery Lane. It was easier than thinking about Felix. An ambulance. Was that how he had arrived? And who was he with? And why? A taxi sailed by with its orange cube of light. What would it cost? The thought delayed her, and she stuck out her arm, too late. Felix would have caught it, whistling, waving, but then if Felix was with her, she wouldn't be out here in the dark, alone. She quickened her pace, her stomach hardening to a knot as wind whipped at her coat, flipping the hem in around her knees, so that she had to stop to wrench it free. A swarm of men poured out of a pub on the corner of Red Lion Street. 'Happy

New Year!' they whooped when they saw her, and they caught her in the thicket of their arms, and spun her round. Rosaleen felt a swell of fury. 'Feck off,' her cursing came out Irish. 'I have to be somewhere! Let go!' Affronted, they unlatched their hands and let her through, although their jeers followed her as she ran. 'Nasty little bitch, what's up with her then ...'

'Imbeciles,' she threw over her shoulder, but she didn't look back.

There was no one on the Holborn Viaduct, only the winged lions and the statues that they guarded – Science, Art, Agriculture, Commerce – all women, as if that was how it was. She stopped for breath in front of Agriculture, oak leaves and olive, a scythe curled in her hand. 'Get the lunch on, woman!' her father boomed between the lamp posts, and there was her mother, smoothing their life along. Soon she was on Fleet Street, her own street, the sparkling black build-ing that housed the *Daily Express*. Rosaleen tilted her neck to where it was rumoured Lord Beaverbrook lived on the top floor, but there was no sign of him, nothing but the fluttering of a flag. At the junction of King Edward Street she rounded the corner. Towers and courtyards, windows in their faceless rows. *But he can talk?* Anastasia's querulous voice caught in her chest, and Rosaleen put a hand to her own mouth. No words. She traced the outline of his lips, leant in against him, felt the nuzzle of his nose. *Please God*, she prayed, *let me feel his hand in mine.* The rain came down with a roar.

The woman at the reception was busy. Rosaleen stood dripping. 'Yes?' she said, eventually.

'There's someone here I need to see.'

'A patient?' She seemed unnecessarily surprised.

'Lichtman. Mr. He's ... he was admitted ...'

Her eyes dropped to the ringless finger of Rosaleen's left hand. 'Visiting hours,' she pointed to a sign, 'are between two and four p.m.' They both looked at a clock on the back wall which showed ten past nine.

'The thing is I've only just now ...' Rosaleen protested. 'I've been away. We were meant to be meeting ...' The woman's eyebrows, plucked high above the bone, left her doubly surprised. 'I have to see him. I need to ...' Tears stopped her voice.

'Then you'll have to come back tomorrow.'

'Tomorrow.' She might as well have said next year, although of course it would be. A small hiccup of hilarity burst from her.

The receptionist bent to her papers and began to write, her pen scratching decisive strokes against a stack of forms. There was no other sound but the rushing of the rain.

A taxi was waiting in the street, its light holy as a shrine. Rosaleen stood at the window and asked if it could take her to Maida Vale. 'Righto,' the man said kindly, and she stepped into the shelter of his cab and closed her eyes.

The flat was colder even than before. If only she'd thought to switch the boiler on she could have had a bath. She stripped off her damp clothes and pulled on a nightdress, a jumper, socks, and lay, shivery and fearful, a hot-water bottle in her arms. Soon she was running down a corridor, Sister Benedict fast on her heels, and when she heard the slam of the front door, for one terrified moment she imagined the nun had broken in.

'Leave it.' A high, sharp female voice, and in response a mumbling, too low to hear. Rosaleen sat up. It was morning and the sky was full of grey. She slid out of bed and tiptoed to the wardrobe, but even as she pulled out clothes she feared being discovered, half naked, tugging a dress over her head. 'Look at this place.' There was a scornful gasp. What had been found? The broken saucer she'd been meaning to glue, or was it the kettle that hadn't been descaled? Rosaleen peered into the cupboard. If she could hide in here she would. Instead she dragged her fingers through her hair, straightened her nightdress and walked out as she was.

A boy turned to face her, pale eyes, Felix's eyes. Behind him stood a woman in a smartly belted mac.

'Who are you?' the woman asked, although from the curl of her lip, she seemed to think she knew.

Rosaleen felt ridiculously young. She folded her arms, protective, and looked at the boy as if she might align herself with him. 'I'm …' What was she asking? Her name?

'I'm just leaving.' That was it. She retreated to the bedroom and pushed clothes, shoes, the still-damp garments from the night before into her unpacked case.

There was silence, and then the sound of paper being ripped and scrunched, a scattering of coal as it was thrown into the fire. 'I'm doing it.' A match was struck, and there was the boy's voice. 'Done.'

When she next opened the door Rosaleen was already in her coat. She'd made the bed and closed the cupboard. She'd found one of Felix's socks, fine and silk, and pushed it into her pocket. Excuse me, she was moving towards the bathroom when she caught sight of a letter propped against the lamp, the blunt pencil print of Felix's writing, her name in his hand. She needed to fold it in with the others – every note and sketch he'd ever sent her was in the pocket of her case – but the woman – it chilled her to think of it – his wife – had seized it up. 'A letter, strictly speaking, belongs to whoever sent it.' She pulled the sheet of paper from the envelope and snapped it open.

Only if the person's dead, Rosaleen couldn't bring herself to say.

My Rosalein, my love. She knew the words. *Now that your secret's out I am fearful. Why go home, when they might never let you leave? The child will be passed off as your mother's, isn't that how it works? Don't go. What I'll do without you I don't know—*

The woman's eyes flicked over Rosaleen's stomach and for one long second they appraised each other's hurt. Then she slid the letter back into its envelope and, unclicking the hard clasp of her handbag, dropped it in. 'Got everything?' Her lip was quivering. Rosaleen stepped on to the landing and, overwhelmed with fear, she asked, 'Will he … do you … ?' but the woman, whose face was ashen, shut the door.

Rosaleen walked towards the canal. The houseboats and the flowers at Little Venice always cheered her, and if nothing else, she could throw herself in. She laughed, but she was shivering, deep inside. She sat on a bench and stared ahead. She could go back to the hospital, plead her case, tell them she was Felix's niece. All she wanted was to sit by his side, listen for what he had to tell her, whether he had words or not. But what if that woman, could it be his wife, was there? A cold wind whipped across the water. She couldn't stay here, not till visiting hour, and on New Year's Day visits might not be allowed. She stood up and, heaving her case with her, set off for the main road. The station, as she'd feared, was closed. There was no one on the streets as she walked towards Marble Arch, no one at the entrance to Hyde Park except two men who appeared from between the scattering of trees and stared. 'All right?' One of them smiled, and she asked if they knew of any buses running.

Together they examined the row of stops. 'Where you heading?'

'Ilford.' Where else could she go?

'Long way,' the older of the men said, and they all three looked along the deserted highway of Park Lane.

'I'd take you myself,' the younger man smiled, he had a sweet, wide-open face, 'if I had some means of transport,' and wishing her good luck, they walked away.

Rosaleen stood at the bus stop alone, and after half an hour when a car approached, she stuck out her thumb. There was a man driving, his wife beside him, two children in the back. He grimaced as if to say, I would but ... and taking courage, she tried again. A car pulled over. It was a large car, two shades of gold, the paintwork swooping over the hubcaps like a gown. Bloody hell, it was a Rolls-Royce, and Rosaleen ran towards it. The driver was in uniform, a peaked cap, black braid along the rim. 'You're not by any chance going in the direction of Ilford?' The man, only hesitating for a moment, said she'd better get in. Rosaleen tugged at the door. 'In the back,' he tutted, and he climbed out and, taking her case, stored it in the boot.

'So where are you on your way to?' she asked as they sped along Oxford Street and up towards Finchley Road. 'Northeast,' he told her, 'the Midlands. I have to collect a poodle, would you believe it, but I can make a detour, for a pretty girl like you.' He looked round then; he had a weaselly moustache. Rosaleen gave him what she hoped was an unencouraging smile. 'Thank you.' She leant back against the leather and glanced at herself in the slithers of mahogany-framed mirror.

The entire household came out when the car pulled up. Mavis, the cousins John and Francis, her Uncle Bob who, even though they'd not exchanged a word, had continued to fold a coin into her palm. There was her Nana Isabelle, her hair in a chignon, her neck draped in jet as if she'd been expecting such a visit. No one spoke as the chauffeur walked round to retrieve Rosaleen's case. 'Thank you so much.' She wondered if she shouldn't give him a tip, but she'd need every penny she had saved and, anyway, hadn't she listened to the story of his disabled wife who knew nothing of the lady friend who was nagging at him day and night to move with her to Margate? 'Good luck,' he said, and she waited for him to roll the car away before she turned to face her aunt.

'To what do we owe this pleasure?' Mavis adopted an unusually grand tone, as if she must live up to the style of Rosaleen's arrival.

Rosaleen wrapped her coat around her. 'The ceiling fell in.' (It had happened to a girl from work and she was grateful now to borrow it.) 'The people upstairs, they left the bath running. I hope you don't mind. If it's not convenient there are other places …' But her Uncle Bob had hold of the case and he was taking it inside.

'You might have called to let us know.' Mavis pursed her mouth. 'I'd have put some extra spuds on. Never mind.'

Rosaleen was back in with her nana. Had it only been six months? She pressed a hand against her belly, the swell of it conveniently subsided. Hunger, she supposed, and shock. She sat at her nana's dressing table and brushed her hair. It was already curling on her shoulders, Felix would be pleased, and she remembered – Felix!

Mavis had a joint of beef, slow-cooking. The smell of it drifted up and clawed at her insides, but even so, once John banged on her door to tell her the dinner was served, she felt so feeble she made her way along the garden path to the privy to see if it would help if she threw up. Nothing came. Just a rolling swell as if she was at sea, and so she came back in and took her seat between the cousins. Yes, she told them, she was only yesterday back from Cork. Everyone was well, and the farm, it was a hard winter of it with the weather. Maybe not so bad as last year, there'd been snow at Easter, and she told them how Mummy had put orphaned lambs in a box in the warming oven of the Aga, and once they were strong enough to go into the yard Daddy had made a pen for them with hay bales and a good strong light, and she, Angela and Kitty had fed them warm milk from a bottle.

'You girls, you're a credit to your da,' Mavis said, 'he's ever so proud of you.' She narrowed her eyes. 'And how are you getting on at the *Express*?'

'I'm getting on all right.' Rosaleen looked at the boys in case they had anything to add. 'I'll be starting back tomorrow, and soon as I can, I'll find somewhere to stay.' She bit on the hot fluff of a potato and scorched her tongue.

'You're looking peaky.' Mavis leant in closer. 'Burning the candle at both ends? Put your feet up while you're here, why don't you?'

Rosaleen glanced over at the clock. 'There's something … I'll need to be going back into the city in an hour.'

'You'll be doing no such thing.' Mavis was stern. 'It's a day of rest. A Sunday, in case you've forgotten.'

'No trains.' Bob made a rare, gruff contribution.

'But surely there's a bus …'

Mavis came in, sharp. 'It's New Year's Day. The whole country is resting. I'm not sure what's so special about you.'

The afternoon was long. Rosaleen sat with the family in the front room. There was a fire that smoked, and Bob smoking beside it, while Mavis clicked her knitting, a fine white bonnet for a baby due across the road. John and Francis shared a car magazine, reading it together so intently it was as if there might be an exam. The clock ticked over the mantelpiece. Visiting hours had begun and there was nothing she could do, no way of getting back to Barts, no Rolls-Royce would be travelling out of Ilford, and although she told herself she'd go tomorrow, would slip away from the post room at lunch and beg to be allowed to see him, the effort of waiting felt like a day's work. Felix — she held his name inside her like a flame — and she stared past her nana sitting at the folding table in the window, gazing out through the net curtains at nothing going by. Rosaleen looked down at her nana's hands, at the gold band loose on her ring finger, and she thought how her father had never missed a chance to warn her that if she continued, wild and defiant, she'd turn out like his mother. The mouth on her, that's what he said, and Rosaleen did her best to gather the whispered pieces of her grandmother's life. Her family disowning her when she eloped, the girl she'd been, jumping from a window into her lover's arms.

Rosaleen woke in the early hours and lay in the lumpy dip of the mattress, her back against her nana's padded spine. She could hear her soft breathing, feel the tickle of her hair. It was cold and she drew her knees up, jammed her hands under each arm, and counted the hours until she could get up. *Dear God*, she started, out of habit, and she remembered her nana as she'd prepared for bed, slowly, painfully sinking to her knees. She had a fine pink rosary, each bead linked with silver, and Rosaleen had listened as she counted them out. *Dear God* … her voice ran soft below the surface … *keep him safe … please … in your goodness … free from harm* … She had considered slipping to the ground herself, but the cold bruise of the convent floor, the gall in her heart for the one unanswered prayer — take me away from here – froze her where she was. *Dear God*, she tried instead from beneath the covers, *what should I do?* But for all that she listened no answer came.

The mountain of post was huge. There had been a skeleton staff over the holidays but there was nothing that would slow the news. The paper was thick with photographs of the Kennedys, Jacqueline, her hair cut into a bonnet, effortless in every outfit – furs, slacks, the perfect little black dress. In the centre was a double-page spread, *Get the Jackie Look*, with a model showing how it could be done. Rosaleen put a hand to her stomach, bound flat as it was with one of her nana's corsets.

'Nice Christmas?' It was Betty, watching as she flipped through the pages.

'Yes, thanks.' Rosaleen snapped to attention, turning to the piles of letters, passing one round that held Lord Beaverbrook personally responsible for the weather.

The girls chatted and giggled, exchanging stories of dances and parties, and when the rush was over the printworkers trailed in for their tea. 'How about you, Rose, out somewhere fancy at New Year?'

She was saved from answering by the Father of the Chapel, as the union representative was known, who produced a packet of Bourbons on which the girls descended.

Every few minutes Rosaleen looked at the clock. Never in her life had time passed so slowly. Ten o'clock, and after an hour, twenty past. *I might be a little late back*, she practised, *I have to* ... but when she glanced at Betty's imperious face the words died in her throat. Eventually the clock ambled round to one. As leisurely as she could she took up her coat, and while the others stood in a huddle deciding which café to choose, she ran. She ran as fast as she could, along Fleet Street, and up King Edward VIII Street, and in under the arch of the clock tower, across a courtyard and through the main doors of the hospital. Her heart beat so sharply she could barely speak. 'My uncle,' she gasped, 'he was admitted last week. Felix Lichtman, I have to see him.' There was a different woman on reception, but she flicked through the same list. When she found his name she paused, and only then did she look up. 'Queen Mary Ward,' she said, not unkindly, and Rosaleen could have kissed her.

'Thank you!' Without asking for directions she ran along a corridor, through swing doors, out again, and back. She was breathless by the time she found the ward. 'Felix Lichtman,' she panted at the nurse who sat in a small office, labelling glass vials, 'my uncle, he'll be expecting me ...' and as she waited to be told to come back later, she craned her eyes along the row of beds, the humps of covers, the still heads.

'Your uncle, did you say?' The nurse led Rosaleen along another, shorter passage. 'Here we are.' She stopped outside a door with a glazed window, and softly opened it on to a room with one high bed. In the bed was an old man. He had the scratchings of a beard, and his face was grey. 'We thought he'd be more comfortable in here.' There was a drip attached to him, and a machine that formed a wavery line.

Rosaleen stared. The man was wearing piped pyjamas and one hand lay curled on the sheet. She knew that hand. It was square and calloused; the thumb, the twist of it, refined. 'Felix?' She stepped closer, and there was his forehead, the beak of his nose, his lovely laughing mouth − not gone, but distant − as if the heat that lived in him had paled. Rosaleen took his fingers and held them in her own. She pressed as tight as she dared, and leaning forward she put her mouth to his and, very gently, blew. His eyelids fluttered. 'Felix.' Tears dropped on to their hands. She bent lower and rubbed at them with her nose. Why is no one helping? She was grateful too to have him to herself. 'My love.' She bent closer and slowly, carefully, certain he could hear, she told him how he'd woken her, changed her, shown her how it felt to be alive. She wished she was a poet so that she could form the kernel of her feelings into words, but she did the best with what she had to pour her heart into his ear. When her voice was hoarse she climbed on to the bed and, turning herself to lie alongside him, she rested her arm across his body and waited for him to wake.

There was a wall clock that read twenty past two. Rosaleen stared at it. She must have drifted off. Felix lay beside her. His breath was shallow, his eyelids palely mauve.

'Nurse!' She rushed to the door, and still calling she ran along the corridor. 'You have to come … Mr Lichtman …'

The young nurse in the matron's station stared at her. 'You still here?' Together they walked back along the corridor and looked into his room. 'He's comfortable, that's the thing.'

'Comfortable!' Why didn't he wake?

The woman was no older than Rosaleen. A student. Maybe not even a nurse at all. There must be someone, something; she ran to the door. 'Help!' she bellowed. 'We need help here! Please.'

The nurse caught her by the arm. 'That's enough,' but she wasn't about to stop shouting, couldn't stop, not until someone came. Soon the room was full of people. 'What's the commotion?' It was Matron, and a doctor, a clipboard in his hand. 'This isn't going to help, not in the slightest.' He gave Rosaleen a stern look, and Matron led her to a chair. 'Drink up.' She handed her a glass of water. 'Wash these down.' Two large capsules were pressed into her palm.

'Were you very close to your uncle, is that it?' The doctor gave the shadow of a smirk, and he glanced at her stomach, just for a second, and up into her eyes.

Rosaleen gulped down the pills, and when she spoke her voice came out like a child's. 'Why won't he wake up?'

The doctor was suitably professional. 'We are doing what we can for him.' He turned, and for the first time, he looked at the patient. They all looked. Felix's proud face, his hair springing short and dark. 'His wife will tell you the same. She usually comes in about now.' He inspected the chart and lowering his voice he spoke sharp instructions to the nurse.

They left her then. Her limbs were heavy, her thoughts unclear. There was something she had to do, she knew, but also, there was nothing. She dragged the chair as close to the bed as she could get, and waited, in the trap of her confusion, her hand curled into Felix's, pulsing small squeezes, feeling for a response. She stroked his rough thumb, the calloused pads on his fingers, kissed his eyebrows, the warm skin of his neck. 'Don't leave me, we've only just begun.' She mopped her tears with his cuff and, unable to remember what it was that might be happening about now, she told him her news. The baby kicking during Christmas lunch. O'Malley winking at her mother.

It was darkening outside the window and her stomach spiked with lack of food. 'I'll have to find something,' she kissed him – even a cup of tea would do – and she drifted off along the corridors, following the old boiled smell of a canteen. She bought a teacake, and ate it at a table in the corner. It was quiet in here; people spoke in whispers, clustered together, or sat, like her, alone. Between sips of tea she let her eyes roam, settling on families, on couples, on the occasional patient well enough to leave their ward, and then on the far side of the room, she saw the boy. He had Felix's straight eyebrows, his same determined mouth, and as she watched he lifted his head to the ceiling and shook it in Felix's own impatient way.

'Will you have your tea now?' Mavis called to her as she came in. She'd thought better of going back to the *Express*, braving Betty's interrogation, the watchful faces of the girls.

'I'm all right, thank you.' It was as much as Rosaleen could manage to walk upstairs. 'I'll have a rest first.' She kicked off her shoes, dropped her coat, and crawled under the covers of the bed. If I could stay here … She was numb, but she knew, tomorrow, she'd have to start again.

It was her nana who came up with a cup of tea, and then went down again and brought her a bread roll. She said nothing, only sat at the dressing table, brushing her long hair, singing a song in some faraway language.

'*Thula thul, thula baba, thula sana,*' her voice was hoarse.

'*Thu'u babuzo ficka, eku seni.*' Rosaleen watched her in the mirror, the lullaby drifting over her.

'*Thula thul, thula baba, thula sana. Thu'u babuzo ficka, eku seni.*'

'Nana,' Rosaleen asked her when she paused. 'Did you sing that to your children?'

'My tannie, in Johannesburg, she sang it to me, long ago. When I came to England, I sang English songs.' Smiling at her through the glass, she started: 'Matthew, Mark, Luke and John, bless the bed that I lie on …'

Rosaleen joined her. 'Four corners to my bed, four angels round my head. One to watch and one to pray, and two to bear my soul away.' She turned on her side and closed her eyes.

★ ★ ★

Betty had the aloof look she adopted when displeased.

'I'm so sorry ...' Rosaleen had a speech prepared, but the postmistress put up her hand. 'If you disappear like that again —' Meg and Sally glanced over at her, concerned '— there'll be no second chance.'

Rosaleen threw herself into the usual flurry, bundling the letters, sliding them into pigeonholes, grateful for the time it devoured, and for the busy morning that made it impossible for the girls to enquire after her story.

'Tea's up,' Betty declared once the first stacks were sorted, and as if they'd heard her, the printworkers came trooping in. Today the Father of the Chapel had custard creams. He drew them from his pocket like a trick. Betty accepted with a small prance of her head and moved away to put them on a plate. The room was warm and steaming up and soon there were more people than could fit. Rosaleen felt faint. 'Go on.' The biscuits were handed round, and when she declined the man beside her grinned. 'Watching your weight, eh?' He shook his head as if to say — Girls! There's nothing I don't know. Rosaleen picked up that day's paper and leafed through, staring into Jackie Kennedy's dark eyes. Wealth, beauty, an enviable marriage. How might it be to swap places even for a day? But there was work to do and Betty was rising, her cigarette held high. 'Righto, fellas, time's up,' and the printworkers drifted out.

Time passed even more slowly than the day before, each second dragged into a minute, each minute an hour. She stood by the one window that looked on to the central shaft and sipped at the cool air. She could feel Betty watching her and so she gathered up the pile of letters addressed to the Agony Aunt and considered the futility of writing one of her own. *I am nineteen, unmarried, pregnant. Please advise where I should turn for help.* If she did write, how would she sign off? *Ignorant*

Imelda. Desperate Deirdre. She and Angela had laughed over the names girls gave themselves. Now she'd have to think up a name of her own.

At one o'clock she was finally released. She kept her head down as she hurried towards the hospital and, when she reached the entrance, she avoided the main desk. No one asked what she was doing. Porters, nurses, patients: they accepted her presence. She found Felix's ward, and tiptoed along the passageway. Light showed through the square of window set into his door.

'Excuse me?' It was Matron, who only yesterday had pressed those pills into her hand. 'May I enquire as to your business?'

Rosaleen felt the familiar jut of her chin. 'You may not.' Her voice was brattish, even to her ears, and she had an image of Sister Benedict, could feel the bat wings of her fingers as they clasped her by the arm; and then, as if she'd spun through time, Matron had hold of her. 'Mind your manners, young lady.' Her grip was steel.

'It's none of your bloody business what I'm doing here. Let go of me.' Her protests spiralled, drawing nurses from their stations, their faces terrified and thrilled. 'No!' She twisted, escaping long enough to press her face against the glazed window, long enough to see Felix, propped up with pillows – his wife at his side. He swerved his eyes away. He'd seen her! Felix, she mouthed, but he did not look around.

Defeated, Rosaleen was handed to a guard. He was a big unwieldy man, embarrassed by her wilted form, who closed his fingers over the bruise above her elbow, and in silence escorted her out. He left her before the fountain in the square. 'No more trouble now,' he warned and, for his sake, she nodded her compliance.

There were four cherubs in the fountain holding up a giant urn, burdened and straining, the weight unnecessarily cruel. Stray splashes caught Rosaleen's face, formed a sheen over her coat. I must get back to work, her thoughts scrambled, and with a supreme effort, she dragged herself away.

The afternoon was long. Her stomach cramped, her skin itched against the ribbing of the corset. *What will I do?* The thought ran in a loop, so fast there was no time to consider, and then it was over, and the girls, Sally and Meg, were waving and calling, 'See you tomorrow, bye, love, bye,' before skipping away down the street.

There were a pair of phone booths outside the station. Rosaleen stepped inside and fished into her purse for change. With numb fingers she dialled the number Anastasia had supplied.

'How many weeks?' The voice at the other end was brisk.

Rosaleen counted back to France. 'Eighteen?'

'You're too far gone.'

'I can pay.' She'd been unsure before what she should do, but now she knew that she was desperate.

'I'm sorry.'

'Couldn't I come by, I might not … it may be less.' She knew that it was more.

'It's too much of a risk.'

'No one would know.'

'If you end up in hospital.' The woman was impatient.

'I wouldn't tell.'

'Sorry.' Before Rosaleen could think of a new way to convince her, she'd put down the phone.

Rosaleen stood in the phone box with the receiver pressed against her ear, and when no queue formed, she slid down the wall, her back against the ridged panels, and cried. At first the sheer work of her grief provided comfort, but her tears were not without their limits and eventually they stopped. She raised her head and stared out at the rain. There was nothing left to do; there never had been. She pushed her way out of the booth, and walked through the streets, glancing at the women hurrying by, wondering how many of them were in a fix. There'd been a piece in the *Express*, she ran over the details, a girl so fearful of discovery she'd hidden in the tunnel of a station to give birth. *Tragic Teresa*, the caption had read, and her first thought had been for her old friend Teresa Donnelly, but the last she'd heard she was living in Chelsea in the house of a professor, escorting him to dinner in lieu of rent.

The train was crowded, although she found a space, squashed in beside a woman so large she overlapped the seat. Tears, unwanted, seeped from her eyes.

'You all right, love?'

Rosaleen startled. 'I'm …' She wanted to say that, yes, she was fine, but no words came.

'Buck up.' The woman touched her arm. 'He'll be back, you'll see, lovely girl like you,' and she squeezed past her and swayed away down the aisle. Rosaleen turned her face to the window, and pressing her forehead to the glass, she looked out at the dark.

That night she sat at her nana's dressing table and wrote:

Dear Teresa,
I'm sorry not to have been in touch for so long, I've been
back from Ireland since the summer, working at the Express.
How are you anyway? I can't believe I've not visited. I know
Chelsea's not so far. But everything has been such a whirl.
Right now I'm living at my Auntie Mavis's. Which is partly
why I'm writing. Could I come and stay for a few days? It

would be super to catch up.
Your friend, as ever,
Rose

Teresa replied by return.

Rosaleen Kelly! I always said that you'd go far. The Daily
Express! *Of course it would be great to have you here. The*
Professor's not too bad, and as long as a girl's young and
presentable [there was a sketch of a woman with a wasp
waist and pneumatic bosom], *he'll be delighted if you stay.*
Write and let me know when to expect you. It will be super to
see you.
Always,
Terrie

While her nana was downstairs filling the hot-water bottle,
Rosaleen unwound the scarves she bound herself with,
unhooked the corset with its hooks and eyes, and examined
her body in the wardrobe mirror. Her legs and arms were
thin as ever, but her breasts were mountainous and her stomach was a smooth round gourd. Slow footsteps on the stairs
alerted her, and she fumbled for her nightdress.

That night she dreamt she was standing in the street calling
to Felix with every bit of her strength. His window wrenched
up, far above, and his wife looked out. 'Get away from here!'
Instead of keys she threw down a black flower, and Rosaleen
woke flailing and battling as the charred petals caught in
her hair.

'Child,' her nana soothed her. She had a hand on her head
and she was stroking. 'We must be strong.'

Rosaleen wrote to Felix before leaving for work. She hoped
he was recovering, that he wasn't in any pain. She longed to

see him, could hardly bear to be apart, and she needed his advice. What was she to do? She took it to the hospital herself first thing.

A week passed in which she heard no news. She wrote again, and delivered it to his flat. She rang the bell and waited, her ear against the grille, and when there was only silence, she forced it through the snap of the letter box and listened to it fall.

Kate

I look out of the cab window at the rain, the people dashing through it, the macs and umbrellas, the bowed heads. Surely it would be quicker to get out and walk, but Matt has a suit on and I've straightened my hair.

'I hope tonight won't be too boring.' Matt takes my hand. 'If there's someone I don't introduce you to ...'

'It's all right.' We've had this conversation before, and I promise to break in and introduce myself, and not, as I did last year, use it as an excuse to sidle away and wait out by the coats.

The lights change and we shunt forward and stop again outside Marylebone Town Hall. Neither of us speak. I press my face against the glass, and screw my eyes up to imagine Freya, six weeks old, a white-wrapped bundle in my arms. I wonder, as I wondered then, was my own birth registered? Did my mother take me to a town hall? This town hall? And what did she name me? I listen for it in the hiss of the rain, the splash of the wheels, but the cab lurches forward and we sail on.

Matt's brother's investment company has merged with another, larger corporation, and the employees from both sides are slapping each other on the back. I stand beside Matt's suited shoulder while he drains his glass. 'Matthew!' A man approaches, and I feel him shrink as he is cross-examined.

I wait for a chance to put out my hand, but no chance comes. If Matt has forgotten this man's name, it seems possible he's forgotten mine, and as he reaches for another drink I walk around the outskirts of the room where I'm embroiled in a conversation with Matt's brother who reprimands me, while keeping one eye on the guests, for not visiting his mother. I find my way to the ladies and stand at the mirror looking into it, wondering how long before we can leave.

'You're probably right,' a voice drifts out from behind the cubicle door. 'It's just ...' the owner gives a sniff '... before, he used to pass my desk, like twenty times a day, any excuse, and now ...'

I take a lipstick from my bag and smudge it against the centre of my mouth. Her friend in the next stall sighs, sympathetic.

'It's as if he's avoiding me, although when I ask him he denies it ...'

I press my lips together, let the red bleed out.

'... and then tonight, why did he have to bring his wife, can you believe that?'

I look through the mirror at the two closed doors. There is a rustle and a flush. 'I suppose if he didn't it might look suspicious?'

'Coward.'

The friend has nothing more to add, and she emerges from her cubicle. She drops her eyes when she sees me. 'Sarah,' she hisses, 'I'll be outside,' and passing her fingers momentarily under the tap, she totters out into the party.

I don't wait for the other door to open. I pick up my glass and fight my way into the crowd. 'Hello,' I put out my hand,

'I'm Kate. We've not been introduced.' I look from Matt to his colleague, and flash them both a smile.

'Ken,' he greets me, vigorous, and then his attention is caught by someone across the room, and he is waving and gesticulating. 'You know Sarah?' He turns to Matt, and in case he doesn't, he draws her towards us — a tussled blonde with make-up recently retouched, who apologises for the drink and cigarette that makes it impossible to shake hands. 'Sarah's in Accounts.'

Matt swipes a fresh glass from a tray and takes a thirsty swallow.

'Accounts? Of course. Hi, Sarah.'

'Hi.' There's an uncomfortable pause, and when it seems there's nothing more to say, Sarah smiles tightly and she moves away.

'You OK?' Matt is unsteady as we brush our teeth, jostling for space to spit.

I look at my eyes, guarded. 'Just tired,' I tell him, and while he stumbles through into the bedroom and flings away his clothes, railing in an exaggerated whisper, louder possibly than his actual voice, about the bloody awful people at the party, how he'd get out if he could, I turn on to my side and pretend to sleep.

That weekend we're out again. I check over my words before I say them, check again, and when I speak my voice sounds false. 'I've been thinking … tonight … could you try, maybe, drinking a bit less?'

'Sure.' His face snaps shut.

'It's just … Mum and Dad … Alice — she's bringing someone.' I'm primed for an argument, ridicule, a case for his defence, but instead he lifts the glass of beer he's poured and tips it down the sink.

Now Matt strides ahead of me as we walk towards the bus. 'Listen, I didn't mean ... ' My heart lies heavy. For fuck's sake! I'd like to scream, but we're paying a babysitter by the hour, and it's not worth it, to argue in the street. The bus is pulling in as we round the corner. We run, waving for it, exclaiming with relief as we leap on. We sit at the front and our two known bodies press together as it rocks. Neither of us speak and I search for the image of Matt as I first knew him, his hand reaching out to me, the promise of it as he drew me in. I am lying beside him in the dark. 'There's nothing I wouldn't do for you,' the words rose out of me, and he'd laughed – had I scared him? – and uncurling a strand of my hair, he'd stretched and straightened it until it snapped.

Alice is already at the restaurant. She leaps up when she sees us and introduces Jamie. 'Kate,' I put out my hand, 'Alice's sister,' and Jamie who's tall and tanned kisses both my cheeks. Matt greets Alice, and shakes Jamie's hand, and we sit down, the four of us, and wait.

'So how are they?' Alice leans towards me.

I look at her, unsure.

'Our parents!'

'They're fine. At least I saw Mum, and she was ...' How was she?

'And Dad, when did you last see him?'

I shake my head. I don't remember.

'When I spoke to him ...' Alice frowns, but the waiter has come to take our order. 'What do you think, shall we ... ?'

Jamie puts up his hand. 'We'll have champagne.' Across the table I feel my sister quiver.

'So ...' There really is no other subject. 'How did you two meet?' They pause, and stammer, but it's clear I've asked their favourite question, and they're off, overlapping, contradicting, lingering on each other's every phrase. I reach down and take Matt's hand.

'Terrible horrible traffic.' Our mother arrives in a fluster. 'We got to Victoria, and then, clearly, it was a mistake to take a taxi. I did say, but your …'

Dad stands stoically by, waiting for her to finish.

Jamie is introduced. Sir, he calls our father, and he kisses Mum on the cheek. I glance at Matt, but he doesn't catch my eye.

Everyone is seated when the champagne arrives. A silver bucket, a frosted, smoking bottle. We wait in silence for the ceremonial pouring.

'Wait one second.' Alice's fair face flushes. 'There's something we wanted … Jamie and I … something we wanted to let you know.' We lower our glasses.

Jamie is pale. 'I know you've only just met me, but Alice and I, we didn't want to keep it from you, from anybody really …'

'We're engaged.' She is so joyful, so sure, that we all clink glasses and, amid a ripple of relief, we drink. All except Matt who lowers his glass untouched. I nudge him. It's not what I meant.

'So have you thought at all about the wedding?' Mum is awash with happiness.

Alice's eyes mirror her own. 'We have, but for now, we're just enjoying being engaged.'

'But you'll be relocated?' It is the only direct question Dad asks all night, and when Alice hesitates, his body folds.

'Atlanta is a lovely place to live. In some areas at least,' Jamie says.

'Clapboard houses, cherry trees …' Alice agrees.

'You should both come and visit.' He is eager. 'All of you.' He turns to us. 'Bring your little girl,' and when no one answers, Alice adds, 'Although it can get very hot.'

For three long weeks Matt doesn't drink. He comes home from work and slumps on to the sofa. 'Maybe we could go out one night?' I suggest, but without a beer he prefers to go to bed. He's upstairs by nine, hunched under the covers, and it is only when Ian calls to set up a rehearsal, he concedes there may be something wrong. 'It's probably a bug of some kind.' He isn't keen, though, when I suggest it, on going to the doctor.

'Has there been no news,' I'm wary of sounding like my mother – his mother – who he loathes, 'about the band?' When he doesn't answer, I press on. 'You were good, it's not just me who's saying it.' I push away the missing hours of that night.

'There was a manager in,' Matt turns away, 'but he's not interested.'

'There are other managers. Do you have more dates lined up?'

'What's the point?' Matt sighs.

What's the point of anything if you look at it like that? 'I think you're brilliant.' I'm fighting to stay afloat, and I wonder how it is that even my admiration presents itself as an attack.

That night my tree is the oak. Alice and I have climbed it and are inching along the slope of its branch. 'Careful,' our mother calls, and we move slowly, two riders, bareback, the barrel of its girth between our knees. Below lies the shadowed ground, leaves and dust, the scuff marks of feet, and I roll under, hang for a minute, and before I have a chance I'm falling, a corridor rising up to meet me, Matt, a fingertip from reach. I jolt awake and lie still in the bed. My heart is racing, my nightdress drenched with sweat. 'Matt?' I whisper but his back is to me and he doesn't wake.

I pull on my dressing gown and go downstairs. I twist the handle of my workroom and step inside. It's like standing in a forest: the shadows of the branches, the leaves dappling the floor. I think of the requests I've had to mount a show, art-school friends mostly, one gallery owner who asked me to get in touch, but I can't part with anything, not yet. First my trees must grow to their full height. My eye is caught by the stencilling knife, stored for safety on a shelf, and heaving up a roll of lining paper, I carry it into the kitchen and spread it out over the floor. I begin with the roots, sketch in the trunk, crawl after it across the lintel and along the hall. I'm crouched by the front door when Matt appears. 'What are you doing?'

I look up. He's wearing striped boxers, a faded T-shirt, socks. It's the socks that catch me, remind me that it's him. 'What's it for?' he asks, and although I hadn't known it until now, I tell him that I've got a plan to brighten up the yard.

'Which yard?'

'At work.'

We look at each other. *Whatever the distance* … I take a breath. 'I'm making a stencil of an oak tree. I'll spray it on to hardboard panels, I'll need to paint them, attach them to the wall.' I bend back over the sweep of the crown.

Matt waits. 'Night then.' He stumbles up the stairs.

'Muuum.' Freya must have heard him creak across the landing.

'Matt! Can't you …?' In answer there's the click of the bedroom door.

Freya lies still under the covers. 'What if I die?' Tears streak her face. 'And you're still alive?'

'Then you'll wait for me in heaven,' I have a stick of charcoal in my hand, 'where waiting is the most fun thing and no one minds.' I've got it wrong. *That will never happen* is what I should have said, and I clench my fist so tight the charcoal snaps.

Freya's shoulders are hunched up by her ears, and her eyelashes are spiked and black. I climb in beside her and wrap myself around her small, held body. 'Everything is scarier in the middle of the night.' I breathe slow and deep, I'd breathe for her if I could. 'Shhh.' I count to five, to twenty-five, to fifty, when I feel her soften into sleep. Slowly, stiffly, I ease myself from the room. I hover on the landing – the pull is strong to go back downstairs – but Matt is in the doorway. 'Come to bed.' He has his hand stretched out and I take it and let myself be led. 'Hey.' His breath is clean, his eyes bright, and I laugh, nervous, and lay my head on the cushion of his shoulder, and it occurs to me I can't remember the last time we had sex when he wasn't hungover or drunk. We examine each other, self-conscious, and I think how strange it is to have his attention, when for so long if I wanted it I had to stand in front of him and shout. 'Kate,' he says, and I open my eyes. I hadn't known that they'd been closed. 'Stay with me.'

'I'm here,' I say, unblinking.

Aoife

That first Christmas after the war we went across to Joe and Elsie for our dinner, do you remember? She laid on such a spread. They had their own girl back from Ireland, and the two of them, Rosaleen and Patricia, eyeing each other like they'd gone for the same job. They'd let her run wild, that's what Elsie said, over at Kilcrea, and the quicker she lost the accent, or how was she ever to get on? At least Rosaleen didn't gabber like a peasant, we agreed on that, but the truth was our daughter didn't say much of anything at all – *no*, and *won't* – so how was anyone to know?

Mock duck, Elsie made us, with sausage, apples, onion and sage. We clapped when she brought it to the table and not one of us thought to mention that it didn't look like duck, or taste like duck. No. We were delighted with it as it was. She served it with potato floddies. That's when their girl set down her knife and fork. She said the floddies looked like cowpats – well, she should know, five years on the farm – and she refused to eat them, and Rosaleen, it took less than that to put her off her food. The two of them, they were sent out of the room. We could hear them, they must have been jumping off the bed, and then didn't Elsie storm upstairs and there was silence. Floddies. I was thinking I might make some for my tea. I've got everything I need: a potato for grating, herbs and flour and the fat I saved from last night's chop. There was no butter to spare then, not for frying, and I'm after the taste of how it was when it was just the two of us, when there was no one and nothing to come between us, not even the war.

Squeeze my hand, Cash. Go on. Just this once. Or blink, you stubborn man. Right so, then I'll wait. I'll sit here, for as long as it takes. I'll wait until you find a way to tell me what you know.

Rosaleen

It was only another fortnight before Betty asked to have a word. She took her out into the corridor, their voices shielded by the rumble of the press. 'You won't be able to stay on here – you know that, don't you?'

When had she guessed?

'All sorted, are you?' Betty's tone suggested there was only one answer she'd prefer to hear, and so Rosaleen assured her that everything was settled. 'Good girl. You'll be paid until the end of the week.'

'You mean today?'

Betty nodded. She wanted her gone.

Rosaleen took her coat and walked down to the river. There was an ice wind rippling the water, and the people she passed looked chapped and raw. *Now what am I to do?* The old question started up again, but what amazed her was that it ever went away. *Maybe I'll die.* It was the only comfort she could give herself, and less bitter than the image of Felix, swerving away from her as he sat in that hospital room beside his wife.

Rosaleen kept walking until she reached the Embankment and from there she trudged up to Trafalgar Square where even the pigeons looked sparse and shivering, without a kernel of corn in sight. She cut through Chinatown and, although she'd not intended it, found herself in Soho. She stood outside the French pub and dared herself to go in. What if he was in there? With her? Would she have the strength to make a scene, run an elbow down the length of the bar, smash glasses, ashtrays to the floor? She pressed her face against the window but could see nothing through the fug of smoke. A man lurched round the corner, his jacket high around his ears. She didn't know him, and as she made to step in after, the door swung back and hit her in the face. A woman came out in a burst of noise, followed by another. They glanced at her, incurious, and linking arms they strode away. Rosaleen stood undecided. Ten minutes. Half an hour. Then she turned and, walking blindly, found herself on Meard Street, outside the coffee shop where, in that miraculous year before she'd gone to Ireland, she'd spent her afternoons. She looked in through the window and saw herself as she was then, talking and laughing, mapping out her future, catching her first sight of Felix. He'd been leaning up against a wall, white shirt, the sleeves rolled up, his dark head dipped towards his cup. She'd kept looking, it was hard to force herself away and when he'd turned and caught her, there it was, the brilliance of his stare. 'How have I not seen you here before?' He had the accent of a foreigner, but he held himself, at home.

'You've seen me now,' she answered boldly, and she felt her face crack open in a smile.

'I have.' He didn't look away and, draining his coffee, he said he was already looking forward to seeing her again. 'In fact,' he set his cup down, 'if I leave now, the pleasure of it can begin.' With a last devouring stare he swung out into the street.

'Bless me, Father …' She'd stepped into St Patrick's Church, a cavernous building made almost invisible by the squash of Soho Square. 'For I have sinned.'

'What is the nature of your sin, my child?'

'I have been with a man,' and in case that wasn't clear, Rosaleen resorted to the ugly words he'd understand. Lustful, carnal, impure. The facts established, she recited the formal act of contrition and was given a penance of six Hail Marys, but before absolving her, the priest directed her to a passage from the Gospel of Matthew: *Blessed are the pure of heart, for they shall see God.* Then, in a voice rising above a whisper and with a gesture of blessing just visible through the grill, he pronounced: *'Ego te absolvo a peccatis tuis in nomine Patris et Filii et Spiritus Sancti. Amen.'*

'But what am I to do?' After all, it was why she was here.

The priest scribbled something – she could hear his pen – and then he passed a slip of paper to her through the grille. *The Sisters of Mercy.* There was a telephone number with a familiar code. 'Put yourself in their good hands,' he counselled. 'May God go with you.' He bowed his head and began to pray, and Rosaleen ducked out of the confessional, skirted the empty nave and stepped through the door into the dark. She stopped under a street lamp and unfurled the paper. *Convent of the Sacred Heart.* The code was for Cork.

There was a news-stand on the corner of Tottenham Court Road where she broke her wages into shillings, buying a newspaper although it was the last thing she needed, and finding a phone box she arranged her coins on the cold ashy shelf and took out the slip of paper. How many times – she examined the priest's cramped hand – had he written this number. Judging by how swiftly he'd set it down she guessed he must have it by heart.

'A trunk call to Ireland,' she told the operator. There were crackles and clicks and a thirty-second silence as her ears strained across the sea. 'Putting you through now.' The girl sounded breezy. Rosaleen thanked her and listened to the long-distance ring. Once, twice, four times. Maybe there's no one there? Her heart lifted, but there was always someone at a convent. Where else would the nuns go?

'Sacred Heart.'

With trembling fingers Rosaleen slotted in her coins.

'How can we help you?'

She swallowed.

'Hello? Who is this?'

'I was advised ...' The call was costing her three shillings. 'Father Gogarty suggested that I call ...'

'Do you find yourself in trouble?'

'I do.'

'How far along, would you say?'

'Six ...' She swallowed again. She mustn't cry. 'Seven months.'

'And where is it that you're calling from?'

Rosaleen looked out through the glass panes of the phone box, at the people rushing to their homes: men with umbrellas; girls in rain macs, chattering and scattering along the street. 'London.'

'Can you get yourself here to us in Cork?'

Dread twisted inside her, but what else was she to do? 'I can.'

'So you'll write and say when it is you'll be arriving, and we'll send a car to meet you from the ferry. After that you'll not have to worry. We'll take care of it all.'

'I will.' Tears ran into the receiver. 'I'll be there soon.'

'Bessoborough, Blackrock. Ask for Sister Ignatius …' The shrieking demand for money drowned out the voice. She scrabbled for another shilling, but the line went dead.

The next morning Rosaleen bound her corset as tightly as she dared and, forgoing breakfast – she'd come downstairs in her coat – she took the early train to Liverpool Street. She felt like an imposter, pressed against the hordes of real workers, but there was a travel agent she'd used before in Holborn, and she didn't want word spreading back to Auntie Mavis. Small, nosy place that Ilford was.

'Will that be a single journey?' The man glanced up from writing out her ticket. Rosaleen started. Was he expecting her to stay? 'It's a return I'm after,' but all she could see was the white swell of the waves as the ferry headed back across the Irish Sea without her.

Rosaleen said nothing to Mavis until the night before the boat, and then, coming in, as if from work, she explained that one of the girls at the paper was looking for someone to share digs. The place was in Chelsea, and so as not to lose the chance of it, she might as well go over there tomorrow, take her things, and move in.

Mavis frowned. 'You couldn't wait till the weekend?'

'If she wants to go …' Bob surprised them. 'Let her have some fun. Sharing a bed with her nana. It's no life for a young girl.' He smiled at her, and she thought of the warm coins pressed against her palm.

That night, while Nana Isabelle knelt beside the bed, Rosaleen sent up a prayer of her own. Please God they are good people at the Sacred Heart, that they'll deliver my baby safely, and keep us from harm, and she realised it had been some time since she'd allowed herself to believe there was a baby, and not a bomb that had the power to derail her life.

'Amen.' Her nana creaked to her feet. She blew out the candle and stood there looking at her in the gloom. 'I'll miss you.' She began tugging at her knuckle.

'Get in,' Rosaleen urged, 'you'll catch your death,' but she kept working at her finger until the ring she wore came off.

'Take this.' She sank on to the bed.

'I couldn't. It's all you—'

Her grandmother took her hand and slid the gold disc on to her finger. 'You'll need it more than me now,' and with a determined pat she arranged the covers round them both.

Rosaleen lay with her feet on their shared hot-water bottle, the ring warming on her hand, and too fearful to sleep, she waited for dawn.

Kate

We've been drinking wine on the bench by the back door, watching our girls as they parade in fancy dress. I examine them, escalating praise, but Krissie, whose daughter Freya has befriended, tells them in her American drawl to get the hell out of here and play. It works. Now we have the garden to ourselves. We discuss the school, the distractingly handsome father of the boy in Year 1 who carries him in each morning on his shoulders, Krissie's husband who she's known since high school – how smart he is, how kind – how twenty years is enough!

I laugh. I'm not in the habit of discussing Matt. *When I'm away from you*, he used to sing to me down the warm line of the phone, our missing disproportionate to the time we spent apart, *I dream my dreams for two* … But in recent years the searching for what we had, for what we do still sometimes have, it is a full-time job.

'What?' Krissie nudges, but I only shake my head.

'The thing is,' she confides, 'I'd like another child, but I can't face it – all the … trying. It's not the same for you,' she insists. 'I've seen your man, he's dreamy.'

'Maybe,' I concede. Where is Matt anyway?

'I guess I should just close my eyes and think of them.' She looks up at the ceiling from where we hear the muted sounds of bickering. 'A sibling. Then they can gang up on us.'

It's almost seven-thirty when Krissie and Mia leave, navigating the cracked tiles of the path, and as soon as I can politely shut the door I run through to the kitchen to check the phone. I would have heard Matt if he'd called, the answerphone would have noisily clicked on, but even so I listen for a message. Nothing. A chill settles over me, and I drag myself upstairs.

Freya is sitting amongst her dolls, her mermaid dress trailing out around her. 'I told you,' she says, violence barely contained, 'sit there and don't move. Don't move, I said!' I put a hand on her shoulder and she jumps. 'Time for bed.' Too tired to protest, she lets me tug the multicoloured outfit over her head.

'Once upon a time there was a small gorilla ...' I make a start on her story.

'Mum! "Baby Day".' And so, for possibly the hundredth time, I tell her the story of a school that asks the children to bring their baby siblings in on a certain day each month. 'Freya's baby was called Max. As soon as Freya settled him with the other babies he started to roll away over the carpet ...' What will I do, I wonder, when term ends and the six weeks of summer holidays begin? 'Max rolled fast across—'

'No, Mum, "fast and faster ..."'

'Fast and faster across the carpet until he had rolled out through the door, and when he was in the playground he remembered that although he was only newborn, he could crawl.'

'Mum,' Freya says when 'Baby Day' is mercifully over. 'When will I get one?'

'Get what?' I look into my daughter's eyes, the rim of black encircling the blue.

'Mia says she's getting a baby.'

'It's nice like this though, isn't it, just us?'

Freya looks unconvinced. 'Do you know that when you die you get smaller? It's to make room for all the others, waiting.'

I kiss her, and hold her hand for the agreed number of minutes, and then slowly, carefully, back out of the room.

'Mum?' She's caught me on the threshold.

'What?'

'I'd like to make a bear with orange paws.'

'Not tonight.' I hold my breath.

'When, then?'

'I don't know! Tomorrow. On the weekend. Any time, just not right now!'

There's silence. Then she starts to whimper.

It's another half an hour before I'm downstairs. I check the answerphone again, although I know it's pointless. Fuck it. I clear away the children's supper, pour out the warm dregs of the wine, and forcing myself to eat a bowl of cereal I sit on the sofa in oddly formal silence until it occurs to me to switch on the TV. *Murder, She Wrote* has just begun, and despite the knowledge that almost anyone who crosses this lady detective's path is sure to meet their end, I'm drawn in by the sparky glamour of Angela Lansbury herself. I gaze into her discerning eyes and, on the search as ever for my mother, I guess at her age, count back the years, and decide it's unlikely, but not impossible, she may have had her reasons for giving up a child. A love child. Did she even marry? Or perhaps a baby would have interfered with her career. I've played this game before, I play it often, although by the time the crime is solved, the perpetrator taken off in shackles, I've dismissed Angela Lansbury as any kind of relative, and in the same breath I've decided Matt must have a work thing – it's possible I forgot – and relieved he's not still drinking, I flick through the channels.

I'm watching a late-night talk show when I catch the splash of keys. There's the slur of Matt's cursing, and before I've even risen, the door flies open and I hear the thud of a body as it hits the floor.

Matt lies face down in the hall. 'Christ.' I'm beside him, testing, checking, rolling him on to his side. His skin is clammy, his breath brewed. I run into the kitchen, dash back with water which I hold against his mouth, and when he doesn't stir I fling it fast across his face. 'Wake up!' His breathing quickens and then slows. I pick up the phone. My fingers hover over the 9, but I can see the look on the paramedic's face. *You wasted my time on this?*

I drag the Yellow Pages from a cupboard, look down the line of A. There is an emergency number, Alcoholics Anonymous, and although Matt has said it, how can he be an alcoholic – he goes to work, he's not lying in a ditch – I can't think who else to call. A soft-voiced man is at the other end.

'Sorry.' I'm struggling to speak.

'It's all right.' I can see him in a yellow mac, shining his light into a storm. 'Whenever you're ready.'

I gulp, and swat away my tears, and after half an hour which may have been five minutes, I put down the phone.

It's morning before Matt stirs, and although I've pleaded for it, bargaining through the night, I'm dangerous with rage. 'Why do you do it when you've stopped? Why be such an idiot!'

'Sorry.' He attempts a smile. 'I thought I'd have one small ... you know, with the boys ...' He is saved from my assault by the alarm of Freya calling.

I bend down so he can put an arm around my shoulder, and we walk, three-legged, to the sofa where he falls into the dent made by my worrying weight. 'Hey.' He tries to tug me down.

'Coming!' I'm enveloped in the steam cloud of his breath. 'Let go!' But Matt grips harder, searching for a kiss.

'Muuuuum!'

Freya has tears of fury on her face. 'Why weren't you here!'

'Daddy isn't well.'

'Sick?' She narrows her eyes.

'He's sleeping, on the sofa.' We both know what this means. No TV. In an effort to distract her, I promise to teach her how to make a bracelet. It was something I used to do with Alice, sitting on the terrace with our plastic looms. Freya has no loom, so we use a breadboard, tapping in nails at either end, and as she weaves her beads between the lines of thread, I think of my sister and what friends we were that summer, our bracelets gathering on our arms, blocks of colour, alternating stripes. It was the year that I turned ten. Alice was already nine, and I was fixing a choker round her neck, a wave design of pink and white, when our parents trailed out of the house. They waited while I fumbled with the knot. 'There's something we'd like to talk to you about.' Our mother was wearing a mauve dress, our father awkward in his weekend clothes. 'We've been thinking,' Mum swallowed, 'for a while, that it might be best, would be best, to tell you ...' Her mouth looked worried as she scratched around for words, and I was consumed by a falling kind of dread. *Don't tell me!* I let the choker drop. My father took charge. 'When you were born,' he hesitated as if to check this was allowed, 'another mummy who wasn't able to look after you ...' He began to cough. 'She let us have you.'

Mum nodded, vehemently, as if she wanted me to know that she agreed. 'We love you very much.'

I couldn't think of a single thing to say, and I wonder now as I scoop up beads how I knew it was me they were addressing. But it *was* me. That at least was clear, and when I didn't speak our mother continued. 'What's wonderful is that you are extra-special. You were chosen. By us.'

Alice turned her gaze on me, and then her eyes flew out to our parents, and I saw her as I never had before, her moon face, the pale hang of her hair. 'Not you, Alice.' Our father put a hand on her shoulder. 'You were a surprise. It happens sometimes. People who've longed for a child, like we had, for years, when they give up, sometimes that's when they get one of their own.'

Mum nudged him. 'Not given up exactly, because obviously we had Katie here …'

I'd stopped listening. I was reeling through the news … Another mummy … I looked at my parents and it was as if I'd always known that they weren't mine.

'Mum!' Freya has the needle in her mouth. 'I can't find yellow!'

I dip my hands into the tin and let the beads pour through my fingers. 'Here we are.' I scoop one with my nail.

At first I didn't think about my real mother, only about the one I'd lost. But then I saw her. She was serving tea at a fete in the next village, standing with a group of women behind a table spread with cakes. She had dark hair, parted in the centre, and as she leant forward to pick out a date slice, two plaits, braided with red thread, flipped over her shoulders. She wore a green dress, printed with leaves, and there was a gold band on her finger. 'You look like my mother,' I told her as she handed over a caramel square, and she hesitated, unsure whether to serve the next person or not. 'Thank you,' she smiled.

Later I went back to the stall. 'What would you like?' It was another mother. Mine was nowhere to be seen, and so I bought a butterfly cake and ate the wings, throwing its sponge body into the hedge.

'How are we this morning?' There's a bruise risen on Matt's forehead, and he does his best to smile as he stumbles in. When I say nothing he catches hold of me. My neck is jammed into his shoulder, my right breast squeezed against his ribs. Out of the corner of my eye I see Freya climb down from her chair. She burrows into the tent of us, jutting out an elbow. 'Aghhh.' Matt winces. 'Bloody hell, where did you come from?' but Freya has her limpet arms around my waist and she is steering me away.

'You little minx!' Matt snatches her up and lifts her high above his head. 'Are you my little minx?' He turns her upside down and tickles her and I watch, my heart scattered, as she begins to laugh.

★ ★ ★

For three fine days Matt doesn't drink. We eat supper in the kitchen, play cards with Freya, blow Fairy Liquid bubbles into the darkening sky, but on the fourth he starts again with a vengeance. He has a beer as soon as he gets home, ripping a can from the webbing of its six-pack before demolishing the rest. I pretend not to notice, not to care. Sometimes six beers are enough and he remains sprawled in front of the TV, raised voices drifting up to where I am reciting 'Baby Day' for the one hundred and seventeenth time, but often he needs more.

Tonight I find him standing in the hall, an enquiring look as he watches me walk down. 'I might go out for a bit.' There is a tilt to his voice as if he's asking, although we both know that he's not. 'I won't be long.'

I pause before replying, because how can I compete with the warm fug of the White Horse?

The door closed, the house still, I retreat to my workroom. My stencil is rolled into a corner, flimsy with its shredding, and between the boards of my trees are canvases, turned to the wall. I check the bleakness of my mood before dismissing them, but even so there is nothing here to admire. I take the smallest picture and I paint it out, and while it dries I stare into its whiteness. All I can see there is an empty can of beer. I look into the bin and I retrieve one, but one it seems is not enough, and so I tip the dustbin up, assembling a week's worth of supplies. The cans give off a stale smell. They wheeze and crackle, the fish eyes of their ring-pulled holes observing me as I take a sharp grey pencil and begin to sketch.

I'm still working when I hear the door. 'Hello!' Matt is looking in at me. He's happy. Soppy. Home. I stand with my back to the tower of cans. 'What you up to?' He approaches, unsteady.

'Nothing much.'

Soulful, he dances me from side to side. 'I love you, Kate.' There are tears in his eyes.

'I love you too.' We sway into the silence until Matt catches his foot against a chair and, for one excruciating moment, I'm sure we will both fall. 'Let's get to bed,' I tell him when we steady, and I nudge him up the stairs.

Matt runs his hot hands over my body. He's too drunk for sex and I'm too weary, and so we settle, tucked against each other, his mouth beside my ear so that I hear him as he sinks into sleep. I search for my river, and when I find it the current ripples past me fast under a sluice gate and drags me out to sea. With the greatest effort I turn around, battling upstream until I'm in open water, and I breathe. My tree is mine for nothing. A lime, its leaves like flowers.

I stretch under its canopy and bask. I'm reluctant to move to the next stage, to meet my Feeling Self, and I'm right to resist because, when I do, I find that I'm in hospital, lying in a high white bed, my body bandaged, nothing visible but my face.

Rosaleen

The drive from the ferry had not been long enough, and as the car turned in through a five-bar gate and rumbled on past low, rough fields, Rosaleen was seized with terror. Slow down, was what she needed to say, but the man's neck below his cap looked obstinate. Rosaleen twisted her fingers, re-examining the events of the last months, re-thinking, re-calculating, still hoping she might land upon any other outcome, but each path she sloped down ended in a wall. 'Excuse me,' she tried, 'could we, might we …?' Even the driver's ears were disapproving, and her request that they might stop for five minutes faded away to nothing.

'Here we are then.' The car slowed, and there it was before her, the Sacred Heart Convent, a grey stone mansion, three rows of windows stretching away on either side of the front door. The driver left the engine running as he lifted her case out of the boot, and for a moment he caught her eye as she took it from him. 'All right,' he nodded, and he folded his body safe behind the wheel.

There were six steps leading to the front door, spotless but for stains of water drying unevenly in patches. The door itself gave off a gleaming tang of polish. Rosaleen lifted the brass knocker and, shifting her eyes from her miserable reflection, let it fall. Once, twice, she daren't knock a third time, and as the echo faded she listened for a strain of comfort, the voices of girls, of children, but there was silence. She glanced behind her at the car, already halfway off along the drive, and clasped the handle of her case as if it was a hand. Was it too late to run? She stood there, considering where to go, when she heard the heels of a nun tapping across tiles. A latch was lifted; the door creaked open. 'Yes?' The nun was old, and dressed in a black habit, her eyes huge behind the bug ends of her glasses.

'Rosaleen Kelly.' A new fear flared in her: what if she was sent away? 'I was told you'd be expecting me.'

The nun glanced down at Rosaleen's stomach, disguised, but clearly not disguised entirely, because a sour look of resignation turned down the corners of her mouth. 'Sister Augustine,' she introduced herself. 'Come inside.' She held the door unnecessarily wide as Rosaleen lifted her case in over the step. She'd packed up everything, clothes and books, every last word she'd had from Felix, even his one silk sock, and, wrapped in tissue, a minuscule white matinee jacket she'd seen hanging in the window of a launderette, the lady who'd knitted it sitting happily behind her counter, thread-ing ribbon through a pair of booties. I should have bought the booties too, she thought now, looking at the many hard surfaces, the empty hall, the row of panelled doors, all closed. 'This way.' Sister Augustine led her into a smartly furnished room, a rug at its centre, Jesus with his heart aflame above the fire. There was a desk spread with papers, and behind it sat a fiercely shrivelled nun, so old she made Sister Augustine look spritely.

'Reverend Mother, Rosaleen Kelly is arrived.'

The Reverend Mother did not look up. She was reading through her pile of papers, and as they waited, mutely, she continued to compile small stacks of figures, ticking them off, crossing them out, as if she was marking the results of an exam. Rosaleen stood on the edge of the rug, and with each minute that passed, she felt herself more desperate. Her arm was aching, she'd forgotten to set down her case, and her skin pricked cold with sweat. This is only what I deserve, the thought bore down on her; it is what I have brought upon myself. Her shoulders drooped, her belly clenched, and she wondered why she hadn't thrown herself into the sea. She'd considered it, tested how easy it would be to hurl herself over the railings of the ferry, but as she'd leant into the roar of spray, a lilting, tuneless voice had breezed in on the wind and sung the Itsy Bitsy Bikini song, and there was Felix watching from the funnels, his smile amused, his eyes piercing, forcing her back from the edge. She was that girl still, she remembered, and she stood tall.

Reverend Mother's head snapped sharply up. 'Can you tell us the date you're due?'

Rosaleen counted, nine months since the South of France. Mid-April.

'And the person who should be contacted in case of an emergency?'

Rosaleen paused.

'Would that be your mother?'

'No!' There would be no emergency, not as long as she had breath. Reluctant, she gave them Angela, and the address of the farm.

'While you're here,' Reverend Mother's pen was poised, 'we advise each girl to take a name.'

'A name?' She wasn't sure she understood.

'You won't want to be using the one you were baptised with.' Even her name, it seemed, must avoid contamination.

Who could she be? The nun was waiting. 'Patricia.' She shivered to be heaping this new misfortune on her cousin.

The Mother Superior wrote it down and shuffled the papers into order. 'Sister Augustine will show you to your room.' Rosaleen clasped the handle of her case but the nun said, stern, 'You won't be needing that.' Too shocked to answer, or enquire when, if ever, she'd be reunited with her belongings, she followed her from the room. They walked across the polished hall and up the staircase, along a corridor, and up another set of stairs, the ceilings lower, the paint faded and scuffed. She was grateful for the old nun's halting steps. Each time she paused, Rosaleen took a rest herself, tired to sickness after the long night. The nun stopped outside a door. She took a breath and pushed it open. A young girl leapt to her feet. She'd been sitting bent over a letter, and the sheet of paper, lined with a round blue scrawl, fluttered to the floor. She kicked it fast under the bed. 'This is Carmel.' Carmel had orange hair, and her rabbity teeth pushed her top lip out. 'Her due date is just ahead of yours.'

The room was sparsely furnished. Two small chests of drawers. Two metal beds. 'This is Patricia,' and Rosaleen looked behind her before remembering who she had become. 'Carmel, you'll show her where to get new clothes.' The girl was wearing a uniform of limp blue denim. 'When she's changed,' Sister Augustine narrowed her eyes at Rosaleen's coat, a soft faun wool bought with her wages, 'send her down to Sister Ignatius.' She turned to Rosaleen and barked with such ferocity as to make her jump, ' Take off those shoes!' before hobbling away along the hall.

Rosaleen sank down on to the bed, but Carmel remained standing. 'They don't want the floors marked. You'd better take them off and quick. We only wear socks inside.' Rosaleen slipped off her shoes and, stowing them with her coat under the bed, followed Carmel back along the corridor, down a flight of stairs, across a landing and into a large storeroom. Here there were cupboards lining one wall and folded in stacks were uniforms in variously faded shades of blue. Carmel lifted one and shook it out. 'You'll be lost in that.' The dress was the size of a tent. 'How far along do you say you are?'

Rosaleen pulled up her shirt to show the old grey corset and the wrap of scarves that held her in. The girl giggled. 'No good pretending now,' and Rosaleen unhooked herself, releasing her squashed, creased stomach and the soreness of her breasts. Carmel held an aproned smock against her. 'This will do.'

Once Rosaleen was changed they slithered in their socked feet down a back staircase, Carmel stopping to push open a door into a bathroom as they passed. The cold came off the walls in gusts. 'About twenty of us share, so it's a bit of a scrum first thing. Not that you'd want to linger. Quick now, if you need to go.' Rosaleen shook her head, and they hurried on to the ground floor.

Sister Ignatius was waiting. She was a tall woman with a sallow face and the dark shadow of a moustache. 'You have been assigned to cleaning and maintenance duties,' she consulted a chart. 'In the convent you will be expected to work hard, as we do, to rise early and use the day productively, as we do, to attend Mass and ask the Lord's forgiveness ...' Here the nun added nothing more. Instead she pointed to a row of wellingtons. 'You can assist the girls on the side lawn.' She handed her a pair of scissors.

There were coarse brown overalls hanging from pegs. Rosaleen pulled one round her, holding her breath against the staleness of sweat. She looked for Carmel but the girl had

gone. She worked in the laundry, she'd told her as they'd skid-
ded along corridors. It was the worst job, heaving the soiled
nappies to be soaked, lifting them with poles out of the steam.
'I have the morning off today,' she'd smiled. 'Thanks to you.'

Rosaleen trudged through the yard and out under an arch
to the side of the house where a group of girls were crouched,
snipping at the grass. No one looked up as she approached.
For a moment she gazed down at the heads, at the streak of
partings in the women's hair, some blonde, others dark, one
ginger, another grey, and fearful of a reprimand she dropped
her own body to the ground and pressed her knees to the wet
earth. Snip, her scissors were small and blunt. Snip. The grass
brought with it a sod of mud. She glanced sideways and saw
backs bent low, fingers clipping, brushing away the shorn tips
of the grass. Rosaleen pressed the roots back into the earth,
and tried again, keeping the scissors straight. A small harvest
fell from the blades, five stalks, no more. She looked up and
across the lawn. A sea of grass and clover. She turned her eyes
to the sky and wondered if it could be the same sun that illuminated the world she'd left behind.

It wasn't until the next morning that Rosaleen saw every girl
together. Three hundred and fifty of them, assembled for Mass.
She'd been woken early, the voice of a nun barking through
the door, and Carmel, in the bed beside her, jolted upright,
for all that her whimpers had kept them awake half the night.
They'd hurried together to the bathroom and joined a row
of women, eyes ringed dark, hair lank, queuing for their turn.
The water at the sink was cold, a gulp of air ushered from the
hot tap, nothing more, and so she'd splashed herself beneath
her nightdress, a swift wipe under each arm, aware of the sin
of appearing naked, especially here in this room. There was no

mirror, and she was grateful as she cupped her hands around her face, and for one moment she allowed herself forgetfulness, her breath held, the ice water pressed against her eyes.

Surely now it will be breakfast? They'd had bread and margarine for tea – but, much like at St Joseph's, first the beds were to be made, then Mass endured. They went in their stockinged feet, careful, down the cold stone staircase. 'Whatever the state of our souls,' she whispered, thinking of Teresa, 'at least the floors shine bright.'

Carmel flashed her a fearful smile and clutched at the banister.

On the ground floor there was a long, dim corridor that led to the chapel. Hunched figures hurried along it. Rosaleen followed, breathing in the damp and incense smell, and once inside she squeezed herself on to the end of a pew and sat with her head bowed. She could hear the familiar murmurs of mouths moving, Carmel lisping through a prayer: *Hail Mary, full of grace, the Lord is with you … blessed art thou among women, and blessed is the fruit …* and without thinking she herself started in on an *Our Father, who art in heaven, hallowed be thy name,* before she stopped herself, reciting slowly and with care, the names in descending order of the twenty-one children – seventeen surviving – of the cowman at Barraghmore. She halted when she reached Frances, number twelve, who once took her to their cottage for a visit and showed her upstairs to the bedroom where she slept with nine of her brothers and sisters and a grandmother in two double beds, their brass headboards pressed together, their shoes thrown down into the gap between. There were two babies hardly more than a year apart, grimed, their noses bunged, still in with the parents, and the lot of them came tumbling out and followed, gaping, as Frances took her to check the hens.

It wasn't until the first intonations of the priest that Rosaleen looked up. All around her were the watchful faces of other pregnant girls, and across the aisle, the faded reflections of their future selves – thin, bedraggled women, their stomachs flat. From habit Rosaleen shielded her own stomach with an arm, and as the priest proceeded with his sermon she stole wary glances at the papery thinness of their skin.

Facing them sat the Mother Superior, her gaze upturned and fixed on the pulpit. The priest's voice floated out to her, rising, swelling, spreading through the chapel where it fell, or so it seemed, on Rosaleen – sin, weakness, the evils of the flesh – until her skull was burning. *Please God*, she heard herself murmur, and her hand was rising to form a cross when a girl, two pews ahead, slumped forward, and there was the dull sound of her head as it hit wood. Rosaleen's hand dropped to her lap. *Please God, my arse*, and as she watched, the girls on either side, one of them surely no older than Angela, used all their strength to haul her upright. 'Mam?' the girl cried out, and then coming round she saw where she was, and she fell quiet.

Rosaleen glanced over at the row of nuns, none of whom had stirred. Surely she should be taken out into the air, given a glass of water at the very least? But the nuns maintained their serene smiles, and the sermon continued, stretched to the full hour.

Breakfast was bread again, with margarine. The tea, already milked, was poured from a huge pot. Rosaleen gulped hers, finishing too soon, reminding herself to eat the bread slowly, an old trick from school, to last it out. Even so her stomach griped with hunger, clenching, painful, clawing at her sides.

'Tuesday and Friday,' Carmel whispered, catching her looking for scraps along the rows, 'we get an egg with our tea, and on Sunday,' she flicked her eyes anxious in the direction of the nuns, 'they bring a pan of sausage, boiled in the oven, and there's one each, although the mothers, they take them for their babies, or they must thrive on nothing but pandy and goody.'

Goody, she knew, was a mush of bread, milk and tea, but all the same her own baby gave a kick of expectation. She put a hand to the nub of a limb as Sister Augustine turned her eyes in their direction. 'Silence!' She struck a knife against her cup.

Work began directly after breakfast. The sky had lightened, but the grass was wet with dew, and as Rosaleen crawled forward she distracted herself by riffling through the clumps of clover that dotted the lawn. She'd played this game with Angela, each one determined to be the first to find a four-leafed stem, remembering how she'd pressed two stalks together, torn off the extra leaves, and convinced her sister she'd won. Now Rosaleen dragged her body over the grass, the baby hanging in the hammock of her belly, her breasts, braless, as was the rule, rubbing against coarse cotton, her thoughts running through the list of her sins until she had convinced herself that, for the crime of pretending to be lucky, her punishment was fair.

That evening, after clearing plates from the canteen, she staggered up the last flight to her room. Carmel was already in her nightdress, hunched over her letter.

'Who is it you're writing to?' Rosaleen asked.

'My ma.' Tears pooled in her eyes, and her words were broken up with sniffing. 'I'm giving her my news ... I'm a waitress, you see, over in Dublin.' She lifted the page and showed her the blue lies. 'What a grand time I'm having, and a dance to look forward to on Saturday ... '

'Does no one know you're here?'

Carmel looked startled. 'Not a soul. Only the friend, the one who helped me. Can you imagine, if they were to guess?'

'And what about the father?' Rosaleen sat across from her.

'He's married, isn't he? With a child to support. So what can *he* do to help me?' She was reciting his own argument, and Rosaleen thought of Felix, dropping to his knees, pressing his mouth against the curve of her belly. 'I'm sorry.' She shook herself. 'That's awful.'

'Not as awful as getting pregnant and only then finding out he'd got a family.' Tears splashed on to the sheet of paper. 'I'm a fool, that's what I am.' She searched under her pillow and found a handkerchief, stained and crumpled, and wiped it angrily across her face. 'I still love him − much good it'll do me. But mostly ...' she swallowed a great new gulp of tears '... I miss my ma.'

Rosaleen did her best to soothe her, but the girl cried harder. 'What if they find out where I am? The shame will kill her, honest to God it will.'

'How can they?' Rosaleen reached out to touch her arm. 'Unless ...' the blotched words lay between them, 'they trace your letters?'

'I post them to Dublin and my friend, the one who helped me, she sends them on for me. Oh Patricia, what a time I'm having in the city, the dinners and the walks along the Liffey, and the tips I get at work − soon I'll have saved enough to go to England.' She blew her nose. 'And what about you? You're the talk of the place, do you know? With your fancy accent, and your smart coat. You'll not be staying, that's for sure.'

'What do you mean, not staying?'

'The three years.'

Rosaleen looked at her. 'Three years …?'

'To work off your debt.'

Rosaleen stood up. 'They can't keep us, surely?' Even now there was nowhere to go, and forgetting Carmel didn't have a job in Dublin, that she wasn't even Carmel, she asked what kind of a boss did she have anyway, three years, and with no visit home?

Carmel shrugged. 'The manager, he's put a word in for me with a friend in London. The new job won't wait, and I must save every last penny for the trip. It'll break my heart, but there'll be no time to travel home before I go.'

'And me?' Rosaleen asked. 'How is it I'll get out?'

'You'll have some fancy fella – a hundred pounds, they don't accept a penny less – and you'll be out of here within ten days of the birth, that's what they're saying in the laundry.'

'A hundred pounds!' It was an unfathomable amount. 'Where would I go –' Rosaleen saw herself aboard the ferry, her baby wrapped tight in a shawl '– with such a young child?'

Carmel's eyes grew wide. 'You'll not be taking any child. There's no amount of money you can give the nuns – they'll not let you keep it.'

'The priest, he said they'd help me. He said they'd see I was all right.'

'And so they will.' Carmel clasped her hand. 'If it wasn't for the nuns, just think what would become of us. The disgrace, for you, and for the baby.' Firmly, she made sure the door was shut.

'The priest …' Rosaleen was trapped behind the grilled wall of Confession. She could hear the scratching of his pen. 'There wasn't one word about giving up the baby.'

'They find good Catholic homes for them. Couples come from England, they travel from America.'

There was a shout for the lights to be turned off. 'It's for the best.' They stood in darkness. 'We'd better sleep now,' and so, still clothed, Rosaleen climbed in under the covers where she lay with her nose inches from the wall. Felix, she allowed herself, and she took his hand and placed it on the warm wall of her stomach. Tears slipped over her face, but it was her mother who was with her on the gangplank of the ferry. 'Look after yourself now,' she embraced her as they said goodbye, and for a brief moment their eyes met.

Aoife

Aoife didn't know how she came to be standing on the beach. Rain stung her face and the waves rolled in, high over the sand. She'd never seen the sea so wild and she looked at her small car and wondered how it was she had driven here to Ardmore. Humphrey cowered at her side as she set off along the strand. The wind was fierce, the whole bay shook, and as she trudged, head down, clinging to the curve of the bay, she was grateful for the roar of the sea drowning out her thoughts. A wave crashed ahead of her and a salt spray stung her legs. The tide was never in so high, and she looked up at the sand and grasses of the dune and wondered if she might be forced to climb, dragging the great weight of the dog behind. Humphrey shivered. His ears were back, his fur was dark with wet. 'Good boy,' she told him, 'who's my good boy,' and she kept walking.

There was a letter from Rosaleen when she left Ilford. *I'm off to share with a couple of girls. I'll let you know when I'm settled in Chelsea.* But a year, more than a year, had passed and there'd been nothing. There had been a storm that day too, she was surprised the post had got to them at all; the water came in so hard the sea wall at Youghal collapsed from the very force of it, the concrete broken up and thrown into the park.

Windows were taken out all along the front, nothing left of them but the frames, and a ketch in the harbour was smashed away to nothing. Aoife stopped and looked back the way she'd come. She couldn't see the car. There was nothing but rain and wind, the waves crashing and beating, retreating just enough to leave a ragged path below the cliff. *What is it I'm doing here?* She shouted to Humphrey and ran. She could feel him at her back, lumbering, as the spray of the waves crashed against them, so that by the time she reached the path the pair of them were shaking.

She put Humphrey in the back and wrapped him in a rug. 'The state of us.' She held his loyal body in her arms as she rubbed him dry, but as she moved round to the driving seat the door wrenched away in the wind and would have thrown her over the front if she hadn't clung to the handle. *I still have two daughters.* She gave herself a scolding. *Good girls who've done nothing to deserve me, and a husband, God bless his soul, who's worked every day of his life to keep us safe.* She thought of them arriving home to find the kitchen empty, no smell but the old cold mess of meat she'd boiled that morning for the dog. *Our Father, who art in heaven,* she said it slowly, pondering each word as she'd only ever done during the worst days of the war. *Forgive us our trespasses, as we forgive those …* For all she knew the girl was thriving, living the high life, too busy for her family. 'Blooming.' That's what everyone had said the last time she was home.

Calmed, Aoife drove away from the sea, marvelling at the roads she'd no memory of taking, the slashing rain, the hedges rattled through with wind. It was dark by the time she crossed the Tinnabinna Bridge, the Blackwater vicious below, and with her lights sweeping the empty streets, she made for home.

Cashel was waiting when she stepped through the door. 'Where have you been, woman?' Humphrey, great soft lump that he was, stood with his flank between them. 'I went for a drive, I was worrying about ...' Without having to say her name, Angela and Kitty hung their heads.

There was a silence then as Aoife took off her coat. 'It's desperate out there.' She'd make light and, wet through as she was, she opened the larder and reached in for the spuds. 'Come on, girls, let's make a start on the tea,' and they sat at the table, peeling, while Cash leafed through *Farmers Weekly* and Humphrey rested himself against the stove.

Kate

I see my mother in John Lewis. She is with her daughter, her real daughter, and they are choosing wool. I hover near and listen as they leaf through patterns. Such a pretty one, they sigh, would this be too difficult? They choose a cardigan, a soft cream patchwork in stocking stitch and purl. I follow them, assessing their dresses, their bags, the shape of their ankles, the curved lobes of their ears. I'm staring so hard I give myself away. My mother turns towards me, and that's when I know. She isn't mine. Of course she's not. There's nothing searching, nothing hurt, she's as easeful as a pudding. I stumble to the far end of the department. What has she done with my actual mother? I choose an embroidery kit, a house with a red tile roof, the threads of wool included, and although I was buying it for Freya I start on the orange path on my way to work.

'You all right?' Beck has coffee waiting.

'I am.' I offer him a smile.

Donica is sitting in the foyer bunched amongst the safety of her plastic bags.

'Will you be joining the class today?' She is sucking a blue drink through a straw. She's shown an interest in art, that's what they told me, at some point in the past, and I remember then what else they told me, and I gulp it down and ask what's in the bags.

'The right pen for the right job.' She lifts a carrier and, releasing its knot, rustles through it until she finds a zip-locked case. Inside there is a biro. 'Very organised,' I say, and, encouraged, Donica draws out a flip-flop, secured with rings of multicoloured bands.

'You're very welcome to come into the room.'

Donica looks fleetingly at the open door. She nods her head, and then, as if considering, she unwraps a layer of silver foil, and then another, and lifts out a bun. 'I would,' she says through a squelch of icing, 'but I have commitments.' And using the stick that supports her twisted leg, she sweeps the outlying bags in under her chair.

My group is preparing for an exhibition. 'I don't think I'll be well enough.' Jen lays her head on the table, and even though it won't be for a month she asks if she can go home. I say she can, of course, but first I ask if she could copy me some leaves? I hand her an illustrated sheet – grey poplar, hawthorn, plane – and sharpen her a pencil. I'm still waiting for permission to spray my tree on to the wall. 'I can't do this.' Jen slumps, but once I turn away she makes a first quick sketch.

Alec and Marjorie have finished their Scots pines. I slide them into the exhibition folder, along with Naina's leopard and a collection of flowers. Neil is outside smoking – he's refused to deviate from his study of the female form – and Sam, missing for two weeks – pale, a little shadowy – is drawing an elk. I stand beside him and watch him work. 'You all right, miss?'

I shake myself, and walk outside.

'Nice day today.' Neil blows a plume of smoke, and he asks if I believe in angels.

'I don't *not* believe in them.'

'Who knew mine would be Miguel?' Out of his pocket he lifts a slither of gold tin. 'Go on, ask him what he's called.'

I put the angel to my ear. Nothing. I move it to the other side. Maybe it reminds me of a conch shell in which my father once told me to listen for the sea, because the name that comes to me is Shellwyn.

Neil beams. 'There you go! He'll look after you.' When I try and hand the angel back he shakes his head. 'He's yours now, keep him safe. I've got a load of them.' He taps his pocket.

At the end of the day Donica is still there. I have a meeting with the centre's supervisor and I can't risk missing my allotted slot of time. 'Next week?' I call out to her as I hurry past the café. 'Roberta,' I mouth to Beck and he makes a gratifyingly fearful face.

Roberta looks concerned as I outline my plan for the mural of the tree, present my invoices, explain how I intend to attach the panels to the wall. 'I'm happy to waive my fee.' She visibly relaxes. 'But I do need money for materials.'

Resources are so low, Roberta tells me, it's a miracle my job exists, and although she laughs, her words have their effect. Threatened, I regroup. I ask her to look over my reports. The progress made by Jen, the attendance rate of Neil. Marjorie and Alec who have spent the afternoon making invitations to the show. Neither of us mention Donica who has not stepped through the door.

'I'll let you know.' She flips shut the folder.

Let me know now! I feel myself hectic. 'Thank you,' I say instead, but once I am outside I press my forehead against the cooling wall and breathe.

I can see Freya, skipping, through the glass of the front door. 'Five, six, seven …' Celine is counting in her precise accented

English and I imagine her, a child at school, reciting the numbers with her class.

'Mummy!' Freya hears the rattle of the catch, and she drops her rope and hurtles towards me. 'Wait.' My arms are full, but she's jumpy as a dog, and while I'm still untangling my bag she hoists herself on to my back. I carry her through to the kitchen where Celine is winding up the rope. 'How was everything?' I ask and she says that everything was good. They went to the playground, they paddled in the pool.

I ask her how it went on Tuesday. She was going for a drink with a man she'd met on a bus. 'But how?' I'd been intrigued. 'How did that even happen?' She'd looked at me, as if she didn't understand. 'Just starting to talk, you know. He was cute.'

Today Celine has the temerity to blush, and changing the subject she asks about my work. 'What about *my* work?' Freya has climbed on to my lap.

'What is your work?' I ask her.

She reaches across the table for a book, the pages stapled at the spine. She flips open the first one to reveal the paper densely filled with dots.

'Is it rain?'

'Rain?' She looks disgusted. 'It's the A page, silly.'

I inspect it again. 'Ants!'

There is nothing on any of the other pages. 'What will you call it?'

She pauses to run through the alphabet; I can hear the song of it under her breath. '"Ant Zoo".' And consumed by the genius of her idea, she makes a start on B.

Once I've paid Celine and tidied up the kitchen, I go upstairs to run Freya a bath. The closed door of our bedroom stops me in my tracks. Is Matt still sleeping? I clasp the handle and slowly turn. The room is dark, the curtains drawn. There is a hump in the near side of the bed. 'Matt?' I move towards him, but it isn't Matt, only the toss and mound of the quilt, the upend of a pillow. I stand quite still. The air is stale. The room, despite the summer day, is cold.

'Mum?' Freya is calling and, closing the door behind me, I go into the bathroom and turn on the hot tap. I kneel and stare into the water, the gurgling wash of it, waterfalls and clifftop birds. Freya sidles in and lies against my back; I feel her small hands dip into each pocket. 'What's this?' She has the angel, and she's examining its flimsy frame.

'If you put him to your ear—' but Freya is dangling him over the water, and although I tell her to stop, she drops him in.

'No!' I fish for his tail but the water is scalding. 'Damn you.'

Tears slip from Freya's eyes but my anger is electric. 'Why would you do that,' I yank her arm, 'when I told you …?' I catch myself and turn my voice around. 'Shellwyn!' I call in mock-despair. 'We'll save you!' But he is floating, buoyed up by a cloud of bubbles, in heaven where he belongs.

Aoife

We thought she might come home for Angela's wedding. That was a day. Your speech, Cash – I could cry to think of it, even now. Blessed with such a daughter, never a moment's worry. Dutiful. That was the word you used, and you were right. But there was a shadow in the room and we all felt it.

I don't want to hear a word about her; you were stern as I pinned on your carnation. Don't let her spoil things. Not today.

We held hands in the church. Our daughter married. Even if we had hoped she might have had a career, but married it was she wanted to be. Seventeen and, for all we'd done to educate the girls, already thinking about babies.

Mavis was there with her gang, and your mother – it was the last time she was strong enough to travel. Later, when I'd had a glass – even though I'd promised myself I wouldn't – I sat with her and I asked: Isabelle, tell me, have you seen her?

Have I seen who? She sat up very straight. She always was a beauty, and she made me say it. She made me say her name. Rosaleen, I whispered. I know you two were friends.

No, she shook her head. I've not seen her. Not that I remember. She put out a hand to comfort me and that's when

I noticed. She'd lost her ring. What lovely hands you have. She did, for all that they were worn and spotted, much as mine are now, but not a ring on any of her fingers, for all that she'd been married twice.

She didn't last long after that. I worried it was the crossing that weakened her, always rough, even in summer, but better that way, fast, and not to suffer. Oh, Cash. And then who should turn up for the funeral? A great lanky fellow with your mother's face, saying he was after something to remember her by. How could you have failed to mention you had a brother? A watch, he wanted, that had belonged to his father, but by the look of him he would have taken anything – a comb, a handkerchief, a scrap of lace – which was a piece of luck, because he never did get what he came for. Wasn't that so, Cash? And why was that? You'd tell me if you could, is that it? Or would you say, Enough now, woman? Or would you say nothing at all?

★ ★ ★

Aoife lay awake, her thoughts spiralling, her heart spongy with the image of her daughter, holding that tiny child in her arms. She was on the ward, a room of dazed and happy mothers, flowers, chocolates, so many visitors Cash had been forced to go searching for a chair. Grandparents. That's what they were now. Nana and Pops. Aoife was assailed with the memory of her own first night as a mother. 'If the sirens start,' they'd told her, 'pull the metal trolley over your head.' She'd given birth in a makeshift ward formed from a lecture theatre, chalkboards and tables pushed to one side. A hospital in Liverpool had been hit the week before, and for safety her baby had been secreted away in the basement, as she'd waited for morning, longing for Cash who was out fighting a fire, a leaflet urging evacuation already in his pocket.

When Aoife and Cash next visited, Angela was home. Declan had started back at work and his mother, the other nana – Nana Shaughnessy – had taken charge of the kitchen, bringing them cups of tea and white triangles of sandwich, the edges trimmed, a scattering of crisps, as if it was a hotel. 'You shouldn't have gone to so much trouble.' Aoife was embarrassed, but Fran Shaughnessy, already a nana five times over, told her it was no trouble at all.

'Will you look at all these cards!' Aoife examined each and every one. 'Oh, well that's nice now, isn't it?' Her voice sounded false even to her. 'A card from the O'Malleys, and would you believe it, that was quick, here's one from Mavis.' There were cards with prams, with rattles, with bonnets. *It's a Girl*. A spray of flowers. A stork delivering a bundle. She inspected one after another, pretending, even to herself, she wasn't hoping to find a word from Rosaleen. 'That's lovely, isn't it so, Uncle Joe and Auntie Bess, and was that Colette with the red hair from Loreto?' She glanced at Angela. Was there a card that she was hiding? But her daughter had a milky opaque look and Aoife bit her tongue. 'Let me have a hold of the little dote.' She consoled herself with a cuddle of the baby. Jacqueline, they'd named her. 'Not for the president's … not for that poor woman.' Angela was quick to let them know. It was a name they liked.

Aoife took Jacqueline into the garden, a bare yard, still scarred with the tracks of diggers building the estate, families starting off together, a view out towards the convent at Blackrock. 'Aren't we the lucky ones?' She looked into the baby's sleeping face, and she stood with her under the pale sky and she counted the years, two, the months, ten, the days, thirteen, since that New Year when Rosaleen had waved from the ferry. Whatever can be keeping her away so long? A stab of pain streaked through her, and she'd pressed her face into Jacqueline's warm towelling body and breathed in her powdery scent.

'Cash?' she whispered now, turning towards him, sliding an arm across his back. Cash grunted, and she heard in the grumble of his throat: What is it, woman?

Nothing, Aoife answered, silent, and she pressed herself closer and lay with open eyes, one of God's poor creatures, repenting her sins.

Rosaleen

The next week it was the windows that must be cleaned. They started to the right of the front door, smearing on the stinking purple liquid, rubbing at the glass with rags. They had stools to stand on, she and the two girls in her team – one of them not a girl at all but a primary schoolteacher from Tralee who'd taken the name Siobhan.

How do you come to be here? Rosaleen wondered, but she was saved from asking by Marie, young and so unwieldy she crossed herself each time she stepped on to the stool.

Siobhan looked anxious. There was to be no talking. No exchange of information while they were at the home. It would be best – the nuns were clear – if they kept the details of their lives to themselves. But there was no one in the hall, only Maisie, simple in the head, down on her knees at the foot of the stairs, scrubbing at the parquet with a brush. 'I was seeing a widower,' Siobhan whispered, 'and I was sure it was only a matter of time before he asked me …' a wash of colour streaked her face, 'but when I told him what had happened – we'd been stepping out six months – he said if I was stupid enough to get caught at my age, I'd better sort it out myself.'

'The nasty piece of work,' Marie exclaimed and she launched into her own tale. How she'd been offered a lift home after a dance on the crossbar of a bike, and when they'd reached the house, the boy whose bike it was, he'd said she owed him: "'Sure, doesn't everyone do it, for the crossbar?" And anyway, wouldn't he be seeing me the following week?' She paused then, as if in disbelief. 'I hadn't any idea it was that quick to get a baby!'

Rosaleen placed a hand on her stomach. There were minutes, whole half hours, when she forgot there was the beginning and the end of life there, and the jolt was the same sharp knifing she received when she thought of Felix and how he'd turned away.

'I thought I must be ill – run down, you know.' Marie was still talking. 'And then I started getting fatter, and when the zipper on my skirt wouldn't fasten my mother took me to the priest.' Marie gave a dangerous wobble and steadied herself with a smeary hand. 'It was Christmas when I came in, not that you'd have known, except that Sister went off to Cork carousing with her friends and there was a girl whose baby was a breech. No cake, no pudding, no ham boiling on the stove, and that poor girl, howling fit to wake the dead.'

Rosaleen ripped a length of cloth from what must once have been a sheet and, stepping on to the stool, she doused it with purple. Looking down, she saw the roots along Siobhan's parting, the old dyed hair escaped from its bun. It was only a matter of time before they asked her, what's your story, and as she rubbed at the glass she felt the sun streaming through the hotel window in Marseilles, caught the two of them entwined on the bed. No. She'd not bring Felix in here, however he'd behaved, and she balled a strip of paper in her fist and rubbed the pane so hard it squeaked.

'Patricia?' Marie was waiting, but she was saved by the unexpected sight of a car, rolling towards them up the drive, a large, dark car, gleaming brighter than the glass.

'Lord, there'll be tears tonight.' They watched as the driver curved on to the tarmac and stopped. With a clip he was out and swinging open the back door. A lady stepped down, a short fur cape, a hat perched on the side of her head. From the other side a man uncoiled himself, and he walked round, slow as you like, and stood beside her and together they looked, a kind of wonder on their faces, at the house, the lawns, the statue of the Virgin Mary, as if this was indeed a holy place.

The three of them at the window hardly blinked. A nun appeared, stretching out her arm as she approached, and shook their hands. They stood there talking; *you've been blessed with a clear day*, is that what they were saying? Then, after a word with the driver whose hand she also shook, the nun led them round the side of the house and out of sight.

No one spoke.

They worked till lunch, rubbing and polishing, squinting for smears, and then outside they went, where the ground was lower, and a nun came with a set of steps so old and rickety they hardly dared risk them. Rosaleen volunteered to climb, volunteered Patricia who was less unsteady than the others, who cared nothing if she fell. The window looked on to the entrance hall. Maisie was gone but two girls had come to mop the stairs. Rosaleen waved but they kept their heads down. 'Careful,' Siobhan hissed, as the ladder quivered.

They moved across the front of the building, peering through into a library, bound books lining a wall, a hard cold bench set into an alcove, and on to the far end of the house where Rosaleen found herself staring into the Reverend Mother's office. Reverend Mother was at her desk, sorting and shuffling papers, and before her, on straight-backed chairs, sat the couple from the car, and with them was a baby. It was dressed smart in a blue knitted jacket, a matching hat buttoned below the chin.

'What is it?' Marie hissed.

Rosaleen swallowed. The child sat awkward on the woman's lap, his eyes, surprised, gazing round the room. 'They have a baby.' She felt the steps beneath her shudder.

'Let me see.' Marie rattled the wood, but Rosaleen wasn't ready to come down. The baby looked to be about a year old, his skin milky, a curl of yellow hair slipped from his cap.

'Wait,' she said too loudly, and the Reverend Mother's head shot up. Their eyes met. Cold and hard. Disgusted. Away with you. She flicked her hand. The couple noticed nothing. The woman was fussing with the child, while the man lifted banknotes from an envelope, and as Rosaleen stepped slowly down, she saw the nun's beady, counting face as he passed them over.

There was a hand on her calf, another on her hip, a firm grip on her shoulder as she reached the ground, and then Marie was scrambling up.

'They're taking Mikey!'

'Mikey!' Siobhan echoed her. 'Dear God. Poor Irene.' They stood there, the three of them, in the spring afternoon, and it seemed they could hear it, the sound of weeping from high up in the home.

That evening Irene didn't come down for her tea. Rosaleen looked at her empty place, and wondered about her rations. Sin, upon sin, she berated herself for coveting the girl's bread and margarine, and she had to stop herself resting her head on the table as she'd been punished for at school.

For a week Irene didn't eat. Rosaleen caught sight of her, cutting wood in the yard. She had hold of a cross saw, two mothers holding the long limb of a branch, while another loaded the wheelbarrow and one more swept away the dust. She had a hollow look and her eyes were raw, but no tears were going to bring Mikey back; he was away over in America, and would not be seen again.

'She thought to have him two more years.' Carmel sat with her feet pulled up. 'If the babies are bonny, sometimes they go early.'

She and Rosaleen looked at each other across the narrow alley between their beds. 'I hope this one,' Carmel glanced at the mound of her stomach, 'isn't too much of a looker, or is that an awful thing to say?'

'Why is she still here?' Rosaleen asked.

'Irene? She'll have to work out the three years. To pay the nuns back for their care.'

It was lights-off and Rosaleen rolled on to her side. Carmel did the same. 'Do you have any news?' she whispered.

'News of what?'

'Who it is that will send over the hundred pounds?'

When she was silent Carmel tried again. 'Patricia?'

Maybe I'll die, was all Rosaleen could think. We'll all die – me, Patricia, the baby – and there will be an end to it. 'Not yet,' she said instead, and she closed her eyes and turned towards the wall. There, waiting for her, was Felix. He was wearing a white shirt, the cotton stiff and smelling of the wash. Where's the fight in you? he challenged, and seeming to forget he had betrayed her, he sang into her ear, *Itsy bitsy teenie weenie yellow polka-dot* … until she gave in and sang along.

Kate

Once a week now, sometimes twice, Matt fails to go into work. There are messages on the answerphone, increasingly hostile, asking where he is. I watch his face as I replay them. 'Idiots,' he looks astounded. 'They said take the day off,' and he glares as if it's me who's been delaying him.

On those nights when he comes home he's gentle. 'I think I'm going to knock it on the head, this drinking business,' and we spend the evening, softly on the sofa, watching quiz shows, holding hands. My hope is such a hungry thing that I believe him, and maybe he believes it too, but on the third night, or occasionally, the fourth, he reaches for a beer and we are back at the beginning. Or not at the beginning, further on, because each time he stops, and starts again, his tolerance for it lessens. Maybe it's stopping that's the problem, and not the drink at all? I don't offer this suggestion because either he's sober and he's never going to drink again, or he's roaring, falling, telling me he loves me, and he can't hear anything I say.

Tonight it is a fourth night and I'm waiting up. A bus rumbles past the end of the road. The windows shudder, and I shudder too, alert, in case it's the door. It isn't the door, and I take the punch of disappointment, promise myself I'll sleep, although it isn't long before I'm glancing at the clock, charting Matt's progress: the pub, the lock-in, the stagger home. It's like an equation that I've set myself. *If the pub closes, officially, at eleven, the regulars locked-in till twelve, the walk home, ten minutes, with an extra five for stumbling, pissing ...* I stop myself and take a breath. Enough! And then I'm sure I hear him. I throw off the covers and I run downstairs, but if it is Matt, he's walked on. I go to the door and yank it open. The gate hangs lopsided on its hinge, the path is cracked, one tile raised, just as it always was. A car's headlamps flood across the road, and I imagine the driver, catching me, frantic, in my slip.

I walk into the kitchen and pick up the phone. I'll ring the White Horse. I have the number somewhere, but as I search through the scrappy pages at the back of my address book, I find that other number, the one for alcoholics, and I remember the kind voice of the man from AA, telling me to take my time. Tonight a woman answers, and it's not long before I wish I hadn't called. 'There's nothing you can do,' she's blunt. 'If he's drinking, he won't stop until he's ready.'

'If he said he'd stop ...'

The woman lets me cry.

'Have you thought about getting support yourself? There are groups for families and friends affected by another person's drinking.' She's giving me the names of churches, the days and times of meetings. 'This disease is too hard to manage on our own.'

I'm silent. I don't want to go to any meeting, I don't want to sit in any fucking church. 'Thanks,' I say, and I put down the phone, and I go upstairs and I pull the sheet over my head.

The next morning I find Matt face down on the sofa. I squeeze myself against his body and Freya, sensing competition, crawls on to his back. Matt moans, 'Get off,' and he rolls away from us so violently we slide on to the floor. I laugh, and Freya laughs too. 'Why's Daddy grumpy?'

I rub my nose against her tummy and I say he's grumpy because he drank too much beer.

Matt pulls a cushion over his ear. 'Get out!' he barks, and I scoop Freya up and carry her through to the kitchen. I tune the radio to music, take her hands and dance her round the room. The more irritable Matt is, the happier I must become.

There's a note for me when I arrive at work – my request for the tree stencil has been granted. I'm so relieved I run through to the café and pass the news to Beck. 'Well done.' He puts out a hand and there's an awkward moment as we reach for each other and withdraw. 'If you need help, holding the ladder, knocking in nails. Biscuits … ?' I thank him and say I'll let him know.

I flip through my diary and block out the following weekend. It'll take all of Saturday to secure the boards, tape down the stencil, spray. Matt has a rehearsal on Friday evening. *Not that there's much point*, but apart from that he's free.

'I'll need you to be around, just in the days, to keep an eye on Freya,' I tell him.

'Sure.' He sounds confounded. 'What else would I be doing?'

I thank him anyway.

'You don't have to thank me for looking after my own child.'

We stare past each other in silence.

All week I pray that it won't rain. I scrutinise the forecast, track the drifts of cloud, unravel the stencil on the kitchen floor to check each twig and groove. I trial a miniature version, slicing, spraying, re-setting it a centimetre to the left to give an edge of shadow, and I imagine how easily it might go wrong, the look on the faces of my group as they arrive to find the mess of it, indelible, on the wall.

That Friday I don't wait up for Matt. I get into bed early, pick up my sleep book and, as directed, take three breaths. My thoughts are scratched and wired. I scramble through the mud and scurf of the Thames, searching for treasure, sifting through debris, until I'm out in the fast flow of the current, floating past boats and barges, face up to the sky. Calmed, I turn to my tree and there's my oak, its branch intact, rooted, in full leaf. My Feeling Self is still in hospital. How can I support you? the book tells me to ask, and although a part of me has split off and is laughing, I dip a hand inside my gown and draw out the pulped mess of my heart.

I wake to a pool of vomit in the hall. I rush Freya into the kitchen and stand her on a chair. Flour, eggs, milk. I take out a mixing bowl and before she can protest I've started whisking. 'Who wants pancakes?' I say as if a horde of children's voices might rise up, and I spoon the mixture into the hot pan. We watch in silence as the edges frill.

'Keep guard,' I instruct her. I grab hold of yesterday's newspaper and, running back into the hall, I fling it over the sick. Eyes closed, I scrunch it up, wiping and swiping at the floor, bashing away gobbets with the mop, erasing every smear. I tip the contents into the outside bin, wash my hands, and returning to the pan I flip the pancake so expertly there is only one fine line of white. I take a breath and lay the table, unscrew the rusted maple syrup. I sit Freya on her chair, a napkin tucked around her neck, and when it's ready I somersault her breakfast through the air and land it on her plate. 'Ta-dah!' You see, I tell myself, I can manage on my own, but when Freya pours the syrup, too fast in a lake, I seize her arm, and scream at her to stop.

The day, at least, is fine and blue. I lift the boards from where they're stored and lay them out across the garden. I tell Freya she can help hold the stencil down while I unroll. I have a can of spray mount, but it doesn't always stick, so I rip lengths of masking tape and wrestle with it as I paste it into place. 'Keep holding!' The tree is taking shape. Roots, trunk, branches, but the more intricate the pattern, the more delicate the paper, the harder it is to attach. By the time I reach the twigs, Freya is bored. 'I'm going in to do my own work,' she informs me, grand, from the back door.

A breeze has sprung up. There's a danger it will rip the stencil if I stop. 'Not long now,' I tell her, but it's mid-afternoon before I have the pattern down. Clouds have gathered, and the wind is buffeting. I go inside and butter Freya toast, smear it with Marmite, pour her a glass of milk. 'You'll need to stay in the house …' I'm pulling on gloves, a mask, collecting up the cans of car spray. 'Will you do more colouring?' But Freya only blinks. Matt is standing in the doorway.

'Why the fuck didn't you wake me?' He peers, disgusted at the hour.

I rattle my can, defiant. 'I've got to get the stencil finished, Beck's coming tomorrow first thing with a van.' I pull the mask over my face and back into the garden, where I rattle it again, and crouch over the tree roots. A squelch of black oozes out. Damn. I shake the can, fierce, and a fine sheen settles. I crawl forward, stopping only to change the nozzle when it clogs, leaning close in to keep the spray from drifting even as I choke.

'Mum!' Freya is calling.

I rise up on my knees. 'What?' My voice comes muffled.

'Dad's gone.'

I stagger to my feet. 'Out, you mean?' I peel away the ragged rubber of my gloves, walk into the house and lift the mask. Bloody hell. I gulp down water. I shouldn't have stopped, or should have stopped before.

'Matt?' I bellow. There's no answer. 'Did he say anything?'

'Who?' She looks at me.

'Dad.'

Freya begins to doodle. She has reached the letter E in her 'Ant Zoo' book. 'He said "bollocks".'

'Sweetheart,' I'm laughing, 'I have to finish this ...' The paper tree bristles in the wind. 'I won't be long.' I hand her a banana, pull my mask down, tug on new gloves, and step across the blackened grass. 'Come on!' I pray for progress, but the more I rush the faster the paint clogs. Shake, spray, stop. The first spit of rain catches me, and I rattle the can so vigorously the nozzle flies off, and I scrabble for it, press it on, and lean in over the topmost branches, shielding the paper with my body, keeping the can upright, trying not to breathe. There are small crooked twigs that must not be missed and I hunt them out – it's easier than thinking – press the paper flat, and ink them in.

'Mum!'

'No!' I cling to my board as if it is a cliff. It's too dangerous even to look down.

'Muuuum!'

'Not now!' I roar so loudly that my throat feels torn.

There is silence, not even the grating sound of snivels, and I keep working. Shake, spray, stop, until every bud is in.

It's dark in the house when I remove the mask. My hair is gritted into metal curls, and my nails even through the gloves are dyed. In the kitchen there are pencils scattered on the floor and the 'Ant Zoo' book has been attacked by biro.

I trudge upstairs and glance into Freya's bedroom, swing the door open into mine. 'Hello?' I check the bathroom. Consider pressing the angel to my ear. I walk back into the garden. My tree glowers from its paper frill. 'Freya?'

There is a bush in the corner where she sometimes hides. I tiptoe towards it, part its scraggy leaves, imagine her grinning up at me, but she isn't there. I turn and run to the front door.

Outside the street lights have come on, and the road is wreathed in dusk. It's a short street, small squat houses, a tower block looming at either end. I wedge the door and bend to a shadow as it flits between the wheels of a car. 'Freya!' My heart flips, but it's not Freya, it's a cat. I hold its stare. Where is she? The cat narrows its green eyes and, when I uncoil, the man from Number 37 is peering round at me. You OK? his glance enquires, but when I turn to him, he twitches, nervous, and walks away.

I rush inside. 'Freya!' I'll frighten her out from wherever she's hiding, and then it occurs to me – she's with Matt. That's it. I calm myself. He must have come for her, of course, and I see them, eating pizza in the window of a restaurant, drinking lemonade. I slide down the hall wall, my back pressed into the skirting. I'll stay here, however long it takes, and I listen to the traffic, the brakes and tyres, a siren screaming in the distance, and wait.

When the gate rattles my legs are so numb I can hardly stand. With clumsy fingers I yank the door. 'Where is she?'

'Who? I haven't ...' Lies and avowals scatter in Matt's eyes. 'Our daughter!'

He veers towards me, his forehead creasing.

I want to pummel him but I've already wasted too much time. 'I'll call the police.'

'I don't … what's … where … ?' I have the phone in my hand and the look I throw stops him into silence. I have dialled the first 9 when I see him slump, and as I turn to dial again I hear the click of the catch as he falls against my workroom door. Only his legs are visible as I listen to the ring.

'Emergency.' It is a woman who has answered. 'What service do you require?'

'Kate!' Matt has scrambled to his knees.

'Fire, police or ambulance? Hello?' a voice insists, but Matt is waving to me, mouthing, and I run back along the hall and there, under my work table, on a bed of paper leaves, is Freya.

'It's all right,' I whisper into the receiver. 'She's been found.'

We stand together and stare in at our sleeping child. A sob breaks out of me, and Matt holds me as I cry.

That night we embark on a long, slow conversation. I kiss him and he bites my neck, and I hold him hard inside me. Once we have our rhythm my eyes close, and I follow the sweet seam of our fucking, keeping to the thread of it, grateful to be here, with him, and not, as so often, outside my hollow body. Tonight, of all nights, I can't risk being alone, and so with every effort I travel with him, moving, moaning, fixing our two selves together until we reach a peak.

It's the early hours of the morning when the doorbell rings. 'What the hell … ?' Matt pulls a pillow over his head, but when I reach for the clock I see it's seven-thirty.

'Hello,' I greet Beck, fingers combing out my hair. 'Come in. I'll just …' I'm not fooling anyone. 'I'm going to need ten minutes.' I lead him into the kitchen and watch as his eyes flick round the room: the cookbooks, Freya's first school photograph, a picture of Matt with his guitar. He lifts down my postcard of Lichtman's *The Secret*. 'Is this you?' He stares at the girl's stone curves.

'Muuuum.' It was only a matter of time, and pointing out the tea, the milk, the mugs, I leave him there and run upstairs.

Together we stand in the bathroom and brush our teeth, and I tell Freya how we're going to take the tree stencil and spray it on a wall. She can help hold the ladder. I don't mention Beck, waiting downstairs, only introduce him, casually, when we find him making breakfast. 'Would you like your egg sunny side up?' He cracks a shell against the side of a pan, and too surprised to ask what that might mean, Freya sits at the table and picks up her fork. I sit beside her, and lift my own fork, laughing at the unfamiliarity of being served.

'You and your mum,' Beck says as he slides the food on to our plates, 'you're two peas in a pod.' Freya looks at me, and I at her, and we examine each other's faces. 'Yes,' I'm happy to agree, although it's not entirely true. She has Matthew in the sweet round of her chin, and there are hints at mysterious others in the fierce blue of her stare.

'Beck,' I say as I glance at the clock, 'I really am so sorry,' and I remember agreeing to start early so he could get on with the rest of his day.

'No worries.' He has ignored the dusty box of teabags and brewed a pot of coffee. He pours me a cup.

I leave our breakfast plates stacked in the sink and we load the boards into the van. The paper is still attached, and as we inch them through the house, Beck in the lead, Freya unhelpful in the middle, I catch the shadow of myself the night before, wild and desperate.

'One minute,' I say, once we're settled in the van, and I run back into the house. 'Matt.' I nudge the pillow.

His voice comes muffled. 'I'm going into work to put up the …' It's pointless to explain. 'I'm taking Freya.' That is the important part, and although he doesn't stir I lean down and imprint it in his ear. 'I've got her.' It's all he needs to know.

Aoife

Aoife walked along St Patrick Street, her hair newly set, her handbag swinging. If she chose carefully she could wear the outfit again, in September for her own Silver Wedding, and she caught herself – making do, even after twenty-five years, for the sake of Mavis. Aoife pushed through the door of the department store, and stopped for a minute to savour the smell. Luxury. She breathed it in, and as she made her way to Ladies' Fashion, an old rhyme of her mother's floated up.

> *I'll buy my baby stockings*
> *I'll buy my baby shoes*
> *I'll buy my baby stockings*
> *And I'll send her off to school*
> *She was the doll in Cash's window …*

Not that her mother had ever ventured into such a fancy shop; a year might pass without her coming into Cork at all, and Aoife was lucky to have shoes, even if they were her brothers', handed down.

'Can I help you today?' There was a girl beside her, with the new style for false lashes. 'Thank you.' Aoife fished a suit off the rail: neat jacket, narrow skirt, in bright bold check. 'This might be just what I'm after.' She took it into the changing room, appraising herself in the mirror as she slipped it on, allowing a smile as the zip slid snugly over her hip, the button fastened at her waist. And aren't I still the same size as when I married? She gave a little shimmy – not like Mavis who never went back after the first baby, and after the second … Aoife crossed herself. There was a sharp voice in her head today, may God forgive her, and she knew it was only luck, her skinniness; she'd got it from her father, never a pick on him, whatever he ate.

'You look only gorgeous, and that's the truth.' The young assistant was admiring when she stepped out from behind the curtain, and Aoife forgave her spidery eyes. She did look fine, and wouldn't Cash be proud, and wouldn't Mavis be that little bit envious?

She paid with a roll of notes, money from the milk, and walked out with the big boxy cardboard bag, its tissue paper rustling, but even by the time she was home her faith in the suit was gone. The bag sat in the corner of the room. She eyed it from the bed but she couldn't bring herself to unpack it. 'Aren't you going to ask me what I've gone and bought?' But it wasn't Cash she'd bought the suit for, it wasn't even Mavis. It was Rosaleen, and Rosaleen wouldn't be there. She wouldn't be at the celebrations, she couldn't be at the house, and even if Aoife scanned the streets of Ilford, she'd not find her. Her only chance was to slip away from the party, search for that flat in Chelsea, for which she never did have an address, or, if she could bring herself to do it, traipse through Soho. Hadn't Angela said they'd had a drink on Greek Street at the Coach and Horses? She'd look up the number, wait for the landlord to answer as she'd answered herself, always a woman at the other end: Is my husband there? Sorry to ask. There'd be the sound of squalling babies, the swallow of pride, and she'd nod to your man, sitting at the bar, and when he'd shake his head, she'd recite the well-worn phrase: If he comes in, shall I tell him you were asking?

'It's not right.' Aoife passed the suit over to the same girl who had admired it, and she searched the rails until she found another, beige with a black trim. 'That looks very smart.' This time there was no smile between them, and when the suit cost half as much and she left, her purse fat with the refunded money, she'd felt none the richer.

That night she modelled it for Cash. 'Very nice.' He had his glasses on, a copy of the paper propped against his knees. 'Indeed,' he yawned and he went back to his reading.

It was almost four years since they'd visited London. There'd been no reason for it once they'd let go of the pub. The scale of the place amazed her, grand and substantial, and hadn't the two of them flown in on a plane! They'd both been terrified, Cash squeezing her hand so tight he nearly crushed it, her stomach fluttery, grateful for the air hostess walking along the aisle with a basket of sweets.

They travelled into the city by coach, and out again by train to Ilford, and every time they saw a foreigner Cash nudged her: That's why we got out. Aoife pressed his arm and looked away. No one wanted trouble. Not when they were celebrating twenty-five years. As they neared, Aoife took out her compact. She patted on a layer of powder and checked her teeth for lipstick, and then she leant over and straightened Cash's tie. They made a handsome couple, they always had, even with Cash's moustache stained yellow with tobacco, and his hair clinging on above the ears, but he was strong, and ruddy from outdoors, and his eyes when he chose to use them still flashed green.

The whole family were at Mavis's when they arrived. Bob and the two boys – John had a fiancée! And wasn't Francis doing well. There was Joan and her gang, and Doris back from the United States with the GI husband she'd met during the war, and a daughter tall as a man.

Mavis had a tea urn, she must have borrowed it, and three types of biscuits, none of them home-made. They squeezed out into the patch of garden where they waited in the sunshine with their saucers. 'And how is Angela?' That's the news that everyone wanted to know. How is the baby? The look on their faces when Aoife told them she was expecting another.

A grandmother! She was the first, and she stood in the huddle of her in-laws, holding her breath for the moment when she'd be questioned about Rosaleen. But no one said a word. Not until later, not till the cricket club reception when Doris came and sat beside her. She'd adopted an American twang and her attitude was forthright, and without a blush or stammer she asked if she and Cash hadn't thought to hire a detective. 'People don't just disappear,' she told her. 'I'm surprised you haven't been in touch with the police.'

Aoife couldn't think how to reply, so instead she picked herself up and walked around the edge of the room until she found the first spare man, who happened to be Bob. She took his hand and led him on to the dance floor, and she danced with him, her silent brother-in-law, until the music and the steps had cleared her head. She danced until the night was done, until the last drinks were drunk, and the slow couples hung around each other's necks; she danced until Cash came for her. 'We need to find her,' she whispered into the damp collar of his shirt, 'it's been long enough,' and he held her by the shoulders and looked into her face. 'She's made her bed,' his eyes were hard, two bottle ends of gin, 'now she must lie on it.' He swayed her stiff body to the last refrains of the band.

Rosaleen

'This is where the dead babies are buried. Here, under our feet.' Carmel looked down at the dense green of the grass. They were standing in the garden of the chapel, its stone walls a shelter from the wind. 'You see,' she pointed, and there against the wall dark crosses hovered. Rosaleen shivered. 'Do many of them die?'

Carmel didn't know.

'And the mothers?' They looked at each other in fear.

To one side of the graveyard was a statue of Jesus. He stood on a small mound, his arm raised in benediction; his robe, his hair, his beard, carved in intricate detail. He'd been formed from some white stone – not marble, she was sure of it – and Rosaleen thought how on their last evening she'd bent to her own statue's naked form and asked that it keep Felix company while she was away.

'Girls!' It was a nun, calling from the gate. 'Have you no work to do?'

'We're only after paying our respects.' Carmel dipped her head, but as they hurried back over the grass Rosaleen saw that there were names on the crosses. Mother Genevieve, Sister Eustrella. It was not reserved for babies at all.

Rosaleen was on mopping duty. She took a bucket from the hall and carried it the length of the corridor. From here she worked backwards, dunking the mop head into water, swishing and swiping, smoothing it over the already spotless floor. It was this corridor along which Mikey had been carried. Irene had held him, his face pressed against her cheek. 'Why don't they slip the child away?' Rosaleen had clutched at Carmel. 'It would be easier on them both.' And Carmel had hissed back that this was the tradition, there was no breaking with it, not for anyone, not even if you came up with the hundred pounds. 'Dada,' the baby had gurgled, and Rosaleen wondered where the father was. Did he ever stop to think what might have happened to Irene? Did he even know? 'Dada.' Mikey clapped his hands, and one girl gave an unearthly groan and covered her mouth.

At the far end of the hallway was a door and, before it, Sister waiting. They'd watched as Irene moved along the corridor. Her steps were heavy, her neck mottled red. Every breath was held as she passed by. They all knew the door led to the outside. As she approached, the nun reached out her arms.

'No!' Irene tightened her grip, but Sister was practised. She swooped round in a flap of white and all Rosaleen saw was the child's frozen face, eyes, arms, empty, and Irene, fallen to the floor.

Rosaleen wrung out her mop. *It's super being a single mum.* She fought to remember the details of the story, but the article was tucked into an envelope, packed into her case, and her case was in the care of the nuns. *Without the support of my father …* That was it.

Rosaleen continued mopping, and when she reached the front hall, there was Maisie, on her knees. She had a brush and a bar of Sunlight soap, and her hands were swollen from the suds. When each section was done she took a square of blanket, ripped along its length, and using the threadbare strip she rubbed a shine into the wood. This was her second time, impregnated – or so they said – by the same man on her release. 'Hello.' Rosaleen stood above her, but Maisie didn't look up.

That evening Rosaleen knelt beside her bed and, stretching an arm into the far corner, she eased out her coat. 'Watch out or they'll have that off you.' Carmel looked anxious.

Rosaleen checked the pockets. There was her return ticket and her nana's ring.

'They left me nothing, except my Bible.' Carmel was working on another letter.

'How do you even send the letters out?' Rosaleen asked, and Carmel whispered that the farm girls took them when they pedalled into market with the eggs. They'd post anything in exchange for a breakfast.

Rosaleen's stomach cramped at the thought of the lost bread and margarine. 'Do they let you at least drink a cup of tea?'

'They do.'

Rosaleen pushed the coat back out of sight. There must be someone she could write to, and she wondered if she addressed a letter to the French pub – the York Minster as it was officially known – would the landlord pass it on?

Dear Anastasia – Rosaleen knew she'd brand her half-witted for not sorting things out when there was time. *If you could find a way of sending me a postal order for £100 I'd be most terrifically grateful. I know it's awfully large, but I will repay you even if it takes five years, which it won't. Please, on no account, mention this to anyone. I'm sure you understand.*

The next morning, in the slither of time before Mass, she wrote it out, and adding the name of the convent – Sacred Heart, Blackrock, Cork – she signed it. *Yours, in need, Rosaleen Kelly.*

It was hard lasting until lunch on a milky gulp of tea, and she'd reckoned without window-cleaning duty. She was working with Marie, and a new girl, Fiametta – making their way around the back of the home, staring into a small sitting room where a cluster of nuns had discarded their shoes and were toasting their toes against the bars of an electric fire.

'Will you look at that?' They pressed their faces to the glass. There was a brown teapot, milk in a white jug. A sponge cake, a quarter of it sliced.

'I can taste the jam.'

'Raspberry,' Fiametta sighed.

'Strawberry. It's my favourite.' Marie's breath clouded the pane.

Rosaleen's stomach squeezed and clenched. She gripped Marie's shoulder, and with her help she clambered to the ground.

'Is it the baby?' Fiametta was alarmed.

'I'll be all right,' Rosaleen insisted. 'If there was a glass of water?'

Fiametta risked a scolding by trudging round to the back hall and fetching her a cup from the boot-room sink. The water helped. It fooled her into fullness, and she struggled on till lunch.

That night Rosaleen looked with new-found admiration at Carmel as she slipped off her pinafore for bed.

'If the letter runs to two pages you have to give an egg,' she told her. 'But it's worth it, to have my ma know I'm doing well.' She sniffed and tugged sharp at the straggle ends of her hair. 'What'll I say when I get there?'

'Get where?'

'To London. It's not long now and I'll be heading over.'

What could she tell them? 'There's a rose garden at Regent's Park. The Royal Albert Hall is round. There are boats to take you up and down the Thames.'

'Where will I live?'

'Brixton. You can stay with my friend Michele. She lives by the market. The Granville Arcade – there's nothing you can't get there. Vegetables shipped from the West Indies. Bananas, mango, jackfruit, yams.' Rosaleen was pushing through the crowds, racks of meat swinging, bright cloths unfolding from their rolls. 'Underwear, sweets, toys. When the sun shines, the girls, they jive on the pavement … Michele will take you. Saturday. That's when they play music.'

Carmel had her thumb in her mouth.

'There's a coffee bar, that's where we used to go. In Soho.'

'A coffee bar!'

'It's an Italian place.'

'They'll want to be hiring their own, I suppose.'

'You'd be better off in Kilburn, for a job.'

'That's it. Kilburn.'

'There are hardware shops. Nothing you can't get. Caffs on every corner, egg and chips. A bakery that sells iced buns.' Rosaleen had to remind herself that for the next three years Carmel would be staying here.

The next day Rosaleen was back out on the lawn, crawling forward over the grass, her breasts heavy as they rubbed against coarse cloth. Already she regretted the letter. *Dear Anastasia*: her face burned as she imagined the circle of Felix's friends, the artist, who for all she knew may be in possession of a fortune, gloating over the request. Maybe there were others she could try. *Dear …* She frowned away the names of her parents, turned her face from Angela who'd stop at nothing to release her, Teresa who couldn't afford rent. And then she remembered: even with the money, the nuns wouldn't let you take your baby out.

The sky pressed down on her, the heavens above were grey, and soon her knees were stinging, the knuckles of one hand swollen where the scissors stuck. Beside her, women moved forward in a row, hanging their hopeless heads. *We'll get away from here*, she promised as she clipped at the stalks of grass. *We'll leave this place together.*

Kate

The evening of the exhibition is cloudy and warm. Alec and Marjorie come in together. I wait apprehensive while they examine their Scots pines. 'Mine's a disgrace,' Marjorie shrieks. Alec says nothing, although I hope he knows it's good. Sam arrives with the care worker who found him living in the Hyde Park underpass, camped out on a cardboard bed. Who were the other homeless? I strain past him down the slope of a tunnel, and I see my mother in a sleeping bag, a sign before her: HELP. 'Sam!' I greet him. 'How are you?' His features bleached, he tells me that he's fine.

Neil arrives late, followed unexpectedly by Donica. Beck offers her a drink but she has provisions, labelled, and she finds a seat and proceeds to unpack.

I watch as the guests circle. Naina has a niece. Alec, a careful, haunted ex. I stand with Neil beside his nude, and we talk about the weather. 'It's been a fuck of a summer,' he says, 'but what can you expect?' He has a brother, disabled, living in Reading.

There's a shout, and Jen, who has wandered into the yard, puts her head back through the door. 'See this!'

I file out after the others, glancing round for Matt who'd promised he'd come straight from work, who'd said he'd be there for the unveiling. Instead there is Beck. I flush, we've caught each other unaware, and when I turn everyone is staring at the tree. They stand in silence, and the wall light, around which we had to cut, flicks automatically on. 'The moon!' Marjorie gives a gratifying gasp and there is a scattering of applause.

Neil slaps me on the back. 'Speech!' He is insistent, and so I climb on to a chair and thank the centre for their support, the guests for coming, and more than anything, the artists for their contribution. Beck watches from the doorway, his apron off, and I'm about to thank him, for the van, the ladder, for spending what turned out to be most of a day fixing the panels to the wall, feeding us with home-made pizza so delicious that even Freya stopped talking long enough to eat, but I don't get a chance because Beck is tussling with a new arrival and everyone has turned towards the door.

I do my best to draw them back. I tell them why I chose an oak. How symmetrically it grows, how deep the roots are, how it is possible to count its age without chopping through the trunk. 'The oak is the best-known and loved of British trees, it produces male – the catkin – and female flowers, and its fruit – the acorn – is a nut.' I've lost them. There's a shout and Beck is flailing – I see one arm swing out before he disappears – and there is Matt, his suit jacket catching on the handle so that for a moment he is yanked back as he storms into the yard. I take a beat and continue. 'There are live oaks, white oaks, red oaks of North America. Turkey has oaks, and Hungary ...' People drift off, crumpling their cups, whispering to each other.

'It's beautiful.' Matt staggers towards me. I don't look at him. I can't. 'Kate.' He reaches for me.

I step away.

'Don't do that.' He grips my arm. 'Let me guess. Why is it you don't want me here?'

'This is my work.' I tear myself free. 'Don't ruin it.' I'm halfway across the yard when he has me by the hair. The pain is searing but I don't call out. He pulls me against him, one arm round my neck. 'Do you take me for a fool, is that it?' And then, from nowhere, his grip loosens and he is stumbling backwards, and as he falls his head cracks against the ground. I spin round to see Neil, white-faced, his fist still clenched.

'Fuck.' Neil shakes his hand.

I heave Matt's shoulder but he doesn't move.

'Oh fuck,' Neil says again. 'That's me done for.' But Matt's eyes flutter and they open.

'How's your head?' I kneel down.

'Ow,' he says and, despite himself, he smiles.

I leave him and go inside for water. I see Beck, a button missing, his pocket torn. 'I've called a cab.'

'Thanks.' And although when I return Matt is sitting up, insisting that he's fine, there's nothing else to do but leave.

We don't talk in the taxi. I'd direct it towards A&E, but Matt wouldn't get out even if we stopped there, so we rumble towards home. I pay Celine as he slopes away upstairs, and ask after Freya's evening. What she ate, what games she played, how happily she got into the bath. It seems my capacity for news of her is infinite. Do I think by knowing I'll reclaim lost hours? When Celine is gone I stand in the kitchen alone. I'm hungry now, and tired. I think for a moment I might call my mother. Darling? I can hear the panic in her voice – is that how rarely we speak? I consider phoning Alice, but Alice has gone back to Georgia, the Peach State of America, and she will be at work, five peach hours behind. I take a biscuit and sit at the kitchen table. My throat is tight and the crumbs catch in my jaw. I lay my head on my folded arms and do my best not to think. Not about my job, the night, my life. Not now when there's nothing I can do.

The following Monday I stand in the dim light of the vestry, breathing in the quiet. There's no one here, not even a priest, and when the clock chimes high above me I hurry out into the churchyard. A man shuffles by, his trousers tied with string. He'll know where I'm supposed to be. There are dark trees, fir and yew, and the stones are green with lichen. Unsteady, he makes his way down a drop of steps, one step, two, then veers off along a path. This can't be the way. I check the address, and when I look up the man has sunk on to a bench and is draining liquid from a bottle. Down another flight I find a door tucked into an alcove. The wood is dense and seamed with iron. I knock and wait, but no one comes. I've tried, I tell myself, surely now I can go home? and I walk on round the building, glancing in at lino floors, stacked chairs, children's drawings pinned around the walls. I'm at the far corner when I find I'm staring in at a circle of bent heads. I duck away but a woman has caught sight of me, and jumping up, she motions for me to walk back the way I've come. My face burns. No – I gesture – I'm not sure … but the woman has decided, this is where I'm meant to be, and so I hurry, as she is hurrying, back past the empty rooms, round the side of the building, up a flight of steps to where she is waiting. 'The door usually stays open. Sorry.' She is short and sturdy and her eyes are warm.

'Is this … ?' I'd like at least to check, but she's herded me into the silent room and is pointing out an empty seat.

'Resentment.' A girl in leggings and a voluminous jumper leans across and whispers.

I stare at her.

'Today's topic.'

'Ahh.' I nod, as if I understand.

'So,' a man on the far side clears his throat, 'I may as well come in,' and after declaring himself a grateful member of this fellowship, he tells the room how hard it has been, spending the weekend with his family when everyone ignores the fact his mother is so bloody sloshed she drops the lamb roast on the floor, burns her hands as she scoops it up, falls asleep half-way through the meal. 'Morning,' they say, when she appears the next day, and they start all over again.

There is a pause and, just like the man's family, no one says a word. 'It's good to be here.'

There is a small shift in the room and again we sit in silence.

An elderly woman is the next to speak. 'Clara. Grateful member of Al-Anon.' There is a pause as she gathers herself, the lines scored into her cheeks straining with the effort of disclosure. 'Last week, my … my qualifier …' she takes a jagged breath, 'he was out in the street, he'd gone to buy provisions …' her eyes flick fast, 'when he fell. An ambulance was called. I was at work. I have to go to work!' and her face collapses and she is sobbing, great gulps of sorrow breaking out between her fingers.

There is another pause and then two people speak at the same time.

'You.'

'No, you.'

They slither into an agony of politeness and once again we sit.

'Right,' the girl beside me starts. She doesn't look much older than eighteen. She hasn't spoken to her father for three years, but now he's been diagnosed with cirrhosis of the liver, her sister, who's stayed loyal, is begging her to visit. She will, she probably will … She shakes her head slowly. Her mother died when she was ten. That's when her father started drinking.

I'm too busy worrying what might be the best thing for her to do to listen to the next few speakers, but then a woman comes in, cheerful. 'Resentment: always a good topic. Although you may be surprised to hear, for all the hours I've gone on about him, it's not my husband I resent. Not any more. Mental cruelty. It was worse than the punches. I couldn't do a thing right. One time he had his hand round my neck, had me up against the wall, and there was one of those light-switch thingies, and I said, stop, there's something sticking into my fucking head. I got a punch for swearing. He was a bully from the start, although what did I know? I was sixteen when we married. Another thing, he'd never take his keys when he went out. Didn't believe in it, however late it was, I had to let him in. I'd run down and open the door, but if I took too long, I'd get a kicking, or if I opened the door too fast – what are you doing up at this hour? – I was beaten for that too. I thought it was normal. Must do better. The thing was, in my own way, I was happy. I had my babies. My man.' There's a crucifix nestled in the deep crease of her cleavage. 'Ahhh, for those days of denial,' her laugh is throaty. 'As I said, I don't resent my husband, not any more. It's myself I can't forgive, for being such a sap.'

A card is raised. White with a red heart. 'Time up already? I only just got going.'

The woman with the book flips over a page. 'We are now into newcomers' time.' All eyes glance my way. 'If you would like to introduce yourself and say a few words.'

'I'm Kate, I'm really not sure why I'm …' I do my best to rise for air but my legs are kicked from under me, my head held in the rip pull of a wave. 'I … I … my … ' Tears swallow me, and I choke to a halt.

'If you have questions, or would like support, you can talk to one of us after the meeting.' It's the woman with the cheery smile.

After! We stand, a mumbled verse – serenity, courage, wisdom – pattering between us while hands are stretched on either side and, not taking them, I keep my eyes fixed on a card, *Detach with love*, and wonder what it means.

Aoife

You hated her for how I suffered. Forget about the girl. But the pain of it would seize me, and I'd take the car and I'd drive. Across Waterford, up to Kilkenny, down through West Cork to Bantry Bay. I'd travel so far that once I had to park and wait out the night. I called. You never did believe me, but I found a phone box on the way to Skibbereen and I dialled home to let you know that I was safe. It was early morning. There was no one about, the gulls so loud I could hardly hear the ringing, but you must have been out on the farm, and I didn't want to stop again, not till I was home.

And how are we to manage a day's work? You were livid. I can see you now. With no hot breakfast inside us?

You can have your breakfast. I wasn't losing face, not in front of the men: Patsy – who'd taken a shine to me, did you ever guess? – and Eamon, who could never think what to do with his hands.

Don't be daft, woman, you told me, it's too late now, and the men, who were cleaning themselves up, nodded their goodbyes and trudged off across the yard.

You came to me later, I'd gone straight to bed. Her bed. With the cover she liked, Harvest, pulled up round my neck. My sweet, you stroked my back. Whatever you do, don't run off like that again. Promise me now. Your voice was thick, but I couldn't promise, even though I did. The next day I went to early Mass. Poor Father O'Reardon, wasn't he tired of my sorrowing? But he listened, as he always did. It's God's will. It wasn't the first time he'd said it. God is watching over Rosaleen, and whatever shame she has brought down on her head, He'll be the one to absolve her.

With each of Angela's babies, the missing of Rosaleen eased. That first girl, Jackie, and then a boy, born within a year. A boy! You were as pleased as punch, and then another boy, and two more girls, until it seemed there was no space for anything but celebration. There were days when Angela brought them over to the farm, the tribe of them rollicking round the yard, and Angela, so patient, never a cross word out of her. That's when I fretted: did we do right by our children?

Times were different – you had no truck with doubts. Wasn't it an education that we wanted for them, and isn't that what they got? I'd retreat to my room then and let the cool beads of the rosary fall between my fingers, and I'd stay there until the comfort of the prayers washed away my fears.

Rosaleen

Most evenings the girls nearest to their time gathered in the day room to knit. They must make clothes for their babies, or their babies would have nothing to wear. Rosaleen thought of the matinee jacket tucked away in her case, but there was no knowing where her case was, and she'd searched through every window of the home. She bent over the pattern for a bonnet stretched across her knee. For all that talking was prohibited small flurries rippled through the room. There was a girl among them whose baby had been stillborn. They'd heard her cries – three days it lasted – and then a mighty hush. Word had whipped along the corridor. *The child was starved of air. A doctor might have saved it.* But no doctor was called. Now the girl was knitting trousers, stitches dropped in a ladder to one foot. 'I never had a sight of him.' Tears smeared her face. 'They told me – look away – but when the midwife cleaned me up she let slip it was a boy.'

'At least now you'll have the free leg out of this place,' Carmel whispered, but the girl cried all the harder. 'I would have traded. Even if I had to stay forever in this jail.' There were veins, broken, on her cheeks, and her eyes were red. 'He was to be called Gabriel.'

Carmel crossed herself with wool, and Rosaleen, fumbling with her knitting, imagined the tiny, shrouded body laid into the ground. Where would Gabriel be buried? Not in the nuns' graveyard, that was certain, and the spectre of an unmarked field, ruts and mounds, rose up before her. She laced her hands across her bump and, lowering her head, felt for a reassuring kick. *Not long now.* She ran over her plan: her dawn escape, the lift she'd hitch to the ferry, the return ticket safe in the pocket of her coat. She'd squeezed herself into it the night before; her nana's ring still fitted.

'Where will you go?'

Rosaleen's head shot up.

'Back to my da.' It was the bereaved girl they'd been addressing. 'He's old, and not so well, he'll be glad to see me whatever anyone says.' There was a pause in which she unravelled a row. 'At least my ma is spared the shame.' She bent over the stitches, and as she gave in to her tears two moons of milk bloomed against her smock.

They knitted in silence, with only the sniffing and the clacking and the occasional squeak of chair legs as a girl shifted her weight. Rosaleen glanced towards the door. It was unusual to go unsupervised for so long. Most nights a nun would have appeared by now to offer some reproach. *Knit two together.* The bonnet, forming, turned pleasingly to cradle a small head.

'What wouldn't I give now for a slice of soda bread and butter,' Carmel, beside her, whispered. It was a game she liked to play, and Rosaleen, although it pained her, conjured up oysters on their own indented plate, skate with capers, and then, unasked for, her mother's lime and tangerine jelly. 'Did you ever … ?' Was it only Mummy who stirred in fruit segments from a tin, presenting the dish so grandly that even now Rosaleen wasn't sure if its rubbery green coolness constituted sophistication or not. Sharp pangs of hunger riddled through her. 'A meat pie, with gravy ...' Carmel continued, and before Rosaleen could beg her to stop, they were interrupted by the thud of the front door. Voices rose; there was the echo of a shout. Every one of them sat tall, their needles still. Fast steps approached, and when their door flew open there stood Sister Gerarda, holding the arm of a young girl. Her hair hung lank, her freckled face was bare, and under her thin dress was the tight strain of a belly.

'Peg,' the nun pronounced the name as if only now introducing it. 'Sit here and settle yourself down.'

The girl looked wildly round as Sister Gerarda chose a ball of wool and, with lightning fingers, cast on. 'You'll work in stocking stitch,' she said. 'Start with plain,' she placed the needles in her hand, 'then a row of purl, and repeat.' She surveyed the room, reminding them, not unkindly, 'We are in silence here, best not to forget it.' She put a warning finger to her lips and turned towards the door, but before she reached it Peg was up. She seized a pair of scissors, and with the needles flashing she advanced. Sister Gerarda fell against the wall, and Peg, the white wool trailing, skittered from the room.

There was a beat of silence as they all stared after her. The nun's shocked mouth hung open. 'Quick,' she found her voice, and she plucked at a girl, pale and heavy, before turning to Rosaleen. 'She'll do herself an injury.'

Rosaleen ran in her socked feet. She could feel the others lumbering behind. Ahead of them Peg had reached the hall and was tugging at the door.

'Quick!' Sister Gerarda shouted, but the door was opening, the girl was stepping out.

'Don't just stand there.' The nun was at Rosaleen's side, and together they hurried on to the step. The night was clear; a sickle moon hung low above the trees.

'Will I find some boots?' The heavy girl had joined them. She had a hand below the shelf of her stomach and her face swam green.

'No time for that!' Sister Gerarda flitted across the drive, taking them with her on to the lawn. Rosaleen felt the grass mulch between her toes.

'There she goes.' They caught a flash of Peg's white legs across the field, and as they rounded on her, tacking back and forth, Rosaleen was reminded of the lamb loose on the lane above the farm and how they'd cornered it on their way home from the O'Malleys', pushing its wool body through the hedge to where its mother bleated in the field.

'Peg!' Sister Gerarda called into the night. 'Stop the foolishness.' The girl was backed against a tree. They could hear her breath, ragged. 'It'll go better for you …' Was the nun searching for her real name? If so, she couldn't get a hold of it. 'Come into the house, will you?' Her voice was pleading. A pound a week they got for every one of them, or so it was said. 'You'll be safe inside with us.'

They were closing in, not more than a yard or two away. They could see the light of the girl's eyes, and a trickle of blood where she'd caught her cheek. *Run*, Rosaleen willed her.

'Come on, there's a pet.' Sister Gerarda stretched out an arm. 'You'll get a nice warm cup of tea.' Peg let out a piercing scream. The scissors flashed, the needles formed a spear. The girl beside Rosaleen fell and did not rise.

'Stop this nonsense!' The nun's voice trembled. 'It'll go against you, that's a fact.'

Peg advanced, her weapons low. She was shivering and growling, and when she lunged Sister Gerarda gave a fearful gasp and fled across the field.

Rosaleen held Peg in a stare. She moved backwards, hoping to reassure her, but there was a ridge of earth, and her ankle wrenched. The pain of it, white-hot and dizzying, dropped her to her knees.

'I've wet myself.' The other girl lay near. Her teeth were chattering. 'What a scolding I'll get.' She whimpered into the pillow of her arms.

Rosaleen had no time for comfort. She must make her escape, but all she could do was sit on the damp grass and look on as Peg hared away towards the trees.

The girl let out a long, low wail. 'My pains,' she stammered when she had the breath. 'I've started!'

'No!' Rosaleen was determined. She might still have the strength to run. 'It'll be the shock.'

The girl gripped her hand. 'Don't leave me.' There it was again, a rolling moan.

'I'll get you help.'

'I mustn't have the baby here,' she begged, and so together, staggering and hopping, they doubled back towards the home.

Rosaleen was in the infirmary when Peg was returned. The Gardai had her arms behind her back. 'Only doing our job,' they smirked as they cast their eyes the length of her twig legs, dirty with scabs and bruises, minding her until the doctor came, until he'd quietened her with a shot. Swift as anything, the spirit went from her, and she was hauled away.

'You still here?' A nun glanced round. 'Away with you. To bed.'

Rosaleen, her ankle bandaged, hobbled up the stairs.

'Lord!' Carmel exclaimed in the dim light from the hall. 'Now what will you do?'

Rosaleen was too tired to reply. She stripped off her muddied pinafore, the calico knickers that stiffened with each wash, and wrapping the blanket round her she lay down and faced the wall. 'You won't get far like that,' Carmel sighed.

Hot tears scorched her eyes. *Felix*, and the love she felt for him, the hate, burned through her as she mumbled out their song.

Kate

'How are things?' Beck hands down the higher pictures, although I could quite easily have stood on a chair.

'Fine.'

He shoots me a look. 'I'm glad.' It's clear he expects more.

I've come in early to dismantle the show, and once everything is packed and accounted for, I step into the yard. A bench has been pulled up before my tree, and the plastic chairs are arranged on either side. Beck follows and stands at my shoulder. 'I may have to start smoking again.' He is admiring, and I laugh, and even though he wears his usual floury apron, I check for the missing button at his waist.

'Why do you stay with him?'

'We have a child,' I answer, fierce, and I walk across the yard and in through the glass doors.

It's hard to leave a man who isn't really there.

That afternoon I hand out sheets of paper and ask my group to drip patterns on to them with ink. What was I thinking? Sam is shaking, and Jen has smears across both cheeks. Soon the table, walls and floor are scattered black.

The day before, I went back to the meeting. '"We come to Al-Anon because our lives have been affected by the disease of alcoholism,"' a man reads calmly. '"It is too difficult a thing to manage on one's own."'

It is? And then, because I still hope that it might not be: too difficult for most?

'"To find contentment, and even happiness, whether the alcoholic is drinking or not,"' the reading continued, '"we have to accept that we are powerless."'

I'd sat on my chair, fear mangling my senses. 'I'm Val,' the woman to my left had said. 'I'm grateful to be here today.'

'I'm Kate,' I managed, 'and I'm ...' but my name was a dam holding back tears, and before I started, I was lost.

'Welcome, Kate.' A soft chorus of voices rose, and the man on my other side handed me a tissue. 'I'm Gideon. I'm feeling – excuse my language – fucked off.'

Helen was tired. Fatimah was confused. The young girl whose father was in hospital told us how, when she'd gone to visit, her sister had stolen the money from her purse.

I am powerless. I sank down in my seat.

There was an Irish woman with hoop earrings and aubergine-dyed hair. She was back from her home town where she'd been attending a funeral. 'I'm glad that I forgave him, before he passed ...' Tears shone, even as she smiled, and she reached up an arm clattery with bangles and for a minute she covered her eyes.

'Bloody hell!' Neil curses from the far side of the table. 'I've ruined it,' and he holds up what can only be a penis, and we all watch as the ink begins to run.

'Let's go away somewhere.' Matt is dancing me around the kitchen.

'Where?'

'Ireland.'

I do my best to keep from frowning. A frown could smash the whole sweet castle to the ground.

'In Ireland artists are respected. Musicians get given tax exemptions. We could find a place, by the sea.'

I smile encouragement; I've made these journeys before – by train through Europe, to South America by plane, one night we set up home in Wales – but I've come to understand Matt's dreams need beer, and by the morning they are sunk.

'When we're settled,' he nuzzles my neck, 'maybe we should think about another child.'

My throat tightens. 'I'm not sure.'

All evening the radio has been playing hits of the eighties, as if the eighties were the distant past. Matt pours his raw, warm voice into my ear. 'We could start thinking about it before then, if you like.' He twirls me round as the music soars, our bodies jolting against cupboards, chairs, the ironing board which sways one way and then the other, rocking the iron which I had no time to switch off when Matt swooped in and rushed me off my feet. It topples sideways before it dives. I lunge for the cord and, missing, catch its hot face in my palm.

'Damn!' I douse my hand with water, drowning out the sound of Matt's recriminations. 'What a stupid fucking idiot I am!'

'It's OK.' The burn stings, but I keep my hand under the cold tap, wait there until it's numb, until, by the time we go to bed, our new life is forgotten.

I buy a gauze plaster on my way to work. I'll ask Beck for a dish of ice before I seal it on, but when I arrive Donica is already in the foyer. She has unpacked a can of drink, a box of raisins, a ribbed support sock and laid them on the table. I stand before her. 'Will you be joining us today?'

She doesn't answer. She unwraps a pack of paper clips and arranges them by colour. 'We'd love to have you, even if you only stay for half an hour. You never know, you might enjoy it, seeing as you're here.'

Donica lifts the catch on her fizzy drink. There is a burst and a sigh as bubbles are released, but before she can raise it to her mouth I've fallen to my knees. 'I'm begging you.'

Donica is as startled as I am. She opens her mouth and closes it again.

'I want you to try the class.'

She looks round. 'You're embarrassing yourself. Get up.'

'I won't get up, not until you promise.'

I can feel Beck watching from the counter. Donica riffles through a bag, and not finding what she wants she tries another, pulling out a large book bound in bubble wrap. 'Seeing as I'm prepared.' She shows me the label, *Sketchbook*, and scrabbling again, she brings out a pencil in its own transparent case. 'In my experience this is the best kind to use.'

'So you're coming in?'

She lifts her chin. 'I've never been begged for anything before.'

I rise to my feet. 'This way.'

No one speaks as Donica manoeuvres into the room. Her bags rustle, her voluminous clothes catch against the backs of chairs. She sits herself at a table and takes out a pot of yoghurt.

Jen spins round to me, eyes wide. FOOD TO BE CONSUMED IN THE CAFÉ AREA ONLY. There is a sign. I say nothing as Donica peels off the lid and licks it, and as she searches for a spoon I pass round photocopy paintings by Monet, Degas, Gauguin. There is a hush as one by one each member of the group appropriates a picture: a lily pond, a wheatfield, the garden at Givenchy. Donica chooses a Tahitian beauty surrounded by fruits and flowers. Yoghurt drips on to it as she opens up her sketchbook, takes up her pencil and begins to draw.

I leave them and run to the kitchen. 'Do you have a bag of peas?'

'Still life?' Beck's sleeves are rolled above the elbow. His arms are brown and flecked with fine gold hairs. I hold out my hand. 'Ouch.' The burn scalds across his face.

'It's not so bad.'

Beck dips into the freezer, pulls out an ice pack. 'Do you have a bandage?' And before I can tell him that I do he fetches down a first-aid box and, peeling away a strip of gauze, he smooths it on. 'Take care now.' He has hold of my fingers.

'Thanks.' I ease them away.

'You've got to have the right equipment,' Donica is telling the group. 'This is the only kind of pencil worth using.' The others examine the pencils I've provided and look at me, accusing. 'That's coming on nicely,' I tell Sam who has drawn three ears of corn, and I move across to Jen and admire the tilt of a Van Gogh chair. I take a sheet of paper for myself and sketch a woman. She has long kinked hair, parted in the centre, and her dress is thick with leaves. 'Who's that by, then?' Neil asks, and I tell him I know I've seen it, but I can't think where.

It's a glorious day and the meeting is full. Extra chairs are fetched, the circle widened, and I sit against the wall of windows and let the heat beat against my back. *I'm happy … grateful …* The sunshine has heightened everybody's mood and, when the introductions reach me, I add, as others have before: *it's good to be here.*

The woman beside me – deep shadows smudged below her eyes – is having trouble with her husband. She has twins that wake each morning before six, which wouldn't matter if she could get a full night's sleep, but her husband staggers in and wakes her in the early hours. 'He could use the spare room, is that an unreasonable request?' She blinks. There's every chance he'll be affronted, which is why she hasn't asked.

I bite my lip and search the faces of the group. They are for the most part attentive, although a girl eating from a Tupperware box continues crunching rounds of celery and carrot. The mother of twins blows her nose. 'I expect it will become clear.' She laughs, defeated, and I wonder whose rule it is – not to offer the most obvious advice. The next woman needs to talk about her daughter. She blames her for the way they live, just the two of them together, but her family, they didn't want to hear it, when she spoke up about the abuse. Troublemaker, they called her. They were the ones who forced her out.

A young Italian tells us he's happy for the day. The smiling faces in the street, the trees – there are so many trees in London. The front gardens. Full of flowers. Every little patch of ground has blossom. We wait for him to tell us why he's here. 'My girlfriend,' he says after a pause. 'It's lonely since she's gone into rehab.' He looks pained. 'This is my third meeting.'

There are murmurs of 'Welcome', of 'Keep coming back'.

'I'm a grateful member of this fellowship.' It is the Irish woman with the aubergine hair. She pauses, and it seems she may not be able to go on. 'Last week I had a message …' Her eyes are fearful. 'My daughter … the one I gave up … she's been in touch, not with me, directly, but someone official, they called to let me know.' Her face dissolves. 'I've waited for this day. Thirty-nine years.' She manages an almighty gulp. 'She's not asking to see me, at least that's not been mentioned. It's medical records she's after, information … that's what they're saying, but maybe one day we could meet and then I'd have a chance, after all this time, to let her know …' Her smile breaks through, and the earrings and the freckles, the fine gold of the cross, spangle out into the room. 'I've always loved her. Never stopped.' The heart card has been raised. I will her to ignore it and she does. 'It's what I've prayed for, ever since she turned eighteen. I put my name down on the register when they changed the law, 1975 it was, but there's been nothing, until now.'

What register? The woman, her name is Ciara, is blowing her nose. I watch her as the voices circle. *Confused, relieved, pissed off.* Thirty-nine years! I wonder if my own mother has been counting, and not simply skipped away to a new life? I'm surprised when there's a move to stand.

'God grant me the serenity,' hands on either side reach out, 'to accept the things I cannot change, courage to change the things I can,' I squeeze them, grateful, 'and wisdom to know the difference.'

I walk into the hot glare of the afternoon and find I've boarded the wrong bus. I'm heading out of habit towards work, and I'm tempted to continue, to stand at the counter of the café. Instead I get off and cross the road and wait for a bus to take me home.

I have half an hour before collecting Freya. I cool my face with water and stare into the mirror. Has she been waiting, worrying, is it me that abandoned *her*? I run upstairs and dig through the mound of trinkets in my wooden box. Freya's newborn tag, a puzzle ring dull with disuse, and there she is, my mother, her hair a tangle as mine is now and I hold her image, and I see Ciara and the lake of her tears.

Freya sits alone on the carpet. 'Mummy!' She leaps up, butting against me with her head, and, guilty for being late, I give in when she demands a treat. 'Wait till we get home,' I say, as she clutches the chosen bar of caramel but when we stop to cross at a red light I see she's peeled off the wrapper and the chocolate, melted, has oozed over her hand. She does her best to lick it off, toffee binding her in strings, and then the sticky mess of it slips between her fingers and falls on to the road. Her lip trembles. She tugs at my arm. 'No!' I'm not going back to the shop. Her feet drag, but I am stronger. 'There are biscuits,' I tell her, 'and Ribena lollies,' but if Freya can't have chocolate she wants nothing at all. Thwarted, she throws herself down in the hall. I stand above her, terrible, and as if from a great height I watch her mouth widen in a howl. Fine, I decide, she can lie there as long as she likes, and I go through to the kitchen and turn the radio up loud. It's the hottest day of the year so far, and I search through cupboards for the paddling pool, and when I find it I remember the last time I tried to blow it up the pump was nowhere to be seen. I slump back on my heels. 'I want to watch TV!' Freya screams from the hall, and although I consider it, I can't give in. Our mother managed with nothing but *Blue Peter* and there were hot days then. She rushes through and pummels at my back.

'Freya!' I swing round and catch her wrists. 'Stop it. Now!' But she roars into my face that she wishes she had another mummy, a mummy who was nice, and in a chalky haze I strike her, sharp, across the side of her head. She stops, and I stop. Her eyes are wide, her body shocked. 'I'm sorry,' I tell her and, all tension dissolved, she folds into my arms.

The next day I call my mother and ask if we can visit. 'Of course.' She sounds wary. It's a long time since I've been home.

All week my stomach knots and gripes, and there's a tightness in my throat. 'I'm going to try and talk to them,' I tell Matt the night before, 'about, you know, how they ... when I was given up.' But on Saturday morning it's he who is unwell. 'You don't mind, do you, if I stay here?'

I seize my bag, take Freya and slam out of the door.

'Are we late?' Freya asks as we rush along the street.

We're not late, in fact we're so early that we take the slow, meandering bus from Chalk Farm to Victoria. We sit at the top, above the driver, and to distract myself I tell Freya stories about the stops we pass. A flat I lived in when I was a student, an art-supply shop where I worked until I was sacked for stealing a tube of Naples yellow paint. At Cambridge Circus I remember a girl who had a studio high up, opposite the theatre. There was nothing in it except a mattress, an easel, and three eels lying listless in the bath. 'If you want to be an artist,' she'd said, 'there can be nothing else important in your life,' and although I'd hoped this wasn't true, I returned the next day and rang the bell, but there was no reply.

I kiss Freya's straggled head as we swing round past the National Gallery and point out the stone lions and the fountains of Trafalgar Square. I tell her how when I was her age there were stands selling corn to feed the pigeons, and that when we get to Gran and Grandad's I'll show her a photograph, Alice and me, half obscured by birds.

The bus fills and empties, fills again as we career round Parliament Square, past Westminster Abbey, a fairy-tale cathedral, dwarfed only by the clock faces of Big Ben. It's warm and hazy, our hilltop home, but as we near Victoria station my stomach quakes and I consider staying on and heading back the way we've come.

'Where's Daddy?' Freya stops on the wind of the staircase as if she's only now noticed he's not with us.

'We'll see him tomorrow, when we're home.'

My mother asks the same question an hour later as we come through the barrier.

'We'll see him tomorrow,' Freya answers for me, and I put a hand on her newly plaited hair.

'Not well?' my mother mouths to me, and I nod and look away from her alarm.

'So ...' My father's voice is breezy as we sit out on the terrace. 'To what do we owe the pleasure of your company?'

I swallow. 'I missed you, that's all,' and when he looks bemused, 'it's nice to be out in the fresh air.'

My mother appears with a quiche. She smiles, innocent, as she serves it up. 'What a lovely surprise. Any special reason?'

I blush. 'I ... it's just ...' Their suspicions stall me. Words settle and disperse, and I cough so hard when I attempt a bite of pastry I am forced to rise from the table. My mother turns her attention to Freya.

'And how are you?'

'Mia might be going to have a baby brother,' she tells her.

'I see.' My mother gathers herself for more, but Freya is sliding from her seat. 'Careful!' she calls as she tracks across the lawn. 'The stream!' But the stream is a trickle of its former self, and even though the fence has been removed, the water was only ever ankle-deep. 'Look at the sweet thing, amusing herself, all on her own,' and her eyes fly open and she turns to me. 'Kate?' she asks, expectant.

'No!' I protest, and my hand goes to the flat of my stomach. 'Can I really not just visit?'

We sit in silence. There's nothing I can say now. Nothing that I'd planned. 'I was telling Freya about Trafalgar Square,' I try instead. 'How we used to feed the pigeons. I said I'd show her the photograph.'

My mother frowns. 'I wonder where that is.'

On the hall table! But of course, some years ago they'd had the house redecorated, and old photographs were replaced, for the most part, with prints of ferns.

That night we climb into the attic. There is a metal ladder that can be latched down with a pole and, as my mother expertly hooks and pulls, I think how we'd heave the step-ladder in from the shed, and push the trapdoor up. Inside are the same shelves, built against the slope, the same stack of files, labelled in my father's upright hand. Our doll's house is here, flanked by a trunk of clothes for dressing-up, and the farm with red-brick paper walls. I ask if I can bring the farm down, but she hesitates and my heart falls. Who is she keeping it for, if not Freya?

'Is there a date then?' I clutch the cracked back of a chair. 'For the wedding?'

My mother has her head inside a box, but she springs to attention. 'They're thinking of venues, here in Sussex. We should go shopping together.' She runs a finger along the farmyard wall, squints at the pad of dust. 'We must.'

I cast my eyes across the stack of files. *Household. Volvo. Guarantees.* 'I thought they were going for a long engagement.'

My mother laughs, indulgent. 'There's never enough time to find the right thing to wear. Fenwick's have lovely hats …'

'Let me look, I might already—'

'No,' she interjects. 'We're going shopping. We'll put some-thing in the diary. It'll be my treat.'

I perch on a crate of paperback books: *The Foundling, Lady of Quality, Charity Girl.* I can see my mother in the embrace of Georgette Heyer, lying on a lounger on the lawn. 'Of course,' she says, smearing the dust against a doorstop. 'We'll lift down the farm.'

That's when I see them, two rectangular folders: *Alice*, the label is inked with high fine letters. *Kate*.

'Found it.' My mother draws out a bubble-wrapped frame and there we are, under the watery plastic, our hair bobbled up in bunches, our identical clothes failing to make us match.

I put the farm with the animals arranged beside it on the rug in Freya's room. When she wakes I may gain half an hour. The photograph I stand on my bedside table. 'Goodnight, darling.' My mother hovers by the door, soft and feathery in her wrap-around gown. 'Your father's turned in.'

'Goodnight.' I want to keep her there, for questioning, forever, but her kiss is a peck, and she is gone.

I wake in the night and summon up the folders. They stand on a shelf, side by side, the only difference – our names. What could be inside? School reports, piano certificates? The rosette I won at the horticultural show for a painting of a pineapple? My mouth is dry as I peel back the covers and creak on to the landing. I stand and stare at the square of the trapdoor. How quietly could I hook down the ladder, and I imagine my parents storming out from their twin room; me, a thief in my own home.

'Katie? Is that you?' There's the rustling of a quilt.

'Night,' I call, and I hurry back to my room.

All morning my blood fizzes and the words I have prepared stick in my throat. We walk down to the Splash and across the common to look at the Big Oak. The ladder still leans against it and I climb and inspect the oval of its scar. Below me Freya walks along its fallen branch, my mother hovering.

I'd like to know, I take a moment to practise, *I need to know . . .* I lay my head against the trunk as a tribe of children race across the field.

If you could give me … I try out phrases as I help prepare the lunch, but my mother is explaining the best way to make gravy and I don't interrupt. Afterwards she takes Freya to say goodbye to the bees. She has three hives, white clapboard, a surprising hobby for someone so concerned with peril. I sit on the terrace and wait. If I'm going to ask my questions it had better be soon. *I need* … My nerve dissolves and my own hand clamps itself across my mouth. I check the time of my train.

'Back to the Big Smoke?'

'Dad?' I look up at him, and thinking himself safe he leans in. 'I was wondering …'

He nods, encouraging.

'When I was adopted …'

He rears back, his forehead shooting up into the bald dome of his head, but I've started − I've started! − and so I go on. 'Was it through an agency? Or how was it arranged?'

My father's lips are white. His grey cheeks quiver.

'I'm sorry.' I reach out and touch his hand. 'I need to—'

'No.' He snaps into action. 'You have every right … It's only that your mother …'

We look at each other. Which mother?

'Your mother.' He makes it plain. 'We don't want to upset her.'

'Of course.'

He pulls out a chair and sits across from me. 'Cork,' he says as if he hopes this may be enough. I shake my head to show him that it isn't. 'There was a home there, run by nuns. The Convent of the Sacred Heart, Bessborough. Babies were available, as long as you were Catholic.' His face is close and I look at him, at the shadow of his shave, his pebbled eyes, so tired. It's as if I've never looked at him before. 'The girl, your mother, she was from a good family, young, unmarried.'

'You met her?'

He jumps, as if accused. 'It was the nuns who handed you over, perfect, and so beautifully dressed, in a white knitted jacket and a bonnet. We were going to stay, there was a hotel booked, but once we'd got you, we made a dash for it, found a car to take us to Rosslare, took the shortest crossing home.' His whisper is so low I hang my head to hear. 'Your mother was terrified, we both were, that there would be a change of heart.'

I hear Freya before I see her, skipping across the lawn. 'Not a word!' My father looks at me with such severity that *How old was I? What was my name?* are as nothing beside his fear.

'We'd better make a move,' my mother calls happily and my father staggers up and takes hold of my bag.

'Bye, old girl, don't let it be too long.' He's walking us towards the garage, and we follow him and pack ourselves into the car.

'What a treat!' My mother wriggles.

'Gran,' Freya asks. 'Could I have one bee? To keep?'

'No.' She hands over an emergency supply of sandwiches. 'Bees need to live together. You remember I told you about the queen? They live in hives, they work together, one bee on its own would die.'

'Not if I looked after it.' Freya is adamant and on the train she makes a drawing of an independent bee, its striped body held up by silvery wings.

I take out my notebook and I write:

Dear Mother Superior,
I was born in your home on 10th April 1961 and adopted by
a Mr and Mrs Hayes from East Sussex, England. Could you

kindly provide me with the name of my mother, and any other
information that may be useful in finding her.
Yours ... sincerely,
appreciatively,
desperately?
Catherine Hayes (Kate).

As soon as I am home I call the Irish directory enquiries. A woman answers, her accent swooping me across the sea, and when I ask for the Convent of the Sacred Heart, Bessborough, her voice softens and stalls. 'Is that the Mother and Baby Home you're wanting?'

I say it is, at least I think that's it, and she whispers me the number as if we may be overheard. My pen scratches out the digits. 'The address?' She seems to press the phone closer to her ear as if she has something of her own to add. 'Bessborough, Blackrock, Cork.'

I thank her, and she pauses. 'Take care now.' The line goes dead.

I copy out the letter, consider what else there is to write, but there's nothing else, or too much, so I seal the envelope, paste on a stamp, another for good luck, and unable to wait for tomorrow I pull open the front door.

'You're home.' It's Matt, standing on the step, and with a thrill of shock I realise I hadn't noticed he'd been gone.

Rosaleen

It had been hard to sleep with the sound of Carmel's snif-
fling, but when her time neared, and she was ordered to the
dormitory, Rosaleen was distraught. 'I'll miss you.' They clung
together, their stomachs knocking.

'I won't start, not while Sister is on duty.' Carmel crossed
herself and turned her eyes to heaven. 'Pray for me, Patricia.'

Rosaleen promised, although what good it would do she'd
no idea, and she thought of the stories whispered, how Sister
would have you sitting on the bedpan, would slap you if you
made a sound, whereas the midwife, a woman not much older
than themselves, would at least allow a girl on to the bed.

That first night alone, Rosaleen spread her palms over the
stretched skin of her belly. She was too tired to imagine any
future. All there was to do was wait, and afterwards – in the
After Life, as she imagined it – she'd make a plan. She listened
for her baby. It lay still and low, and she was almost asleep
before she felt the familiar flutter as it waved.

On her third night a knocking started. A tapping, scraping, drawing in of breath – not painful, but insistent; it
tunnelled through to where she lay on a forest floor, the
warm earth twisting, tight and tighter, a fist, closing and
releasing, until it punched her awake. It's too soon! Her
due date wasn't for a fortnight, and even as she thought it, a

wave started close in to her spine. It rolled up through her, gathering force, bringing blood, small stones and seaweed, until it dropped her on the shore. Fidgety with fear, she made her way to the bathroom where she sat on the cold bowl, soothed as the minutes passed by the comfort of her peeing. It's a false start, surely, she said as she wiped herself, but there on the waxed paper was a smear of blood. Rosaleen shook so violently her teeth clattered in her head. Please, she moaned. There was no mirror, but all the same she saw her eyes dilated, her nostrils flared, a horse girding itself for an impossible jump.

She was at the basin when the next contraction caught her. It bent her to the floor where she would have stayed, pressed against the damp check of the tiles, if a spider hanging between the claw legs of the bath hadn't made a scuttling dash. There'll be hell to pay, Rosaleen feared for the girl who'd failed to dust there, and she pulled herself upright.

Through the rest of that night she kept to her room, a cloth between her teeth, biting down on each new swell of pain. Gulls circled, cawing, flying out from the port, or was it her own voice, moaning? Soon her mattress was soaked through. She crawled across and lay on Carmel's bed. 'Please, Lord,' she had no other words, 'have mercy.' Sweat ran down her sides. She struggled free of her nightdress, pressed her face into the musty pillow, added her own tears to those already soaked into its feathers.

As dawn broke her door flew open. 'Will you stop the racket!' It was Sister Ignatius. 'You know the rules.' She forced the damp material back over Rosaleen's head and yanked her by the arm. 'Get up now, won't you.'

Rosaleen did her best to stand. 'That's it.' The nun led her towards the stairs, but halfway down, she buckled. 'There's something wrong.' The pain was searing.

'There's nothing wrong,' the woman hissed. 'Nothing that you haven't brought upon yourself. Nothing that couldn't have been avoided by keeping your legs together.'

Vomit flew from her mouth, but Sister Ignatius pushed her on.

'What a fuss!' Sister was sour-faced when they arrived. 'A first offender, is it?' She forced Rosaleen on to the bedpan, and measured her dilation in the copper gleam. 'And only three centimetres.'

When Rosaleen tried to rise, she held her down. 'Is there nothing you can give me?' Rosaleen grasped at the white cloth of Sister's habit. Surely there were powders, gas, an injection of some kind?

Sister said nothing, only passed her a clipboard. 'Sign here.' A pen was folded into her fist, and eager, the words swimming before her, she began to write: *P a t r …*

'No.' Sister crossed it out. 'The name you came in with.'

Rosaleen was gripped by a new pain, so fierce she lost sight of the form, the room, the home. *Rosaleen Kelly*, she managed at last. 'Now let me have something!'

The nun smiled and, taking the form, she left the room.

How long Rosaleen sat there she couldn't tell. The bedpan turned from ice to fire, scalding as the edges slipped with sweat. Her contractions roared, the spaces between each one so short she could hardly catch her breath. 'Help me,' she sobbed, but no one came. Only Bess, who'd been there twenty years, who had nowhere else to go. She stroked her brow and told her to be patient. 'The midwife'll be back from her day off,' she whispered. 'I'll try to keep the witch away till then. Hold on.'

Later, much later, a softer voice came through to her. 'Get her up.' Hands were in her armpits, on her back, and she was on the bed, the pain of a sharp instrument, a gash, and warm water gushed between her legs.

'It'll be a while yet.' It was the midwife. How long is a while? She had no breath to ask. How many heartbeats? How many screams? The price of sin, it seemed, was ever-lasting, and she saw that God, as she'd suspected, was godless. I can't go on. She forgot there was no choice, and then she remembered the child. She must keep on for the sake of the baby. Please, she gasped, the child is without sin. She fought to find a sky, a sea, the comfort of her nana's singing, but God did not want respite for her, and the pain that seized her was so violent it grew dark. There were raised voices, then, that weren't her own. Shouts. A hush.

A banging started in her head, and then a falling, and for a sweet while she was adrift. She floated, high above her body. I'll go now, she was calm, I'm ready for what is next, but she was tugged back, and the wave, when it found her, left less than a second before the screams ripped out.

This time no one told her to shut up. She could hear prayers, mumbling, voices rushing. She had no tears left to cry, and then a new pain bore down. 'That's it, keep going.' She gritted her teeth and fought. For the baby. She would pay the price for her child. She pushed, and pushed again, the very centre of her splitting, until not a thing was left.

'A girl.'

The girl was placed in Rosaleen's arms. A scrap of fury, blood and slime, with Felix's face, squashed and angry, and a black slick of hair. 'Shhh,' she soothed, amazed to find that she could speak, and she held her, trembling, and the two of them looked into each other's eyes.

Around her people were moving; a dab of some sharp spirit stung her wounds. 'Stitches?' she heard the midwife. 'Surely in this instance?'

Sister, irritable: 'Come now. You know we don't offer that service here.'

There must have been some word of dissent because Sister, when she spoke again, was ice. 'Women all over the world give birth in the most appalling and unsanitary conditions every minute of every day, and these girls ...' she paused to emphasise what kind of girls she meant, 'these girls would do well to remember they're lucky to have the support they do.'

The midwife was silent, and it wasn't until later, when the baby was removed and Rosaleen had been helped, limping, to an another room, that the bruise of her insides began to burn. She suffered the flame of it, lighting her baby in a delirium of pain, her child, someone of her own to love, and her arms ached above all else to have her back. She forced open her eyes and watched the clock, ticking lightly, and saw that every minute that passed was a countdown to their parting. Three years. So short a time! Was that all she'd be allowed? Three years, less an hour, and she urged the morning on when they would bring her daughter in to her; three years, less a day, when she'd hold her tight and memorise her face.

For one short week Rosaleen kept her child beside her. She wasn't going to let her go, not after the first morning when she'd woken to a siren wail, its source far along the corridor, a baby – her baby – crying.

'She's awake.' It was Bess, her mop dropped as she ran across the ward.

Rosaleen attempted to sit up. 'Where is she?'

'Shh.' Bess held a hand to her forehead as if she may be ill, or raving, as if the red-hot squalling of a desperate child didn't warrant their attention. 'You need to rest.'

'No.' She slid a leg towards the floor, but a shard of glass splintered through her and she couldn't help herself, she screamed.

The midwife was there then, on her other side. 'Let's see how you're getting on.' She peeled back the sheet and removed a sodden pad. There was no disguising the hiss of air as she drew in her breath. 'Right.' Her voice turned bright and bustling. 'What's to be done here?' She reached for the Dettol which she applied with stinging dabs. The baby's crying had reached a feverish pitch, drilling through the walls and floor. The others ignored it, rolling her deftly to one side, stripping the sheet from under her, tucking in a new one. 'A hot, sweet cup of tea, that'll set you straight,' Bess determined, and she was left alone with the midwife who busied herself with her trolley.

'Can you not bring her?' Rosaleen begged, but the midwife turned away, and fearful – what did she know that didn't bear telling? – Rosaleen folded her arms around herself and pressed down with her nails.

When the tray arrived she was hoisted to a sitting position, a cup held to her lips. 'That's better,' the midwife nodded, as if the pain-relieving drugs she'd begged for had been admin-istered, and she was handed a plate of toast. Rosaleen ate obediently, and then with a ferocious hunger. How long was it since she'd tasted butter? She licked up every crumb, and then, when she listened, there was silence. Terror gripped her. Where had her baby gone? Had they made a note of her desire to keep her, did they not hear it when she told them she could sleep beside her in a drawer? But the lull may have been a gathering of breath because the screaming started with the force of an electric bell. 'Please!' She would crawl from the ward if she had to, and she was making ready to throw herself from the bed when Sister appeared, a swaddled bundle in her arms. 'The little devil!' She dropped her into Rosaleen's lap where she lay, shivering and scarlet with distress.

Rosaleen held her tight against her heart. 'I've got you,' she sobbed and her daughter's screams softened to gulps, to hiccups, to small stuttery breaths. Rosaleen didn't look up. If she couldn't see those bitches, then maybe they'd disappear, and she unbuttoned her nightdress and pressed a nipple to the child's mouth. The baby took it and began to suck, the gummy hardness of her palate drawing out a feed, and with it, a softening so deep she felt it in her bones.

'And what will you be calling her?' Sister was still there.

When Rosaleen didn't answer – what business was it of hers? – the nun persisted. 'We'll be needing a name for the certificate. Although of course,' she added, 'it'll be half the usual size, for illegitimates.'

Rosaleen kept her eyes on her baby. She'd been washed and dressed since she'd last seen her, but there was the same black tuft of hair, the arc of eyebrow, the eye moving mauve beneath closed lids. Her ears were Felix's, as was the shape of her head, and her mouth – when she stopped sucking and for a moment looked up – was all her own. 'Isabelle,' she decided.

'Isabelle.' Sister scratched it on to the form. 'That'll do. For now.'

That night Rosaleen hardly slept. She had Isabelle beside her in a crib and was unable to look away, her face so familiar that she couldn't keep from smiling. Look at our baby, she sought Felix in the shadows, and she stretched out an arm and gripped the bars of the cot. 'It'll be all right.' She stroked the tiny hand, splay-fingered as a bird's, and her heart clenched. Who was she to reassure their child?

She was still sleeping when Rosaleen heaved herself up and crept through to breakfast, each step a trial, where she sat with other new mothers on a bench. Girls, still pregnant, looked across, and away. With Reverend Mother at the top table, no one risked a word.

By the time she got back, seeping blood and sweating with the effort, Isabelle was crying. She washed her and folded her into a fresh nappy before lifting her on to the bed where she grappled with the pinafore of her dress – no slovenly nightwear in the dining room – and, clutching her tight, she quietened her with a feed.

On the third day Rosaleen woke to a new trial. Her milk had thickened to cement, clogging and blocking, turning her breasts to stone. Her poor child could barely scale their bouldering surface, floundering to catch hold of a nipple, and when she did clamp down the soreness of it made her break into a sweat. By the fifth day her nipples were blistered, but Isabelle's face was filling out, her skin smoothing, her eyes as deep and beautiful as glass. Someone of my own to love; Rosaleen stroked her tiny ankle, and she watched the girls and women, those arriving and others removing to the farm where, once their babies had been settled in the nursery, they would be set to work in the fields. For months she'd watched these girls at Mass, pitying them the long incarceration. Three years! Now she saw three years would never be enough.

On the sixth day Carmel joined her. Carmel's baby had been late. A boy, red-haired, with the same sweet groove above his lip. She sat on Rosaleen's bed and showed him off, and the tears gushed from her as she wept for her mam who wasn't here to see him.

That night, once more, they lay side by side. 'How was it?' Rosaleen whispered. Carmel's labour had been quick, that's what she'd heard, and the girl had a shocked look to be so soon on the other side.

'Not so very bad,' a shadow settled over her. 'Although I was scared witless, all the girls are, after what happened to you.'

Rosaleen frowned. She'd not had a word of pity and she didn't want to risk one now.

'When the priest came ...'

'The priest?'

'Did they not tell you?' Carmel propped herself on an elbow and relayed in a dramatic hiss what everyone else knew. How they thought they were to lose her, she'd been in that much danger that the priest was called to deliver the last rites; how, before he could do that, they'd rung the emergency number, they must have, or why would her father have come by?

Rosaleen felt her blood still. 'He wouldn't.'

'He was here at the back door. Fiametta saw him, a dark-skinned man ...' Carmel coughed and made a quick correction '... weather-worn. He had an overcoat, bottle-green, and a brown hat.'

Rosaleen was shaking. Her father was here. He knew she was in danger and he'd gone away again without a word. 'Was he alone?' she managed.

'He was.'

Surely he'd told Mummy? Why had no one come? A wail threatened to fly out of her.

'It was while they were giving the last rites the baby woke you. A fighter. It's what they're saying. She needed you to push.'

They both looked across at Isabelle, her face framed in the swaddle of her blanket, her chest rising gently with each breath.

'Your pa,' Carmel wasn't finished. 'They must have given him the news you were delivered because he was off away along the drive, and later ...' she paused, and for so long Rosaleen was forced to urge her on, 'he came back, parked by the front door, broad daylight it was then, and he walked through to the Mother Superior's office ... Oh, Patricia, I always knew there'd be someone to hand over the one hundred pounds.'

'No.' Rosaleen shook her head.

'Why do you think it is Sister is off out today? There's a party of them gone for tea in Cork.'

Rosaleen flew from the bed, her cuts and sores as nothing, and seized Isabelle up.

'You have the free leg!' Carmel whispered. 'It's what he wanted for you. Your da.'

Rosaleen was trembling.

'I always said best not to have a bonny one.' Carmel was crying again now. 'Look at mine, he'll be with me till the end.'

'Ten days.' Rosaleen clutched the child so tight she made a strangled sound.

'I'm sorry,' Carmel sobbed, and they both looked into her peaceful sleeping face.

It was the next evening they came for her. 'It's only been a week!' She'd lost three years; she couldn't lose a moment more.

'Stop that nonsense.' Sister was stern. 'The child must be made ready. No one wants her returned.'

They gave Rosaleen a dish with which to collect her milk, showing her how to push it out with the flat of her hand where it sprayed in pinpricks, so pitifully little for the effort involved. They collected milk from other girls too. Scraps, unused, their babies taken to the nursery. Rosaleen's tears plinked into the dish, and she imagined her daughter's eyes sprung open as she tasted the surprise of salt.

That night Isabelle's crying seared into her soul. Hunger, hopelessness, the discomfort of a cold wet nappy. She recognised each yell. She'd been moved into a room below the nursery, one more punishment to add to the rest, and not just for her — no baby over a week old must be attended to during the night. *I'll not walk down that corridor, I'll not give them the pleasure*, Rosaleen swore near dawn when the anguished chorus reached a pitch, and in the half light she picked up the bonnet she'd been knitting and stitched a message into the white rim. But by the tenth day she was so hungry for a hold of her child that she would have begged, if she'd been asked to, for the chance of one more minute. She glanced briefly through the window at the car pulled up, at a woman, stiff and fearful, her husband moving around her in a nervous dance, and she ran as fast as her socked feet would take her to the start of the corridor, where she waited for her baby to be placed, for the last time, into her arms.

Aoife

Aoife flicked on the light. Who could it be, calling at this hour? She reached for her robe but Cash was up, pulling on his trousers, looping the braces over his vest. 'You stay here now.' She nodded, only tiptoeing to the landing as he lifted the phone in the hall below. 'Barraghmore 153. Cashel Kelly speaking.' There was a pause. 'No, she isn't here.'

Who isn't here? Their two girls were tucked into bed. Everyone was here, but Rosaleen. She strained her ears – it couldn't be O'Malley, the great fool, calling for her, he didn't have a phone. She crept a little closer, risking the creak of the third step, but all she could hear was the sound of her husband, listening. 'I'm on my way.'

He came up then, neither fast nor slow. 'What is it?' She had scrambled back into bed.

'Trouble over at the Foley place. There's been an acc—' He shook his head, not wanting to worry her, and he slid a fresh shirt from its hanger and buttoned it methodically, starting as he always did, at the top. He put on his good suit, and the black shoes reserved for Mass, and looping his tie, and knotting it, he came round to her side. 'You get some sleep now. I'll not be long.'

There's been a death, Aoife knew it. No one dresses in their Sunday best if they're called out for a fire, and as soon as she heard the car, crunching away over the gravel, she got up and went down to the kitchen where Humphrey watched her from his basket, his velvety face creased with concern. Who had they been asking for when they called? The confusion of it wouldn't let her alone, and it kept her sitting in the chair so long that it was nearly time to start the breakfast before she went up to get changed.

Cash arrived back as the men trooped in. 'Morning.' Patsy gave her his shy smile, and Tim and Eamon grunted as they washed their hands. Cash sat at the table without a word, and so without a word she served him, only once catching his eye as she handed him his plate: sausage, mushroom, bacon; three rashers, crispy as he liked it. 'Business,' he muttered when Tim asked what had kept him from the milking, and whatever it was, it had robbed him of his appetite. She could see Patsy looking hungrily at his plate, the sausage half eaten, the tomato untouched, and when he failed to take his slice of toast, the men ate it between them, scraping the last of the jam.

She'd catch him, Aoife decided, when he went up to change, but as she began to clear the table he filed out behind the men, and she could hear him giving orders in the yard. She scraped the plates, throwing the rind to Humphrey the end of the sausage, although she knew she shouldn't or they'd suffer for it later, and by the time she'd filled the sink, wiped down the table, swept the floor, he'd started up the car. She ran through the house to the front door in time to see the tail end of it slip through the gate. 'Cash!' She had a dishcloth in her hand and she waved it, but it was too late, he was gone.

She waited, and would have waited longer if it hadn't been her morning for a set and dry. She turned the radio on, listening for the local news, an ear out for accidental shootings, barns burned down, a body found drowned in a stream, but there was nothing, and if there had been, wouldn't it have been all the talk among the men?

Maureen was finishing with a customer and as soon as she was done she relieved Aoife of her coat and settled her at the sink. As she eased her backwards, the jet of water prickling her scalp, she began to tell her about the child of a neighbour – not that she was one to gossip – but the girl had gone across to England, to Liverpool, to work as a domestic, and she'd not been there three months before she found herself in trouble. Maureen gave a sniff as if it pained her to go on, and Aoife felt the cold slick of the shampoo eased into her hair. 'Now, this is the surprise of it. When she sought help she was told the English no longer wanted to be saddled with the worry and expense of girls like her, and she was directed to a Repatriation Scheme, they're calling it.' She lifted her hand to cross herself and a stinging drop dripped into Aoife's eye. Aoife bolted up and dabbed it with a towel, but the froth of the lather slid down her forehead and she lay quickly back. 'Would you believe it,' Maureen began to rinse, 'they pay for those girls' tickets, and when they've set them on the ferry there's a nurse, and a taxi at the dock to take them …' she lowered her voice, 'to the comfort of a home?'

She sat Aoife up and bound her hair into a towel, and led her over to the mirror. 'Those nuns,' Maureen's face was flushed, 'they wear themselves out for girls like that, teaching them morals, caring for them, finding new parents for their brats.'

Aoife saw, reflected, that she was shivering. 'It's God's work they do,' she agreed and she slapped away the image of her daughter, waving to her from the boat.

'Now then,' Maureen brushed out the wet hair, 'let's make a start, shall we, or you'll be here at teatime,' and, slicing a segment with her fingers, she wound it into a roller and pinned it to Aoife's head. 'And how are your own lovely family?' She'd need to have her roots done when she next came in but neither of them mentioned it.

'We're all well, thank you. And yours?'

'Mustn't complain.' Her face turned sour, and then catching herself she sighed and took another roller and wound the hair expertly, setting it beside the other, so that soon Aoife's head was a halo of hollow curls, and she was placed under the drier beside old Mrs Fitzpatrick, with whom mercifully the whirr of the air made it impossible to converse.

That evening Cash was in a teasing mood, asking Angela, and even Kitty, did they have boyfriends – surely there were one or two they had their eye on? – until they were both helpless with protesting, and when they'd cleared, and swept the floor, and the kitchen was set to rights for the morning, he insisted Aoife's lipstick was a shade brighter than usual and hadn't he better check it with a kiss?

'Are you not going to tell me where you dashed off to in such a hurry?' Aoife looked into his eyes but he answered that he had to see a man about a dog, and although she nudged him and gave him a pinch, he held her tight and hummed into her new-set hair.

Later, as he slept, Aoife lay beside him, Maureen's nuns filing through her mind, until, tormented, she crept from the room and sat at the desk, where she wrote to the Sisters of the Sacred Heart to enquire: Had they any news of her daughter? She knew it was unlikely, but could they reassure her she was safely in their care?

Kate

My letter is waiting by the door. I'm not sure I have the courage to send it. I examine the address and I put it into my work bag with my ink and paints.

On the bus I keep my eyes averted. My mother is in Ireland, and not staring at me from a billboard. She's not the woman whose bicycle we overtake, back straight, hair streaming, although — I can't help myself — I turn around to check. And then, for all that I'm determined to stop searching, she's there! So familiar I start out of my seat. Her hair is speckled black and grey, cut severe into a helmet, and she has on a short-sleeved shirt. I know that shirt, those arms, her elbows, as if they are my own. Hello. I roll the word, consider offering up my seat, and then it comes to me: she's not my mother, she's the attendant from the playground on the heath. I've seen her standing by her brick-tight hut, handing out plasters, splashing antiseptic over wounds. Idiot. I turn away and close my eyes and I daren't open them until I reach my stop.

There's a postbox on the corner, but as I approach a sheen of sweat washes cold over my skin. *Keep quiet.* Whose voice is that? A hand presses on my head. Later, I decide, I'll post the letter later, and I stop outside the main door of the centre and I gulp for air, three gasps before I catch enough to breathe.

Donica is already settled. She's prising the lid off a Tupperware box, unrolling a wad of tissue to reveal a pen with multicoloured nibs. Jen arrives as I am pasting a sheet of paper to a board. 'Do I get one?' she asks, panicked, and before I can tell her that yes, there will be enough for everyone, Donica pronounces: 'God giveth, and he taketh away.'

Jen looks unnerved so I set the first board before her. 'The theme is summer.' Summer is safe. Or safer. I considered dreams, but dreams take you inward, and my job is to ease my people from themselves. I spread out materials – glitter, tissue paper, wool.

'Can't you … ?' Jen begs me to start for her, and although my fingers itch, I wait until she takes up her brush, squirts paint into a bowl and slants grey rain across her page.

Neil is in a manic mood. He paces the room, describing a dispute he's having with a long-stay resident at the hostel where he lives. 'Summer.' I feed the word into his ear, and he takes a pencil, and still talking, he draws the pendulous shape of a breast.

Sam limps in, and when I ask what's wrong he rolls up a trouser leg to expose a gash. 'No idea how that happened.' I lay down a board and wait for him to begin but half an hour later he's done nothing.

Soon Donica's collage is bursting with words. *Bless. Almighty. Halleluja.* In the centre is a fist. She discards my materials in favour of her own, unwrapping and rewrapping – pencils, rubbers, crayons, chalk. 'The Lord works in mysterious ways,' she proclaims to Sam and she takes out a box and, dislodging the foil and the elastic bands, starts on her lunch.

At half past twelve I call an official break. I've packed the last of my mother's sandwiches and I take them into the yard. *Bye, darling*, she is waving at the barrier, and I wonder how she'll take Dad's news – *there were bound to be questions* – but of course my father will never say a word. There are no words she can stand to hear.

'Any supplies needed?' I have adopted my adopted mother's voice, and I make a list: coffee for Neil, strong and sweet. 'Like me,' he cracks the usual joke. Teas, Fanta, Victoria sponge, although Sam needs nothing. He is sucking on a roll-up, fuelling himself with smoke.

There is a new assistant in the café, cornflower eyes petalled with mascara. I begin my order, but Beck intervenes, sliding me a slab of cake. 'If this doesn't help …' His gentleness unnerves me.

'I'm fine.' But the treacly denseness, the kick of ginger, swells my throat so sweetly that it hurts.

All afternoon we snip and paste. I keep my eye on Sam who has glued his dog end to the centre of his page, and Marjorie who is making a sketch of the mansion where for three decades she lived incarcerated, or, depending on her mood, as mistress of the house. Alec's serpent is a replica of his tattoo, Jen's picture has an elaborate link-chain frame, and all the while Donica mutters 'Praise be!' in admiration of her work.

At ten to five I issue a warning to leave all boards on the side. Donica protests. She wants to take hers home with her, and she folds her arms proprietorially around it. I wait, anxious, for others to demand the same, but they have learnt not to ask for anything, and on no account to complain.

I'm helping Donica down the ramp when Beck appears. 'God is our refuge and our strength,' she points her stick at him, and turning on us both she declares, 'I have seen your detestable acts on the hills and in the fields. Woe to you, Jerusalem,' before pulling open the door of her cab and climbing in.

We stand and watch as she sails off into the traffic. I lift my own bag on to my shoulder. 'Bye, then.' I turn to Beck but he is heading in the same direction. For a short while we step along in silence. 'Woe to you, Jerusalem,' he says and laughter bubbles out of us. I'm still laughing as I pass the postbox, and I hesitate, but Beck is telling me about a wedding he's been asked to cater, a sit-down meal for a hundred, the name of each guest painted on a leaf beside their plate. He blushes at his own enthusiasm and rushes on to say that what he really meant was that he'll be away for a few days, so if I don't see him, that's where they'll be, Dorset.

The flower face of his assistant swims before me and I tell him that I may be going away myself.

'Oh yes?'

'Ireland.'

Beck waits for elaboration, and when I say nothing adds that he was in Ireland himself, last year. Dublin. With mates, for the craic.

Blood flushes through me. The craic. The good times, is it? My letter burns through my bag. 'I'll probably visit Cork.' We reach my stop as the bus heaves into view. 'I hope the wedding's a success.'

Beck looks at me. 'Let's hope for sunshine,' and he steps forward, and there's a fumble as I put out my hand. 'Take care now.' He has me in a hug. His shirt smells of biscuit; his neck, familiar, of turps. 'You smell of paint!'

He laughs. 'That's you.'

'It's definitely you.' I ease myself away.

There's a seat free near the back. My head's so light I close my eyes, but as the bus gears itself to pick up speed I feel the force of his attention, and when I flick them open there he is, looking in at me. I lift my arm and wave.

The next morning I post my letter, and I wait. I wait even while it is lying in the hollow of the postbox where I deposited it at twenty minutes past nine. The next collection is at noon, but the waiting twists so tight and painfully I consider running out when the postman does arrive and begging for it back. How will I last forty-eight hours – I daren't hope for twenty-four – and I imagine my letter's journey from sack to depot to airport – or was it to go by boat? – picturing its arrival at the sorting office, the cream of the envelope, the address in large letters, EIRE underlined in black. The soft-voiced girl from directory enquiries is there to receive it, smoothing her hands over the known name of the home, and it is she who packs it into a stack and binds it with elastic, for surely I can't be the only one writing. *Dear Mother Superior. Dear Sacred Heart.* The post van rattles to a stop outside the convent, and a nun takes hold of the papery bundle, carries it to her office and in deep silence, amidst the waft of incense, flicks through the letters until she comes to mine. *Urgent*, this should alert her, and I listen for the sound of the telephone ringing although it is still only half past nine.

That afternoon I collect Freya and take her to the paddling pool on the heath. We stay there until the heat of the day has bleached us and we are sticky with shared snacks.

'Your mother rang,' Matt calls as we come in.

Already? I don't move. And then I catch myself. 'What did she want?'

'I don't know.' He frowns at Freya, bedraggled, a towel knotted round her neck.

'I'll ring her.' I take the bag through to the kitchen. 'Can you run a bath?'

Matt has followed and is searching for his keys. He opens his mouth, begins, regretful, but he's saved by the ringing of the phone. It's Mum again. 'Are you all right?'

'Shouldn't I be?' She sounds affronted, and when I turn, Matt is sidling off along the hall. 'Wait.' I press the receiver against my side. 'When will you be back?'

He stops and mimes confusion, and pointing to the phone from which there is a cry of 'Kate?' he edges through the door.

'Sorry. It's just … how are you?'

'Fine,' my mother says, emphatic, as if to clear the question once and for all, and now I'm listening there is a prize-day burble to her voice. Alice has set a date for the wedding and although it's not until next May she wants to take advantage of the summer sales in July.

I hesitate. Freya will have broken up from school by then. I will be on leave. 'I'll have to let you know.'

Her disappointment barrels down the phone. 'If not then … ?' I hear her deflating.

'It's just what to do with Freya …' I can't stand to make a plan, not now, while I'm so busy, waiting.

'I would have thought there's time to make arrangements.'

'There is, I'm sure …' I do my best to reel her in, make a note of the suggested day. 'How's Dad?'

'Your father's fine,' she clips. 'Would you like a word?'

Such tragedy! But even as I roll my eyes I know, I've always known, I have the power to shoot her down, ever since she told me: *God chose you for us.* Ever since she lied.

'Hello?' My father's scared.

'Dad?'

'Yes?'

For several minutes we discuss the weather. How warm it was today, how likely it is that there will be a storm. By the time we say goodbye I am exhausted.

I trudge upstairs and run the bath, and without waiting for Freya I get in. I let myself drift under, the tendrils of my hair floating above me, my breath forming small bubbles. When I resurface she is looking at me, solemn. She dips her sticky hands into the water. 'How do we even know that we're *not* dead?'

Late that night it starts to rain. I wake to the drum of it, the rushing of the wind. Matt is climbing in beside me. 'There's something ... I need to talk,' I try but he mutters, unintelligible, and pulls the quilt over his head.

God grant me the serenity. I mutter the words as I hurry back from dropping Freya at school, and I stifle a sob as I think how roughly I buttoned her into her mac. *God. Grant. Me.* I try breaking up the words, but as I reach *serenity* again I can feel my fingers itching to tear the covers from Matt's body, to scream at him until he hears.

I slam the door to warn him. 'Matt!' my voice shrieks up the stairs, but when I rush into the room, he's gone. I sit on the bed. *Detach with love.* The phrase is like a see-saw: detach, and the love flings into the air.

That day no one calls. I'd told myself they wouldn't, but even so I check the phone to see that it is working, testing the answerphone, switching it off and on again, re-recording the message. 'Hi, if you'd like to leave a message for Kate, or Matt, speak after the tone.'

'That's what it said before.' Freya speaks when I'm still recording, and I have to start again. 'For Kate and Matt.'

'And Freya.'

'For Freya, Kate or/and Matt. Satisfied?' I kiss her so hard she squirms.

'Why did it used to work?' I ask Matt that evening when I come down from the multiple tasks of settling our daughter to sleep.

'What work?'

'Us.' I notice he's made himself a cup of tea.

'You made it work.'

I'm so used to arguing: *That isn't true. Don't be ridiculous.* I have to swallow the words. 'And now?' He is moving away from me, out through the door, towards the comfort of the television. He turns to me and shrugs.

I re-record the answerphone message. 'For anything urgent, try Kate Hayes on ...' I leave the number for the centre, imagine Beck summoning me, his face insistent in the square of glass, but Beck is away, the grille of the café pulled down and locked, and I must make my own coffee in the staffroom.

'Where's your boyfriend got to?' Donica eyes me as she unpacks her board, peeling away bubble wrap, snipping at industrial quantities of tape. The others trail in and wait to see what she'll unveil. 'All right,' she looks up before removing a last fine layer of gauze, 'prepare to be amazed.'

There is a ripple of appreciation as we see each word cut from material. *Hallelujah* in an orange swirl. *Bless* in green zigzag.

'It's beautiful.' I put a hand on her shoulder. She flinches, and I remove it fast.

'It's not finished, if that's what you mean.' And she settles herself at the table and begins to unpack embroidery thread, sealed for safety in three layers of tinfoil.

It is raining in short bursts now, interspersed with sun, and galvanised by Donica's industriousness we set to work. *For anything urgent, try Kate ...* Should I have put *Catherine*?

'Miss?' Sam is calling to me and I spring up, but all he wants to know is whether he can use the toilet. 'Of course.' I watch him weave across the room. Some new medication has interfered with his perception of space and it takes three goes to grasp at the handle of the door.

'So where's he gone then?' We all miss Beck at lunchtime. 'Given up, has he? Retreated, defeated?'

'The café is closed, if that's what you mean, Beck and …'

'Zoe,' Donica prompts.

'… have gone to cook at a wedding. It'll be open soon. Next week, let's hope.'

'Let's hope.' Donica raises her eyes as if she is dependent on Beck's food for her survival, and the others, who are provided for the most part with sandwiches by the hostels, nod as if much longer and they'll perish.

No one calls. They must have thought better of it, decided they'd prefer to leave a message on the machine at home. I close the class up early, and run to the bus. I sigh and tap my feet and huff at every stop, standing; even if there'd been a seat, too restless to sit down. What will she sound like? My heart swells, painful, for now it's not the convent that is calling, but my mother. *You made contact!* – is that what she'll say? – and as I scrabble for my key, white fear shoots through me. *Keep away*, her voice spits in my ear.

'Hello!' Celine and Freya are spooning cake mixture into crinkled paper cases.

I push past to the red bead of No New Messages. I press it anyway. *There are no new messages.* I press it again.

Freya watches me. She has a fingerful of mixture and her eyelids droop in a swoon. *There are no new messages.* I can't stop.

'Celine, has anybody called?' Celine slides the tray of cakes into the oven and gives a small French shrug.

I forgo my usual questions – will never know how much broccoli was eaten, or whether Freya scratched her head. I pay Celine in silence and show her to the door. 'Bye,' she says, perplexed, and a minute later she's shouting through the letter box. 'Fifteen minutes, cakes are cook. OK?'

Fifteen minutes come and go, and it is only when smoke seeps from the oven that we remember the cakes. Freya cries as I scrape the molten mess into the bin, sling the tray into the garden where coils of black rise from the scorch. 'Paddling pool.' Freya reverts to the language of a toddler, and I tell her, with the strained patience of its mother, that I can't find the pump, and anyway, it's raining. Freya empties out her toy box and, resigned, I rummage through the dresser, tug open the coat cupboard, where tucked behind the broken Hoover, not only do I find the pump, but Matt's suede jacket, fallen from a peg. I lift it out and shake it. One side is dense with cobwebs, incubating spiders gritted to the sleeve, and as I peel away the sticky mess I imagine it displayed for exhibition on the very day they hatch. Tomorrow I'll take it to the dry cleaner's, and I slide my hand into a pocket. There's a pen, and a guitar pick, a twenty-pence coin. In the other is a square of foil. Quality. The foil is cold against my fingers. Durex. The lube inside so slick I'm sure it's leaked. I fling it away and Freya lunges. 'What's this?'

'Nothing.' I seize it from her and, slipping it back into the pocket, I shove the jacket into the corner as if it was never found.

I don't even try and find my river. I have no interest in my tree. There is a damp patch on the ceiling, large, and getting larger, and I stare at it: loose tiles, a dripping tank, I add the repair to the list of things I have to do. I'm still awake when Matt comes in. I hear him shudder the door closed, fail to double-lock it.

He stamps into the kitchen, there's the gurgle of the tap, and now he's trailing up the stairs.

'Hello.' He's surprised to find me sitting up.

I don't answer, only look at the clock.

'There were drinks, at work, and … I lost track of time.' He's easing out to the bathroom.

'Matt.' Our eyes meet, and for a moment I waver.

'What's up?'

'I want you to leave.'

The air goes out of him. 'Kate!' He slumps towards me.

'No.' I'm fierce, and he staggers as if it's him that has been stung.

'But, Katie, don't be—'

'If you don't leave,' I leap up, wild, 'then I'll go. I will.'

'All right.' I've scared him.

There's nothing else to say, and it must be what I want, because I wait, silent, as he shuffles down the stairs.

The next morning he's gone. There is no dent in the sofa, no smell of smoke or beer. I take Freya to school, rush to avoid Krissie, walk as far as the corner with the handsome father from Year One who can do nothing to distract me, and arrive home to the unblinking phone. I'd like to pull it out of the wall, hurl it into the garden, but instead I climb the stairs and get back into bed.

That weekend we stay inside. The choices are stark – kill myself, or glue pasta on to card. We make a frieze of *The Three Little Pigs*, and while Freya forms a wolf from macaroni I attempt the first pig's house, the one who thinks he can protect himself with straw. I use egg noodles for the walls, vermicelli for the roof. 'I'll huff and I'll puff,' Freya mutters as she sticks on a spiral tail.

Every half an hour I lift the receiver and hold it to my ear – 'Hello?' – and, convinced that I have answered in the moment before it rang, I listen for a whisper, *Is that you, Kate?*, but there's only the dialling tone's dead purr.

As Freya embarks on a house of bricks, I examine the address scrawled on to the pad, and I'm consumed by a new worry: did I copy it down right? I think back to the pale cream envelope, the dash along the hall, and I'm so busy agonising over whether I remembered to write *Blackrock*, that at first I don't see it, the number climbing vertically up the page. What if I were to call? I count the digits. Does that include the code? My stomach quakes, my throat is strangled, and I can feel it, how very much they don't want me to dial.

I move to the back door, and still in my nightie I step out and tilt my head into the rain. It stripes my cheeks and settles on my hair and I think how I'd be happy to lie down in it and drown. *God. Grant. Me.* I keep my eyes closed and examine each word. *Serenity. Accept. Cannot. Change.* And when this only perplexes me, I revert to the Lord's prayer and reel it off: *Our Father, who art in heaven, hallowed be thy name, thy kingdom come* ... Soon I'm looking for another. *Go placidly amid the noise and haste, and remember what peace there may be in silence. As far as possible, without surrender* ...

'Mum?' Freya's voice is small. I feel her hand in mine. 'Let's finish our pig houses.' She's borrowed my own most practical tone and she leads me inside and waits till I sit down.

It's late afternoon when Krissie calls. 'Sorry,' I say when she suggests meeting for a drink. 'No babysitter.' And when she hears I'm there alone she orders me to get myself over to her house. 'Mia would love company,' adding, with emphasis, 'we can chat.'

I check and double-check the answerphone, open the cupboard, and ignoring the jacket crumpled at my feet, I pull out both our macs. But I can't do it. I stand on the step, and even then I'm sure I hear it, the ringing of the phone. I call Krissie back and I tell her it's best we stay at home.

'You all right?'

'Fine,' I manage. Even now someone may be trying to get through.

It isn't until Sunday that Freya asks after Matt.

'He had to go …' I've always been a useless liar ' … away.'

She doesn't ask where, and I swallow the story about him visiting his mother, her other granny, Granny P, who she hardly ever sees. Instead we look through her book bag, read three pages of Biff and Chip, discover a note informing us that there are children in the class who *still* have head lice. 'We'll make popcorn,' I tell her when she slumps, and putting her in charge of monitoring the pops I fill a bowl with water, assemble tissues, conditioner, comb. Together we search through the videos. 'Not *Bambi*,' but she's determined, so we settle to the combing as Bambi stands on trembly legs, learns the word for butterfly and bird, is befriended by a rabbit and a skunk, bracing ourselves for what is to come – the gunshot echoing through the forest, his mother unable to follow. There's a reprieve as slowly Bambi recovers, grows into a stag and falls in love, but only, that is, until the fire. Today the fire is more than we can take, and we cling together, the nits abandoned as trees crash and animals run screaming from the flames.

It's then I hear the phone. It rings above the cacophony of sound, a high insistent calling that I have no choice but to ignore.

Aoife

He'd asked her to go with him when she met him in the lane, slowed his car, and leant his elbow out, even though she'd told him, straight, she never would again. 'There's a place in Cork, down by the docks ...' Startled, she remembered her brother Jim's shebeen, but of course – she'd told him about it on one of their drives, and wasn't he pulling her leg? Aoife looked at him through the open window. 'Out drinking,' she shook her head, 'and on a Tuesday.'

'Tell me, Aoife, when did you last go dancing?'

'That's enough now.' Whatever was between them was in the past.

She'd watched him drive away. Could see his teasing face in the mirror. He never could take no. She'd turned and walked towards home, slow now, poor Humphrey would rather lie by the stove, but that evening as Aoife started on the meal – ham salad and a bowl of potatoes, sweet and yellow from the ground – she was away with Patrick O'Malley in that long white car, the smell of aftershave and dog, the two of them singing as they sailed along. How many more times would he have to ask before she said: *Go on with you*. Before she got in?

'Are you listening to me, woman?' Cash was squinting at her. He looked amused.

'I am always listening.' The crumble was singed. 'Just one minute.' She took it into the pantry where she did her best to slice off the burnt peaks. 'What was it you were asking?' She brought it back with a jug of cream, and it came to her in a flash of luck. 'What should we do to increase the yield?'

When the men came the next morning they were full of it. The car, buckled and twisted, wrapped round a tree. Aoife held tight to the rail of the range, but all the same she felt herself flung up and over, the breath knocked out of her as she crashed against the trunk. 'No one but himself was hurt.' They crossed themselves. 'Praise be to God.'

The breakfast was prepared. There was only the toast to make, and she watched it with a hawk eye as it turned.

'It was after midnight ...'

'Woken by it ... '

'Foley, who lives out by the ...'

'The collision ...'

'Instant. That's what they're saying.'

'Better that way.'

'It is, so.'

There was silence then as Cashel and the three men ate. The eggs had hardened, a skin over the yolk, and the mushrooms had shrivelled in the pan.

'You're a good woman, Mrs Kelly.' Patsy gazed at her, happy for the excuse, and Tim and Eamon nodded.

'It's a shocking thing.' Cash stood beside her as the men filed out. He had his boots on and his farm jacket, and he kissed her, gentle, on the forehead. 'Have yourself a rest. Later we'll go to Mrs O'Malley and we'll pay our respects.'

Aoife didn't pay her respects, not that day. She took to her bed and Cash went up without her. The son was there, smart as they'd never seen him, and Mrs O'Malley had put on a spread. Cake and sandwiches and some kind of pie. She must have started baking as soon as she heard the news. Was that decent? The question of it tumbled in her thoughts.

Aoife kept to her bed for two days. She might have stayed there longer but it was best, she knew it, to get up and escape her dreams, Patrick O'Malley driving through them, from bar to bar, and she with him, his arm around her shoulder, and in every room of every bar there was Rosaleen. The girl raised a toast to them. Good for you, Mummy, she lifted her glass. It's time you had yourself some fun. But where was the baby? What in God's name had become of the child?

Rosaleen

It was Rosaleen's turn to go out with the Professor. She could hear him fussing as he came up from the basement. 'I thought I had Teresa tonight,' he muttered, 'is that too much to ask?'

Rosaleen didn't blame him. She was no fun, they all knew that, but she had to make an effort or the arrangement was off, and where else was she to go?

'What are we up to then?' she rallied.

'You girls, can you remember nothing?' He tapped his stick against the banister. 'Poulenc. Wigmore Hall.'

Rosaleen creaked open the front door. It was a stickily warm evening, the trees heavy with spores, the scent of wild raspberry rising from the basement yards. A troupe of boys were playing football, skittering against the railings, while girls scraped a rope against the ground. Rosaleen searched for things to say as they made their way along the street. 'Was Poulenc a favourite of your wife?' His wife had played the oboe. They'd held concerts in the house before she died.

'Not particularly,' he said.

Conversation stuttered, and stopped. Rosaleen hoped there might be time for a drink. If they managed a drink in the interval too, they wouldn't have to have one after, and she could pack them both into a cab and speed home to Chelsea where the other girls – whose night it wasn't – would be talking and smoking, grateful to have the place to themselves. It had been rumoured that Chloe would be visiting. Chloe Hazell who had once lived in the house, and was talked of with awe; half French, her hair cropped short, she'd left when she was discovered to be pregnant. Rosaleen pressed her nails, sharp, into the palms of her hands. 'Rosie!' the Professor reprimanded her as a taxi sailed by, and she mumbled an apology, and strained her eyes the length of the King's Road.

They managed one whisky before the concert started, and fuelled with the heat of it they settled into their seats. At least we won't have to talk. They usually went to the Italian on the corner and then to an out-of-the-way pub where there was little chance of meeting anyone they knew. It was undivided attention the Professor was after, and he made sure that was what he got. The girls moaned about him, shared anecdotes, but were grateful too for the minimal rent, the large rooms and occasional hot water, the kitchen with its dark wood table where they sat up late playing gin rummy. 'He won't want to touch, only to look,' Teresa had assured Rosaleen that first day, secreting her into her room. 'When you're feeling perkier, that is.' She'd gone through to the kitchen to make tea and while she was alone Rosaleen had kicked off her boots, tugged at her clothes and, wrapping herself in a nightgown, climbed under the covers. Her breasts were leaking, she was seeping blood, but that was nothing to the rip of pain where Isabelle had been.

'What's up?' Teresa sat on the edge of the bed and narrowed her eyes.

Rosaleen had no words to tell her. Instead she recited the lines she'd prepared. She'd fallen ill at Christmas, stayed on at home, and now her job wouldn't have her back. None of this was strictly a lie. She was weak, she told Teresa, but getting stronger, and so damn grateful to be here or she'd be holed up with Auntie Mavis, and then she may never recover.

It was a fortnight before Rosaleen was able to get up. The girls – Teresa, Suzette, Diane, Esme – brought her hot toddies, and visitors, one of them, Eddie, who climbed in through the window in the early mornings, hoping for Teresa's attention, and, when she turned her back on him, fell asleep wedged between them. Rosaleen clung to the edge of the bed. Her breasts were still bound down under a vest, and she took every chance to escape to the bathroom and change the wet dressings, secreting the bloody pads into the bin, pressing out the milk with the flat of her hand, any thought of her baby causing them to release a fine warm spray. 'Did he drop you, then?' Teresa had whispered that first night. 'Who was it you were with? A foreign gentleman …' She fixed her eyes on the ceiling, trying to catch hold of what she had heard, and then, maybe she remembered, because she rolled towards her and laid an arm across the cottony quilt. 'We'll look after you.' Hot tears had swelled under Rosaleen's lids.

She hardly dared think of this as the music started up. A flute trilled, drums boomed, and she placed a hand on her soft stomach. There was a light reprieve and the flute floated high above the strings as she tugged the denim of her dress towards her knees. It was the dress she'd worn the first day she got up, short-sleeved with buttons down the front. It had no waist and had always been loose, but even so she was surprised to find how easily it slipped on. Where was Patricia? She examined her silhouette, and although she was unusually pale, and her hair had lost its sheen, it seemed that with the return of her suitcase she'd been reunited with herself. 'Enchanted to meet you.' The Professor had welcomed her as if she'd just arrived. He liked a new girl, and he'd booked her that first evening where she managed a bowl of minestrone and was relieved to find he required only that she let him talk.

'Beautiful music,' he declared now as they stood crammed into the bar. He drained his whisky and gave her a shrewd look. 'Do you agree?'

'Oh yes!' Rosaleen nodded. She'd been startled by the audience's applause, had been standing in the French pub, staring over at their table, where Felix sat, not with his wife, but with a girl, willowy and fair, every ounce of his attention settled on her. She'd stood, unable to move, and it was only when the girl looked up, dazzled, a flush of red high up on each cheek, that she turned around and ran. Blindly she'd swung out through the door and careered through Soho, on into Mayfair where she avoided Felix's old gallery, across the lanes of Marble Arch and into Hyde Park. She kept up her pace, past the Serpentine, through Knightsbridge, never slowing until she came out on the long straight safety of the King's Road.

Rosaleen shook herself and flicked through the programme. 'Which is your favourite piece?'

'My favourite, let me see ...' The Professor was away, describing for her the scope of Poulenc's work, his religious influence, his versatility – chamber music, orchestral compositions, opera – as she accompanied her own destroyed self through the stuccoed squares of Chelsea to the Professor's house at World's End. 'Listen carefully.' He fixed her with stern attention. 'Then you can tell me which piece *you* like best.'

The second half continued much as before, but towards the end was a sonata for oboe and piano, *Élégie*, composed short months before Poulenc's death. Regret, sweetness, clouds closing in. The music had her heart and it was wringing it. She pushed a fist against her mouth, but she was walking down that corridor, the oboe weeping, the piano urging her to run. 'I'll take her now.' Sister's smile was greedy, and the oboe rose up on a high wire as Isabelle was wrenched away. Rosaleen's teeth grazed her knuckle. Every note flayed her skin. She choked, and bit down hard, but her grief was bursting at the seams. Now what will I do? Her skin turned cold. Where will I go? She'd seen the Professor inform a girl she was not only messy but inconvenient. She wiped her face on her bare arm, sniffed into her elbow, and felt a hand nudging hers. 'Take this.' It was a handkerchief, and glancing at the Professor she saw a tear slip below the frame of his glasses.

Afterwards they were both silent. She found a cab and helped him to climb in, and as they rumbled through the summer streets, the moon low in the light sky, the music travelled with them.

'Will you play cards?' she offered as they came in through the door. She could hear the chatter of the girls in the kitchen. The old man shook his head. 'Not tonight,' he said, and he descended to the burrow of his room.

Chloe was sitting in the armchair, her child asleep on her lap. 'Rosaleen. It must be?' A flick of recognition lit her eyes. 'We've been talking about you.'

'Oh?' she paled, but Teresa whispered, 'How was the old goat?' and the others turned, eager for entertainment.

'The whisky helped,' she gave them that. 'The second, even more.' There was laughter and agreement, and a joint was passed around.

They stayed up late, chatting and smoking, interrupted by the occasional banging of the Professor as he struck a stick against his ceiling. 'Sleep in with us,' Teresa told Chloe as they retreated to their room, and tucking her lion-headed boy on to a quilt folded in the corner, she climbed into the bed and lay with her silk skin, warm, between them.

Rosaleen woke with the chattering of birds to find Chloe's body folded round her. She tensed with alarm, and did her best to ease away, but a sleepy voice rose from the shared pillow, so gentle that she stopped. 'What did you have?'

'What did … ?'

'You can always tell, if you've been through it.'

Rosaleen lay still. 'A girl.'

'As soon as I saw you. Shh.' The well of her tears seemed never to run dry. 'It's all right.'

But it wasn't all right. It would never be all right.

'You'll feel better …' Chloe insisted.

'No.'

'When you have another one.'

Rosaleen twisted round to face her. 'I'm not like you. Not brave.'

'You're brave.' Chloe's eyes looked into hers. 'Don't wait too long. Believe me, I know.' She leant forward and put her soft mouth, for a moment, on hers, and to Rosaleen's surprise they drifted back to sleep.

Each morning when Rosaleen woke she made an inventory of her baby. The starfish hands, the lock of hair, the petal of her mouth. She traced Isabelle's ears, the high creased shoulders, the narrow legs. She counted, once again, the pearl tips of her nails, and in her palm she held a heel, feeling the soft thud of its kick. For those minutes, for that half hour, she kept her baby close, but then the bed heaved, Teresa sat up, Eddie was at the window. 'Go away!' Teresa harangued him, more often now than not, and when he'd climbed in anyway, and fallen hard asleep, she leant across to Rosaleen. 'I just can't,' she whispered. Eddie was whippet-thin and pale. He had the look of a man who'd be grateful even for a kiss.

'He's lovely,' Rosaleen said.

'Maybe I've turned lesbian,' she giggled, they both did, and then Teresa asked, solemn, 'Would you?'

'With Eddie?'

'Did you, with your artist?'

They lay in bed and Rosaleen told her how it had been with Felix. How time had warped and lost itself, how once they'd lain down for thirty minutes and when they'd next looked up five hours had passed. It was after midnight and the restaurant they were going to was closed. Hungry, they'd walked through London, their arms entwined, stopping to kiss at every kerb, arriving as the sun rose over the meat market at Smithfield so ravenous they'd ordered three break-fasts, plates piled high with black pudding and poached egg. She described for Teresa how he'd made love to her, gentle and then fierce, the sparks that travelled through her when he stroked her skin.

'Stroked how?'

'So light, his fingertips were air ...'

'Try it,' she murmured, and ignoring the sleeping Eddie, Teresa flung away her slip and rolled on to her front. Rosaleen sat astride her.

'Bony!' Teresa protested, but Rosaleen was comfortable on the pad of her friend's bum, and she trailed her fingers across Teresa's shoulders, along the skin of her arms. Lighter. Firmer. She used the very edge of her nails. Felix had shivered, goose-bumps rising, a fire that bucked them both. Teresa lay stolid as blancmange. 'They must have slippered it out of me,' she yawned, and then, quiet, 'Why do you not see him?'

Rosaleen lay back down on her side. 'I can't.'

'Never?'

She took so long to answer that Teresa began to dress. She had a job typing for a publisher's, and it was some time since the alarm had rattled its tin ears. 'Got to get to work.'

Got to get a job, Rosaleen thought wearily when she'd gone. She'd written to Betty in the post room only to learn her place was filled. She bought a paper and searched through. There was a health-food shop opening in Camden. An antique arcade needed part-time staff. She took out her old notebook and looked over ideas. *Skirt lengths in sixties Britain. Support for servicemen. The first man on the moon? Patricia*, she added. *Carmel.* These weren't stories people wanted told.

Another week passed and she took a job at a pub on the Fulham Road. 'All right, sweetheart?' the regulars appraised her. 'Who do we have here?'

Soon they were clicking their fingers, whispering invitations, telling her to take one for herself. Rosaleen was practised in keeping herself secret and she thought of Margaret and how she'd taught her to tuck away the money, not too little or too much, all the while evading the lumbering body of the landlord, who did his best to brush against her as she moved between the spirits and the pumps. My father, he was landlord of the Black Horse in Brixton; she thought that might jolt him into keeping those hands to himself, but she couldn't bring herself to use her father's name, not since she'd seen it, signed at the end of the letter. *You've made your bed.* Sister Ignatius had handed it over with her case. *Now you must lie on it.* She hadn't at first recognised his writing. It was Mummy who had kept in touch through all the years of school, but it was him all right because, after requesting that she never show her face again at Barraghmore — her mother would not bear the shame of it — he'd signed it, *Mr Cashel Kelly*.

★ ★ ★

The summer had reached its height, and it was Rosaleen's turn to accompany the Professor to the chiropodist where his bunions were examined, the horny yellow nails clipped short with such a snap she jumped. They hobbled home, it was too near for a cab, and she sat listening to his reminiscences, stories of the friends who'd crowded in to hear the music played in the house. Later she helped him down into the basement. He'd retreated to one room after his wife's death, stuffy, the window grimed with dirt, but at the back, along a linoed corridor, was a door into the garden. 'Do you mind?' She dragged it free, and they stood and looked out. Nettles and ragwort, dog rose, lavender, half strangled by convolvulus.

Rosaleen found a pair of gloves under the sink and, buttoning herself into a shirt, she waded out. The bindweed came away easily enough, bringing with it a shower of petals, but at its root it had wound itself so tight around each stem it clung like wire. Rosaleen clipped and tore, and flung it into piles, ignoring the frilly plaintive faces of its flowers. 'Rosie,' Teresa entreated her. 'We're going out. Come with us.' She attempted to lure her with the coffee shop she used to love in Soho, but Rosaleen wasn't ready to leave the safe square-mile of World's End. 'At least stop for five minutes,' Teresa said, exasperated. Rosaleen shook her head. She had hold of a clinging string of bindweed and she would not let it go.

Late into the evening she worked, ripping, flinging it on to the stone yard where it lay, only waiting, Rosaleen was sure of it, to dig its tendrils back into the earth. The next day she found a metal bin and, stoking it with paper, she made a fire and gloried as it burned.

The girls were admiring and perturbed. They clucked over her scratched arms, the welts and stings, and whispered that the rent was so little surely a shift or two at the Queen's Elm would be enough to cover it. But Rosaleen had had enough of pubs. *My daughter, she's one of those Chelsea girls*; she could see her father leaning on the bar, and although she knew he was safely on the farm, picking off rabbits with his shotgun, she felt the sting of his sneer. *You've made your bed.* She caught at the root of a clump of nettles and tugged. *Now you must lie on it.* She'd lie on it, all right. A thorn razored through her glove and, cursing freely, she felt the hot blood swell.

Kate

'You were gone for a whole week!'

Beck, his apron loose, is setting out a tray of cornbread. He looks amused. 'I said I might take a few extra days.'

I shake my head, and tears, unasked for, scatter from my eyes. He lifts the hatch, and before I can protest he steers me out into the yard. 'What's up?' We are standing under the branches of my tree.

'I missed my morning coffee.' I do my best to smile.

Beck puts out an arm and draws me close. I'd like to stay here. I'd like to stay until my tears are spent.

'You need a holiday.'

'Maybe.'

'When are you off to Ireland?'

'Ireland?' I think of my unanswered letter, the phone call unreceived, and for the first time it occurs to me that I could go. 'When Freya breaks up from school, after that, I might … '

'Do you have family there?'

'No!'

Beck's eyes widen, and before I can begin to explain, Neil is in the yard, rolling tobacco, no attempt to hide his smirk. 'You're in demand,' he calls to Beck. 'That girl, pretty as she is, can't manage on her own.'

Beck sighs. 'I'll see you later.' He turns, and as he does he mouths 'hopeless' before he disappears inside.

At the end of the day we line our boards along the ledges of the windows and examine each created world. 'Amen.' Donica bows her head, but it doesn't stop her swathing her board in bubble wrap and taking it with her when she leaves. 'Do not covet your neighbour's possessions.' She gives me a sharp look, and knowing it is pointless to argue I watch as she rumbles away in her cab. I wait until she's turned the corner, and then I wait a little longer. When Beck doesn't appear I set off for my bus. Maybe he left early, maybe he's with Zoe? and to banish further thoughts of him, I replay the phone calls of the last few days. *Andy?* I'd practised until my voice was calm. *I was wondering. Is Matt with you, by any chance?*

When Andy knew nothing I tried Ian, but Ian knew even less, and so I called his work. 'Is Matt ... Matthew Jensen ... is he in today?' I asked the woman on reception.

'Can I ask who's calling?'

There was a surprised pause when I said it was his wife, and I was put on hold. 'Matthew doesn't work for us any more ... last month, let me see ...' She sounded embarrassed. 'Three weeks it is now since we parted ways.'

'Of course!' I pretended. 'I meant to ring—There's another number somewhere, for his new job.'

Three weeks? I think of the mornings when I'd questioned him – board meetings, financial reviews – of all the ways he shot me down.

Tonight, I decide, I am going to call his brother. If I don't try his brother then I can't call the police. I can't call the police and report a missing person. A person who I asked to disappear. I'll have to explain I hadn't expected Matt to go, not when he never usually does anything I ask. *But did you*

287

mean it? I am deep in conversation with a detective. His eyes are brown, his face cheerful, he looks remarkably like Beck, and I'm pondering the question *Did I mean it?* when a man jumps out at me. I shriek and clasp my bag. It seems I'd risk my life for sheets of coloured card and tissue.

'Kate, it's me. My God.'

My vision clears and I see that it is Beck.

'I'm so sorry.' I can't stop shaking, and he takes my arm. 'You need a drink,' and as if he has arranged it there's a pub on the corner, empty except for two women, laughing as they stir ice with their straws. 'What will you have?' He keeps hold of me, and when I hesitate he suggests a brandy and orders two. 'What's going on?' he asks once we're at a table.

If there was a pill that dried tears I'd take it. 'It's Matt,' I say, because it's easier, 'a week ago, he left.' But I can't withstand his puzzled face, and I grip his hand, strong enough to hurt, and whisper, 'My mother. I've found her.'

'In Ireland?'

'Why do you say that?'

'No one goes that pale when they mention a weekend break.'

'When I say I've found her ... it's not actually that I *have* found her.' I tell him about the Sacred Heart, the babies given up to Catholic homes, that I am one of them. Beck moves round to sit beside me. I drain my drink and the heat of it burns through me.

'I read somewhere,' he is hesitant, 'that if you're going to trace your birth parents, it's best to do it at a time ...' he looks at me, 'when you're happy and stable.'

'But what if I'm never happy and stable?'

He laughs and, despite myself, I laugh too.

'I can't wait. That's the thing.'

'Then don't.'

It's not long before I've made a promise that, if I've heard nothing by the time Freya's school finishes for the summer, I'll go to Cork, to the home at Blackrock, and I will ask for information. Whatever else, it will be a start.

That night I call Matt's brother. 'Kate.' His voice is jovial. 'How are you getting on?'

'I'm worried … Matt, he's not been home. I'm not sure if you know, but apparently he's not working for you any more, and he's been—'

'He is working for me. I saw him this morning—'

'But I rang—'

'Kate. Listen. It's all rather hush-hush, and it is a bit of a sideways move, but I've set up a bespoke service for our most, shall we say … valuable clients, and I've asked Matthew to join the team. He's got potential. I know you'd rather have him messing around with his guitar … the amount of time he's missed … anyone else would have … but let's face it, Kate, he's never—'

A stone drops into the well of me. 'Is he there?' I imagine him in the next room, sitting round the family table, eating poached salmon, drinking wine.

'Not just at the moment. No.'

'Where is he, then?'

I have him, finally, flustered. 'He … he's staying with a colleague.'

A colleague. Does Matt have colleagues now?

'Who is it?' I take up a pen.

'Someone … from Accounts.' He pauses as if searching. 'Sarah.'

S— I don't write the rest of it. For a few seconds neither of us speak.

'We must make time to see Freya.'
I put down the phone.

It's only later, as I slide off my ring and put it on the bathroom shelf, that I realise I don't have a name. Not for myself. Or for her. How will I find my mother with nothing but a date?

Aoife

There were sheep that needed shearing, and Cash had the trailer attached. He was whistling for the dogs when Aoife hurried out in her jacket and her boots. 'If you're after a bit of company?'

Cash grunted. His publican's talk had quieted over the years, the long days seeing to the cattle and the crops, but it was she that needed company, four paying guests the whole of the last month, and now a couple from Kilkenny with eyes only for each other. Cash whistled again, and the dogs streaked round the side of the house. 'Get in then, if you're coming,' he told her, and Aoife slid into the front seat.

They rattled along the farm track, the hedgerows green on either side, the hay in the far field cut, the stalks so even she might have smoothed her hand across the tops.

'Philip is growing into a fine lad.' Aoife smiled at the thought of her grandson, the bristles of his scythed hair springing, much the same.

Cash grunted again, and Aoife twisted in her seat to look at him. 'And Jackie, so good to her nana.' Still she had no response. Aoife sighed and stared out of the window, remembering the barrage of her talk. If you wanted a word you had to slip the girl a sweet. She'd bought a packet, orange and yellow, the same boiled pastilles they'd handed out on the plane that time they flew to London. She had one now in the pocket of her skirt, left over from a visit, the boys out in the garden kicking a ball, a great bare patch of dirt it was, the flowers in the borders with their heads blown off, not that Angela minded. She sat inside with the new baby, and let her oldest daughter chatter.

'Cashel.' She rested her hand on his arm, sidling a finger under the cuff of his shirt. She hoped to rouse him with her touch, and found instead the glass dome of a watch. 'What's this?'

Cashel turned sharp into the lane.

'Aren't you afraid, wearing it for work?' Aoife knew what it was, and she was back at his mother's funeral asking the name of the stranger who helped carry the coffin. It had been Mavis who had taken her round to the side of the church and told her what her husband wouldn't say, how Isabelle had married again when Cash was just a baby, had had another son. They'd lived happily, until it was discovered Dad – as they all called him – already had a wife, and although he was a criminal in the eyes of the law, the law allowed it that he take the child. Did Cash never say? 'If he'd been a girl,' Mavis whispered, 'Isabelle might have kept him.'

Cash braked hard and the dogs leapt from the back and ran low and fast across the field, slipping like water over the far fence, the sheep scattering before them. Cash spun the trailer round and backed it up against the gate. He secured the panels of the fence, helped form a tunnel for the dogs who rounded the sheep into a flock, doubling back for stragglers, then forced them up the ramp. *Clang*, and they were in the trailer. The dogs lay down, paws out, and Cash nodded to them, trained as they were, to expect nothing more.

It was something of his mother's he was after. That's why he'd come.

Mavis showed him to the room where Isabelle had lived out her last years. There was her dressing table, the brush she'd used, a silver strand threaded through the bristles, and a box of trinkets, a brooch, a bracelet. Her rosary was buried with her, strung around her hands.

'My da said there was a watch.'

'There is a watch. He gave it to her when he had to go.' Mavis pulled open a drawer, but hard as they looked there was no watch now.

Cash had stayed in the front room, making conversation. Old ladies, hungry with mourning, sloshing their tea.

'Turn out your pockets,' the brother had demanded, but Cash advanced, much as he had rounded on troublemakers in the pub.

'Maybe,' Mavis stepped between them, 'it was somebody else took it?'

That was a cowardly thing to do, to pick on the one who wasn't there.

'A ring went missing,' she explained, 'the last time Rosaleen was here.'

There was a silence then, and Cash let his hands fall to his sides, and the man was seen off with a shamrock brooch, although if anyone had wanted to retrieve it they could have trawled the pawn shops the next day.

The dogs sprang up and into the open back of the car. You let them suspect her. There were days even now when Aoife's heart was hard with unforgiving, but children, they left you, and the man you married, he was there for better or for worse.

Cash started the car, and they bumped across the fields. As they drove she slid her fingers around the back of his neck, felt how he'd weathered, dark and creased, and when he didn't shrug her off, she trailed the tips under his collar to where his skin was smooth. Cash said nothing, but his breath softened, slowed, and they drove along the border of their land, speaking in a language that was safe.

Rosaleen

In the Professor's house no men were allowed to stay over-
night. Men visited, friends, admirers — Suzette and Esme both
had boyfriends — but much as if the girls were indeed 'young
ladies', once they heard the Professor's stick thump against
his ceiling, they accepted the rule and made do with a doorstep kiss. The girls complained, but Rosaleen wondered if
they might like it. No entanglements, no domestic ties, no
mess or rows. They twittered through the rooms like birds,
scattering clothes and wisdom, indulging the Professor, who,
fortified with their youth and beauty, arranged it so that he
was almost never alone. It was only Eddie who flouted the
rules, arguing there was no mention of the morning, and so
he returned in the early hours, still in the same slick suit, and
Rosaleen would wake to the sound of the window sliding
up and watch drowsily while his clothes came off and his
white body in white Y-fronts slipped in beside her. She held
her breath, her eyes half closed, as he clambered over her, into
the narrow space between her and Teresa, and Rosaleen felt
his hard bones and the rise of his desire. 'Damn you, Eddie.'
Now they were all awake, and Teresa allowed him an embrace,
endured a little snuffling and stroking, before insisting he get
off. 'Some of us have jobs.'

'And where d'you think I've been?' There was much talk about the dubious nature of Eddie's night-time activities.

'I'm not sure I want to know.' All this in a whisper so as not to wake her, but whatever he'd been up to, Eddie was left exhausted, and once Teresa had bestowed a last irritable kiss and left the room, he descended into sleep.

Rosaleen waited for the slam of the front door before flipping open her eyes. Eddie slept on his side, one arm stretched towards her. He had silk black hair, and the green tracks of his veins flowed smooth to his wrists. His lips were blushed, his jaw stubbled, and an unfamiliar scent rose from him, the sharp edge of cologne. A longing knifed through her, for dust and heat and turps, and she eased herself from the bed. She dressed and washed and tiptoed down into the basement to look in on the old man who snored hard enough to lift his covers, before pushing open the door to the back garden. Here she held herself and sobbed.

The wilderness was receding. Her efforts had revealed a stretch of land bordered with shrub roses, dense with artichoke and rhubarb. The bindweed was gone, tugged out at the roots, although she knew, next spring, with the tenacity of evil, it would come creeping back. The Professor had looked unsure as she'd brought the place to life. 'My wife, she was in charge of the garden.' He stared at the clumps of ox-eye daisies, the hollyhocks and asters, as if he'd never expected to see any of them again.

One morning, once Teresa had hurried out, Rosaleen drifted back to sleep, and when she woke there was Eddie still beside her. A hand hovered by her thigh. *Touch me*, she willed him. She was consumed by need. *Brush a thumb against my skin.* She began to count her baby's fingers, twist a lock of

Isabelle's hair. She stroked her ear, inspected the marvel of her eyes, but all the while she longed for something that might make her forget. In a fever she climbed from the bed and retreated to the bathroom. Teresa didn't want him; her eyes were in the mirror. Neither, if she was honest, did she. But for a bit of comfort … She knocked her forehead against the wall and allowed herself a brief, hot rush of tears.

Teresa's publisher had a surprise hit. *The Golden Notebook*, by a woman who had left her husband and two children and come to London from South Africa to write. She brought home a copy and they passed it round, discussed the author, Doris Lessing, over cups of tea, alluded to the four strands of a girl's interior life so often during games of rummy, the Professor took it away to his basement to read. Now Teresa leapt up as soon as the alarm rang. Work was busy, and they noticed if she was late. 'Eddie!' She wriggled free of his embrace. 'Is no one missing you at home?'

Eddie yawned and reached out blindly, 'Don't have a home,' but neither of them believed him. Where, then, did he keep his collection of smart suits, and why, if no one was expecting him, did he sidle off along the street at lunchtime each day?

'He's not going to give up.' Rosaleen caught Teresa in the kitchen. 'He's crazy about you.'

'I told you. I can't, not after my sister … I'll never do it with anyone unless I'm married.' She was crunching toast. 'Look what happened to Chloe Hazell.'

'But Chloe's working, *and* she's got her child.'

'It's illegitimate.' She made the word sound dirty, and Rosaleen saw Teresa's mother in her, a small suspicious woman, and remembered how, in the school holidays, her father would take his belt to her, not caring where it left its mark. Teresa clattered her knife into the sink. 'I wouldn't risk this for anything. Books to read and films to see. When I walk down the King's Road, I get this feeling,' she filled her lungs as if she could taste it, 'my life's about to happen. Aren't we the lucky ones?' She took hold of her friend's hands.

Rosaleen nodded, but hard as she tried she couldn't find herself among those carefree girls.

The leaves on the trees were turning when Rosaleen arranged a picnic supper in the garden. She'd clipped and weeded, deadheaded the last of the roses, and spread a blanket on the meadow that must once have been a lawn. She dared herself to travel to the delicatessen on Brewer Street, and using wages saved from the pub she bought olives, smoked ham, bread. Afterwards she walked through Berwick Street market, eyes guarded for anyone she might know, and chose mussels from the fish stall, dipping into Foyles where she memorised a recipe from a book.

I did it, she congratulated herself, but there, taped to the glass of the window, was an advert for an exhibition. It was a group show. There were names she recognised, and at the bottom: *The Secret – New Work*. Felix Lichtman.

She put a hand to her own image. *I couldn't love you more*; his eyes bored into her, his arms held her up. He *couldn't*. She saw that now, and she ran.

The food was a triumph. The mussels cooked with garlic and cream, they washed down with wine, and Esme contributed a pineapple upside-down cake baked from a recipe in a women's magazine. When they'd finished, Diane fetched her guitar. The Professor sat awkward above them on a chair, disapproving of the music which to his mind wasn't music at all, but he stayed, even after the men arrived. Larry,

Cyril, Eddie and a friend of Cyril's – tall and black – Pascal. Pascal demolished the leftover food. 'Most delicious …' He cast around for who to thank, and his eyes alighted on Rosaleen.

They stayed late in the garden, talking, passing joints through the soft dark. Larry lit a fire, drawing moths that danced amidst the sparks, as the twigs hissed and leaves threw up a coil of smoke. They played Truth or Dare. What's the sexiest thing you've ever done? The knife spun, pointing towards Suzette, but before she could answer the Professor roused himself and asked for a volunteer to escort him to bed, and when she rose they laughed, so idiotically, they were still snickering when she returned. The knife was spun again, and Diane told them how, in her last year at school, she'd written a love letter to the history master who, having seemingly never noticed her before, caught up with her behind the outside loos and put a hand under her skirt. It wasn't actually that sexy, now she came to think about it, but the good thing was it cured her. For two long years she'd thought of little else; after that she hardly thought of him again.

'Rose?' Teresa was asking her. 'The sexiest thing?'

Her eyes fixed on the fire: 'Marseilles.'

'I say. Marseilles,' the others echoed, but for all their begging she added nothing more.

Teresa told them she'd once read a sexy book.

'Maybe that's why you went into publishing.'

'It is!'

They forgot about the game and Larry, in his denim and leather, took over the guitar and strummed a twangy imitation of Elvis, while Eddie rolled another joint.

The next day Rosaleen woke to find herself alone. The sun was high outside the window, the house quiet. Late morning was her most suggestible time and she put a hand to her breast and traced the altered shape of it, the nipple darkened, the wreath around it bloomed. She slipped a finger in between her legs, testing for the silk sheen of her wetness, feeling for the heal of her scars. The door opened, and she froze.

'Hello.' Pascal was more devastating even than the night before.

'I was wondering where you were.' He raised his eyebrows, and shutting the door softly behind him he stepped into the room.

For a minute he sat on the edge of the bed, and then he took her hand and kissed it. 'You one sad lady.' His lips were velvet soft. 'I thought I might drop by and cheer you up.'

Rosaleen looked at him. His eyes were glittery with life. She reached out and he bent his head to her. 'Teresa?' She looked towards the door.

'Gone to church, like a good girl,' and as if to stop all questioning he put his mouth on hers.

It was delicious. The pleasure pulsing, the wiry thrill of being held. 'Hey.' He used the pad of his thumb to wipe away a tear, and she smiled, encouraging, urging him on through the pain. 'You OK?' He paused, and she nodded yes.

'No, I mean, are you *OK*?'

'Oh.' She'd no idea. She'd lost track of her safe time. She assured him that she was.

Afterwards they lay together, dozing, and would have stayed like that if the Professor hadn't banged his stick. Rosaleen started, sure it was her father, damning her further, and then she remembered: he was free of her, as she was free of him. 'Rosaleen!' It was her turn to take the Professor to the Italian for lunch, and sighing she pulled on her clothes.

'So long.' Pascal kissed her on the forehead, and with a grin he eased up the window, waved. He was gone.

Kate

I don't wait for the end of term. I can't. I buy two return tickets from a travel agent in Camden, and book a bed and breakfast in the Blackrock suburb of Cork. The flight is almost too easy. One hour and we're there, and the taxi driver we find waiting, chatting with others at the airport, examines the address of the home and, to my dismay, declares it to be no distance at all.

Freya slips from her seat belt and burrows against my side. 'Who are we visiting?' she wants to know, but my heart is whirring and I don't trust myself to speak.

The sign has been painted in religious font. I hadn't known there was one, but there it is: CONVENT OF THE SACRED HEART. Black letters against white. My stomach tightens as we start along the drive and I stare out of the window, at the hedge of hawthorn, the saplings overshot, the cows arranged in painterly groups, legs folded, draped against the green.

The rain is stronger here, the wipers swipe it back and forth, and as we sweep round in a curve, there it is: the home. Tall windows in a flat-roofed wall, a wrought-iron conservatory, and beyond it, the main building: three storeys, stone steps leading to a dark front door. 'Here we are, right enough.' The man gets out, and he lifts our bag from the boot.

'It's Mary.' Freya points towards a shrine.

I pay the driver, and I turn. The Virgin's statue stands in a canopy of stones. Ivy trails around her head, and her hands are raised in prayer. *Hail Mary, full of grace*, the words reel out, thirteen years of Mass before it occurred to me I didn't have to attend, and I picture Alice waving to me from the rear window of the car. That first Sunday I'd dutifully done homework, remaining, guilty, at my desk, the triumph fading as it occurred to me how easily they'd let me go. The following week I minded less. I lay on my bed and read a magazine. I baked peanut butter cookies, and when they went on to a pub for lunch without me, I devoured them, one by one, until I felt sick.

'Mum?' Freya looks out from her yellow hood. 'Next Christmas, can I be Mary?'

'Maybe.' I take her hand, and we walk up the shallow flight of steps to the front door.

We wait until the car has turned before I ring the bell. It shrills, and we can hear it, startling on the other side. When no one comes I take a breath and ring again, longer, louder, and even before the drill of it has died I seize the round black handle, and I twist. 'Hello?' There is no hint of give, and so I bang a fist against the wood. 'Hello!' I shout again, and would have gone on shouting if Freya hadn't tugged at my coat.

I spin round for the car. It's gone. Of course it's gone. There is nothing but the plume of its exhaust, and desperate for what else there is to do, I see a gate in the fence and I rush us both towards it.

'Was no one there?' Freya has to run.

I look back and, on the second floor, catch the dim glow of a lamp. 'That's right.'

The latched gate opens easily, and we find ourselves in a shaded glade of trees, a mulched path sodden with wet leading between pine and rhododendron, and in the distance, the low hum of the road. At the far end is a rectangle of lawn, and beyond it the ruins of a tower.

'A castle!' Freya races towards it.

'Wait!' Around the edges of the lawn there are black crosses. I bend to one, my breath caught, fearful as I am of finding my mother, but the graves are inscribed with the names of nuns. Sister Augustine. Mother Euphrasia. The most recent, Sister Gerarda, buried two years before.

I saw a face, I'm sure of it, peering out beside the lamp.

On the castle wall, there is a plaque:

IN REMEMBRANCE OF ALL BABIES WHO DIED HERE
BEFORE OR SHORTLY AFTER BIRTH. I GATHER YOU
IN YOUR FRESHNESS BEFORE A SINGLE BREEZE
HAS DAMAGED YOUR PURITY.

'Freya!' Who decides a single breeze is all it takes, but Freya has stepped inside, and is standing with her hood up in a leak of rain.

We wait there until the downpour lightens, and when it does we walk back the way we came. A pale sun has broken through the cloud.

'Excuse me!' There is someone striding from the house. 'Can I help?'

The nun is tall and bent, a straggle of white hair on her upper lip. 'It's private property you're on.'

I swallow and my heart beats sharp. 'I was hoping for information. I'd like to talk to someone who might know … my mother she was here … '

Her eyes widen, and I see her flash a look across the knuckles of my hand. 'Shame on you, dragging the child along.'

'I've come from England to talk to—'

'This is no talk for innocent ears. Now off with you.' She ushers us, with unholy strength, past the front of the house, round to the side, and points us down the drive to the main road.

'My mother. She was here.'

The nun stands squarely. 'You'll find you have it all mixed up.'

My blood rises and I'm spinning in a mist of red. 'And so was I.' I'm flailing, falling, holding out my arms, and when I'm steady, and my vision's cleared, the nun has turned her back and we are left alone.

There's one lumpy divan at the bed and breakfast, and a bathroom along the hall. 'I could have brought in a trestle for the child.' The woman looks aggrieved.

'There's no need, we can share.' Freya gives a yelp. 'And if there's space we'll stay in and have our dinner.' She softens then and offers us the choice between a first course of orange juice or soup.

While we wait we climb under the covers and I tell Freya the story of my mother, how young she was when she had to give me up, how she came and stayed in that big house, it was the place where I was born. It was where Gran and Grandad collected me from when I was ten days old. 'They chose me,' I try out the words, and it helps when Freya wriggles. 'They gave me the name Catherine, although they always called me Kate, or Katie if they were very pleased, and they brought me up and looked after me, but now I want to know what happened to my other mother, I want to let her know I have a girl of my own.' Tomorrow, I tell her, we'll go back and we'll ring the bell, we'll ring it until the door is opened, we'll stand there until they let us in.

The next day the rain is slanting sideways. 'Are you up here for a visit?' this new taxi driver asks and I tell him, 'No, I've come for information. I was born here, you see.'

We've slowed at a hump and the car stalls. 'Right you are,' he says as he jerks it into gear and there's silence as we continue along the drive.

Once again we walk up the steps. I can see the same dim light through a window on the second floor, and I press my finger to the bell. I press so long my finger starts to tremble but before I can release it there's a shout: 'Enough now!' and the clack of shoes.

It is a different nun that pulls open the door. 'What is it I can do for you?' She is younger, dimpled, and she gives Freya a quick smile.

'I came by yesterday,' I tell her. 'I was adopted from here in 1961 … my mother, she was …' The nun holds up her hand. 'Slow down, will you.' Behind her there's a girl, her stomach heavy, dragging a mop across the floor. She hesitates. 'If you could come back …'

'I have come back.'

The young nun falters and it gives me strength, but instead of welcoming us in, she comes out on to the step and closes the door. 'This way,' she says and she hurries round to the side of the house where the building stretches back, ten, eleven windows deep. She lets us in through a narrow door, into a hall with boots and coats where we shake ourselves and follow her along a corridor, damp and incense meshed into its walls. At the far end she opens a door, and we're in a sitting room with windows looking out on to a yard. There is a sofa, armchairs, a low table. 'Now,' she says when we've sat down, 'the thing is …' She pauses and asks if we wouldn't like a cup of tea? 'The thing is,' she continues when I shake my head, 'there was a fire, and if it's records you're after, they have mostly been destroyed.'

'Mostly,' I stop her, 'but not all?'

'When was it you were born?'

I tell her, and she creases her soft forehead. 'You're sure that it was here?'

'I am.' I write down the names of my adoptive parents. 'You'll have a record of them, surely?'

'And your mother's name?'

We look at each other.

'Your given name?' She's quietly cheerful.

'I was hoping you could tell me that.'

There's a silence in which she drops her eyes. 'There's nothing we can do for you,' she says.

'But surely if you search under the date?'

'I told you, there was the fire.'

'When was that?' My voice flares, and as if shouting is a sin that can't be countenanced, she suggests it would be best that we leave.

'Mum?' I've forgotten Freya. 'If you have tea, could I have a biscuit?'

We both look over at the nun. 'I would like tea after all.'

She hesitates. I can see she's tempted to refuse, but she opens another door and she is gone.

It's a long time before she reappears, and when she does the tall, moustachioed nun is with her.

'Sister Ignatius may answer your questions.' She sets down a tray.

Today Sister Ignatius takes a different tack. 'Now I can tell you, if it's information that you're after you'll need to go to St Joseph's, that's where the records are kept.'

'St Joseph's?' I look at the first nun. Why had she not said? 'I'll do that then.' I snatch up a biscuit and hand it to Freya, and without bothering with tea, I stand to go. 'Thank you.'

They both give me the same wan smile.

Once again we hurry down the drive, keeping close in to the hedgerows. We turn right past the lodge, trudge along a winding road until we find a phone box. There's St Joseph's Church, St Joseph's School, and a cemetery of the same name – *Cork City County Archives* in small black print below. When I call I'm told I'll need an appointment. A confirmed appointment. Would I like to make one, there's a space in two weeks' time?

Panic rises. 'Is there any chance of a cancellation?' I've managed the not knowing for so long, now it seems I can't wait one more day. 'It's unlikely,' she tells me, 'although you can always ring again and see.' I risk another question. 'Is there a way to find a birth certificate even if I don't have a name?'

'A birth certificate?' She sounds confused. 'It's death certificates we deal with here. I'm sorry,' she says when I don't speak. 'Were you directed to the wrong place, is that it?'

There's a ringing in my ears, and I ask myself why didn't I say yes, when Beck offered to come with me? Think of me, he'd urged, if you need a friend, but I have my daughter pressed against my side writing *Freya* in the steam cloud of our breath. 'Maybe.' I put down the phone.

That night while Freya's asleep I creep down to the payphone in an alcove under the stairs. 'Dad,' I whisper, my voice carrying in the carpeted hall.

'Kate?'

'Dad?' It's important he's alone.

'Your mother has gone up to bed.' He knows.

Above me, on the landing, a door creaks open, and is closed. 'I'm here, in Cork. I need to know my name.'

There's a pause. I can hear the arguments whirring and when he speaks his voice is very low. 'All we know …' He stops and my heart threatens to stop too. 'It was stitched into the inside of your bonnet. We didn't notice, not at first. The thread was white against white wool. It may not even—'

'Yes?'

'Felicia.'

'Felicia.' I hold the word in my mouth.

'I looked it up.' His voice is close. 'It derives from Felix, and means happy, although,' and here he sounds as if he's reciting some long-ago knowledge, 'it most often occurs in the phrase *tempora felicia* – happy times – and is associated with …' I can hear him trawling through all the things he knows ' … saints, poets, plants.'

I am sitting on the swirling carpet. I don't remember how I got here. 'Dad,' I whisper into the receiver. 'Thanks.'

'Please, for God's sake, don't say anything to your mother.'

I laugh. *Felicia*, I say it to myself. 'I won't.'

'Take care, dear girl.' We wait a while, like lovers, listening to each other's breath.

'Bye for now.' I stand on shaking legs and carefully I put down the phone.

The next day is soft and warm; the fields, as we turn up the drive towards the home, electric green. The door is opened after the first ring, and a woman stands there. She has stringy hair that must once have been red and her protruding teeth are stained. I'm so surprised to find she's not a nun that I don't speak.

'And who do we have here?' Her accent is deeper than those I've heard in Cork. She kneels down to Freya, who, taken aback by her faded face, clutches my leg.

'I'm looking for information about my mother; she was here, in 1961. I came by yesterday ...' I attempt to make it sound as if I may have been invited back.

'April?' She looks up at me. 'April 1961, that's it.'

I stare at her as she is staring at me.

'What day was that, so?' She frowns.

'What day?'

'That you were born?'

'The tenth.'

'The tenth, that's it.' She struggles up and puts out her hand, and when I offer mine, she doesn't let it go. 'Carmel.'

'Kate.'

'Kate, is it?' She looks round, fearful, and seeing no one, she takes Freya by her other hand and runs with us along a hall and into a small back kitchen. She shuts the door and leans against it. 'I told her,' she says in a rush. 'It's not safe to have a bonny one, and look at you, the spit of her.'

'You knew her?'

'We were going to meet when I got out. She said that I should find her, over in London when I went there for my job. Brixton. Or Kilburn. Or Chelsea, was it? There were girls there, jiving, in the afternoon, but I was caught by an infection, too ill to say goodbye.' Pain twitches through her. 'I got to the window, saw her there in her good coat. I waved, but I'm not sure she saw me.' Carmel grips my fingers. 'I always said she'd get out early, and me, that I'd be here till the end.'

'Where did she go?'

'London. It was where she came from. Although she had family, in Ireland. A farm they had. Or was it a pub?' Carmel puts her ear to the door. 'I've a girl just started, along the hall.' She listens. 'She'll be all right, so. I'll check her in another half an hour.'

'Are you a midwife?'

'No!' She looks surprised to hear of it. 'Only helping out. Keeping an eye. Sister will be along soon enough.'

'Carmel.' I lean forward and fix her with my eye. 'There must be some record. A birth certificate. Addresses. Others must come, asking.'

She looks afraid.

'I don't even know her name.'

'Patricia,' she says fondly, and then a shadow darkens her face. 'Not that Patricia was her real name. They said to take a new one. We all did that. I've been Carmel for so long—'

'She never told you?'

'If she did,' she hesitates, 'it's gone.'

'It'll be in the records, surely. They must be somewhere. You must know who adopted your child?'

Carmel stops and tears well in her eyes. 'They said they'd bury him in the chapel. I wanted to lay flowers. A healthy boy when he was born, but he was struck down, the same infection I was caught with, most likely it was me that passed it on. I begged them to get him to a hospital.' She covers her face with her hands. 'But they left him.' She stands quite still then, and when she looks up, she is composed. 'Sometimes I hear his crying.' She lifts the kettle, fills it with water, sets it on the stove to boil.

I have my arms round Freya. Sister Ignatius was right. I never should have brought her. I take paper and a box of pencils from my bag and sit her at the table.

Carmel flings teabags into a pot. 'We'll have a brew,' she's saying, stoic, but when the door opens she startles round. 'Oh, Bess,' she slumps with relief. 'Look who we have paying a visit. Sure you remember Patricia, she was here with me when Brendan was born. Got the free leg when her daddy was after paying the one hundred pounds. Isn't she the spit?'

Bess is old. She has no teeth, and her hair is so thin her scalp is visible beneath the strands. She moves slowly, one leg dragging. 'You're very like. And the child.' She peers at Freya, and she crosses herself. 'If she could see the two of you.'

I take Bess's hand. 'There must be a record of some kind. Surely not everything was destroyed in the fire?'

'The fire?' Bess glances at Carmel but she is pouring in the boiling water and she doesn't catch her eye. 'Is it Sister Ignatius you've been speaking to?'

I nod.

'She said a lot of the documents were destroyed, which means there *are* documents. April the tenth, 1961.'

'Isabelle.' Carmel's eyes light up.

'Was that her name?'

'It's yours.'

'Felicia.' My heart falls.

'I wouldn't know about that … ' There's a loud agonised wail from along the hall and Carmel thumps the pot on the table. 'Although it may have been another of her secrets. Didn't want a soul to know, you see, about her man. She'd sing to him. Kept me awake, talking to him half the night. Tell him every scrap of news. There were times I could have sworn he was there with us in the room. Felix, that was it. She'd ask for strength, when what she should have asked him for was the hundred pounds.' She stands, one hand on the doorknob. 'I'd better go to her.' She gives me a hungry look and I am left alone with Bess.

Felicia, Isabelle, Isabelle Felicia. My new old names rattle in my ears.

A low moan drifts out to us.

'Women aren't still forced to come here, are they?'

'Not forced.' Bess frowns. 'The nuns will help a girl out if she's in trouble, organise it so that no one knows. They give their lives to helping them. There are some that have been here as long as me.'

Carmel puts her head round the door. 'She's giving out something terrible. I'd better call Sister, not that she'll be pleased, you know how she gets on a Sunday with the midwife away. Look in on her for me, will you, if you hear her holler.'

Bess creaks to her feet. 'You'd better make yourselves scarce. If Sister finds you here, it'll be Carmel who gets it.'

I scoop up Freya's pencils and pens. She's been drawing a picture of the castle folly, small black crosses up against the walls. 'I'm sorry,' Bess says, 'not to be more help, but this is the only home I have.' She walks us back along the hall, a hobbling gait that we keep pace with.

'Carmel.' I have to know. 'Why did she stay, after … ?'

Bess looks behind her. 'She'd not leave until she'd seen her son's grave, but they'd not tell her where it was, and she stayed so long she didn't have the courage. You lose the knack of it, the real world.' She unlatches the door.

'Tell her thank you,' I say. 'Tell her goodbye, from Isabelle …'

'And from Freya.' Freya is tugging at my hand. 'And Kate.'

I tear a page from my notebook. 'If she wants to keep in touch …' I jot down my address. 'Maybe she'll find the time to write?'

Bess folds the paper into her pocket. She pats it and smiles. 'She writes a good letter, does Carmel,' but there are steps echoing along the corridor, and fearful, she presses shut the door.

Before we leave we walk back through the gate towards the folly. The lawn is dense, fed rich with rain, the borders of the beds neatly edged. I look again at the black crosses. Sister Augustine. Mother Euphrasia. And I notice something that I hadn't seen before – a board, half shrouded by ivy, on to which words have been scratched inch deep.

BRENDAN

16.4.1961–16.5.1961

NEVER FORGOTTEN. ALWAYS LOVED

MY HEART CRIES OUT IN SORROW

MAM

We go round to the far side of the castle, where there is a low rough field, the earth churned in ruts and grooves. 'When I die,' Freya says, 'I don't want to be buried here.'

We look down at our feet.

'When I die, which won't be for a *very* long time, I'd like a tree planted. A hornbeam or a silver birch.'

Freya looks solemn, as if she'll not forget, and we set off down the path, across the forecourt with its statue of the Virgin and along the long, humped drive.

Aoife

I was in the kitchen when I heard Patsy bellow. I'd been clearing out the larder, had taken every last packet and stacked them on the table, and I was wiping the shelves, a wet cloth and then a dry one, flicking at cobwebs, chasing silverfish, for all that they were never caught. God forgive me, I had the arms of Patrick O'Malley – may he rest in peace – around my waist and we were swaying to a tune, but as soon as I heard Patsy I was alone again with the jar of pearl barley and the jamming sugar seeping at the seams.

We called an ambulance. Straight into Emergency they brought you, and for three long days we thought you were lost. If he's any chance of getting better, they told me when you were through the worst, the farm must be let go. I was ashamed then for all the times that you'd suggested it, for hadn't it been me that didn't want to leave.

We've worked hard enough, I insisted then. From this time on there'll be nothing but relaxing. We'll drive to the beach, we'll visit the girls. We'll take a trip abroad. Remember how we were diddled out of Spain? Had to make do with those two days in the Strand Hotel? You raised your eyebrow at the memory, I was sure you did. Now's our chance to go.

All day, every day I sat by your bed, worrying when I remembered, what was I to do about the paying guests? I had ten booked in over the summer. Most of them regulars, a few that were new. I didn't like to let them down, but Angela must have written and explained, because when I got home there was no one waiting on the doorstep, no one camped in the drive.

If we'd had a son, he might have taken on the farm, but the girls, neither of them wanted it. Declan was tempted, I could see that, the tribe of those children filling up the house, but Angela had no use for being stuck out here with no one but poor Mrs O'Malley along the lane, when she had neighbours where she was at Blackrock, and a shop on the corner, and the children on their bikes up and down the street. Kitty's husband, Con, travelled abroad a week out of every three, so that was no good. They'd met when she had her job at the bank.

I put our names down for a new build on a plot of land on the other side of Youghal. Two bedrooms, in case of guests, and we'd get to choose the fittings. Wardrobes, kitchen. A garage for the car. You'd be out of hospital for sure, before the move, but when the time came, I stood out on the steps of Barraghmore and said goodbye to the oak in the field over the way and the ghost of that old donkey, what was his name, Teddy, and I thought of all the hours I'd tried to coax him, walking backwards with a carrot. I looked into the sheds, and there were our girls, the lambs gulping milk from the bottle, and into the big barn where I breathed in the hot-twine smell of bales. What if she comes back, and we're not here? I couldn't get the sight of her out of my mind. Not when a stranger answered the door and asked who she was. I left our forwarding address; I told the new owners when I handed

315

over the keys – a couple from Donegal with two boys, nearly grown – that they must provide it to anyone who called, and I laid the card on the hall table so they'd not forget. I prayed, I still pray, that she isn't turned away, that wherever she is coming from, no one insists that she go back.

It's Humphrey I missed most when we left the farm, his grave marked by a cross of sticks, his collar buried with him. You, on the other hand, came with me. Your pyjamas, neat under the pillow; your shoes, shined, on a rack. Look how smart we are. I opened the wardrobe and there was your best suit, freshly pressed, your shirts sharp and shivering. In the kitchen I wiped a hand along the surfaces. Oatmeal, I'd chosen, so it wouldn't show the crumbs. The sink was gleaming. Stainless steel. There was a mixer tap and a brand-new basin, blue to match the lino. I brought in photographs. Held them up. The hallway. The doormat. The carpet, also oatmeal. By the bathroom you were growing weary. Quick, I showed you the spare room: the twin beds, the old counterpanes, Harvest and Barley, bearing up so well. Wait – your eyes were drooping. What should we do about the mattress – replace it or make do? You showed no sign of having heard. Blink for making do. Nod for replacing. But your eyes were shut and you had that old familiar look as if to say: Enough now, woman, give me peace.

That evening when I came home to the bungalow I removed my shoes and felt the carpet spring between my toes. I will replace it. But when I stripped the bed there was the wear of the years, the marks and stains, the dip where we'd rolled against each other. I'd turn it over, later, when I had help, but for now I lay down in the fold of quilt and held tight to the pillow.

Sometimes I think I'll drive up past the old place. Have a peek into the yard. They wouldn't mind, I'm sure, if I put my nose round the gate, but once I'm dressed and I've had my tea, and a round of toast and butter, I think better of it. If anyone had called, they'd have passed on the address. The number too. I made sure to leave it, and when the telephone does ring I count to five and send up a prayer. Let it be her. It never is. Angela, usually, or Jackie, who calls her nana every time she's home. She tells me how she's getting on. Dancing. That's what she's crazy for. Jazz, and modern. She's in one of those troupes that entertain the passengers on a cruise, and she tells me all the places that she's been. South Africa she went last year, and she was surprised as anything to hear it's where her grandfather was born. Weeks, it took them. There was a swimming pool aboard, but they didn't stop long, a few days that's all, and they turned round and came home. If it's Sunday, it'll be Kitty ringing to say when she's likely to call round. Her boys are at a Gaelic-speaking school. That was Con's idea. Not that he speaks himself, and he's done with any talk of finding Rosaleen, not after your man came back from England without a shred of news. All his fine ideas of looking in the phone book. He came round himself to tell me. I've bad news. He hung his head, all sombre. There's no trace. That afternoon, at the hospital, I cried. Was it relief, or disappointment, I wasn't sure, but it would have been galling to think that all these years she'd been waiting to be found.

You were very near the end then. Your hand, when I squeezed it, light and warm. I'd given up the begging, I'd stopped asking you to blink, although I did ask if you were listening. I laughed, then, for all the years you'd asked me the same: Are you listening to me, woman? And I'd answer: I'm always listening. Even if it wasn't true. I'm listening now, though. I found the obituary, after, when I cleared your things. *Felix Lichtman, 1921–1970.* A wife he had, although it wasn't Rosaleen, and a child, who survived him. There was a photograph. Your man in officer's uniform, smart as you like. He'd parachuted into Germany in the last months of the war, an agent for the Special Operations Executive, gathering intelligence, never fully recovered from what he saw when they opened up those camps. There was a picture too of his last work, a girl in profile, all rounds and curves, as beautiful as the model herself.

I'm standing in the garden, looking at the stars, and I'm sure there's something that you want to tell me. If I listen hard enough, I'll hear it, whatever it is you have to say.

Rosaleen

When Rosaleen arrived in the village of Oakfield, she wore her button-down denim dress in the hope she wouldn't show. *Housekeeper for a widowed gentleman. Experience with children essential*, the advertisement had read, and she'd written in to say she had experience. She had two young sisters. She could clean and garden. She didn't mention she was nineteen.

Suzette cooked goulash on her last night, Teresa made potato salad, Diane another of her cakes. They lit candles in the kitchen, and played rummy with the Professor, talking about the girls who'd left over the years, who'd vowed to visit, and never did. The girls of a previous era were mythical. There was Julia whose miniature stage sets still cluttered the back bedroom. She'd left to live with a theatre director and had not been heard from again. There'd been Merl who'd damned them all for smoking – she was training to become an opera singer – and Clarissa, an heiress who had run off with an African explorer and whose photograph, above a caption that read *Disgraced*, was pinned, curling, to the bathroom wall.

They didn't mention the men who'd disappeared. Larry, who'd gone to California; Eddie, who'd given up quite suddenly on his seduction of Teresa; and Pascal, who no one but Rosaleen seemed to remember.

'But as for this one,' the Professor predicted, smiling, 'she'll be back, if for no other reason than to see her garden.' Rosaleen nodded and looked out of the window at the black shapes of the bushes, the neat, raked beds, before reminding them that Chloe had come back. Chloe had visited, didn't they remember? She'd come back with her child? But their reflective mood had lifted and they were talking about the new girl who was to arrive next week. 'Barbara,' the Professor sighed. 'Let's hope she knows how to behave.'

Rosaleen took a train from Victoria, and then a bus, and reading the instructions she got off by the church. From there she walked across a common, past a giant oak, a ladder propped against its trunk, downhill to where she must step around a pool of water collected in the dip of the road, and up again, skirting the old wall of an estate, along a lane and into a copse of trees. There was a cottage, half hidden, its front door flaking paint. I've read too many novels, she reprimanded herself; she'd imagined a mansion, a silent widower, grey-jowled and austere, but when she knocked, she found the widower was young, his hair messed, a dab of porridge on his shirt. They looked at each other equally surprised, and after a moment a woman, as young and fair as he was, came out with a baby on her hip. 'I'm Peter's sister—' She stopped. It was clear Rosaleen was not what she'd expected. 'It's pretty isolated,' she warned but as they'd had no other applications they agreed that she should try it for a month.

That first evening Rosaleen stood on the landing and watched while Peter bathed his daughter, splashing her with tiny drops, singing as he soaped her hair. He was a teacher, although he'd liked to have been a writer, and now that he had help he'd be starting back at work. In the meantime he cooked for Rosaleen, and read her poems, and the three of them went walking through the woods, the baby strapped to Peter in a sling.

There was a plot of land behind the house, the remnants of a garden, and although it was too late for planting Rosaleen prepared the ground, digging and clearing, making lists of seeds they'd need to buy. There were pear trees, and old raspberry canes burnt black by frost, and she chose a corner to make compost, throwing in the leaves she raked, mixing it with peelings. She warmed milk for little Sylva and fed her by the fire, holding her slight body against her swelling one, shifting her against her shoulder to be burped.

At the end of that month, Peter asked if she would stay. That's when she told him she was pregnant. 'I thought you might be,' and, blushing, he'd looked at her, although she'd seen him looking before. 'No more secrets, eh?' His eyes were very blue.

'She's to be called Chloe.'

'Is that a fact?'

Rosaleen nodded, so solemn that he'd laughed.

'I didn't expect to be laughing. Not six months after—' She didn't ask, not then, what had happened to his wife. 'Thank you.' He took her hand and squeezed it.

'I will stay.' She didn't say for how long.

Kate

It's high summer as we walk through the streets towards home. Our road looks swept and welcoming, and the nasturtiums planted by an invisible neighbour have flowered, orange and red. Our gate clangs familiarly as Freya swings it open, and avoiding the cracked tile, we step along the path. I'd double-locked the door before we left for Ireland but as I reach up with my key I find it opens on its one loose catch.

'Matt?' I call into the vacant hall.

I run upstairs. The bed is as I left it, the chair beside it piled with books, but when I open the cupboard I am assailed by an empty drift of hangers, a shelf swept free of clothes. I step back, sorrow battling with elation, and when I look into the bathroom and see Matt's toothbrush, hope rises, dipping as I find his shaving brush and razor gone.

Freya is standing on a chair. I put my arms around her, hold her tight until she squirms, and it is only once I have unbolted the back door and she is outside, stirring the dried-mud segments of potion, that I see the red light of the answerphone is flashing, notice the pile of post. My heart loops as I leaf through it. There is a phone bill, an invitation to a studio show – three friends from art school exhibiting their work; *Next time join us* scribbled on the back – and a letter from the Convent of the Sacred Heart. *We are sorry to inform you that there is nothing we can do to help you in this matter.* It was sent before I left.

I want to rip the letter, but I can't. I have so little, I must keep it.

I press the button on the answerphone. *You have two new messages.*

'Hey there. I'm dropping round on Saturday to get some of my stuff.' There's a pause as if Matt is shocked to be giving me this news. 'Sorry.' There's another pause. 'We'll talk.'

The next message is from Beck. His voice is low and inquisitive. 'Just wondering how you got on in Cork. Call me when you get a chance. I'd like to know you're safely back.'

My finger hovers to replay the messages, but first I scan the phone bill. The repeating number isn't hard to find. Twenty-three minutes. Thirty-seven minutes. Eighteen minutes. If nothing else I must send it on to Matt. And then I'm dialling; what is there to lose? 'Hello!' A cheerful voice on an ascending scale. 'Sarah isn't here right now so leave a message!' Sarah is presumably at work, and so most probably is Matt. I speak slowly as if I may be hard to understand. 'This is a message for Matthew Jensen. I'd like to say ...' What is it that I'd like to say? Oh yes. 'Fuck you?'

I've hardly set the phone down when it rings back. 'Yes?' But it isn't Matt, or Sarah, it's Roberta, who wants me to know – I can hear the shuffling of papers – that the board have decided to increase my hours. They've been unusually impressed by recent projects.

I'm so surprised I ask about a raise. Roberta draws a breath. 'That's something that will have to be discussed.'

'The thing is, I'm going to be working towards my own exhibition,' I tell her, and as I speak I push open the door to my studio and I step in among the trees.

'I'll let you know,' she says with a new warmth, 'about the raise.'

We stay close to home those next few days. I set up a shade in the garden and we sit outside with pens and crayons, scissors, glue, and fill the pages of our scrapbooks. Freya's involves much sticking. Mine is a record of our trip. I draw a sketch of the convent, the slope of the stone steps, the fortified front door. I draw a picture of the castle folly, the rectangle of its lawn, the encircled crosses, the names of the nuns. More importantly, I write down Carmel's words.

Patricia.

Her good coat.

Singing to Felix through the night.

How much would a hundred pounds be now? A thousand? Two?

Her father must have loved her.

Isabelle. I set it beside Felicia. Beside Kate.

As ever, I'm not sure who to be.

Rosaleen

They were expected at the hospital, a small clean cottage hospital, where the midwife gave her reassurance that a second baby was almost always easier than a first. There'd be gas and air, and in the event of any complications, an obstetrician would be close at hand.

Rosaleen had been mindful to wear her nana's ring and to refer to Peter as her husband. She looked at Peter now, sleeping, peaceful beside her, the pale form of him, a light in the dark room. Slowly, quietly, she slid from the bed, careful as she creaked over the boards, and holding tight to the banister she crept downstairs.

There was a gathering inside her, cramping, bloody, as she inched open the front door. She'd wait as long as she could bear it – fear broke across her back – and she closed her eyes against the hanging crescent of the moon. Damn this, a contraction swelled, and she fought away the image of herself gripping that basin, doubled in agony as she was forced down the stairs. Slowly she made her way along the path beside the house, and into the wood behind the garden. Branches hung low enough to swipe her face, each leaf damp with dew. She reached a clearing and sat with her back against the trunk of an oak, the wood pressing warm against her spine. The light was grainy, each blade of grass vividly outlined, and as she breathed in, exhaled, breathed in again, the birds began to wake, small cheeps and squawks cut through with song. The melody coiled inside her, twisting and lilting so that she began to hum. She hummed in a low round roll, lifting the pain as it descended, swooping with it, drawing it away.

It was light by the time Peter found her. She was bent over, palms pressed to the wood. 'My love.' He laid his hands on her, but there was no time to answer; she must sing the baby out. 'Sweetheart.' He tried to ease away her hands.

Rosaleen shook him off. She mustn't break the rhythm of her humming. If she stopped for even a moment she'd be lost.

'Rosaleen!' His voice was firm. 'We have to get to the hospital.'

'Mmmmmmm, mmm, mm.' Her eyes were closed.

'I'm bringing the car, stay right here.' She laughed, or would have if she'd had breath to spare. Bring the car, she thought as she rode the swell of a contraction. She'd not be agreeing to anyone's orders again.

When Peter returned he had Sylva with him. Rosaleen caught the bright gleam of her hair. 'Sylva,' she managed before the rolling started, deep down and rising. 'Please,' Peter was begging, but she lost sight of him, and when she next looked up, he had a blanket and a steaming bowl of water. 'They're on their way.' She didn't dare ask who. There was work to do, and she was going to do it.

By the time the ambulance arrived the baby was born. It slithered out on a roar of pain and triumph, and Peter held it up. 'A girl,' he told her, and he kissed her dark head.

'You did well,' the paramedic said, admiring, leaning down to cut the cord, looking to Peter to check he'd noticed the baby wasn't his.

Rosaleen could only make a strangled sound of need, and her daughter, wrapped in a towel, was placed in the crook of her arm. Her eyes were open, blue-black, and watchful. 'Hello.' She felt her whole self falling.

Why had Chloe failed to say that as her heart opened, it would also break?

Aoife

Aoife had a brandy, with ice to make it last, and as she accepted each powdery kiss and squeeze of her poor shoulder, she ran back over the eulogy, searching for her husband. Honest, hard-working, devoted to his family. There was no word of his temper, the dark depths of his mood, or the rhythm of the man who held her in his arms and danced. A good life, the priest called it, industrious, rewarded, and Aoife had kept her eyes fixed on his face, waiting to see how he would evade the subject of their daughter. *The sorrows that we all must bear.* That was all the mention he gave her, but afterwards she thanked him, as they all did, for a job well done.

There was a fine turnout for Cashel's funeral. The sons-in-law helped carry the coffin, with Mavis's boys at one end, and Patsy, Tim and Eamon in the middle. There were gold handles, and his name, shined, on a plaque. Mavis stood beside Aoife and held her arm, and it was she who pressed a sod of soil into her hand. Aoife stepped forward, sure that she would fall, and as she let the fine earth scatter she wanted to nudge him, share the joke that, even now, Mavis was in charge.

There were drinks and sandwiches in the back bar of the pub, with the grandchildren out in the car park, sipping lemonade. So many of them, as if that would make up for the one. 'There's nothing like a funeral to give people an appetite.' Mavis had lost Bob the previous year. As always with Mavis, she'd done everything first.

Kitty and Angela came back with her to the house. They were to sleep, the pair of them, in the spare room, while the aunties and their families bedded down at theirs. There was cake, left over, and a plate of sandwiches. 'Shall I make us something fresh?' Angela's face was smudged with crying, but Aoife wanted nothing and, when pressed, neither did the girls.

The three of them sat in silence and looked out at the bay. 'Do you remember,' Aoife said, 'when I used to read to you from Patricia Lynch?' They didn't remember. Had she read *Brogeen* to herself? The homesickness was terrible that year; maybe it was knowing she'd be going back. 'We'd sit upstairs in the big bed –' she felt her eyes mist for the heft of their warm bodies, the noise of the customers, a dull murmur below '– and I'd read to you about the little dancing leprechaun always in and out of trouble.'

They remembered the bed. They'd slept in it, all three of them, when they were home from school. It had tall wooden panels at the head and the foot, and a mattress stuffed with feathers. They'd played ships and shipwrecks, jumping and falling as gales rocked the vessel, and when there was a calm, they'd sunk into its lumpen softness and talked themselves to sleep.

'The summer we first came to Ireland,' Angela ventured, 'and stayed over at Kilcrea, it was Rosaleen ...' she paused to test the air before continuing '... it was Rosaleen who was the wonder, tugging out the wild oats, working until the field was clear.'

Kitty leant forward. 'The way she'd brave the sea, swim out into the bay at Youghal. I could see her from my window at Loreto, floating on her back.'

'And the dancing,' Angela broke in. 'Now isn't Jackie the spit of her? Not that Rosaleen ever took a lesson. The ankles on her—' They all looked down at their own perfectly fine ankles. 'Never saw such lovely legs. There was no one prettier. The looks she got when she arrived in Cork on a Saturday for the dance.'

'How would you know?' Aoife hoped she hadn't been there, and Angela blushed and said it was Declan who'd told her. Of course, it was Declan Shaughnessy who'd chosen Rosaleen first.

On and on they talked: the elegance of her writing, the grades, the best in the county in her matric. There was her hair, thick and black, how smart it looked when it was smoothed, and her cleverness with a story – did she not sail into that job on the *Express*? Anyone listening would have thought it was Rosaleen that they were mourning, but with Cashel gone and, with him, the ban against her name, they felt themselves, that night at least, to have her back.

Kate

It is July, and the morning of the shopping trip, when the box arrives. I carry it through to the kitchen and set it on the table. It is a proper parcel, tied with string, wrapped in brown paper, covered in a multitude of stamps. My name is in large letters, the name of the street smaller, Great Britain huge. Freya drums her hands as I cut through the tape. Inside, there is a shoebox. Plain, the edges dented, and on the side of the box is written *Isabelle, 10th April 1961*, and in larger letters: *Kelly*.

My hands are shaking as I take off the lid. Inside is a typed form, dated the day before my birth, which states that permission has been granted for adoption, that the mother has given up all rights to her child. It is signed, *P a t r* scratched through, and then again, another, longer signature, scrawled so wildly it's impossible to decipher. I wither. Had I hoped that I'd been taken forcefully? And I hear it, the roar of the corridor, the rushing of my dreams.

Freya is waiting. 'What does it say?'

There are more papers. My parents' names. Caroline and Gavin Hayes. Their signatures, legible. A stamp. A seal.

Below this is a folded sheet of paper. A letter, pale blue, the writing sloped and fluid. The address of the sender is blocked out with black.

Dear Reverend Mother,
I'm writing to enquire whether my daughter ███████ *may be*
residing in your home. I have reason to believe that this may be
so, god willing, as I am sure she will be well looked after there.
All the same I would be put much at ease to know for certain.
Please could you write to me by return?
Bless you for your good work.
Yours faithfully,
Mrs ███████

The letter is dated the week of my birth.

Below this, as if the box had at some point been turned upside down and its contents re-ordered, is an envelope, *November 1975* stamped across the face of the Queen.

I open it, and read the address, untampered with.

Gamekeepers Cottage, Oakfield, Sussex
Tel: Oakfield 325

Reverend Mother,
I would like it known that if my daughter Isabelle is to contact
you enquiring as to my whereabouts, it is my wish that you
pass this letter on to her, so that she might know where to find
me. Please be mindful that in some parts of the civilised world
this is now the law.
Rosaleen Kelly (Patricia)

I read the letter twice before I understand it is from my mother, and then I sit with my back against the kitchen cupboard and I read it again.

'Is it news?' Freya has tucked herself under my arm.

'It is.'

'Good news?'

At the very bottom of the box is my own letter.

I was born in your home on 10th April 1961 and adopted by
a Mr and Mrs Hayes from East Sussex, England. Could you
kindly provide me with the name of my mother, and any other
information that may be useful in finding her.
Yours appreciatively,
Catherine Hayes (Kate)

There is a slip of paper. *Good luck. A friend.* And then, in
brackets, as if it is less likely to count: *Carmel.*

We arrive to meet my mother as arranged in the café at John
Lewis. I kiss her cheek, and I linger, breathing in her floral
scent.

'Hello.' She is flustered by my show of affection, but Freya
has her hand and is pulling her towards the counter. 'Is that
all right?' she mouths, holding up Freya's chosen treat, and
I tell her that it is, and that I'll have a coffee, although even
without one I'm hardly able to sit still. Oakfield. I think of the
times I've driven past the village, up over the hill and down
through the Splash. 'Faster!' Alice and I would whoop as water
cascaded round the car. Rosaleen Kelly. Might she still be
living there, less than ten miles from the place where I grew
up, and I picture her in 1975, posting her letter in the market
square where I'd posted letters of my own.

Freya's cake is large and chocolate. 'Is this a good idea?' my
mother asks, and not sure if she means the cake, which she is
eating carefully with a fork, or her inclusion on the shopping
trip, I reassure her that it is.

My mother outlines her plans. She already has her dress; it's
pale blue. What she needs is a hat. I move through the floors in

a trance. 'Maybe,' I nod, distracted, as she stands before a mirror, and I'm grateful to Freya who beams at each creation until she's so encouraged she buys a hat with grapes and kumquats moulded out of silk. 'Wear it!' Freya demands as it is dropped into a box, five times larger than my shoebox, but my mother says she'll save it for the big day. Now what she needs is shoes.

'Kate ...' My mother pauses as she slips her feet into navy low-heeled courts. 'I know Alice is hoping you'll be maid of honour, and Freya of course will be a bridesmaid, but is there nothing tempting you today? It'll be my treat.'

I shake my head, and she looks at me as if for the first time. 'Darling,' she frowns. 'Are you all right?'

I swallow, and my ears fill with rushing. 'Where's Freya?' I spin around but Freya has barrelled her way into a turnstile of dresses, and there is the dark tuft of her hair sticking out. 'Things haven't been easy.' She'll need to know. 'Matt's left, I asked him to, and—'

My mother's arms are around me and she's holding me so hard I sob. 'I'm sorry.'

I prime myself for what will follow – *We did warn you. It's only what we expected* – but she suggests we go back to the café, and instead of shoes, and bags, we buy sandwiches and soup, and my mother tells us about her life growing up in Ceylon, stories that I've never heard, and how when she was seven she was sent to school in England and didn't see her parents for five years. 'Had they died?' Freya asks, and my mother, with only the smallest tremor, says that's exactly what she'd wondered, but there they were again – she'd just turned twelve – looking much the same as in the photograph she'd kept by her bed. After that, she went out to visit them by ship every summer, until she was grown up, by which time she'd met my father, Grandad, who didn't like to travel.

That night I call Beck, and when he answers I find that I can't ·
speak. He waits, patient on the line, until I manage to squeeze
out my name.

'Kate,' he echoes, and he waits again, coming in at intervals
to say he's not in any hurry, suggesting I might prefer it if he
called me back in a while?

'No,' I manage, and with a heave of breath I ask him to
listen.

Reverend Mother,
I would like it known that if my daughter Isabelle is to contact
you enquiring as to my whereabouts, it is my wish that you
pass this letter on to her, so that she might know where to find
me. Please be mindful that in some parts of the civilised world
this is now the law.
Rosaleen Kelly

I keep Patricia to myself.

There's a pause while the words swirl and settle.

'What will you do?'

'I don't know!'

'Could you write?'

I could, but what if she's moved – I might actually go crazy
waiting for a reply.

'Is there a number?'

'There is.'

'You'll have to call.'

'Who will I say I am?'

'You could pretend to be someone else?'

'I am someone else.'

'Can you wait half an hour?'

'For what?'

'I have an idea.'

I hear Beck's van as it rattles to a stop and even before he knocks I've opened the front door. 'Hello.' I put a finger to my lips so he knows not to wake Freya and he gives me an awkward hug and steps inside. I lead him through to the kitchen where his eyes glide around the room. Can he feel it, the way the house has emptied? Has he noticed the grimed outline where the photograph of Matt with his guitar once hung?

'Would you like … ?' I search around for something to offer, but he shakes his head.

'Shall I?' He picks up the phone.

I hand him the letter.

'We'll need the code.'

I know the code. It's the same code as my parents'. I look up at the clock. It's a quarter past nine.

He dials, and my heart thumps so wildly I'm sure that it will burst. 'Who will you say you are?'

'A friend.'

It rings.

I double over.

It rings again and I hunch down on the floor, but by the seventh ring my terror is subsiding. By the tenth I'm beginning to calm. There's no one at home. I stand, I breathe, and then there is an answer. Beck bends his head to the receiver. 'Hello?' I strain to hear the voice on the other end. 'I was wondering, is Rosaleen Kelly there?'

There is a pause. Don't let her be there! My fear is white, red-hot and burning.

'I'm an old friend,' Beck is saying. 'I wanted to send her something. Can I check the address? Gamekeepers Cottage.

Oakfield. That's it. Thanks so much. And you are? Thanks then, Chloe. Bye.'

I put my hands over my mouth. 'What a coward!' I say through the grille of my fingers.

Beck laughs. 'You're the bravest person I know.'

We sit up late, eating the remainder of the chocolate cake Freya brought home in a napkin, and Beck tells me about his family when I've exhausted the details of mine. The middle son of three brothers, they moved to Devon not long after he was born, and from the age of ten he spent every hour of his spare time surfing. This was how he got the idea for his café. He'd sell cakes and biscuits to the ravenous surfers on the beach, and soon he'd set up in a shack, making wraps and salads, juices, omelettes, and when he needed staff his mother – everything he cooked he'd learnt from her – came and worked with him, and once he left for college in London, she took the place over and extended it. Now even he can hardly get a table. 'I'd love to take you there. And Freya. She could learn to surf.'

It is beginning to get light when he stands and stretches. 'I'd better go.'

'Yes.' I could ask him to stay, and I glimpse the sweetness of a future, sea spray and hunger, another night like this.

'Bye then.' He reaches out but I find that I've stepped back. Nothing surely can be this easy, and there's Freya, horizontal in my bed.

I show him to the door.

Dear Rosaleen, I write on a thick cream sheet of drawing paper. *I have a great desire to talk to you about Isabelle, and also Felicia. Would you call me when you receive this letter?*

I draw a picture of a face. Wild hair, wide mouth, my own startled eyes. I seal it, paste on a stamp and run out to the post-box where I drop it in before I change my mind.

It seems now I may never leave the house. The first day I float, ghostly, up and down the stairs; on the second, it is a full-time job, listening for the phone. Freya is in a manic mood. She demands potato prints, stick whittling, animals cut from felt. Exhausted, I throw a sheet over the washing line to make a tent. '"Baby Day",' Freya pleads, and when I don't immediately respond she recites the story herself, adding a new section in which Max, while on his way to school, is adopted by a family so kind he stays for lunch.

Lunch. I've forgotten we need to eat, and I'm cutting carrots, setting glasses on a tray when the phone rings. I stare at it for so long the pasta boils over, and the tomato sauce I'm heating crinkles in the pan. Hello, I practise before I pick it up.

It's Matt.

'Oh,' I say, deflated. I can't think of anything to add.

'We should talk.'

'We should.' We should have talked.

'I'll give you money for Freya, of course.'

'Of course.'

When there is another silence he spits, 'She's not just yours, you know.'

'No.' I force the word out. 'I'm sorry.'

'I'm sorry too.'

We hold the line.

'I'll call by soon.'

'Do that.'

I listen while he puts down the phone.

Rosaleen

Each summer, in the triangle of field behind the house, there was a horticultural show. A poster pasted on to the window of the village shop announced the categories: Flower arrangement. Flower arrangement by a man. Biscuits decorated by a child. Jam. Marmalade. Lemon curd. A fancy dress parade. And every kind of vegetable.

Rosaleen roamed her garden, fingering the fronds of carrots, the red veins of the chard. She fetched a trug and arranged in it potatoes turned that morning from the earth; three long beets, bushy with their tails; a spray of beans and one cob lettuce. She added parsley, rosemary, a royally purple artichoke, remembering the first year they entered when the girls had dressed as a horse, making a head from papier mâché, painting it silver, pasting on a mane of wool. That was the year Peter ripped a bunch of flowers from the borders of the garden – marigolds and daisies, stems of ripening corn – and jammed them into the top of an old engine-oil tin, and won. They'd arrived, as a family, through the side gate of the field. Peter, with red braces over his white shirt; Rosaleen, in a green dress. It seemed the whole village watched as they advanced: their neighbours, strangers then who passed them on the hill, the windows of their Volvos wound.

'Haven't you made a splendid effort!' It was the woman from the Coach House, her steel-grey hair set in a wave; her husband, in cravat and slacks, grinning by her side. 'What a delight to meet you. We have been intrigued.'

Peter had steered them towards the tent where earlier that day Rosaleen had dropped off her trug of vegetables. Even before they entered they could hear the flutter of excitement. Men and women in their summer best were bent over tables on which sat rows of paper plates. Further along were jars of jam, each with a mouse-sized spoonful missing; bouquets of sweet peas in narrow-throated vases; and, at the far end, misshapen vegetables: a carrot with its legs crossed, a parsnip with one unseemly bulge.

'Where's yours?' The girls rushed from one table to the next. Carrots, trimmed; onions with their topknots sheared; potatoes, polished. Rosettes sat in clusters – first prize; second – intercepted by small harsh comments. *Only seven gooseberries in this category allowed. Courgette outside specified size.*

Rosaleen's entry sat on a side table. Wild and hairy, it looked positively obscene.

'What does it mean, disqual-i-fied?' Sylva attempted, and Rosaleen had snatched up the slip of paper, and scrunched it in her hand.

'Bastards!' Her anger was explosive and she glared at Peter who was laughing with the landlord of the pub.

'Isn't that you?' he called to her as a loudspeaker asked for cake-stall volunteers, and she'd stamped away, still swearing, past the shortbread entries and the sausage rolls.

Now fashion had exonerated her. Radishes were exhibited in all their frilly glory, potatoes clotted with earth. That weekend had been a turning point. The neighbours congratulating Peter on his win, patting the horse which was garlanded with a rosette, bending to talk to Chloe and Sylva as they unfolded themselves from their disguise: Chloe, strong and dark, her hair in braids; Sylva as slight and fair as an elf.

This weekend they were both home. They loved the fete, made an effort not to miss it, relishing the strictness of the judging, the imperious comments, enjoying the chance to see old friends.

Rosaleen uprooted a thistle, and wondered if she'd imagined the girl. *You look like my mother.* She'd been so shaken that as soon as she'd been able she'd slipped through the gap in the hedge, and retreated to her bed.

'What is it?' Peter was gentle. He was used to her despairing moods. 'All you have to do if you're that desperate to win is trim the bloody beetroot.'

She couldn't tell him. It was the only thing she had – her secret – and she needed it for herself.

'Mum,' Chloe was standing on the path, 'I meant to say, there was an odd phone call last night, when you and Dad were out.'

Rosaleen cut a trail of nasturtiums. 'Odd how?'

'Just someone, said they were an old friend.'

Rosaleen looked up.

'But you don't have any old friends.' It was a common tease between them. 'A man, he wanted to check the address.'

Rosaleen paled.

'Mum?'

She forced herself to look at Chloe. Whoever it was, no one could take anything from her now.

'Are you OK?'

'I'm fine. For God's sake, let me get ready or I'll be late getting to the tent.'

'Disqualified.' It was a family joke.

'Before I've even entered!'

'Quick!' Chloe looked at her watch. 'I'll get my cake. Sylva,' she bellowed. Sylva had baked a loaf of soda bread. 'We have to run!'

Kate

'Mum?' Freya is whispering, soft against my hair. 'What?' I turn towards her, surprised to find it's morning, but even as I do I hear the ringing of the phone. I push back the covers. It's too early, surely, for anyone to call, although when I glance at the clock I see it's after nine.

My feet are swift and clumsy on the stairs. The phone is slowing, I can feel it as I fling around the banister, and as I scoot along the hall and lunge for the receiver I'm convinced I've caught the last ring.

'Hello?'

The air is still.

'Am I speaking to Isabelle Felicia?' A light, clear voice.

I grip the receiver so hard it stings my ear. The silence deepens. Rivers run through it. Trees blossom and leaf. 'You are.'

There's a strangled sound. I think it might be choking, but then there's a quiver, and she's laughing, and I'm laughing too, peals and trills, an echo of each other.

'I'd like to see you.'

'I'd like to see you too.'

She begins to explain about the journey, or where would I like to meet? But I say I'll find her. I'll catch a bus, get off by the church, and walk up the hill.

★ ★ ★

'Where's Gran?' Freya asks when we push through the barrier, and I tell her that she'll see her soon, just not today. Rosaleen offered to collect us, but in my hurry I need all the time I can get. We take the bus, a double-decker, swaying greenly above hedgerows, and when we step down I breathe in the familiar air, grass and bracken, the open sky. We walk across the common, past the oak, the fallen branch of which Freya smooths with her hand, uphill and down again, across the trickle of the Splash and along beside the wall of the estate. There, as directed, is the copse of trees, straight and rustling among the stumps of those struck down in the storm. We push open a gate and walk along a path and there it is, as she described, a red painted door. I knock, and wait, and when there's no answer I turn away; and that's when I see her, standing by the side of the house. Her hair is long. It hangs almost to her waist, and the black is streaked with grey.

'Isabelle.' She says it quiet, and she walks towards us and she takes hold of my spare hand.

Acknowledgements

In 2011 I supported the charity Action Against Hunger by offering to name a character in my forthcoming novel after the highest bidder. Chloe Hazell did not fit into *Mr Mac and Me*, but I found a place for her here; although Sarah de Lisle, who, in 2016 bid to be immortalised in support of Freedom from Torture, was too distracting to include in full, she will, I hope, be satisfied to know that she is indeed Sarah.

Among the books I read during the writing of this novel I'd like to credit: *The Light in the Window* by June Goulding, *The Baby Laundry for Unmarried Mothers* by Angela Patrick, and *A Good Likeness* by Paul Arnott. My thanks go to my lifelong friend and editor Alexandra Pringle, my agent Clare Conville, and, in America, Anna Stein, Dan Halpern and Gabriella Doob. I am grateful to my loyal first readers Xandra Bingley, Delia Woodman, and Kitty Aldridge, and to Justine Picardie who appeared as if by magic when she was needed most. Many thanks also to Deirdre Terry, Julie Terry, Michele Macey and Angela Shaw, and to Georgia Shearman, Sarah Shearman, Isabella Tree and Paul Arnott for their help with research, and to John Kelly for his careful reading and advice on Catholic doctrine.

I would also like to thank Gerry Simpson, who has provided much more than the title.

But mostly I am indebted to my much-missed mother, who, at eighteen, found herself pregnant and unmarried. Terrified she'd be discovered and sent to a Home – a workhouse for morally defective women – she kept the news a secret. This novel was written in response to the idea: what would have happened if she'd been found out, or if she'd asked for help from the wrong people? Would her story have followed the path of so many thousands of other girls and women, and would anyone have intervened?

A Note on the Author

Esther Freud trained as an actress before writing her first novel, *Hideous Kinky*, which was shortlisted for the John Llewellyn Rhys prize and made into a film starring Kate Winslet. After publishing her second novel, *Peerless Flats*, she was chosen as one of *Granta's* Best Young British novelists. Her other books include *The Sea House, Lucky Break*, and *Mr Mac and Me*, which won Best Novel in the East Anglian Book Awards. She contributes regularly to newspapers and magazines, and teaches creative writing with her own local group. Her first full length play *Stitchers* was produced at the Jermyn St Theatre in 2018, and in 2019 she was made a fellow of the Royal Society of Literature. *I Couldn't Love You More* is her ninth novel. She lives in London.

www.estherfreud.co.uk

A Note on the Type

The text of this book is set in Bembo, which was first used in 1495 by the Venetian printer Aldus Manutius for Cardinal Bembo's *De Aetna*. The original types were cut for Manutius by Francesco Griffo. Bembo was one of the types used by Claude Garamond (1480–1561) as a model for his Romain de l'Université, and so it was a forerunner of what became the standard European type for the following two centuries. Its modern form follows the original types and was designed for Monotype in 1929.